When the Saints Come Home

Dorothy Stewart

Published by Zaccmedia
www.zaccmedia.com
info@zaccmedia.com

Published December 2014
Copyright © 2014 Dorothy Stewart

The right of Dorothy Stewart to be identified as author of this work has been asserted by her in accordance with the Copyright, Designs and Patents Act 1988.

ISBN: 9781909824676

British Library Cataloguing-in-Publication Data
A catalogue record for this book is available from the British Library.

ACKNOWLEDGEMENTS

First, special thanks to Alice and Peter Blackburn for their kindness, excellent lunches after morning service at Pulham Market Methodist Church, and the original conversation that grew into this book.

A key figure in the book is the real-life evangelist Jock Troup. I have drawn information about Jock and his activities during this period from a number of reliable publications listed below and I hope my portrayal of Jock and his work honours him, his memory, his work, and his Lord. Thank you to Anne Dunnett, Lord Lieutenant of Caithness, for the James Alexander Stewart booklet, *Our Beloved Jock*.

Researching in Great Yarmouth and Wick, I was met with generous assistance and great kindness and should like to record my thanks to Peter Warner for lots of useful architectural details; Patricia Day and Johanna O'Donoghue at the Time and Tide Museum in Great Yarmouth; Simon Townsley and Elaine Ellis of English Heritage at The Row Houses, Great Yarmouth; the staff at Wick Heritage Centre, Wick Library, and Caithness Archive Centre; Great Yarmouth Library; Lowestoft Maritime Museum; British Library Newspapers, Colindale.

Online research led me to even more helpful folk who supplied really useful information. Amongst them, I'd like to thank Howard Geddes and John Roake of the Highland Railway Society; Iain Grant, Editor of *The John O'Groat Journal*, and Tim Williams, Managing Editor, Archant Norfolk (*Yarmouth Mercury*), for permission to include excerpts from 1921 and 1922. Cover photographs are from The Johnston Collection by kind permission of The Wick Society. Thank you to Harry Gray and Fergus Mather.

Extracts from the Authorized Version of the Bible (The King James Bible), the rights in which are vested in the Crown, are reproduced by permission of the Crown's Patentee, Cambridge University Press.

Among the many books I consulted the following were particularly valuable:

Our Beloved Jock: Revival Days in Scotland and England by James Alexander Stewart (Revival Literature, Philadelphia, 1964); *Revival Man: The Jock Troup Story* by George Mitchell (Christian Focus, 2002); *Glory in the Glen: A History of Evangelical Revivals in Scotland 1880–1940* by Tom Lennie (Christian Focus, 2009); *A Forgotten Revival: Recollections of the Great Revivals of East Anglia and North East Scotland of 1921* by Stanley C. Griffin (Day One Publications, 2000); *Floods upon the Dry Ground* by Jack Ritchie, www.bibleteachingprogram.com/floods/floods.htm; *In a World A Wir Ane: A Shetland Herring Girl's Story* by Susan Telford (Shetland Times, 1998)

CHAPTER 1

Wick, late September 1921

Lydia Alexander ruffled her young son's dark hair affectionately before going back to the task of buttoning up his coat and winding the warm woollen scarf round his neck. Five-year-old Ewen was wriggling with impatience, itching to be away.

'Is everybody ready?'

Lydia's mother, Jean Ross, closed the sitting room door behind her to keep the warmth in the room and joined her daughter and grandson in the lobby. Drawing on her gloves, she smiled approvingly at them.

'We're nearly there,' Lydia assured her, adding with a laugh, 'if this one would just stand still...'

'Och, he's excited,' her mother said. She smiled down at the little boy. 'Never fear, my dearie. We'll get there in plenty of time.'

The apple of their eyes gazed up at her.

'We have to, Granny. I promised Granddad I'd be there,' Ewen told her.

'Yes, my love, and you'll keep your promise, good boy that you are.'

Appeased, Ewen submitted to his mother's ministrations, even to the placing of a cap on his head to keep out the cold.

'There, now,' Jean said. 'Don't we all look fine!'

The trio turned to leave, Lydia, a mite taller than her mother, holding Ewen's hand firmly in hers. Both women were respectably dressed in warm cloth coats, maybe not the finest or the newest, but clean and neat and well looked after. Their hair was tidily pulled back into buns resting on the nape of their necks as was the fashion of the time and the place, Lydia's a fine chestnut colour while her mother's was showing silver threads, and each wore a felt cloche hat. Automatically they both stopped at the little mirror on the lobby wall and checked their appearance one last time.

'Come on!' Ewen protested impatiently.

Mother and daughter laughed and Jean reached for the door knob.

A sharp knock at the door startled them.

'Whoever can that be?' Jean asked.

She opened the door to reveal a thin elderly woman in a long black Astrakhan fur coat and hat and a severe expression. Ewen took one look at the woman on the doorstep and scuttled away behind his mother, clutching her skirts and peeking out around her. Lydia backed away. She did not want to catch Granny Leslie's eye or sharp tongue.

'Well?' the woman demanded. 'Am I to stand here all day? Are you not going to invite me in?'

Lydia could see her mother shrink in on herself, her shoulders tense.

'Mother,' Jean said.

'Well, at least you know who I am,' Mary-Anne Leslie said with a sour smile. 'My own daughter...' She took a decisive step forward.

2

Jean hesitated, then said in a low apologetic voice, 'We were just going out...'

Her mother paused. 'Oh, were you? And where might you be going at this time of day?'

Ewen pushed his head from behind Lydia's skirts and announced, 'We're going to wave my Granddad off. He's away to the Yarmouth fishing today...' Ewen paused before adding with a proud flourish, 'On his boat!'

Mary-Anne sniffed.

'Is he now?' she said. 'I thought he'd be gone by now.'

Lydia and Jean wisely held their tongues. They knew Granny Leslie would never have come to the house if there was any chance of David Ross still being at home.

Ewen however jumped into the breach.

'Well, he's not. And we're going to say goodbye so we need to go *now*!' He tugged at Lydia's hand, looking up at her anxiously.

'Children should be seen and not heard, young man,' Granny Leslie announced frostily. 'I see, Lydia Alexander' – the stress on the surname spoke volumes of disdain – 'what a fine job you're doing of bringing your son up on your own. It's time you married again and gave that boy a father who will teach him right from wrong. Though perhaps that's too much to ask of this family!'

At that attack on her family, Lydia saw her mother square her shoulders and pull herself up to her full height.

'If you'll excuse us, we do need to be going,' Jean told her mother in carefully polite tones. 'As Ewen says, we need to get to the harbour before his granddad's boat has gone.'

'I'd have thought you were past all that now,' her mother said with a sneer.

Jean's cheeks reddened but she answered quietly, 'Then you'd be wrong.'

'Am I?' her mother interrupted. 'I'm not so sure about that. We told you, your father and I, when you determined to marry that...'

'Lydia!' Jean's voice cut quietly but firmly across her mother's. 'I think it's time we were going. Ewen, come along now!'

Quickly she gathered her small family and got them out of the house, turning her back on her mother as she locked the door after them. Then she turned to face her.

'We'll be going now,' Jean said, adding with the slightest twitch of her lip, 'unless you want to come with us?'

She swiftly ushered her daughter and grandson down the street towards the harbour, leaving her mother's bitter tongue for once without words.

~

David Ross pushed past his men waiting on the deck of the steam drifter, *Bonnie Jean*. The fleet of boats, herring drifters under sail and steam that had filled Wick harbour, was thinning now. It would soon be their turn to put out to sea and there was still no sign of his youngest son. Hearing the discontented muttering from his crew, his anger grew.

He knew he had let Jean persuade him against his better judgment. And now he was paying the price.

'Give Robbie a chance,' she had begged. 'You're too hard on him.'

David crashed his huge reddened hands onto the rail of the boat as he stared out at the little grey town. Jean's words echoed bitter in his memory. Too hard on Robbie? He got only what he deserved. He had never been any good. Not like Alec.

And the pain of grief washed through him again, sudden and acid. Why did it have to be Robbie who came back from the slaughter of the Great War while his brother Alec lay cold and

4

dead in a grave in Flanders? Alec would have been standing here by his father's side, alive and cheerful as he always had been, here where he belonged, on their boat setting out for the autumn fishing in Yarmouth. By now Alec would have had a wife to wave farewell to, and a clutch of bairns at her knee. Grandchildren.

David swallowed hard. It did not help to think of the might-have-beens. The terrible waste of that war. His own crew, like so many others, decimated by death and injury. Alec gone and now there was only Robbie left.

Robbie. The son who had let him down the first time he came out on the boat. He had been seasick for the whole of his first voyage, green and shaking. Alec had had to wrap him in a blanket and put him in the little boat till the end of the trip, so the men could get on with their work. His mother had come down to the harbour to meet them on their return and what a fuss she had kicked up. As if seasickness was something worth bothering about. But then she had always been soft with Robbie.

It had been as clear as daylight to everyone that Alec was the son after his own heart. And Alec had captured that heart from the first sight he had of the squally red-faced bairn in his proud mother's arms.

David pounded the rail in frustration. It should have been Alec sailing with him to Yarmouth today. Not Robbie, whatever his mother said.

The bitter scene was clear in his mind. The boy being carried off the boat. His mother scolding him. *Him!* As if it had been his fault her precious mollycoddled boy had no stomach for the sea.

Alec had come up on deck then and stood by his shoulder.

'Well, at least you've got me,' Alec had said. 'I won't let you down.'

'Aye,' David had said. 'You're a true son of mine...'

He maybe should not have said that, for Jean's head had come up then and she had fixed him with such a look. Things had never been the same between them after that.

And the boy had declared he would never step foot on the boat again, and neither he had. He had gone his own way.

But with Alec gone and the rest of his crew shrunk by the war, it had not been easy to find enough men for this voyage. And Jean had used that. She had swallowed her pride and pleaded for Robbie to be allowed aboard. To take his rightful place, as she put it.

And when that did not do the trick, she had thrown down her ace. Not that such a strict Wee Free as Jean would ever think in such worldly terms! Still, it was what she had done.

'For my sake,' she had said.

The one appeal he had no defence against. Despite every-thing, despite all that had torn them apart over the years, he still loved her.

For a moment, David wished he had a drink on him to dull the pain, but he was skipper and his decree was no drink on board, so that applied to himself too. And it would have to apply to that no-use Robbie, if and when he chose to put in an appearance.

Fool that he was to have given in to Jean's pleading to give Robbie one last chance. To show him what herring fishing was about – the best of it, the Yarmouth fishing – so he would see what his future could be if he would just knuckle down.

David cracked his own work-rough knuckles. One son remain-ing to leave the boat to. Well, if he did not turn up in the next few minutes it would be too late. The boats ahead of the *Bonnie Jean* were on the move, easing their way carefully out of the narrow harbour entrance and into the bay.

As skipper of the boat, he had to think of his crew. So far it had been the worst year's fishing anyone could remember. They needed to get to Yarmouth and recoup their losses or they would all be in debt by Christmas.

He could not – he would not – wait for a disobedient, worthless wastrel like Robbie, whatever he had promised Jean.

~

There was a giggle from behind the high stone wall.

'Robbie! Stop that!' The pretty dark-haired girl gave the young man a playful push. 'You're late already! Your father's going to be furious...'

Though his eyes darkened with sudden anger, Robbie ignored her words, holding her firmly in his arms in the shelter of the concealing wall, and kissed her again with slow deliberation.

'Robbie, stop!' Chrissie protested more firmly now. She pulled away from him and drew her dark blue woollen shawl more tightly around her, fighting to hide her smile.

'You must go!' she told him, as sternly as she was able. 'Or the *Bonnie Jean* will put to sea and leave you behind.' Her eyes betrayed her anxiety.

'I've got plenty of time,' Robbie assured her, reaching out to draw her back into his embrace. 'I did my bit earlier before the old man turned up. We got all the barrels stacked and the coal taken on, the food delivered... everything's done and ready for the voyage to Yarmouth, and I'll soon get back across the harbour. He'll never notice I'm not there – he never sees me anyway – and if he does...'

'Oh, Robbie!' Chrissie seized his hands and turned back to face him, forcing him to pay attention to her. 'You mustn't anger him now! After all the persuading your poor mother had to do to get him to take you with him! You mustn't let her down now.'

Robbie snorted. 'Fat chance!' he said. 'You know how it is – damned before I ever set foot on the *Bonnie Jean*. Might as well give him something real to complain about. And if I'm not good enough for him, then good riddance to him. I can go back to Aberdeen. I'll soon find work on the trawlers there again.'

Chrissie gazed gravely into his eyes. Everyone in the little grey town knew there was bad feeling between Robbie and his father, but work was hard to come by these days, even for able-bodied young men like Robbie. Better by far for him to knuckle down and take his place on his father's boat. With his older brother dead in the Great War, Robbie was in line to inherit the boat, and that was surely worth knuckling down for. But Robbie was not the knuckling-down type.

Twitching her shawl closer to keep out the chilly autumn air, Chrissie gave him a quick mischievous grin.

'Since I'll be in Yarmouth myself next week, there's no use you staying here if you want to see me!'

Seeing him consider that, she added teasingly, 'And we won't have to huddle behind walls in draughty corners there! Yarmouth's a great place. We'll have a good time. So, go on with you now!'

With a final smile to him, she turned to walk away, but he caught her hand.

'He won't go without me...' Robbie said.

Chrissie turned back, her eyes searching past him to the harbour packed close with its fleet of drifters waiting their turn to leave and start the long journey south.

'I wouldn't be too sure of that,' she said.

~

Out in the bay, beneath the bright September sky, the flotilla of boats spread out into a long line, heading south for the autumn herring fishing at Great Yarmouth and Lowestoft, in formation like a skein of migrating geese.

In the harbour itself, there seemed still to be hundreds of boats waiting their turn, skinny woodbine funnels sending out puffs of smoke as engines readied themselves for the voyage. Lining the decks were men and boys impatient to be away. Everywhere there was noise from the drifters' engines, the smell of the smoke from the chimneys overlaying the crisp freshness of the day and the green sea smell of the harbour.

Lydia, with Ewen by the hand, stood with her mother at the quayside, eyes fixed on where the *Bonnie Jean* rode high in the water, sandwiched between the other Wick drifters on the far side of the harbour.

Just at that moment she spied a figure scrambling from boat to boat, taking a dangerous shortcut across the harbour. Lydia narrowed her eyes as she tried to follow Robbie's progress from the deck of one boat over to the next, grinning widely and laughing carelessly at the protests of the skippers, as he made his way across the drifter-filled harbour to the *Bonnie Jean*.

The sudden stiffening in her mother told her that she too had spotted Robbie. His mother's darling – and her despair – he had turned up after years away from home. 'Like the proverbial bad penny,' his father had muttered.

Then just a week ago she had heard her mother pleading with her father that Robbie be allowed to go on this voyage down to Yarmouth. Robbie needed the work, and the crew were a man short. It seemed like a hopeful solution for them all. But by the look of it, it was not going to start out well for Robbie – if it started at all.

'Look, Mum! Look, Granny!' Ewen pointed. 'There's Uncle Robbie. He should have been on the boat with Granddad by now! He'll have to hurry!'

'Yes, my dear,' Jean Ross said with a sigh. 'I've seen him.'

'Granddad will be furious,' Ewen continued. 'Uncle Robbie's going to be in trouble with him.'

The two women and the small boy watched as Robbie clambered on board the *Bonnie Jean* and was confronted by the burly figure of his father. From this distance and amidst the hubbub of farewells and the steam engines noisily powering the boats, they could hear no words but they could read the actions of the figures as clearly as in a mime. A very angry mime.

~

'And just what do you think you're doing?' David Ross demanded. 'You should have been here long since, helping the others. There's work to be done.'

Robbie waved his arm round the boat. 'Seems to be all done. And I'm here now. I don't see any problem.'

'Problem?' David Ross exploded, his face purple with rage. 'Problem? *You're* the problem! Just like you've always been. You should have been here at the same time as everyone else...'

'Well, I'm here now and by the look of it, it's time we were going,' Robbie replied.

The gasp from the crew told him he had gone too far. On board the drifter, his father was skipper and his word was law – his word that decided when to put to sea and when to stay in harbour, when to shoot the nets and when to haul them in. Stepping on board the boat was stepping into his father's kingdom, and it was a kingdom where Robbie knew he was already unwelcome.

Robbie tried a careless shrug. His father's eyes narrowed, then he turned on his heel back towards the wheelhouse.

Robbie laughed. He had got away with it, for the moment. He turned to the rail and, spotting Chrissie high up on the brae, waved his farewell.

~

Lydia, watching from the quayside, saw the wave. She noted that it was not in the direction of her mother and Ewen and herself. Curiously, she scanned the crowds that had come to see the boats off for an answering wave. She wondered which of the local girls was Robbie's latest sweetheart.

There.

An arm in a pale blue cardigan with a darker blue shawl. The typical dress of the fisher girls. Lydia could not see from this distance who it was. Dark hair and sure to be pretty. Robbie liked them pretty. But a fisher girl?

And if she was one of the fisher girls, had she and Robbie arranged to meet up in Yarmouth? The special trains for the shore workers – the women and girls who gutted the fish and the coopers who made the barrels to pack them in – would be leaving soon and Yarmouth, far away from the prying eyes of their families, was famous for romances amongst the fisher folk.

Was that why Robbie had been willing to go? He had always professed contempt for the life of the drifterman. Old-fashioned and a waste of time, he said, though not in his father's hearing. Lydia often wondered whether Robbie had deliberately chosen to work on the trawlers so hated by driftermen as a deliberate insult to his father.

She saw the fisher lassie turn and leave. Lydia hoped this would be one more short-lived romance. Her mother seemed able to turn a blind eye to most of Robbie's shortcomings, including his many girlfriends, but she would surely want better for her only remaining son than one of the fisher lassies? They were not exactly respectable. Their nomadic way of life, travelling around the herring ports to gut the fish, put them outside polite society to say the least. And they had a certain reputation... 'No better than they should be'. No, it would not do.

And what Granny Leslie would say was beyond contemplation! After all, according to Granny Leslie, Mum had married beneath herself when she had married a fisherman. Granny Leslie had made no bones about it and still made her disapproval loud and clear, even though that fisherman was now skipper of his own boat and had provided well for his family.

If Robbie married one of the fisher lassies! No, it was too terrible to think of. Surely Robbie would have more sense?

They waited, watching, as the harbour emptied. Lydia saw her father hesitate a moment just outside the wheelhouse. Ewen jumped up and waved, attracting his attention. David Ross's gaze reached across the harbour to them. Lydia saw her mother acknowledge him with a little nod of her head and then he turned back to the wheelhouse and a few moments later, the *Bonnie Jean* moved out.

Maybe that was how it was with long-married folk, Lydia thought, but it seemed a pity. He would be gone two months or more. And the sea was a dangerous place. To let him go with just a nod...

She noticed her mother's lips were moving and leaned closer to hear.

'Look after them, Lord Jesus. May there be peace between them and bring them home safe. Amen.'

Once upon a time she had prayed, Lydia remembered. When her older brother, Alec, and his best friend, Danny, set off in high spirits for the war in France, she had prayed for them – the two men she had loved most of all in the world, loved, she often thought, from her cradle.

They had been eager to enlist in the first few months of the war. 'It'll be over by the New Year!' they had told her cheerily, delighted to be going off together on such an adventure. And she who had tagged along after them since she was old enough to walk was left behind.

But she had prayed – earnestly, and then when the fighting did not end in the New Year, she had prayed more and more urgently through that long winter, and a spring and a summer which felt empty and meaningless without them. She had kept praying till at last they came home on leave in the autumn. And her life changed – because her adored Danny had married her during those four short days.

But then they had gone back to the war and one day a letter arrived, announcing that Alec and Danny were dead. Killed in action. In Bourlon Wood, Cambrai. Two amongst the 45,000 British men and lads slaughtered there.

Maybe if she had prayed more? She still cudgelled herself with the questions. If she had only prayed more, would it have made any difference? Would they be alive today?

~

On the top of the brae, Chrissie watched a little longer. She had no use for prayers but she was glad that Robbie had come to her before he left. Maybe he cared for her a little. She would have to be careful. She did not want her own heart broken and she knew he had a bad reputation among the girls.

She turned to go. She had to finish packing her kist ready for the long train journey from Wick to Yarmouth on Monday. She had done it enough times and knew it would be good fun travelling with the other girls. She was looking forward to Yarmouth with its dance halls and cinemas and a lot more freedom. And when she got there, she would see Robbie again.

CHAPTER 2

'Dear wife...'

David Ross licked the end of the pencil and stared at the sheet of paper as if he could force it to produce the words he needed. She had to be told. But how?

He sat in the skipper's cabin – fine words for such a tiny space – listening to the creaking of the boat timbers and the quiet lapping of the barely existent waves in Yarmouth harbour. They had been stuck here how many days now? The weather too hot and calm to lure the herring near enough and in big enough numbers to make it worth spending the exorbitant amount that coal now cost to get to the fishing grounds. So the boats had come back to Yarmouth and sat in the harbour in the heat of an unseasonal sun, their crews idling away their time in the pubs and on the street corners. Doing nothing productive but still needing fed – at their skipper's expense. Always more expense!

'The devil makes work for idle hands,' was one of Jean's favourite sayings – and idle minds too. Maybe it was not surprising that the boy had got bored and impatient. But that was no excuse for what he had done. Challenging the skipper! Aye, Robbie always thought he knew better and when he had told him to mind his place, the boy had had the cheek to argue back... How he had argued!

There can be only one boss on a boat and the boy needed to learn his lesson. But shouting him down had not worked. And it had only drawn more attention to them and their dispute.

Maybe he had lost his temper. Maybe both of them had. But fisticuffs! He had had no choice. The boy deserved to have the book thrown at him. On another boat it would have been the constables called and he would have been off to the Yarmouth gaol. Maybe it would have taught him a lesson.

But he could not face Jean if he had done that to her blue-eyed boy. So he had turned him off the boat. Let him try and see how his fine ideas would help him now! He would be back soon enough. Robbie knew which side his bread was buttered on!

~

'Dear wife...'

How she hated the way he wrote to her now. It used to be 'My lovely Jean', 'My darling girl...' Long ago when they were newly wed, his letters full of longing and words of love for her and their baby son – who had arrived a bit early for her parents' comfort but was the apple of her and his father's eye.

Jean's eyes misted. Her baby son. Lost in the Great War. One of the so very many who never came back. Like his best pal, Danny. Lydia's husband. She had thought them too young to marry but Lydia had had stars in her eyes. How could she grudge them their brief time of happiness? She had fought for her own marriage to David Ross, herself no older than Lydia had been.

But like hers, the happiness did not last. Danny was buried in Flanders and Lydia was trying to hide herself in her widowhood, going out only to her work at the primary school. It was not at all what she had hoped for her daughter. And there was Ewen to consider. A fine lad and much loved, but fatherless and Lydia adamant she would not look at another man again. Still, she reminded herself, the Lord worked in mysterious ways and could bring good out of the worst situations. She had to trust.

Jean settled to read the letter.

~

'I'm home, Mum.'

Lydia dropped her bags and books thankfully on the hall table, unwrapped her warm scarf and hung up both coat and scarf on one of the big hooks on the wall of the lobby. She pulled off her close-fitting cloche hat and patted her hair, smoothing stray strands of chestnut brown back into its confining bun at the nape of her neck. The best you could say about it, she thought, was that it was tidy.

She checked her appearance in the mirror. A pale face with huge brown eyes. She looked even paler than usual. Tired, that was what it was. The last day of school before the weekend meant the children in her class were in high spirits. A few of the bigger boys had already gone to help with the potato harvest on their home crofts and more would join them in an unofficial holiday next week to get the last of the potatoes in before the first frosts of the winter. Her class of ten-year-olds would be sadly shrunken by Monday. Though the youngsters knew the tattie picking would be hard work, they were looking forward to the freedom from school and the mischief they would get up to. Their help was needed more than ever now with so few able-bodied men back from the War...

So many that never came back, like Alec and Danny. She pushed down the emotions that seemed to rise automatically in her throat.

No need to think of that now. She turned instead to open the living room door, realising that she had heard no reply to her call.

'Mum?'

Jean Ross was sitting in her usual chair by the table in the front window where the light was best. The sewing that she took in to earn a few extra shillings was pushed away from her in an uncharacteristically untidy heap, still caught under the metal foot of her hand-operated sewing machine. Glazed eyes were fixed on a letter she gripped in her hands.

'Mum!' Lydia repeated and hurried to her mother's side. The last time she had seen her mother like this was when the letter came with the news of her brother Alec's death.

'What is it?' she asked urgently, then thinking the unthinkable, forced the words out. 'Is it Dad?'

Jean's head came up then.

'No, my dear. Your Dad's fine...' she reassured her, though her eyes were still troubled.

'So what is it?' Lydia looked down at the letter. Her father's handwriting. 'What's Dad saying?'

'It's Robbie,' Jean said.

'Oh no, Mum. What's he done now? What's happened?' Lydia asked.

Wordlessly Jean passed the letter over to Lydia, pointing at the relevant passage.

'*The boy has gone too far this time. The men know I could have had him up before the magistrate in Yarmouth for what he did. Maybe a month in prison would do him good, but I could not do it. So I have thrown him off the boat and I wash my hands of him.*'

It then went on in a matter-of-fact tone to detail the poor catches and the strange over-hot weather.

'I wonder what Robbie's done?' Lydia pondered. 'It must have been something really bad this time...'

'We'll find out soon enough, I'm sure,' Jean said, pulling herself together. 'This won't be the only letter from Yarmouth delivered in Wick today. You put the kettle on and set out the tea things. I'll tidy up here. I've some fresh-baked scones we can put out...'

It was not long before there was first one knock on the door then another, as David Ross's gossipy younger sisters, Ina and then Lena, came running with their news.

'You poor thing,' Ina said with mock sympathy as she settled into the chair nearest the fire and accepted a cup of tea and the buttered scone Jean offered. 'That boy is such a worry for you!'

'A sore trial,' Lena put in, taking the next closest chair. She reached for the plate of scones and helped herself.

'Disobeying an order is bad enough but lifting a fist to his faither!' Ina declared with relish and bit into her scone.

'Just as well David is a big man. They say he fair whipped him before he threw him off the boat.' Then seeing Jean and Lydia exchange glances, Lena added triumphantly, 'Haven't you heard? I had a letter from my man today.'

'And me,' Ina put in, hastily swallowing her mouthful of buttered scone. The Rosses were a fishing family and both David's sisters had married driftermen.

Lydia spoke up. 'We had a letter from Dad but he didn't say much...'

'Ah well, he wouldn't, would he?' Ina said with a knowing sideways smile. 'Close as a clam about his business nowadays, isn't he?'

Jean drew her dignity around her. So the estrangement between David and herself was common knowledge, was it? But she had to know. '*Blessed are the meek*' she reminded herself wryly and swallowed down her pride.

'Do tell us what you know,' she said, trying to squash the edge to her voice.

Ina gave her a sharp glance but the temptation to reveal what she knew was too strong. She launched into her tale.

'Seems the pair of them were arguing about taking the boat out. The fishing's been that poor and the coal expensive, it wisna worth the cost of going out...'

'But the boy thought he knew better...' Lena chipped in.

'There was an argument...'

'Well, David is skipper. His word goes.'

'Aye, but the boy wisna having it. He ups and tells him to his face...'

'They'd both had a drink. Lying in harbour day after day... it's no good for anyone.'

'So his faither tells him to pipe down and the boy squares up to him.'

'By then there was a good lot of the men watching...'

The two women paused and sipped their tea.

The implication was clear. The story would be all round Wick by now.

Lydia saw her mother's cheeks flame and then pale.

'I hear none of the other skippers will take him on,' Jean's sister-in-law Ina announced. 'Insubordinate is what they're saying. Naebody will have him. And they've all got full crews they can trust.'

'I hear he's sleeping in the coopers' bothies in your brother Bill's yard,' Lena added spitefully.

'He tried to get work in the curing yards but that was no good. He's not got the training.'

'He even went to the Yarmouth coal heavers, I heard...'

Lydia kept the teapot filled, politely refilling cups and handing round the buttered scones, inwardly seething at the knowing looks and spiteful delight of the gossips.

When they had finally departed to their own homes, Lydia knelt before her mother's chair and put her arms round her.

'He'll be all right,' she told her. 'You know it always works out for Robbie.'

Jean sighed unhappily. 'Yes, but he's far from home. That makes a difference. And he's got nowhere to stay. You know he has a weak chest after the gas in the war...'

They sat together in silent contemplation of Robbie's situation.

Finally Jean announced, 'He can't stay down there. He needs to come home.'

'But Mum, if Robbie's not working, he won't have any money to get home and he won't get any dole money either, being on a drifter now, not a trawler.'

'Yes, I know that but I've still got some savings.'

'Mum, it's not fair to use that. Robbie got himself into this...'

'I know, my dear, but...' Her voice tailed off.

They sat in silence. Lydia could see her mother worrying at the problem, chewing her lip, her brow furrowed. Finally she said, 'Well, if you're sure you think the best thing is for Robbie to come home...'

Then, remembering the girl in the shawl who waved to Robbie from the brae head, Lydia asked, 'Do you think he'd be willing to come home? I mean, we could send the money down to him and he could just hang on to it and spend it down there. For a young man, footloose and fancy free, Yarmouth could be a bit of an adventure once he had some money to spend as well as time on his hands.'

'You're right,' Jean agreed sadly. 'There's little point just sending the money in a letter...'

Lydia rose to tidy away the tea things, carrying them through to the back kitchen. When she returned, she was surprised to see her mother looking a lot more cheerful.

'I still think he should come home,' Jean told her. 'And I think I know how we can do it.'

'Oh yes?' Lydia replied with a quiet smile. 'As if anyone can make Robbie do anything!'

'You can,' her mother said. 'You've always been able to manage Robbie.'

'Maybe when he was younger, Mum...'

'It's the tattie-picking next week, isn't it?' Jean continued. 'And nearly all the bairns in your class will be off for that?'

'Yes,' Lydia agreed slowly, wondering what plot her mother was thinking up.

'So it wouldn't be too difficult for you to get the week off and go down to Yarmouth after Robbie.'

Lydia was startled. 'Me? Go to Yarmouth?'

They heard the outside door slam, then a cheerful young voice, 'Mum! Granny! I'm home!'

'But I've got Ewen to think of,' Lydia pointed out.

'I'll look after Ewen. He's no bother,' Jean said. 'And anyway, why shouldn't you have a few days away? You always said you enjoyed the train journey when you were at college.'

'Well, yes,' Lydia said. 'But that was a long time ago.' A long time ago, she thought, when she was a different girl, when life held hope and maybe even adventure...

Her son rushed in, bright-cheeked from the cold air and the exertion of playing outside with his friends after school.

'I'm hungry!' he declared cheerfully, planting himself between his mother and grandmother.

'Go and look in the kitchen, lovie. There's some scones left over from our afternoon tea,' Jean said. After Ewen rushed off, she said, 'I think it might be the only way.'

She paused and sent up a little prayer, 'Your will be done, Lord Jesus, but I think both my children need rescuing.'

'Will you do it?' she asked Lydia. 'You always used to be game for a little adventure.'

A little adventure? Oh yes, and look at where that had got her – her impetuous marriage to Danny, now lying in a grave in Flanders, and the birth of her son. No, she did not regret Ewen, not in the least, but she was not that carefree young girl any more, game for adventure. She was a respectable widow trying to make a decent living for her son and herself.

Her mother was waiting for an answer.

Lydia sighed. When her mother was determined, nothing and nobody could budge her. It was true Lydia had not been out of Wick for years now. And she could trust her mother to look after Ewen. But to go to Yarmouth?

As she thought of it, a tiny spark of interest lit. She had never been there. And it would only be one day on the train, find Robbie and bring him home, maybe the next day. She would not be gone for long.

Maybe it would even be... fun? That was a word she had not used in a long time. She suppressed the tiny emerging bubble of excitement and turned a carefully serious face to her mother.

'If it's the only way, and you'll look after Ewen, then yes. I'll go,' Lydia said.

CHAPTER 3

It was nothing like the train journeys to college in Edinburgh that Lydia had so enjoyed, though the early start was familiar. Half-past seven on a cold dark morning and a long day and a night's travelling ahead. And instead of being part of a proud send-off of young ladies and lads who had done well in school and were now set to achieve even more, she found herself surrounded by a noisy gaggle of fisher lassies, giggling and pushing to get into the train. With a decided whiff of fish about them.

Lydia's natural instinct was to draw back. She did not belong here, and she was already drawing curious glances as she peered at the labels on the carriage windows to find those that had been reserved by her Uncle Bill's curing firm for his shore staff.

It reminded her of the Bible story of Ruth and Boaz. Ruth had gone to glean and had been noticed by Boaz who told her to stay with his female workers where she would be safe. Lydia looked at the bold-eyed fisher lassies, loudly sorting themselves out in the compartments. She was not at all sure she would be safe amongst them. She would stick out like a sore thumb.

It took all her courage and determination to climb into the third-class carriage when her heart longed for her to sail past with her nose in the air down to the second-class carriage where she belonged. But she had no choice. Her mother had persuaded Uncle Bill's clerk to issue a fish-worker's subsidised ticket for her so here she had to be. She hesitated at the door to the compartment.

The girls went quiet and turned to stare at her. She took a step forward.

'You're in the wrong place,' one of the girls told her bluntly. 'These are for us going to Yarmouth. You should be in the posh carriages at the front.'

Unspeaking, Lydia held up her special ticket. All eyes fixed on it.

'Leave her alone,' another girl spoke up, a pretty dark-haired girl in a brown tweed skirt and Fair Isle patterned jumper. 'If she wants to travel with us, we can't stop her.' She turned to Lydia with a cheeky grin. 'But you'd be more comfortable up the front.'

'My ticket's for this carriage,' Lydia said, already feeling very uncomfortable.

'We can see that. Come in, then, and make yourself at home,' the girl said. 'I'm Chrissie Anderson, that's...' A stream of names that she was sure she would never remember flowed past Lydia. Some of the girls smiled a greeting when their name was spoken. Others scowled.

'I'm Lydia Alexander,' she began.

'We know,' Chrissie said, and turned her back to finish putting her bag in the net above her head.

Wick was a small town but here Lydia felt she was at a disadvantage. Although she vaguely recognised some of them, fisher lassies were not people that she *knew*. Granny Leslie's voice echoed in her head: 'Not our kind of people.' So how did these girls know her? The answer came: they would know her as their employer's niece. That would be it.

They budged up and made room for her although she felt she wanted to shrink down into the tiniest space. And she was desperate not to show how aware she was of the all-pervading smell of fish. Although the girls seemed to be wearing quite smart clothes for the journey, there still was a definite aroma. Lydia's nose tickled. She knew it would be unforgivable to let it show. She concentrated hard on trying to distract herself.

It was not difficult. Packed like sardines into the special compartments boldly labelled with the names of the curing firms that had hired the fisher lassies for the Yarmouth season, Lydia felt completely out of her depth. Around her, chattering away excitedly, nineteen to the dozen in broad Wick dialect like a flock of noisy seagulls, the fisher lassies were clearly enjoying themselves – and her discomfort.

She tried to make herself inconspicuous but it was hard to avoid the curious eyes of these girls – girls she recognised from living in the same town, who had been at the same school when she was growing up, and no doubt some of whom were related to her through her father's family. Though Granny Leslie always made it clear that her side of the family was a cut above the Rosses and the other fisher folk, despite Grandpa Leslie, and now Uncle Bill, owning the biggest fish-curing yard in town.

The train slowly left Wick, the big steam engine puffing out into the darkness, whistle shrieking above the clatter of the wheels on the rails. The girls settled down to gossip. It was clear they knew all about Robbie's fight with his father but they were curious to know why Lydia was on her way to Yarmouth.

'But you're a teacher, aren't you?'

'Yes. But it's the tattie-picking holidays so I've got a few days off.'

'But Yarmouth?'

'For a holiday?'

Unsurprisingly they did not believe her. Chrissie snorted and the other girls laughed. They were avid for more details but soon tired in the face of Lydia's determined silence.

'Leave her alone,' Chrissie finally told them, and they seemed willing to do what she said.

It was obvious they thought she was being stuck-up and she was aware of some unfriendly looks, but she was grateful to Chrissie for stopping the inquisition. Lydia settled herself to ignore them all but she could not help but hear their conversation.

They seemed to talk about anything and everything, quite shamelessly, and their comments made her blush. A married woman like her! Though admittedly, she and Danny had only had the two days before Danny went back to the Front. She seemed to know less than some of the fifteen-year-olds! It made her feel both ancient and ignorant. Even more a fish out of water. And the occasional peals of laughter accompanied by sideways glances at her just added to her discomfort.

She was happier when they talked about where they were going and what they expected to be doing. She listened intently then in the hope of gathering useful information. Her mother had, as usual, organised everything efficiently and all in a few days. She had sat Lydia down to write a letter to the Education Board saying she needed a week off because of 'urgent family matters', then she had managed to get one of the special tickets for the train from her brother Bill who ran the curing yard after Grandpa Leslie's death. His clerk had brought it round to the house.

'It's got the date on of when you're going but it's open for coming back. You've got six months, but you'll no' be needing that! The other lassies will be staying till the end of the season and coming home for Christmas but you just come home when you're ready,' the clerk explained. 'The other lassies will look after you,' he added. As if she was not able to look after herself, she had thought resentfully at the time.

But after a few hours in the train, she began to understand. Most of the women and girls had done this trip many times and knew how to make themselves comfortable. They even seemed to be enjoying it, as if it were a holiday.

They were a lively bunch, laughing and joking, knitting and singing to pass the time. They compared notes on what they had packed in their kists – everything they would need for their stay in Yarmouth. Their oilies – the long oilskin aprons – and their working clothes of warm tweed skirts and hand-knitted jumpers and cardigans, and their 'good clothes' for Saturday nights and Sundays. Some even brought a mattress to sleep on and bed linen. Lydia had never guessed how much was involved in this annual migration.

The train steamed slowly into Inverness station at half past one, the platform loud and musical with the Gaelic of the fisher lassies from the West Coast waiting to board. The Wick girls leaned precariously out of windows and doors, waving to old friends and shouting greetings and enquiries. Chrissie called to a plump young girl to join them and once again, space was made for the newcomer.

Chrissie introduced her to Lydia as Johann, from one of the Western Isles. She spoke with Chrissie in a low soft voice. There seemed to be a lot of catching up to do and a few tears. There was obviously some boyfriend trouble but Chrissie seemed to have a wisdom beyond her years and as Lydia watched, Chrissie listened, comforted, advised and cheered the girl up.

By the time the train slowed and pulled in to Perth station at nearly six o'clock in the evening, it was full dark again. Lydia was tired and sore, but strangely comfortable now with the fisher lassies who unselfconsciously included her in their chat and their songs and their laughter. They really were not a bad lot of companions, she mused, and then had to budge up again as Chrissie welcomed another, older woman into their midst.

'Janet Foubister,' Chrissie introduced her. 'She's from Lewis originally, but she married a fisherman from Orkney. The three of us – me, Johann and Janet – we work together in the same crew.'

'I came on the Aberdeen train,' Janet explained. 'It brings all the women from the Brough, Aberdeen and Fraserburgh, and us from Orkney.'

She described to the amusement of the other girls how, when the coaches from Aberdeen were being coupled to the Inverness train, she had jumped down and run along the platform till she spotted Chrissie leaning out of the window. Lydia looked admiringly at Janet's trim figure. She was lithe and young-looking though, Lydia guessed, in her forties.

'Aye,' she said, 'there's a good lot of us', and it was plain when the train started up again that the loudly puffing engine was straining to pull a heavier load.

On their way again, the women and girls settled down to chat and Lydia to listen. Some of the women like Janet had menfolk on boats which had already arrived in Yarmouth. Others like Johann had boyfriends they had met at the earlier fishing season in Orkney, including lads from Yarmouth, and they were keenly looking forward to seeing them again.

The train drew into England. Carlisle, then Nottingham. Somehow along the way Lydia managed to get a little sleep. The singing of the West Coast girls was soothing and she was grateful that the train was steam-heated and had lavatories. Third-class carriages maybe, but bearable.

The Wick lassies took pity on her when her bottle of tea and packet of sandwiches ran out. Janet had a little stove she lit in the corridor of the train to brew up fresh tea. 'Share and share alike' seemed to be their motto and they shared cheerfully with her, making her feel a bit ashamed of her earlier attitude toward them. They seemed good-hearted folk.

Gradually the pitch black of the night turned once more to grey as morning arrived. Five o'clock and time to change trains. They dragged themselves out of the warm fug of their compartments and into a chilly morning. After what felt like a long wait, they piled on to what Chrissie said was the milk train. It puffed slowly along the track, seeming to stop at every station. The window showed a flat landscape, almost as flat as home, Lydia thought. But there were more trees, some beginning to change to the golds and reds of autumn colours. There were flat fields with fat cows and slow drizzly rain. One of the girls spotted some men working in a field. The train was going so slowly she leaned out of the window and shouted to them, asking them the time and laughing as she tried to catch their answers.

Then at last they arrived at Yarmouth Beach Station. It was the middle of the day. The journey from Wick had taken over twenty-four hours.

'You've got your lodgings fixed?' Chrissie asked.

'Yes, my mother arranged it. She's given me the name of the hotel and the directions,' Lydia began.

'Oooh!' one of the other girls declared, mimicking her cruelly. 'A hotel!'

'Never mind her,' Chrissie told Lydia. 'You'll be fine there. But you would have a lot more fun in wi' us in the Rows.'

Whatever the Rows were, it sounded as though the girls were definitely planning on having fun – and by the sound of it, it was not the kind of fun Granny Leslie would approve of.

Though the other girls were pinched with tiredness, they were still in high spirits, planning to get to their lodgings and have a good sleep. Lydia yawned and stretched, trying to unkink her tired and sore muscles.

How she would love to have a good long sleep but she knew she did not have time to spare. She had to find Robbie as soon as possible and persuade him to come home. She had only managed to get a few days' leave of absence. She had to succeed swiftly and get back on the train home, with Robbie at her side.

CHAPTER 4

Gripping her little suitcase in one hand and in the other the piece of paper her mother had written out for her with directions to the hotel, Lydia set off from Beach Station and into Great Yarmouth.

First, she decided, she would need to get something to eat to recover her strength. She knew she would need her wits about her to persuade her brother to come home. It was different when he was little and she was his beloved big sister. Now at 22, he was a man – and a man who had seen terrible things in the Great War, things that had changed him. Things he would not speak of even to his family. Maybe especially to his family. The biddable wee boy was long gone.

Lydia found a respectable-looking café and ordered tea and toast.

'Come off the morning train, did you?' the motherly woman in charge of the café asked.

'Yes,' Lydia said.

'From where?'

'Wick.'

The woman beamed at her. 'My sister married a Wick fisherman,' she said and when she brought the tea and toast, there was a boiled egg too.

'I didn't order...' Lydia began but the woman brushed aside her protests.

'You need something inside you after a long journey like that. You're too thin as it is. And it's on the house so eat it up!' She stood by the table, hands on hips and waited till Lydia gave in and started to eat. Satisfied, she went back to her chores.

Lydia enjoyed the fresh egg. The woman was right. She did need more than just a piece of toast. Thinking of the bowls of steaming porridge on the breakfast table at home, she thought her mother would be horrified...

Reminded, she reached into her bag and drew out writing paper and a pen.

'*Dear Mother,*' she began. '*Well, I've arrived in Yarmouth. It was a long journey but I managed to get some sleep. It was a bit crowded but I tried to keep myself to myself.*'

She paused, chewing the end of her pencil, remembering the fisher girls' laughter and the jokes, the flirting with the men at each station they stopped at. No, there was no need to tell her mother about that.

She continued in scrupulous honesty: '*The other girls were kind, though. They even shared their sandwiches and tea with me.*'

~

Jean Ross smiled as she read Lydia's letter. So she was launched onto her adventure, even if she did not realise it yet. She had felt Lydia had become rather withdrawn after Danny's death and needed something to pull her out of it. But what was this 'tried to keep herself to herself'? That was not quite what she would have advised Lydia. She had got... not quite stuck-up, but her solitariness made it almost seem so. But sharing tea and sandwiches with the fisher lassies.

That was an excellent sign. The fisher lassies were good-hearted and she would come to no harm.

'Letter from your Mummy,' she told Ewen who came rushing in from school.

'Oh good,' he said carelessly. 'Can I go out and play?'

Jean laughed. 'Of course, darling.'

Poor Lydia had worried about leaving him. He was not going to come to any harm from this little adventure either!

Well-pleased, she reached for her cup of tea and re-read the letter, trying to read between the lines and imagine what her daughter was doing.

~

After a good breakfast, Lydia thanked the café owner and tried to pay for the egg as well as her tea and toast. But the woman was having nothing of it.

'I could be entertaining angels unawares and anyway, for all you know we could be related,' she teased Lydia. 'Anyway, think of it as one for the Lord.' She paused, then continued, 'Do you know the Lord Jesus?'

Lydia hesitated. Once upon a time, she would have said yes without hesitation but now... For a moment, she felt the sudden pang of loss.

'You've come to Yarmouth at a good time,' the woman was saying. 'The Lord's been moving in Lowestoft and we're hoping for more here in Yarmouth. There are lots of meetings. You'll maybe find your way to one of them.' And she turned away back to her chores.

Meetings? Lydia thought. She was not interested in religious meetings. And anyway she would not have any time. She had to find Robbie and get them both on the train back to Wick as soon as she could. She thanked the woman politely and headed out into the street.

The roads seemed to be set out in a very orderly fashion with a few long streets running the length of the almost-island the town was built on and lots of tiny cobbled alleyways running between them. These were numbered and made it quite easy to find her way.

At last she found the hotel her mother had booked – but a chilly welcome. She had been advised by her uncle's clerk not to dress in her smartest clothes as she would have to mix with the fisher lassies in their third-class compartments, but even so she had felt over-dressed compared to them. Now she felt the receptionist was looking down her nose at her. Maybe the taint of fish had migrated to her!

'Mrs Alexander,' Lydia announced herself with more firmness than she felt and carefully removed her gloves so her wedding ring showed.

The receptionist sniffed and turned the register round for her to sign.

'Room 21,' she was told. 'First floor, last on the right.'

Lydia took the room key and thanked the woman, then trudged up the stairs. By the time she got to the top, her weariness was telling on her. In the room – small but clean – the narrow bed looked welcoming. She thought of the fisher lassies who had been planning a long sleep before meeting up with their friends for a walk round the town. How she would love to sleep.

Resolutely, she put her case on the bed. Then weakening slightly, she allowed herself to sit down for a moment in the armchair by the open window, sure that the fresh air would keep her from dozing off.

~

When she woke, it was growing dark. Lydia felt cramped from sleeping in the chair and chilled by the cold air coming in from the window.

Time was marching on and she had not even begun her search for Robbie. Guiltily, she turned and left the room, locking the door behind her. Downstairs, she handed the key back to the receptionist.

'I'm not sure when I'll be back,' she said. The receptionist took the key and hung it on a hook without a word.

Outside, she hesitated. Where would she be most likely to find Robbie? At the harbour, Lydia decided, and headed straight for one of the little cross streets that cut directly through to the quayside.

It was not like any harbour Lydia had ever seen. More like a wide canal packed tight with boats tied up to both sides. There were more fishing boats than she had ever seen in one place, all crammed in together, bow to the quayside, side by side like sardines. There must have been hundreds of them. Most were simply riding at anchor without even a puff of smoke from the slender chimneys, the few men on board lounging against the rails and smoking cigarettes.

A handful of newly arrived boats were jostling to find a place. A few others already at the quay were unloading their catch, the pulleys creaking as they swung the crans of silvery herring out over the deck and onto the quayside to be scooped up by nimble boys or shovelled into strange double wicker baskets and taken away by horse-drawn cart or motor lorry. Men in smart suits and working clothes moved around between the covered fish market, the fish-merchants' sheds, the salesmen's offices and the refreshment rooms.

There was little of the shouting and laughing she was familiar with when the Wick boats came in laden with their silver harvest. Here the atmosphere was tense, anxious – only the noise of a few engines, and the creak of the boats...

Lydia carefully made her way along the quayside, checking the registration letters on the boats till she found the familiar WK of Wick and began her quest in earnest, glad that there was no sign of her father's boat.

'I'm looking for my brother, Robbie Ross. Do you know where I can find him?' Lydia hailed the men leaning on the rails.

She soon became familiar with the quick lift of eyebrows, the exchanged glances, and the unwilling answers.

'Sorry, haven't seen him.'

'No, no idea.'

Till finally she found a fisherman she knew. Geordie MacDonald had been a friend of her older brother Alec and somebody she had never really liked but he looked up from his work and seemed to recognise her.

'Well, well, well,' he said. 'If it isn't Lydia Ross.' He stepped across the deck towards her. 'And what might you be doing in Yarmouth?'

'Hello, Geordie,' she said peaceably. 'I'm looking for Robbie.'

'Oh aye?' He laughed derisively and spat over the side of the boat. His reaction stung her.

'What's the matter with you men? Is there some kind of secret? Will you not tell me the truth?' she demanded, hands on hips. 'Where will I find Robbie?'

'Well, you won't find him here, that's for sure,' Geordie said with relish. 'None of the Wick skippers will take him on after what happened with your Dad.'

'So where can I find him?'

He shrugged. 'You could try the pubs,' he said carelessly and turned back to his work.

Pubs? She had never been in a pub in her life. But if that was where Robbie was to be found, then she would have to track him down there. Her mother would skin her if she knew. Her father would do worse!

She turned on her heel and marched towards the main streets of the town, aware as the streetlights came on that time was pressing.

At first she simply steeled herself to peek inside the door of the dark, smoky, drink-smelling dens and check that Robbie was not there before moving on to the next. But at the Lamb and Garter, a man just inside the doorway caught her arm and pulled her inside.

'Don't be shy!' he mocked her.

His friends clustered at the bar turned round and stared at her.

'What do we have here?'

'Let me go!' Lydia demanded.

'Ah ha,' he said. 'Just got in on the train this morning, have you?'

Lydia nodded.

'And where might you have come from?'

'Wick,' she admitted.

The men exchanged glances. 'A Wicker are you? That's good. We like Wickers, don't we, boys?' Lydia did not like the knowing grins on their faces. She knew the fisher lassies had a certain reputation...

'Now you're here, you'll have a drink with us,' the man said, drawing her closer to the group. 'To welcome you to Yarmouth.'

Lydia shook her head.

'No, thank you. I'm looking for somebody...' she began.

'Yes, we know that, sweetheart,' the first man said.

Hope flared to sudden life inside Lydia. Had word got round so quickly? Maybe it was going to be easier to find Robbie than she had begun to fear.

'Do you know where he is?' she asked hopefully.

'Oh yes,' the first man said. 'I'll show you where he is,' and taking her arm he led her out of the pub and into the dark alley behind it.

The alley was empty. The man stopped suddenly and Lydia felt sudden alarm.

'Where is he?' she asked. 'Where's my brother?'

'You don't need a brother,' the man said, pressing her back against the wall and seizing her in a hard embrace. 'You said you were looking for somebody. Well, I'm somebody!'

'Let me go!' Lydia began to fight to break free but his mouth came down on hers in a disgusting wet kiss. 'No!' His hands pawed at her clothes and she struggled in horror. 'Help!' she managed to squeak.

Just when she thought she would faint from the horror of it, the man was pulled off her and she was surrounded by a trio of furious women. One of them started scolding him loudly in a strong Wick accent.

'Leave her alone! You should be ashamed of yourself!'

Lydia was left shuddering and trembling against the wall, her eyes tight shut to block out the horror. She heard the man swear at the girl.

'Be off before I call a policeman!' the girl shouted and Lydia heard heavy footsteps hurry away.

'Are you all right?' the girl's voice asked. 'We saw him pull you round here and knew he was up to no good.'

Lydia opened her eyes. It was Chrissie, the girl she had met on the train. With her were Janet and Johann, the other girls on her crew.

'What on earth did you think you were doing?' Chrissie demanded.

'I was looking for Robbie. My brother. That man said he knew where he was...'

'And you fell for it?'

'Yes.'

'I'm surprised your mother lets you out, Lyddie Alexander,' Chrissie said, with a shake of her head.

'Oh don't scold her,' Janet said. She turned to Lydia. 'No harm done?'

'No,' Lydia said with a shudder. 'If you hadn't come...'

'Well, we did,' Chrissie said.

'We couldn't just walk past,' Johann murmured.

'Not at all,' Janet said.

'Thank you...' Lydia told them. 'I don't know how I'd have...'

'What are you going to do now?' Chrissie cut in.

'I've got to keep looking for Robbie till I find him,' Lydia said. 'That's why I'm here. My mother sent me with the money for his ticket home...'

The girls exchanged glances. There was something here that Lydia didn't understand.

'Do you know him?' she asked.

To Lydia's surprise Chrissie burst out laughing.

'She should,' Janet said with a grin. 'She's been his girlfriend this past summer.' They began to laugh again.

Lydia remembered Robbie's farewell wave to the girl on the brae head. The girl in the dark blue shawl. Lydia had not got a clear look at her but she thought now maybe she could make out the resemblance. It was sad how little she seemed to know about her younger brother – or how little he had chosen to tell his family.

'I'm sorry, Chrissie. I didn't know,' Lydia said. 'But I have to find him. Do you know where he is?'

Chrissie seemed to accept the apology. 'I haven't seen him yet,' she said. 'But then we've only just arrived. The lads will all be in the market square tonight so we'll maybe see him there, and then tomorrow's Sunday. There's plenty of time...'

'No there isn't!' Lydia said. 'I've got to get back in a day or so. My ticket...' She stopped, horrified. 'My bag! Where is it?'

Hurriedly she turned back to the alley and peered into the gloom, but there was no sign of it.

'Oh no!' Lydia cried. 'What am I going to do? That man must have taken it. It's got the money for Robbie's ticket in it, and my money for my lodgings, and my ticket and everything! How am I going to manage? How am I going to get home now?'

CHAPTER 5

Chrissie pushed past her and ran down the alley but the man had vanished and there was no sign of Lydia's bag. She came back to where Lydia was waiting with the other two girls.

'I'll have a look in the pub,' she said. 'You stay here.'

She returned a few moments later, shaking her head.

'No,' she said. 'He's not there and they won't say who he is or where he comes from.' She looked curiously at Lydia. 'What are you going to do now? Do you want to go to the police?'

'I don't know what I'm going to do,' Lydia said, 'and I don't think there's much point going to the police. I didn't really get a good look at him...'

'Where are you staying?' Janet asked.

'The Grafton Hotel. I went there first and got a room. I...' Lydia hesitated, feeling suddenly guilty. 'I had a little sleep before I came looking for Robbie.'

'And you thought you'd find him here?' Chrissie demanded hotly. 'In the worst tavern in Yarmouth? Fine opinion your family's got of him. It's no wonder...'

'Leave her alone,' Janet hushed her. 'It's not her fault.' She turned to Lydia. 'Look, with no money you can't stay at the Grafton. You'd best come back with us to our lodgings. We can squeeze in another one.'

She looked to the others for agreement. Chrissie hesitated then nodded. Johann said in her sweet soft voice, 'That would be the best thing to do.'

'That's really good of you,' Lydia said. 'But I left my case at the hotel...'

'Well, they're hardly likely to just let you go in and get it once they find out you've got no money to pay for the room,' Chrissie told her.

'Couldn't I say I'd changed my mind about staying there?'

Chrissie and Janet exchanged glances.

'I don't think so,' Janet said. 'You did use the room...'

'But I slept in the chair... I didn't make a mess...'

'They're not to know that,' Chrissie said.

'And they're in the hotel business to make money,' Janet told her.

'So what am I to do?'

'You're the brains, Chrissie,' Janet said teasingly.

Chrissie grinned. 'In that case,' she said decisively, 'we'd better go and get that suitcase back. Come on!' And to Lydia's surprise, she linked Lydia's arm through hers and the four women set out back towards the hotel.

If Granny Leslie could see her now, Lydia thought, she would be horrified. Walking along the street arm-in-arm with a trio of the fisher lassies she so despised. Fisher lassies who chattered and laughed and seemed to accept her as if she was one of them.

But it felt good.

For the first time in a long while Lydia felt her loneliness ease. Fisher lassies they might be, but they seemed like really nice girls

and they had rescued her and taken pity on her. Now they chattered away, Chrissie in her Wick accent, Janet in a mix of northern
and western dialect, and quiet little Johann in her Gaelic-tinged lilt.
There was a lot of laughter and they made sure to include Lydia when
they could, cheerfully shortening her name to Lyddie, something she
had never known before but thought she rather liked. It felt friendly.

'Oh, there's Walter!' Johann cried suddenly and pulled away from
the girls. 'Walter! Here I am!' she called, excitedly waving at a young
fisherman coming towards them. Bright colour lit her cheeks as she
rushed towards him, stopping him in his tracks. She seized his hands,
then turned back to them to call out, 'I'll be back at the house later!'

'Oh dear,' Chrissie muttered and pulled Lydia and Janet down the
next street away from them.

'Oh dear?' Lydia queried.

'Johann met him at the Orkney fishing in the spring,' Janet
explained. 'She's really sweet on him, but I'm not so sure about
him. Poor Johann.'

'She's so trusting,' Chrissie said. 'A bit like you, Lyddie. A pair of
Babes in the Woods, you two. Myself, I wouldn't trust that one.'

'Oh well, no doubt we'll hear all about it later,' Janet said.

They continued their arm-linked progress on through the town
till they neared the hotel. Steps slowing, Chrissie asked, 'Right,
Lyddie, where's your room?'

'On the first floor, at the back, right at the end of the corridor.'

'First floor – that's going to mean a bit of a scramble,' Janet said.

'You or me?' Chrissie asked her.

'I can climb better than you!' Janet laughed, then seeing Lydia's
bewildered face, she said, 'Lyddie, you just stay with me. It'll be fine.
We'll go round the back and see if there's a window open. Chrissie
will go in the front and make a nuisance of herself...'

'Smelly Wick fisher lassie wanting a room in a genteel hotel! And maybe a little drink taken?' Chrissie explained. 'They won't look any further than their own prejudices!'

Lydia had the grace to blush. It was rather too close a description of her own self climbing on to the train the previous day. But maybe not today?

'Don't overdo it!' Janet warned Chrissie, then turned back to Lydia. 'Anyway, while our girl makes a noise at the front, I'll just pop into your room and get your case.'

The two women grinned.

'Give me long enough, mind!' Janet cheerfully admonished Chrissie.

Chrissie laughed and headed for the front of the hotel.

Still completely bewildered by what was happening, Lydia allowed herself to be led round the back of the hotel.

'Can you point out which is your window?' Janet asked.

Lydia scanned the wall. 'My room's at the end of the corridor so I think it's that one.' She pointed. 'That's the window I left open.'

'That's handy,' Janet said. 'And so is that nicely placed outhouse underneath it. Now you wait here and give me a shout if anyone comes.'

Janet ran quietly across the deserted courtyard and within minutes, she was climbing up on to the roof of the lean-to, and pushing open the window to Lydia's room. She stuck her head inside, then turned back and beckoned to Lydia to come to the side of the outhouse.

'Brown case on the bed?' she whispered.

Lydia nodded and watched, heart in mouth, as Janet clambered over the sill and into the room.

What shall I do if someone comes? she thought. I'm a respectable widow, a teacher. If they call the police I'll lose my job... But strangely it was Janet being caught in the room that mattered more, and she cringed to think what nasty insults Chrissie would be taking from the snooty receptionist. It was bad enough when the woman had looked down her nose at her! How strange. She had only met these girls the previous day, yet here she was caring about what happened to them.

Moments later, Janet reappeared at the window with Lydia's suitcase. She quickly set the case on the lean-to roof, and turned to close the window. She lowered the case down from the roof into Lydia's waiting hands, then she scrambled down and brushed off her skirts. Linking her arm in Lydia's, she said with a satisfied smile, 'Let's go and find Chrissie.'

Chrissie was not hard to find. As they turned the corner, they saw her being ejected forcefully from the hotel. She was screeching her outrage in the broadest terms.

'My money's as good as...'

She caught sight of them and swiftly gave up the fight.

'I understand. Fisher lassies aren't good enough for you.'

With a flounce of her skirts, she swung away from the hotel and stormed past them, giving every appearance of high dudgeon.

'Come on!' Janet whispered and pulled Lydia after her, round the corner.

There Chrissie was waiting, her face red with laughter. 'Oh that was good!' she said. 'I really enjoyed that.' She looked at the case in Lydia's hand. 'Got it? That's good. We'd better be going and get you settled in at our lodgings.'

And again the arms were linked and Lydia was swept along by the two girls, who cheerfully related their adventure to one another, with much laughter and gaiety.

'That was a bit of fun, wasn't it?' Chrissie asked, her face alight with mischief.

And yes, it had been, Lydia realised. She felt strangely carefree, having fun with these women who had accepted her so easily and generously. It was all very strange.

~

Chrissie and her friends had lodgings in one of the Rows, the narrow streets that criss-crossed the town. The houses were so close together that you could almost touch the walls if you stood in the middle with your arms stretched out. Rich merchants' houses rubbed shoulders with pawnbrokers and fishermen's cottages, and children ran and played on the cobblestones. It was a lively, noisy place.

At the tall narrow house where Chrissie, Johann and Janet were staying, Mrs Duff their landlady was a friendly Yarmouth fisherman's widow.

Her eyebrows rose when the girls arrived but Chrissie launched into explanations and wheedling. Mrs Duff heard Chrissie out, exclaiming in dismay at Lydia's misfortune.

'Yes, of course, you'll stay here tonight,' she said to Lydia's relief, and instructed Chrissie and Janet to take her upstairs. Narrow enclosed wooden stairs led to a loft room that ran the length and breadth of the house. High enough to stand up in, the room was filled with beds all neatly made up. Kists were tucked under beds or set out as seating. The walls were lined with brown wrapping paper, and the air was pervaded with the smell of fish.

The girls led Lydia to the corner they had made their own. Chrissie looked at Lydia. 'Are you hungry? We've eaten already but we can see if there's anything left.'

Lydia shook her head. 'No, thank you. I don't need anything...'

'You've had a bit of a shake-up,' motherly Janet said kindly. 'You climb into bed and get to sleep.'

'We'll be back soon,' Chrissie said. 'And if I see Robbie, I'll tell him you're here and what's happened.'

'Don't you worry about anything,' Janet said. 'Once you've had a wee sleep you'll be able to think better what to do.'

And with that the two women went back down the steep stairs. Left alone in the big quiet room, Lydia opened her case and changed into her nightdress. She climbed into the high bed and tried to sleep but her mind would not rest.

It was all very well for Janet to say not to worry about anything, but how was she to manage with no money and no ticket home? Why had she been so stupid as to trust that man? But then what did she know about men? There had only ever been Danny...

Lydia sighed. There was little point beating herself up for her folly. She rolled over in the big bed and tried to get comfortable.

Maybe if she went to her father he would help her? The sudden flare of hope died just as suddenly. She needed enough money for both her own fare home and Robbie's, and she was certain her father would not do anything to help Robbie any more. The only other person she knew in Yarmouth was her uncle at the curing yard. But he had already provided her ticket. She could hardly ask him for a replacement in the circumstances.

Oh, what was she to do? Tears prickled behind her eyelids but then the sheer exhaustion of the past days overcame her and she fell asleep.

CHAPTER 6

The whispering woke her.

It was broad daylight. Chrissie and Janet were sitting on the kist beside the bed, their heads close together. They were fully dressed and by the look of it, all the other inhabitants of the room were up and gone.

Lydia sat up in bed, surprised that she had slept so soundly on the thin mattress – not at all like her comfortable bed at home. And sharing it with the other two girls! She had never shared with anyone in her life, apart from the two nights with her husband Danny. Hurriedly, she pushed that thought away.

Janet and Chrissie had teased her good-naturedly when they returned the previous night, insisting that there was plenty of room since she was so thin. She was grateful that they had put her to one side, with Janet in the middle and Chrissie on the other side. It had made it easier for her to slip shyly out from under the covers in the night to use the chamber pot tucked under the bed.

'What time is it?' Lydia asked.

'It's Sunday.' Chrissie laughed. 'You don't have to worry about the time...'

'Unless you're going to church, Lyddie?' Janet added.

'Umm, well, not really,' Lydia mumbled. In the years since Danny's death, she had occasionally accompanied her mother to church – to please her. But it was not something she had any interest in for herself. Not any more.

'If you want to go to church, there's time. And Janet will go with you. She always goes to church,' Chrissie said with affectionate teasing. 'She's very religious!'

'And if you don't want to go to church, you can go for a walk with Chrissie,' Janet responded placidly.

They waited for her answer, but something new struck Lydia. She had slept in the bed with the other two women – Janet in the middle and Chrissie on the outside. But there was someone else on their team who should have been there.

'Where's Johann?' Lydia asked. 'Did I take her place and she slept somewhere else?'

Janet and Chrissie exchanged glances.

'Well...' Janet began carefully.

'Oh, tell Lyddie the truth,' Chrissie said crossly. 'She's a grown woman.' She turned to Lydia. 'We haven't seen her since she went off with Walter last night. She's probably stayed out with him.'

Lydia's eyes widened. 'All night?' The quiet lass from the Western Isles did not seem the sort of girl to indulge in such loose living.

'Oh, it's not Johann's fault. She's completely besotted with that Walter Smith,' Janet said. 'She'd do anything he tells her.'

'But if that's where she is,' Chrissie continued, 'then we're hoping that means everything's all right.'

'What do you mean?' Lydia asked.

Again Chrissie and Janet exchanged glances.

'It's all right,' Chrissie told Janet. 'Lyddie will probably never set eyes on her again.' She turned back to Lydia. 'The thing is, Johann told me on the train that she's expecting and she was going to tell Walter when she saw him. She was sure he would marry her. She said he'd promised her, she's so...'

'Innocent,' Janet said sadly.

'Soft in the head, more like,' Chrissie snapped. 'She should have known he was only saying it so she would let him...'

'Well, well,' Janet soothed. 'It's done now.' She turned to Lydia. 'So we're hoping that if she's stayed out all night with him, then when she turns up, it will be with good news.'

'If she'd come right back, then we'd know he'd dumped her,' Chrissie said. 'Which is what I would expect from *him*,' she added darkly.

Janet nodded. 'I'm afraid I have to agree. He does not have a good reputation with the girls. But he turned poor Johann's head.'

Chrissie snorted.

'Well, I'm off to church now,' Janet said. 'Maybe a few prayers will help!' She gathered up her coat and hat and Bible. 'If you two are going out for a walk, we can meet up here afterwards.'

'You get dressed,' Chrissie told Lydia, 'and I'll get us a cup of tea.' Chrissie followed Janet down the stairs.

Obediently Lydia followed Chrissie's instructions, tumbling into her clothes, before catching up with her in the kitchen downstairs, one thought uppermost in her mind.

'Have you seen Robbie?' Lydia asked Chrissie. 'Last night?'

'No,' Chrissie said. 'His boat's still out...' She shut her mouth quickly as though she had said something she wished she had not. She turned away and started fussing with the teapot.

Lydia stared at Chrissie's averted face. 'But I thought no one would take him on as crew? That's what Auntie Lena and Auntie Ina said.'

'Cats,' Chrissie said succinctly. 'The pair of them. Just as well some of his family think better of him.'

53

'What do you mean?' Lydia was perplexed.

Chrissie looked over her shoulder at Lydia. 'The Lowestoft lot,' she said unwillingly.

'Lowestoft?'

Chrissie swung round to face her. 'Where his other Granny lives, yes?' she said impatiently. 'Lyddie, you *do* know about her?'

'Well, yes. I know about her.'

She knew that her father's widowed mother had moved to Lowestoft. When she remarried a Lowestoft fisherman after her young husband was lost at sea, she had taken her two girls – Ina and Lena – to live with her, but David was left with his grandmother in Wick. Later, both Ina and Lena had married Wick fishermen and returned home but David had never had any contact with his mother and her new family. And Lydia was aware of bad feelings regarding the estrangement so it was something that was never mentioned at home.

'We don't have anything to do with them,' she added.

'*You* may not,' Chrissie said. 'But Robbie does.'

'Robbie does?'

'Yes!' Chrissie thumped the teapot on the table, clearly irritated with Lydia's response, but then she relented. 'He met up with one of his cousins in the War and they've been good friends ever since,' she explained. 'His Granny was happy to see him whenever he was south with the Aberdeen trawlers. So when his Dad threw him off the *Bonnie Jean*, where else would he go but to his own folk where he knew he was welcome?'

Lydia swallowed hard. This was too much to take in. It was as if a whole new family had materialised who had accepted Robbie and taken care of him... taking the place of his own family in Wick. Who maybe had not been so accepting.

But there was something she needed to know.

'Where is he now?' she asked humbly.

'He's out on his cousin's boat. The English boats work Sundays,' Chrissie told her. 'We'll maybe see him if they come in with a catch this afternoon.'

'So that's what you meant about him maybe not being ready to come home yet? I see,' Lydia said quietly. 'We've been worrying over nothing.'

'As usual,' Chrissie said.

'Oh.'

Lydia drank her tea in silence. If Robbie was in no need of help, then the only problem was how *she* was going to get home before the end of her leave of absence. The thought came: maybe Robbie would help her? She did not want to ask her father. If he knew why she had come, he would be furious. Robbie was her best hope. Her face brightened.

'So we might see Robbie today?' she asked Chrissie.

'Might do,' Chrissie replied. 'The boats won't be in till this afternoon. Do you want to go for a little walk first? You might as well see what sort of a place Yarmouth is now you've got here.'

'That's true,' Lydia agreed. 'I'll get my coat...'

~

Once again, as they stepped out of the house, Chrissie unselfconsciously linked arms with Lydia and the pair of them set off down the street.

'You'll see enough of the harbour this afternoon when we're waiting for Robbie's boat to come in,' Chrissie said. 'So let's go the other way. You can take a look at the beach and the hotels where the posh folk stay on their holidays.'

55

Lydia felt the barb hit. Folk like her, Chrissie was saying. Not like the ordinary working folk – the fisher folk – who stuck together and looked after one another. The people her Granny Leslie so fiercely looked down on – and had taught her to do too.

Only now, as she got to know these girls, Lydia was beginning to see them differently. Yes, maybe on her ultra-strict grandmother's terms, these girls were a bit bold and independent. Un-ladylike. But Lydia was beginning to admire their independence. And they seemed to enjoy their lives. It was all rather topsy-turvy.

Chrissie led her down the length of the Row, and over a couple of streets that ran lengthwise through the town, till they reached the tourist area.

Chrissie had clearly taken it upon herself to give Lydia a thorough guided tour. After they had walked along the beach, she guided her back into the town where she pointed out the best shops.

'That's where we buy the Yarmouth rock we take home to the bairns at the end of the season,' she said.

A little later: 'That's where you get the best price oilies. Aprons, boots,' she explained. Then, 'That's where the girls buy the cotton for their cloots – their bandages. You get them at a good price there.'

'Bandages?' Lydia was horrified. 'Why do the girls need bandages?'

'For wrapping round our fingers when we're gutting, so the knife doesn't slice them up.' Chrissie laughed at Lydia's horrified look. 'You've lived a sheltered life, Lyddie,' she mocked gently. 'Never mind. We'll do our best to sort that out,' and next she pointed out the dance halls and the cinemas, exclaiming with delight at the posters advertising the programme for the week.

Even though it was Sunday and everywhere was closed and quiet, Lydia could see it would be a lively exciting place for young folk away from home. The kind of lively and exciting that the strict older folk at home would frown on!

'And now you've seen what Yarmouth has to offer, we'll have a little stroll along the river,' Chrissie said and with her arm securely in Lydia's, deftly turned her up the next street.

'It's a big place,' Lydia ventured. 'And there's a lot going on.'

'Are you surprised?'

'Well, I didn't know what to expect,' Lydia admitted.

'It's not like Wick!' Chrissie laughed. 'That's for sure!'

Lydia had to laugh and agree with her. 'No, it's very different.'

'And very different from Stornoway and Lerwick,' Chrissie said. 'And that's half the trouble,' she added with a wisdom beyond her years. 'Some of these young ones can go a bit wild down here on their own.'

Johann, Lydia thought. That's who Chrissie means. But surely Chrissie herself was not much older?

'I'm nineteen,' she declared proudly. 'This is my fourth year at the fishing.'

Their gentle stroll around town completed, the two girls turned back towards the lodging house.

As Chrissie opened the door, Janet rushed towards her and seized her arm. 'Oh there you are!' she cried. 'Wherever have you been? I've been waiting and waiting. I didn't know where to find you!'

Chrissie stared at the usually placid Janet in amazement.

'What's the matter with you?' She thought for a moment, then hurried on, 'Oh Janet, it's not Sandy, is it? Has something dreadful happened? Oh no!' and she flung her arms round the distressed woman.

Lydia knew how easily a man was lost at sea, how devastating it was for a family dependent on his earnings. And it had been plain that Janet loved her husband dearly and had been looking forward to seeing him.

She held back, waiting for enlightenment, and was surprised to see Janet push Chrissie away.

'No, no, it's not Sandy, you daft thing! Now come in, the pair of you, and I'll tell you.' Her eyes went from Chrissie to Lydia, her face drawn and unhappy. 'But I warn you, it's bad.'

CHAPTER 7

'We need to be private,' Janet said and led them upstairs to their corner of the big attic room. 'Now, coats off and listen.'

Chrissie and Lydia took their coats off and settled onto the bed, with Janet facing them on the kist.

'Tell us what this is about,' Chrissie demanded.

'Johann,' Janet said.

Chrissie and Lydia exchanged worried glances.

Janet sighed and wiped a hand over her eyes. 'I found out at church.'

'What?' Chrissie persisted. 'What about Johann?'

'You remember she rushed off to Walter last night? We saw her...'

'Yes.'

'And she was going to tell him she was pregnant? She believed he would marry her...'

'Happy ever after,' Chrissie muttered sourly. 'Pretty unlikely with that one...'

'Well, you were right. In fact, he's worse than we thought,' Janet said grimly. 'It seems he told her to her face there in the street in front of the whole world that she was a trollop and the baby wasn't his so he wasn't going to marry her and bring up some other man's...' Janet swallowed hard and changed the ugly word she had been going to use in her anger and distress. 'Some other man's baby.'

'Oh poor Johann!' Lydia whispered. 'What a dreadful thing to say!' She thought of the gentle pretty girl, the stars in her eyes as she ran to meet her lover.

'And he said it where everyone could hear?' Chrissie queried.

Janet nodded, adding 'And *loud*.'

'That...!' Chrissie stumbled to a halt. No word was bad enough. She pulled herself together. 'So where's Johann now?' she demanded. 'Where's she gone? I don't blame her for running and hiding after that but we'd better go and bring her back here. She needs to be with us!'

Chrissie rose from the bed and reached for her coat. But Janet held up her hand to stop her.

'It's too late for that.' She swallowed hard.

Shocked, Lydia could see the tears start to fill Janet's eyes. Janet wiped them away and then reached across and took Chrissie's hands in hers. Then she reached for Lydia's hands with her other hand.

'My dears,' she said with a deep sigh. 'Johann is dead. She jumped into the harbour last night and drowned herself.'

Lydia and Chrissie gasped in shock.

'No!' they echoed.

'Dead?' Lydia gulped.

The sweet-natured, soft-spoken lass she had only met – what was it? – two days ago? A gentle young woman with so much to live for? A girl who had welcomed her, made room for her...

'No!' Chrissie wailed and threw herself in Janet's arms.

As Janet held Chrissie through the storm of weeping, Lydia found herself stroking Chrissie's hair and murmuring the kind of soothing words she would have used on Ewen, and knew her own eyes were brimming with tears.

Gradually Chrissie's wailing eased and she sat back, scrubbing the tears from her eyes.

'I'm all right now,' she said fiercely. 'Tell it all, Janet. What exactly happened? What did Johann do? We need to know.'

She glanced at Lydia who nodded. 'Yes, please. If it's not too...'

'No,' Janet said with a gentle calm. 'No, you do need to know so we can decide what to do next.' She gathered herself visibly and continued.

'People at church said they saw Johann pull away from Walter and go running down the street. Nobody knows where she went. But she must have gone to the harbour a bit later.' Janet went on, 'People saw Walter getting on to his boat as though nothing had happened. But then Johann appeared. Just as the boat was putting out from the quayside, she ran to the very edge of the quay and shouted after him, crying and crying... but he turned his back on her... deliberately.'

Chrissie muttered under her breath. Lydia could not hear the words but she knew she probably agreed with them.

'And when she saw that, she gave a terrible cry and threw herself into the water.' Janet swallowed hard again. 'You know how many boats there are in on a Saturday night. She didn't have a chance. There were boats going out and boats sliding against each other in their berths and the water's deep and...' Her voice caught and the tears spilled over.

'Have they got her out?' Chrissie asked bluntly.

Janet nodded. 'She's in the Hospital mortuary.' She shook her head. 'Oh, I wish we hadn't let her go! I wish we'd been there! She could have come home with me. Sandy wouldn't have minded. We'd have given her a home while she had her baby...'

'But what about her parents?' Lydia asked. 'Hasn't she got any family of her own?'

'Them!' Chrissie spat the word. 'Yes, she's got parents – holy holy Wee Frees! And they disapproved of everything the poor girl did.'

'Now, now,' Janet remonstrated. 'I'm a Wee Free and I try to be holy...'

Chrissie's laughter was bitter.

'Well, we'll agree to differ on that,' Janet said peaceably. 'Let's just say that my kind of Wee Free would have taken the poor girl home and looked after her.'

'And her parents wouldn't have,' Chrissie said bluntly. 'They'd have shown her the door. And she knew that. That's why Walter was her only hope. That's what she told me.'

They fell silent.

It was Lydia who broke the silence. 'Will Johann's parents come from Lewis and arrange the funeral?' she asked.

'I shouldn't think so,' Chrissie said. 'They won't want to know. Their daughter pregnant and a suicide! It would never do. They'll want it hushed up.'

'Poor Johann!' Lydia said again.

'Yes,' said Janet. 'So I think it's up to us to see to things for her, do the best we can. But there's nothing we can do today, so let's have our bite of dinner...'

'Eat?' Chrissie protested. 'I couldn't...'

Janet shook her head. 'We need to keep our strength up – for Johann's sake. Then we can face tomorrow.'

The girls went downstairs to a generous meal of hearty beef stew rich with vegetables and dumplings.

'We order the food from the butcher and the greengrocers,' Chrissie explained to Lydia. 'They deliver it then Mrs Duff cooks it for us.' Chrissie pointed with her knife. 'Do you like your swimmers?'

'Swimmers?' Lydia queried.

'That's what they call dumplings here,' Chrissie explained. 'Norfolk swimmers.'

The light and tasty dumplings did indeed swim in the rich gravy and despite the girls' shock over Johann's death, the food disappeared quickly.

Plates cleared away, Chrissie broached the subject. 'So what do we do now?'

'I expect there will be an inquest before they'll release Johann's body for burial,' Janet said. 'That's the usual thing. We'll just have to wait till it's over.'

'I'm head of the crew that Johann belonged to,' Chrissie said. 'Maybe I should talk to the police and see if they'll tell me what's going on.'

'Good idea,' Janet agreed.

'But if the inquest says it was suicide,' Chrissie continued, 'there could be problems burying her.'

'Does it have to be suicide?' Lydia suggested tentatively. She had been thinking hard. It seemed so wrong for this gentle girl to be further disgraced in death. 'Couldn't she maybe have just fallen in?'

'Everybody heard what Walter said to her,' Janet reminded her. 'It just makes sense.'

'Yes,' Lydia persisted. 'But she could just have tripped, in her distress – not fallen deliberately.'

Chrissie and Janet exchanged glances.

'Nobody knows where Johann went after she spoke to Walter,' Janet said slowly.

'Did anybody hear what she said at the quayside?' Lydia asked.

Janet shook her head. 'Just that she was crying and shouting after him.'

'Could she have been saying "Good riddance"?'

The girls sat for a moment in silence, staring at Lydia, as they took in what she was suggesting.

Chrissie stood up. 'I think I've got something to say to the police.'

'You may have to say it at the inquest. Under oath,' Janet warned her. Fishermen's wives were well aware of the procedures for deaths and accidents at sea.

Chrissie put her hands on her hips and glared at her. 'Do you want Johann taken home and given a decent burial or do you want her disgraced forever and dumped in a pauper's grave down here far away from her own folk?'

Lydia put her hand on Chrissie's arm. 'I'll back you up,' she offered. 'If you want me to? If you were there, then I was there too.'

'Janet?'

'Oh dear,' Janet said.

Chrissie grinned at Lydia. 'Having a conscience is a terrible thing! Just as well I don't have one!' She turned back to Janet. 'Just this once. For Johann. And if you're lucky, maybe nobody will ask you any questions so you won't have to tell any lies!'

'I don't...' Janet started to protest.

'I know. You don't believe in luck. You believe in your God. Well, you ask Him what He's going to do for poor Johann! But I know what I'm going to do!' She thrust her arms into the sleeves of her coat.

'Chrissie, wait a minute,' Lydia said.

'Not coming with me then?' Chrissie turned on her. 'Come on, Lyddie. It's all your idea! And you're posh. They'll listen to you. You have to come!'

'I am coming with you,' Lydia assured her, 'but Janet shouldn't come with us.'

'What do you mean?'

'She was at church this morning. People spoke to her. They told her their version. She reacted – because she didn't know any better,' Lydia explained. 'If she'd been with us and Johann last night, she would have known that we talked Johann round from tears of despair to tears of anger. That Johann was furious with Walter and was shouting "Good riddance" and was going to go home with Janet and Sandy to have her baby and...'

'Slow down!' Janet raised her hand. Lydia subsided. 'Let me think about that.' She was silent for a moment, then a smile spread across her face. 'Lyddie's right. I suppose I could have been canoodling in a corner with Sandy while you two young ones sorted Johann out. And yes, I did react to the news like I knew no better. Because I didn't. Well then, if you're going to do this – you know I disapprove of telling lies, but I agree we have to do our best for Johann. So go on then, off you go. And thank you, Lyddie, that I don't have to.'

Lydia was glad of the linked arms as Chrissie marched the pair of them to the police station and demanded to talk to someone about their friend's terrible accident. The pressure of Chrissie's arm against her side gave her the courage to speak up and play her part. But the pair of them were shaking from relief when – it felt like hours later – they were able to return to their lodgings and the anxiously waiting Janet.

'It's all right,' Chrissie told her. 'They believed us. They'll contact Johann's parents and get them to arrange everything.'

Chrissie slumped on to the kist. She gave Lydia a weary grin.

'Thanks,' she said gruffly. She reached out for Lydia's hand and squeezed it. 'Without you...'

Lydia heard the echo of her own words the night before when Chrissie and Janet and Johann had rescued her from the loathsome attacker in the dark alley outside the pub. If those girls had not come along then... She shuddered at the thought.

'You helped me,' she said. 'Last night. It's only right that I should help you when I can.'

Janet and Chrissie exchanged glances.

'Now, there's a thought,' Chrissie said slowly.

'What?' Lydia asked perplexed.

Again, that exchanged glance.

'I need to think,' Chrissie said, standing up. 'I'm going down to the harbour now to see if Robbie's boat is in yet. Is anybody coming?'

But there was no sign of Robbie or his cousin's boat. The weather had turned nasty, the girls were told, and the Lowestoft boats had all returned to their own port.

'Maybe tomorrow,' Chrissie said hopefully.

'An early night,' Janet recommended and Lydia was happy to agree.

CHAPTER 8

Lydia woke with a jolt. Someone was shaking her.

'C'mon, Lyddie. Up with you!'

Lydia opened her eyes to a room filled with bustle. All the fisher girls were up and about, making ready for the day ahead.

Janet grinned at her and handed her a cup of strong tea. 'Get that down you, then we'll get you sorted.'

'Sorted?' Lydia queried sleepily.

'Drink!' Janet commanded with a chuckle.

Lydia sat up in bed and sipped her tea as slowly full wakefulness dawned. Chrissie and Janet were sitting on the kist, dressed in warm jumpers and skirts, hair tucked away neatly under brightly coloured scarves, busily winding strips of cloth round their fingers. Lydia noticed with interest that Janet was doing all her fingers, while Chrissie was only doing two or three. Once a finger was bandaged, the strips were tied in place with what looked like thin crochet cotton, the girls helping one another.

'We'll put cloots on yours once you're up,' Janet told her.

'Mine?' Lydia asked in surprise.

'Aye.' Chrissie and Janet exchanged quick glances.

'We had a think and this is what we've come up with,' Janet said. 'We've lost Johann from our crew so we're one short.' She swallowed hard and pressed on. 'We can't work with just the two of us. Now, you're stuck here till you find a way of getting a ticket home and you'll need money to live on...'

Lydia nodded, puzzled about where this argument was leading.

'So, if you're willing to give it a try, you can come with us and work at the gutting till you've earned your fare home,' Chrissie said. 'Unless you're too proud for it, Mrs Teacher?' Chrissie threw out the challenge with a twinkle in her eye.

Lydia gulped. Work at the gutting with the fisher lassies? Whatever would her mother say? And Granny Leslie? She shuddered at the thought. But Chrissie was right. Now she had lost her money and ticket, she could see no way of getting back home unless she earned it.

'But I don't know anything about...' she began.

Janet waved it away. 'We all began somewhere. We'll teach you. And you can use Johann's things. She won't need them now and I'm sure she wouldn't mind.'

'You can't work in your own clothes,' Chrissie said. 'You'll ruin them in no time. So?' she prompted. 'Will you give it a try?'

'It will help us out as well as you,' Janet put in softly.

Lydia gulped. She nodded uncertainly. 'Yes. Well, I'll try.' She swallowed hard on her pride. 'Thank you.'

~

Dressed in two of Johann's warm jumpers and a thick tweed skirt, an oilskin apron that reached down over the tops of wellington boots, her hair tied back in a bright floral headscarf, and Johann's knitting bag tied to her waist, Lydia scrambled up the steps onto the back of the lorry that had been sent to take the girls to the gutting yards on the Denes. The others had laughed as they had dressed her, like a child or a doll she had thought.

'Your own uncle won't recognise you,' Chrissie had teased her.

'My uncle?'

'Aye, we're working in his yard, remember.'

Lydia had had a moment of panic then. If her uncle saw her, he would be sure to send her packing – and he would let her mother know. Worse, he would tell *his* mother. Lydia closed her eyes to blot out the picture of Granny Leslie's disgusted fury.

Sharp-eyed Chrissie saw the fear.

'You don't want him to know?'

Lydia shook her head.

'Are you ashamed to be seen with us?' Chrissie demanded fiercely.

'No!' Lydia protested, though she was... slightly. Not for herself. But for her mother who had scraped and saved to put her through college, who had wanted so much for her, been so proud of her. Not to mention the shame of what Granny Leslie would say. Granny Leslie whose opinions of the fisher girls had brought blushes to her cheeks before now.

'It doesn't matter,' Janet said gently. 'If you don't want your uncle to know you're working with us in his yard, we won't tell him.'

'He hardly ever shows his face,' Chrissie added. 'Too stuck-up to mingle with the likes of us!'

Janet put a restraining hand on Chrissie's arm.

'All right,' Chrissie said crossly. 'I'm only telling the truth.'

'Maybe so, but it doesn't help Lyddie.'

'We'll have to square it with the coopers though,' Chrissie reminded her.

'They supervise the yard,' Janet explained, 'and they're sure to notice a new face.'

'Oh,' Lydia blenched. 'What should I do?'

'It's up to you,' Chrissie told her. 'Tell them the truth or pretend to be someone else.'

What a strange idea, Lydia thought. Or was it? Her long-buried secret taunted her. Had she not been pretending to be someone else for a long time: the heartbroken widow with the orphan son, their lives devastated by the tragedy of the Great War. Well, maybe another few days living another pretence would not be so very difficult.

'I'll be someone else.'

And as she said it, Lydia felt a sudden flare of hope. Maybe here, where nobody knew her, she could turn her back on the role she had been playing.

Janet nodded agreement and reached for her hands. Ah, Lydia thought, recoiling, now they will sneer at my white hands that have never done a proper day's work. But all the older woman did was start painstakingly bandaging her fingers and tying the cloots in place.

'So you don't cut yourself,' Janet explained, handing over Johann's wickedly sharp gutting knife. Janet called it a cuttag.

Cut herself? Lydia fingered the knife. It seemed like a foregone conclusion, she thought. Still, the work should not be too hard. She was bright, at least as bright as these women. Surely she would pick it up quickly?

As the motor lorry rolled through Yarmouth picking up more and more fisher girls, Lydia felt it was more like a charabanc outing than a works collection. The girls laughed and sang and called teasingly to any young man they saw on the streets. They were a cheerful bunch, and seemed determined to enjoy themselves.

The lorry dropped them off at the gutting yard and the girls spilled out, still chatting and laughing. They all seemed to know where they were going. For Lydia, still half-asleep at such an early hour – at home she would still be in her bed at 6 o'clock in the morning – it was strangely daunting. She was familiar with the sight of a gutting yard. There were plenty at home in Wick. But she had never stepped foot in one as a potential worker.

Quickly she scanned the yard and gave a sigh of relief that there was no sign of her uncle. At the back of the yard were the bothies where the coopers slept. Where the spiteful aunts had said Robbie had been sleeping. Lydia felt sudden pride that her brother had done much better than that. He had landed on his feet through his own efforts, his own friendships. Maybe his family had underestimated him? She remembered Chrissie's anger with them. A fine if maybe misplaced loyalty, she had thought at the time, but now... Maybe, she thought suddenly, maybe Robbie had never been given a fair chance, always overshadowed by older brother Alec in life, and in death.

The wall of stacked barrels waiting for the herring to be packed in them looked mountainous. Lydia had never realised just how many barrels were new-made for the season. Girls and older women moved in little groups to different places in the yard. Some started working on barrels, others sorting out wooden tubs and baskets.

'We need to get cleared for the day's work,' Chrissie told her. 'I'm the packer and I work over there.' She gestured to one side of the yard. 'You'll be here at the farlin with Janet.' She seemed to be indicating a long table-like affair, set under a rickety corrugated iron lean-to roof. 'You'll need to get ready for the day's catch.'

'If there is one,' Janet said. 'The girls were saying that last week was terrible,' she explained. 'That's why we didn't come down till now.' As she spoke, she busied herself with tubs and baskets which she set out around where they stood. 'We'll be busier tomorrow morning if we get a decent catch today. First thing you do each day is check what was packed the day before.' Seeing Lydia's bemused expression, she laughed. 'Don't worry. You'll soon catch on!'

'Good morning, ladies. Who's this now?'

Lydia jumped guiltily at the loud voice. She glanced worriedly at Janet. Was she going to be found out so soon?

'Good morning, Mr Troup,' Janet replied calmly. 'This is my friend, Mrs Alexander. She's going to work on our crew.'

Lydia peeked under her lashes at the cheerful young man with the huge hands who had confronted them. He must have sharp eyes to have spotted her so quickly.

'She's a widow and was just going to have a few days in Yarmouth but when Johann died...'

'I was right sorry to hear of that,' the young man said and he seemed to mean it. 'Her parents will be grieving hard. And Johann, herself, was she right with the Lord?'

Janet hesitated then said quietly, 'She had a strong faith, Mr Troup. I'm sure the Lord would never fail her.'

She turned back to Lydia. 'If I'm going to teach you the gutting, we'd better be getting on with our work.'

Lydia took the hint and bent to her task.

Soon the motor lorries began to arrive from the quayside with shining loads of herring. The men emptied the unfamiliar double baskets into the farlins.

Seeing Lydia's curiosity, Janet said, 'They call them swills here and it's the only place you'll see them.'

As the herring poured into the farlin, salt was added in handfuls, then the girls got to work.

'Like this,' Janet said. She seized a herring from the deep pile in the farlin, cleanly slit its throat and with a deft flick of her finger pulled out the innards which she tossed into a small tub beside her on the farlin. 'There's three sizes – matties the little ones, mattiefuls the middling, and fulls the big ones.' She pointed at the baskets at her feet. 'One for each.' She threw the gutted fish into one of the baskets. 'Just you watch for a wee while, then you can have a go.'

Around them, Lydia was aware of concentration, skill and most of all speed as the women set to their task. Within moments, the clean oilskin aprons were spattered in blood and guts and scales from the fish, and the baskets on the ground filled steadily as the wicked little knives flashed and cut, and the skilful fingers flew. It seemed to take the women only seconds to gut each fish.

As she watched, Lydia felt cold apprehension. She would never be able to do this. Nothing she had ever done in her life had prepared her for this work. At home she had done a little cooking and sewing, but because of her teaching position and the marking of exercise books, not to mention the preparation for next day's classes, her mother tended to do most of the household tasks.

Lydia had married from her parents' house in Rose Street, then she and Danny had had two nights in a hotel. (She firmly pushed the memories away.) And then she had returned to her parents' house, expecting to have her own home when the war finished and Danny returned.

But he had not returned and so she had remained at Rose Street. Her parents had been happy to include Ewen in their household when he arrived. Now he slept in Alec and Robbie's old room.

In a way, she was still the protected and even pampered girl that she had always been, living with her parents.

As she stood in the cold October morning, watching the fisher girls working steadily through the mounds of silver herring, calm, competent and efficient, Lydia felt like a spoiled child that had never had to do anything much in her life. She felt her pride and her confidence shrivel.

'Your turn now,' Janet said cheerfully. 'Right, grip the knife like this, grab a fish with your left hand...'

Lydia expected the fish to slip out of her grasp but the salt gave it grip. She discovered she could hold it firmly and then slit its throat as she had been shown. The next bit was trickier. Finger in through the cut and hook out the innards. Into the little tub. Check the size against the fish in the three baskets and hope she chose the right one. Next fish...

'Nae fish, nae money,' one of the coopers taunted her when he came over to check her progress. 'You're a bit old to be learning. What's your name?'

'Lyddie,' Janet told him, 'and it's only her first day. Leave the poor girl alone!'

Lydia was grateful for Janet's support but she *was* slow. She knew she *was* slow. The knife was lethally sharp and the work was dirty. But she kept going, determined not to let her new friends down, not to let herself down. '*Mrs Teacher*'. Surely she could learn to do this? But it was so hard. She had never realised how difficult it was, how skilful these girls were.

Maybe she had been stuck-up, filled with pride. As Lydia struggled to build up speed, she realised she was learning a lot more than how to gut fish.

~

'Stop!'

It took a moment for Janet's instruction to penetrate Lydia's brain.

'What?' she asked, confused. The farlin still had plenty of fish piled in it. There was still work to be done.

'The baskets are full,' Janet told her. 'We'll take them over to Chrissie now. Put your knife away in your pocket – never set it down or you'll lose it and that's your job lost. Then you take one handle of that basket and I'll take the other. Careful now. It's heavy.'

Lydia did as she was told and discovered that she was staggering under the weight. Janet however seemed to have no problem and called cheerfully to friends as they made their way across to the other side of the yard where Chrissie was waiting.

'How's she doing?' Chrissie asked Janet as they set the heavy basket down beside her.

Lydia's heart thumped. Suddenly it was important that she should not be found wanting. Again the thought came: what would her grandmother think that what these fisher lassies thought of her had become the most important thing in the world to Lydia! She realised she was holding her breath, waiting for Janet's answer.

'She's doing fine,' Janet said, to Lydia's relief. 'Slow, but you'd expect that. She'll get there.'

'Let's see your hands,' Chrissie demanded.

Lydia found herself automatically obeying. She held her hands out to be examined but it was the bandages on her fingers that Chrissie paid attention to.

'A few near misses but the cloots have held off the worst,' she said. Then the twinkle appeared in her eyes again. 'Not exactly what you expected to be doing on your holidays?' she teased.

'No,' Lydia agreed. 'But I'm learning.'

CHAPTER 9

By the time the girls were taken back to their lodgings for their dinner, Lydia's respect for the fisher lassies had turned to awe. They stood on sopping wet duckboards, ignoring the drips of rain leaking through the rusty corrugated iron roof above their heads, and continued to chatter and laugh through the morning while their hands, as if of their own volition, dealt with herring after herring.

The only break was to lug the heavy filled baskets over to the packers. That was another skilled job. The packer had to place each herring individually into the barrel, head to the outside, tier after tier. The barrels held around nine hundred fish in twenty layers, each one carefully placed and each layer salted. The topmost row of fish was laid belly-up so that when the barrel was opened, there would be the glorious sight of shining silver.

The packer seemed to be the senior girl on the crew, the one in charge. Despite her youth, it was clear that Chrissie had the personality to run a crew. Janet, though significantly older, seemed happy to take orders and just get on with the gutting.

'It makes a bit of extra money,' she explained. 'It helps out what my husband brings home. And I enjoy coming away when he's at sea.' She waved a hand at the scene around them. 'Now that our children have left home, it's company for me, and we have a lot of fun.'

The fisher lassies seemed to find fun in everything they did. After they had lugged the filled baskets of fish over to the packers, the girls took advantage of the change of scene to banter with the men in the yard before returning to their own place and getting back to work. And even there, the chatting and laughter never seemed to stop.

Lydia, unused to working out of doors, was glad that the weather was unseasonably warm and the rain showers though heavy were short-lived, but she found standing over the farlin made her back ache. The other girls and women seemed to demolish the piles of gleaming herring that had been tipped into the farlins in front of them. She felt her own contribution had hardly made any kind of a dent. But she was glad when the farlin was clear of fish and it was time to help Janet hose down their tubs and containers ready for the next day.

Shortly afterwards, Chrissie rejoined them and told her it was time for dinner.

'Dinner?' She had not really been aware of the time but now that she had stopped work, she realised her stomach was empty.

'Aye. The lorry will take us back to our lodgings. It was a poor catch today,' she said. 'We've cleared what was brought in.'

'Better than yesterday,' one of the other women called to her.

'At least there was something for us to do,' another chimed in. 'We'd nothing to do but knit last week!'

'And talk, Annie Matheson!' someone called. 'You never stop that!'

The women were still laughing as they climbed into the lorry for the trip back to their lodgings.

Mrs Duff had another hearty stew waiting for them, with lots of vegetables, plenty of potatoes and the delicious and filling Norfolk swimmers. But first, since the girls were not going back to work, they stood in the paved back yard to remove their oilies and their wellingtons and scrub them down with the yard broom in cold water from the tap in the yard. The aprons were hung on the washing line to dry for the next day. The cloots round their fingers had to be unrolled, rinsed and wrapped round their knife, and then the girls could finally step in their thick boot stockings into the stone-floored scullery where a kettle of hot water awaited them so they could finish off their toilet.

It took almost the last of Lydia's strength to copy the other girls in this ritual. She was glad of the seat at the table in the warm back-kitchen where her dinner awaited her. Although she was tired, she found herself wolfing down her food. She looked up, startled, to realise Janet and Chrissie were staring at her.

'Never seen food before?' Chrissie teased her.

'I was hungry,' Lydia admitted.

'Not surprising. First real day's work she's had to do in her life,' Chrissie said to Janet.

'Oh, leave the poor girl alone,' Janet scolded her. 'She's done a good day's work and I'm glad to have her with me.'

Lydia glowed at the praise, though she felt she was hardly worthy of it.

'Now tell her what you found out about Robbie,' Janet continued.

'You've seen him?' Lydia exclaimed in delight, her tiredness forgotten.

'No,' Chrissie said. 'But I know where he is.'

'Where? Please tell me!'

'He's still at sea.'

'He's gone back out?' Lydia queried.

'He's not on a drifter,' Chrissie reminded her. 'His cousin's a trawlerman. One of his friends had an accident and they've taken Robbie on in the meantime. I thought they might have come in yesterday but one of the Lowestoft women, whose man is on the same boat, told me they're planning to be back in Yarmouth on Saturday so you can see him for yourself then.'

'Saturday?' Lydia repeated in horror. 'But I expected to be going home before then. I have to be back at school on Monday!'

'You'll need to see Robbie when he gets into port on Saturday. Maybe he can help you with a ticket back to Wick. You could be on the train on Monday.'

Just a few extra days, Lydia had to console herself, but she would need to write to her mother and square it with the Education Board.

~

After their dinner, Janet and Chrissie invited her to go with them for a walk along the river.

'You'll be company for me if she finds her man,' Chrissie told her.

'I've seen him already,' Janet protested. She turned to Lydia and explained, 'Most of the boats are lying up till the weather changes and the shoals of herring come nearer in. With the cost of coal to feed the engines, it's not worth it to the skippers to put out to sea and then come back in without a catch. So, depending on what his skipper decides, my man might still be in Yarmouth.'

'We'll go and see,' Chrissie assured her. She winked at Lydia. 'Sweet, isn't it? They've been married more than twenty years and she's still like a bride!'

Janet blushed and laughed but Lydia felt sad. She didn't think she would have still been blushing and laughing after even ten years with Danny. The thought caught her unawares and she was filled with horror at her disloyalty.

Janet must have seen something in her face.

'Oh, I'm sorry,' she said gently. 'You're a widow, aren't you? The war?'

Lydia nodded. She could not tell them what she was thinking. They would be horrified. Even more than she was. How could she think such a thing? But the truth was that she really did not mind being a widow. She did not want to be anyone's wife. She would not ever risk that again.

'Come on. A breath of fresh air will do you good,' Chrissie said briskly.

Lydia hesitated. She was not sure she could get up from the table, let alone walk along the river.

'Trust us,' Janet said. 'We learnt the hard way too. It's better to keep moving.'

'If you stop now, you'll never survive,' Chrissie told her.

Survive. It had a hollow echo. That's what she had been doing for too many years, surviving. Maybe she could learn something from these girls' courage and gaiety. The latter had been sadly lacking in her own life, and her heart, for a long time.

Bravely, she dragged herself upright.

'Let's go,' she said, concentrating on hiding the pain in her joints and muscles, and missing the approving glance that Chrissie and Janet exchanged.

'Let's go,' they echoed and set off for the river, arms linked, talking about everything they saw and waving at the people they met, cheerily carrying Lydia along with them.

CHAPTER 10

'*Dear Mother,*

Please don't worry.'

Of all the words to send terror into a mother's heart, Jean thought, these took the prize. Of course she worried. It was what mothers did.

She took a steadying sip of her tea. She had perfect confidence in her daughter, she reminded herself, and even more in her Lord to whom she had entrusted her.

'Yes, Lord Jesus,' she whispered. 'I'm still trusting You.'

Strengthened, she turned back to the letter.

'*Robbie has found work on a Lowestoft boat. He met one of the Lowestoft cousins during the war and it's his boat. He was a man short so he was happy to take Robbie on. So he's landed on his feet again.*'

That did sound reassuring. Robbie had told Jean about meeting the Lowestoft cousin during the war but it was not a thing to be mentioned in David's hearing, so maybe Lydia hadn't known? Still, that was not a problem, so what was she not to worry about? She read on, trying to hear Lydia's voice in the written words:

'*I'm fine but I won't be home immediately.*'

Now that was interesting. Not a cause for worry, but interesting. She would have thought Lydia would be anxious to return home. Fly back to the nest where she had hidden herself for the past four years. But no. Maybe her daughter was at last emerging from the seclusion she had imposed on herself after Danny's death. That could only be a good thing. But why would she think her mother would worry? Jean read on:

'Because Robbie is working on a trawler, he won't be back in port till Saturday so I'll have to wait till then to see him and make sure everything is all right. Hopefully, I'll be on the train home on Monday. I've written to the Board of Education explaining I need a few more days.

Give my love to Ewen and tell him I'm missing him.'

It sounded straightforward enough. Perfectly reasonable, too, but Jean felt there was something more. Why would her daughter start the letter warning her not to worry, when there was nothing in her news to trigger worry? With Robbie working on his cousin's boat, there was nothing to stop Lydia simply coming straight home. Clearly she was not telling the whole story. What could be keeping her dear reliable sensible daughter so she needed extra days in Yarmouth?

~

'Give Ewen my love and tell him I'm missing him,' Lydia reminded herself. Back home in Wick was a wee boy – *her* wee boy – and if she was any kind of mother she would be missing him. But she was just too tired to think of anything other than the next herring. Grip, cut, hook out innards, toss offal, throw gutted fish in the correct container. Next one...

How many days now and she was still nowhere near the speed of the other girls?

'I feel I'm letting you down,' she had wailed to Janet only that morning. She had cut herself with the razor-sharp knife and Janet had to take her to the dressing station on St Peter's Road where a Red Cross nurse waited to treat their injuries and give them a cup of tea. The shock of the cut had finally broken through her staunch determination not to show her feelings and the tears had come, embarrassing her as they flooded down her cheeks.

Janet had hugged her and mopped up her tears.

'I'm glad of the break and the cup of tea,' she had reassured Lydia cheerfully. 'And you're not letting us down. You've come to our rescue. Without Johann, we were one crew member down.'

The nurse in the dressing station overheard.

'Oh my dear, was that poor girl in your crew?'

Janet's face froze and she turned unwillingly to her interlocutor.

'That was a terrible accident, wasn't it?' the woman continued. 'You must have been awfully upset.'

Janet and Lydia exchanged glances.

'Oh yes,' Lydia said quickly. 'Terrible.'

'We must be getting back,' Janet said. 'Mustn't be slacking!'

Lydia found herself slipping her arm through Janet's as naturally as if she had been doing it all her life.

'Thank you for the tea and the first aid,' she said cheerfully to the Red Cross nurse and the two of them walked hurriedly away.

'Accident?' Lydia said when they got out of earshot. 'They must have accepted it if that's the story that's got round.'

'Well, I suppose it will be easier on her parents,' Janet said quietly. 'But you know I don't approve...'

'It's a lot nicer for Johann,' Lydia said. 'Though that rotten Walter doesn't deserve to be let off so easy!'

At that, Janet laughed, 'Oh Lyddie, you're a right fierce one. Just like Chrissie! Maybe it comes with being a Wicker!'

She laughed again and urged Lydia back over the street to the gutting yard.

~

Returning to her place at the farlin under the corrugated iron roof, Lydia was soon back in the swing of the gutting but her mind was suddenly alive with questions. Chrissie certainly was fierce, especially in defence of Robbie. In fact, Lydia pondered, Chrissie was fierce in defence of anyone who needed it! But was *she* like that? She did not think so.

Had she been like that at Chrissie's age, she wondered, trying to think back. There was the time she caught those terrible Thompson twins bullying little Lizzie Flett. She had seen them off in short order. And then there was the time those other boys were throwing stones at that wee dog in the river. And...

Yes, she realised, once she had been like Chrissie. Fierce and thinking nothing of standing up for what she thought was right. She tossed the gutted fish into the right creel and reached for another herring. She had been so sure that she knew what was right, that she did what was right. Once, her faith had been strong and she had tried to live the way Jesus taught. But it had gone wrong – she had gone wrong – and then everything went disastrously from bad to worse.

Lydia's hands worked while her mind remained focused on far away and long ago. Was it the war that changed people and made them do uncharacteristic things, she wondered. It had changed her – and Danny.

She had adored her older brother Alec – as had everyone else in the family (except Robbie, of course). And somehow that adoration had spilled over to include his good-looking friend Danny. Alec and Danny had been friends from first going to school, a friendship that had lasted through the years. David and Jonathan, people had called them. Inseparable, and the pair of them beautiful young men. She used to to tag along, like a little dog at their heels. A little adoring dog, she thought sadly.

Once she was in her teens and old enough to go to the Saturday night dances in town, Danny would occasionally give her a dance when he saw her standing on the sidelines. Not that she was without other invitations, but since she wanted to dance only with Danny, her constant refusals meant the other lads thought she was stuck-up. She had not cared. She was willing to wait a whole evening for just one dance with her idol.

Maybe that was the clue. Her focus had shifted from Jesus to Danny, and he had become her idol.

She had been as excited as Alec and Danny were about going to France to the war. It was a huge adventure and in her youthful eyes, they were heroic and courageous. She would have gone too if she could. She would have been a nurse or driven an ambulance, but she was too young.

She had devoured the letters Alec sent home and when she heard that he and Danny would be coming on leave she could hardly bear the excitement. When they walked into the house in their smart uniforms, her heart almost burst. They looked like heroes and the stories they told... she would have done anything for them.

Lydia's hands slowed as she remembered. First the amazing joy that Danny had seemed to notice her, not as the nuisance little sister of his friend always tagging along but as a young woman in her own right, and apparently an attractive young woman. Then the night he appeared at her bedroom door. He was staying in their house, sharing Alec's room. But when he slipped into her room... The blush rose in her cheeks, followed swiftly by the hot rise of shame as she saw again her mother's shocked face when she caught them together, and her father's angry voice, using words like betrayal, taking advantage, and insisting that Danny marry her before he went back to the trenches.

'Why not?' Danny had said lightly as if it was of no consequence. 'Who knows what will happen?'

She had wondered later about that. At the time, she had been on a roller-coaster of emotion: excitement, the brief shame that her parents had found Danny with her though they had done no wrong, then the wild exhilaration that she was going to marry her hero, her idol.

Her heart bursting with pride, she had walked on a cloud of happiness from the ceremony, the brand-new ring on her finger and Danny heartbreakingly handsome in his smart uniform at her side. In her imagination she was a heroine in her own right, supporting her man before he left for battle.

Her hands slowed on the fish as she remembered the girl she had been – full of dreams and ideals. She had swallowed whole all the nonsense from storybooks of heroism, knights in shining armour and the beautiful damsels they wooed and won. And when she had proudly said 'I do', she had felt all her dreams had come true as she smiled up at her handsome hero husband.

How long had it taken for her dreams to shatter into disillusion? For her childish adoration to be stripped away by the reality of who Danny really was?

As she gazed adoringly at Danny, it was to see he was not gazing back at her, but exchanging a grin with her brother. And she had felt excluded yet again – as left out as she had felt in her childhood when she had dogged their footsteps... At the time she had determinedly shrugged it off, told herself she was being silly.

But that was nothing to what would follow. Danny was going back to the trenches and time was short. The seductive charmer who had been interrupted by her parents was gone, and in his place was a terrifying stranger. He had ignored her protests and mocked her tears before he got impatient with her and angry. She had trapped him into marriage, he told her, so he would make the most of what he'd got. And what followed was a nightmare. Two nights of it.

Her mother thought the tears were grief that Danny had marched away. The bruises she kept hidden. And the prayers for his safe return stopped.

When the news came of his death in Bourlon Wood there had been few tears for Danny. How could she not be grateful that the monster he had turned out to be would never come back? That the nightmare of her rash marriage was over?

'Lyddie.'

Janet's quiet voice broke through her trance. She lifted her eyes from where she was gripping the knife so tightly that her knuckles were bone-white and realised that tears had been pouring down her face.

'Lyddie, are you all right, love?'

Janet's gentle words nearly undid her completely. She swallowed hard and forced herself to speak.

'I'm fine. Really,' she assured Janet. 'I was just remembering...'

Remembering why she had locked away her dreams and ideals, dead dreams and ideals, as dead as the man whose selfish brutality had killed them. Remembering why she had shut down her heart and her life, safer by far to be alone and lonely than trapped in another nightmare.

Safer maybe, but now she acknowledged her loneliness was a hurting tangible thing. Yet she knew she dared not step out of her safety zone. She could not bear to be hurt again.

She reminded herself of the one good that had come out of her brief disastrous marriage: her beloved son, Ewen. And she was glad, fiercely glad, that his father would never come back and make him into the kind of man he had been.

She grabbed a herring with her left hand and bent once more to her task.

CHAPTER 11

By Friday, news of the poor fishing had reached Wick and the pages of the local newspaper. Jean sat with her cup of tea and reached for the broadsheet pages of the *John O'Groat Journal*. She looked briefly at the births, marriages and deaths on the front page, noting the names she knew, then the public notices and announcements, before turning the page for what she was most interested in.

'*Although the Yarmouth fishing does not show a very bright outlook the number of local workers who have left this season is almost as great as that of previous years. On Friday last the special train which left Wick for the fishing towns of Gorleston and Lowestoft carried 183 women fishworkers and coopers, whilst on Monday morning another 83 workers left by the ordinary train. It is estimated that around 500 workers have now left for the East Anglian ports.*'

And her Lydia amongst them.

She had so far managed to keep the news from Lydia's grandmother but she knew it was only a matter of time before she came calling and commented on Lydia's absence. It would never do for her to know that Lydia had travelled south with the fisher lassies! How she would scold! But it was the only way she had been able to think of to get Lydia to Yarmouth, quickly, safely and economically.

Money had been short for a while. This year's herring fishing had been the worst in living memory. Disastrous, some were calling it. The herrings had been poor quality. Some had blamed the weather, others the mines that had been laid during the war disturbing the shoals and the breeding grounds. Others had said it was God's judgment on the men of violence, the men who had returned from the horrors of Flanders godless and shameless in their drinking and their immoral ways.

But the slump in the herring trade had affected even the prosperous curers like her brother. The aftermath of the war had hit Germany hard and the demand for pickled herring, long a favoured delicacy in Germany and the Baltic states, that had once been the backbone of the trade for Scotch cure herrings and kippers, had all but disappeared.

Everyone had pinned their hopes on the East Anglian autumn fishing season to save their fortunes. But now there was talk of another disappointment. Jean had heard one of the Buckie curers at the harbour saying that unless the government did something to help out the herring industry, it would collapse.

'No, no,' the man he was talking to had replied. 'It's bad but not as bad as all that.'

'I'm telling you,' the Buckie man had said, 'I wouldn't be surprised if the herring fleet don't just give up on the poor catches and come home early from England.'

Jean looked down the page and the dreaded words caught her eye: 'poor results ... Weather still warm ... many boats remaining in port till prospects are brighter.'

If her husband was sitting idle in his boat tied up to Yarmouth quay, maybe he would be thinking he would be as well off at home.

Except, she pondered, how long had it been since David had shown any enthusiasm for being home either?

That was yet another thing to be laid at the door of the war in Flanders. It had torn the heart out of her family – and out of Lydia and David in particular. Maybe if Alec had not been his father's particular favourite, his death might not have hit so hard. But Robbie, a weaker child from birth, had never had a chance against Alec. And if she was honest, she had to admit that Alec made sure of that. Robbie always came out worse. And when he came home so ill with the seasickness from his first trip on the boat, both Alec and David had taunted the poor child. It was no wonder Robbie had turned his back on the pair of them and gone his own way.

She had loved all three of them, very different though they were. Alec always so sure of himself, Robbie the black sheep of the family seemingly determined to live up to his reputation, and David just as determined to prove himself worthy of her in the face of her family's disapproval. His hard work and resolution had bought him his own boat, so proudly and lovingly named *The Bonnie Jean*. And she had been proud too – of the boat, of him, and of their son at his side.

Life had held so much promise then. They had been riding high. Well, all except Robbie who could not settle to anything and seemed to get into trouble with his father or brother every time he encountered them.

And then the war had steamrollered into and across their lives, leaving not one of them the same. She remembered Lydia's shamed expression when, after hearing a noise in the night, she had gone to investigate and found Danny Alexander seducing her daughter. David had been so enraged she had had to hold him back from giving Danny the thrashing he deserved.

Jean sighed. It might have been for the best if she had let him, and then sent Danny packing. But he had insisted Danny 'do the honourable thing'. Poor Lydia was ecstatic. She had adored Danny from the moment she saw him.

Jean had not been happy about the marriage. There was something about Danny that she could not like but she could not say that, so she tried to say that Lydia, at 19, was too young. That was useless.

'Same age as you were when you married Dad, Mum!'

Clever Lydia. There was no answer to that. So the wedding went ahead and the lads went back to the war. And never came back. And nine months later Lydia gave birth to Ewen, who delighted all of them. But along the way, Lydia seemed to have lost herself, and her faith.

Jean sighed again. She hoped against hope that this trip to Yarmouth might awaken Lydia to life once again.

'Help her find herself again, Lord Jesus,' she prayed. 'And please help her find her way back to You.'

CHAPTER 12

Sharp tears came to Lydia's eyes as she plunged her hands into the brine in the barrel. She bit her lip hard. Would she ever get used to the pain of the salt on her cuts? How did the other women endure it?

She looked up to see Chrissie and Janet watching her approvingly.

'It's the only way,' Janet said almost apologetically. 'The first bite of the salt is the worst. Then you'll be fine for the rest of the day.'

'We won't be working long today. The weather's been too warm for the herring. They drop to the bottom and stay there, awkward little creatures!' Chrissie said. 'There's little point going out after them in a drifter if they won't rise to the nets, so very few of the boats will have put out to sea. There will be little for us to do.'

'And tomorrow's a day off,' Janet reminded her. 'So chin up, my dear!'

'We'll be off out having fun this afternoon!' said Chrissie with a grin.

Lydia had to laugh. Their cheerfulness was infectious.

'Let's get on with it, then,' she said and linked arms with Janet back to the farlin as the first lorry rolled into the yard with the results of the night's fishing.

Chrissie was right. It was a poor harvest for a night's work and the girls had leisure to chat and sing as they worked without pressure through the pile of herrings that had been tipped into the farlin.

'Going-home time soon!' Chrissie sang out as they lugged the last of the swills over to her packing station. They went back to the farlin and hastily cleaned up and cleared up while Chrissie skilfully packed the last of the day's barrels, patting down the top layer of silvery fish with evident satisfaction.

'There!' she said. 'Let's be going!'

Then it was back to their lodgings in the Rows and the ritual of cleaning down the oilcloth aprons and their wellingtons with the yard broom and cold water from the outside tap, hanging them up, peeling off the soaked and bloodied cloots round their fingers and washing them thoroughly, then padding in stockinged feet through to the scullery.

But today's personal toilet was a much more thorough job and there was a kettle of hot water ready for them.

'Do your hair too,' Chrissie instructed her when Lydia reached for the towel to dry her face and hands. 'We're going out on the town later and you'll want to look your best.'

'What for?' Lydia demanded. She had no reason to look her best. Chrissie had Robbie to look nice for, Janet had her Sandy, but Lydia was not interested in catching anyone's eye. She would just pin her hair back as usual...

Chrissie spotted the rebellious gleam in Lydia's eyes.

'Well, if you don't mind the fisher lassies showing you up,' she teased.

At that Lydia had to laugh and ducked her head into the basin of warm soapy water. She had to admit she had still a little pride left!

After a heartening dinner, the girls in their best clothes set off into town. Janet and Chrissie were determined to show her more of the shops and the sights, though all Lydia cared about was meeting up with Robbie and getting the money from him to buy her ticket home.

'He'll find us,' Chrissie reassured her. 'Don't you worry!'

Lydia marvelled at the way the members of this strange nomadic community were able to communicate with one another. Both Janet and Chrissie were quietly confident about meeting up with their menfolk and they had made themselves clean and bonnie in anticipation.

First though, they wandered round the shops pointing out to Lydia the best places to buy presents for the family back home.

'You'll want to take something nice home to your mother,' Chrissie said.

'And some rock for wee Ewen,' Janet added.

It was strange, Lydia thought. In just a week these women had become extensions to her family and she had felt free and comfortable about telling them about Ewen and her mother. Free and comfortable. And it felt surprisingly good. She would miss that and them when she went home on Monday's train.

'We're just looking now,' Chrissie said. 'We'll be buying when we get paid at the end of the season.'

'If we get paid enough,' Janet said. 'If the weather doesn't improve...'

'But the weather's lovely,' Lydia protested.

'Aye, for us,' Janet said. 'But not for the herring fishing. This calm warm weather is no good. The herring just stay down deep. They don't come up where they can be caught in the drift nets. The best fishing is always when it's the kind of weather we don't like!'

'Wind and rain,' Chrissie said darkly. 'Then we stand out in it, gutting and packing huge catches. Keeping going till there's not a fish left. All nighters sometimes!' She laughed at Lydia's expression. 'You'll get used to it!'

I hope not, Lydia thought silently to herself. She was within a touch of her ticket home and escape from the hard life of these girls. She vowed she would never again complain about her teaching job or the badly behaved children in her class at school. She knew now how fortunate she was to have such a comfortable job, with civilised hours, and no standing out in the wind and rain with her hands stinging from the salt in the cuts made by that wicked little knife. She admired the girls that did that work but she had no desire to be one of them any longer than she had to.

Yarmouth market was a bustling place with the stallholders doing their best to attract the attention of the little groups of fisher lassies that ambled about, chatting and knitting. As the sun began to set, the streetlights and stall lights came on, and the atmosphere changed to festivity. The girls sang, and flirted with the young men that hung around the street corners in groups. They were all Scots lads whose boats had come in and unloaded and would not be going out on the night's tide, unlike the English boats that fished even on a Sunday.

Janet's Sandy came and found her and led her away.

'They're going dancing,' Chrissie told her. 'Janet loves to dance!'

'But she's a Wee Free!' Lydia protested. 'Don't they disapprove of dancing?'

'Some of them do.' Chrissie shrugged. 'And disapprove of having fun in any way, but Janet's not like that. She's very normal for a *Christian*.'

A loud voice stopped them in their tracks, someone making some kind of announcement. Chrissie tugged Lydia's arm.

'Let's go and see what that's about,' she said. 'There's always something happening!'

By now the market stalls had closed, but by the Plain Stone stood a small group of men. A smartly dressed young man was calling out to the passers-by.

'I've seen him before somewhere,' Lydia said to Chrissie.

Chrissie looked closely. 'Aye, he's one of the coopers in your uncle's yard. Jock Troup's his name. He's awful religious. You don't want to stay...?'

But Jock was addressing the crowd in the loudest voice Lydia had ever heard. His words poured out and seemed to transfix his listeners. Everyone close by stopped in their tracks, and from all corners of the market place more people came, curious to find out what the noise was about.

The loud voice broke into song and the other men joined in. Words floated by Lydia. Words about rescue. Being pulled from disaster. Being saved...

Jock continued his passionate preaching in his loud voice with its strong Wick accent and as he spoke, the crowd began to respond. Lydia saw tears rolling down weather-beaten faces. Broad-shouldered fishermen dropped like stones to their knees in prayer. Something like an electric current seemed to run through the almost one thousand people who had gathered to listen.

'I don't like this!' Chrissie whispered fiercely. 'Come on. We've got to get out of here.'

She seized Lydia's arm and towed her out of the crowd and away from the market place. Behind them was noise and confusion. Shouts and cries as if of pain. Loud voices pleading. Weeping.

Lydia had to admit she was glad to get away from the place. She had felt the wave of emotion in the crowd, felt a sudden compulsion to reach out to the young man with the impassioned message of new life and forgiveness – to ask him could there be any for her. Her heart had suddenly yearned for... for something new. A fresh start. She swiftly dismissed the feeling, angry that she had been infected by the emotion.

Standing there in his smart black jacket and pinstriped trousers and an incongruous bow tie, she had not immediately recognised the young man as the cooper she had spoken to at her uncle's yard. He seemed transformed – in more ways than just his clothes.

He believed what he was saying. That was plain. He believed that God really cared about each one of them and wanted them to turn to Him. Once upon a time, Lydia remembered with a kind of weary sadness, she had believed all that. She knew her mother still did. But it had not done either of them much good.

'Let's find Janet.' Chrissie's words pulled her out of her thoughts and back to earth. 'I fancy a dance. We'll find someone to pay for our ticket.'

'What do you mean?'

'Well, *we* don't have enough money for that kind of thing,' Chrissie said, 'but there will be plenty of lads outside happy to pay for your ticket.'

Lydia tugged her arm out of Chrissie's grasp.

'No,' she said fiercely. 'I don't want anyone buying my ticket.' It felt like putting herself at the mercy of another stranger. 'You go and find Robbie and tell him I want to see him. I'm going back to the lodgings. I'm tired and what I need is an early night. You tell Robbie that I'll see him tomorrow.'

She pulled away and left Chrissie standing in the street.

'Suit yourself,' she heard Chrissie mutter. 'You could have come with me and had some fun...'

CHAPTER 13

When Lydia woke, both Chrissie and Janet had returned and were fast asleep. She dressed quickly and slipped downstairs to fetch cups of tea for all three of them.

Janet, when she woke, accepted the tea gratefully. She sat up in bed and sipped it, smiling.

'Cat got the cream,' Chrissie said tartly.

'What's the matter with you?' Janet asked. 'Robbie taken up with someone else?'

For a moment Lydia thought Chrissie was about to burst into tears.

'Only joking,' Janet said quickly. 'He wouldn't do that,' but Chrissie concentrated on her tea and did not answer. Her face was tight and troubled.

Over breakfast, Chrissie was uncharacteristically quiet and Lydia did not like to ask whether she had seen Robbie or arranged for them to meet. The girls ate their porridge in silence and Lydia was glad to escape the atmosphere at the table as she turned to take their bowls through to the scullery. She could hear a murmur of voices behind her.

'Church?' she heard Janet say in a surprised voice. 'Did I hear you say you're planning on going to church?'

'You mean what would the likes of me be doing going to church?' Chrissie demanded angrily. 'And why shouldn't I go to church if I want to?' She rounded on Lydia when she returned. 'You go to church sometimes, don't you? Will you go to church with me?'

'Yes, of course, if you want to,' Lydia replied in confusion.

It had been a while since she had been to church. There had been Ewen's christening of course. And she went to please her mother at Christmas and Easter. But voluntarily? She had put all that behind her. However, if Chrissie wanted to go to church and needed company, it was the least she could do for her. She was clearly upset about something today.

'Which church do you want to go to?'

'St George's, the Methodist,' Chrissie said uncompromisingly.

Janet and Lydia exchanged puzzled glances but Chrissie offered no further information. The girls went back upstairs for their coats and hats and set off into the town, parting with Janet who was going to the Wee Free service.

When Lydia and Chrissie got to the Methodist Church, Lydia was surprised to see that the building was packed. They squeezed into a pew in the balcony while Chrissie craned her neck looking round at the congregation.

'There's a lot of people here,' Lydia commented.

'Aye. It's that man Troup's preaching that's doing it. He's stirring them up something terrible,' Chrissie hissed. She tensed and sat down suddenly, leaning down and reaching around at her feet as if she had dropped something. When she sat up, her face was pale and she was trembling.

'What's the matter?' Lydia asked. 'Won't you tell me?'

'It's nothing,' Chrissie snapped. 'Mind your own business.'

Her words were drowned out by singing as the congregation joined in a Moody and Sankey hymn. One after another hymn was sung till the atmosphere was expectant and rapt.

As one, the congregation rose when the local minister entered with Jock Troup at his side, once more smart in his black jacket and pinstripe trousers. Once again his preaching was loud and impassioned, calling on the hearers to turn from their sins and accept the salvation bought for them on the Cross by the Lord Jesus.

One by one, men and women rose from their places as if driven by an inner compulsion and went to the bench at the front to be assured of forgiveness, or to go to one of the back rooms for counselling. Burdened men and women stumbled, blinded by their tears, into the rooms and time and again, returned alight with joy.

Lydia watched in amazement. These were tough, hardy people who had seen all of life's hardships and suffering, now brought to their knees by the preaching of this man. But when they returned from the back rooms or stood up from the bench, they were transformed. It was as though the years had rolled back, and their burdens had been removed so they stood young and tall again.

And Lydia discovered envy for them in her heart. Once upon a time she had believed – maybe not like that, not with the amazing shining love and joy that was pouring out of these people. But she had believed in Jesus. She had believed His death had been sufficient to save her. But that was before... before Danny and the implacable hatred that had grown in her heart, culminating in relief and an almost disbelieving joy when she heard of his death. Feelings that were surely sinful.

Yes, she had once believed – when she was an innocent girl with barely any sins needing Jesus's great sacrifice. But now it was too late. Her actions had taken her through the gates of Hell and left her there. Now she felt beyond the reach of this loving, saving Lord.

'Come on.' Chrissie was standing up and tugging at her arm. 'We're getting out of here. Now!' she hissed urgently.

Lydia allowed Chrissie to pull her out of the pew, down the stairs and out of the church into the fresh air. But the strange atmosphere and happenings had spilled over to the street outside the church.

In their path was a middle-aged couple facing one another, tears rolling down their faces.

'Can you forgive me?' the man was asking in a broken voice.

'Aye,' the woman replied robustly. 'As the Lord has forgiven me!'

And Lydia saw that strange wonderful light in their faces as their tears became tears of joy and they embraced.

'Come *on*!' Chrissie cried, desperation in her voice. 'We've got to get away from here.'

'But why?' Lydia asked her. Her heart was strangely reluctant to leave.

'You don't need to know *why*. Let's just do it!' Chrissie insisted and she led Lydia away from the church and on a fast promenade of the river till it was time to go back to the lodgings for their dinner.

'Not a word to Janet,' Chrissie instructed her and when Lydia began to frame the question why, she added, 'And no whys!'

Chrissie remained snappish and clearly unhappy for the rest of the day. Janet by contrast was happy and carefree. Her simple contentment with her life and her love for her husband were obvious to all and seemed to annoy Chrissie beyond measure.

'So go and find him,' she said, rudely interrupting Janet's recounting of their evening's dancing. 'You're not needed here.'

Janet said nothing but kept placidly knitting. Lydia admired her patience and gentleness. It was as if Chrissie was determined to pick a fight, but Janet would not tangle with her and carefully stepped in to protect Lydia when Chrissie's acid tongue turned her way.

It was an uncomfortable afternoon and evening, relieved only when Chrissie went out for another walk. That night in bed Janet and Lydia could hear her sobbing in the darkness.

In the morning, when Janet brought up their tea, Lydia could see that Chrissie's eyes were bloodshot and swollen from weeping.

'Oh my dearie!' Janet said and enfolded Chrissie in her arms.

Lydia held her breath waiting for Chrissie's furious reaction but all the fight had gone out of her and she sat within Janet's embrace like a beaten child.

'What am I going to do?' she kept repeating, a terrible dullness in her voice. 'What am I going to do?'

'You'll have to tell us what the matter is,' Janet said gently, 'or we'll have no idea what we can tell you to do.'

That brought a thin wavering smile but it was quickly replaced by hopelessness and desperation. Chrissie's eyes fixed on Lydia. She seemed to be pleading – for understanding? And she seemed afraid.

'Come on,' Janet coaxed her. 'It can't be that bad. Spit it out. You'll feel better...'

'No,' Chrissie wailed. 'How can I ever feel better?'

'You will if you tell us,' Janet persisted.

Finally Chrissie took a deep breath, and still with her pleading eyes fixed on Lydia she stammered, 'I'm expecting. And the bairn's Robbie's.'

Janet and Lydia exchanged glances. Lydia reached out and took Chrissie's hand, squeezing it encouragingly.

'And?' Janet prompted, for surely there was more to Chrissie's distress than this simple statement.

Chrissie gulped. 'And Robbie was at that meeting on Saturday night,' she said. 'I saw him afterwards and he was full of all that stuff – all that religion stuff!' she said wildly. 'All the stuff you believe!' she flung at Janet and broke into noisy sobs.

Janet soothed her, stroking her hair like a child's till she calmed and was able to continue. 'He told me he'd be going to the church on Sunday and he was there,' Chrissie said. 'I saw him.'

So that was why they had gone to church, Lydia thought, and why Chrissie had ducked her head, hiding from someone. Hiding from Robbie. But surely they had not fallen out? If her brother had rejected his pregnant girlfriend the way Walter had spurned poor Johann – well, he would have his big sister to answer to.

Chrissie's voice broke into Lydia's vengeful thoughts.

'And then he went forward,' Chrissie said. 'After we left,' she said to Lydia. 'He's been...'

'Saved?' Janet prompted.

Chrissie nodded. 'I heard from some of his friends last night.'

Fresh tears began to flow and Janet tried to staunch them with a fresh handkerchief.

Lydia was puzzled. Chrissie was behaving as if it was the end of the world, but she could not see it.

'So yes, you're pregnant,' Lydia said. 'And maybe you don't want to be, and Robbie's been saved, but...'

'Oh, Lyddie, don't you see?' Chrissie cried in desperation. 'He won't want the likes of me now! I'm part of his *past*, his *sinful* past. He'll never want anything to do with me now! And there's the babe to think of! Oh, what am I going to do?' She flung herself on the bed wailing.

Janet took her hand and indicated for Lydia to take the other. She stroked Chrissie's hair with her free hand.

'There, there,' she murmured. 'So Robbie's turned to the Lord. Well, in itself that's no bad thing. But what of you? You say you're part of his sinful past. Is that how you feel?'

Lydia could feel the tremor in the girl as she nodded her head in assent.

'I'm no good,' Chrissie said brokenly. 'I heard that man Troup. I'm a sinner – and this babe just goes to show how much of a sinner I am. And I can't even jump into the harbour like Johann because I'll go straight to Hell if I do! Whatever I do, I'm lost!' Her voice rose to a crescendo, competing with sudden shouting from outside. The morning lorry had come to fetch the girls to the curing yard.

Janet gently disentangled herself and motioned for Lydia to stay, comforting Chrissie.

'I must go, my dears,' she said. 'The lorry is here and someone needs to go to the yard and tell them you won't be in this morning. Don't you worry. I'll sort it out and I'll be back as soon as I can.' She turned to Lydia and put a hand on her shoulder. 'Can you get her dressed? She'll feel much better, and yourself too. And then try and keep her as calm as you can. And pray,' Janet said softly

Lydia looked up in surprise.

'Yes,' Janet said. 'You do whatever praying you can, because poor Chrissie is in sore need of it now.'

They heard the lorry's engine revving up in the street.

Janet said, 'I must go. I'll tell the cooper that you're not well enough to come to work today.'

Lydia heard Janet hurrying downstairs. A few moments later she heard the lorry move away and they were left in the quiet of the big empty loft room.

CHAPTER 14

Lydia sat and stroked Chrissie's hair, murmuring soothingly to her as she would have to Ewen. Chrissie's wild cries had died down to a heartbroken sobbing but she clutched at Lydia's free hand as if it were her only lifeline. She had acquiesced numbly to Lydia's suggestion that they get dressed, and had half-heartedly splashed water from the basin on to her red-rimmed eyes and blotchy face.

What to do now, Lydia worried. Janet had told her to pray for Chrissie: 'Do whatever praying you can.'

It did not sound as if Janet had much confidence in her. Rightly, Lydia thought, as she tried to cobble together some kind of a prayer for Chrissie. Oh, she could find words but you really needed more than that. You needed faith that the words would be heard and listened to.

Back when Alec and Danny had marched off so proudly to the Great War, she had prayed fervently for their safe return. She had felt her prayers answered when they came home on leave. But then, after a few short days when her emotions went from ecstasy to shocked horror, they had marched off again and everyone expected her to pray with even more fervency. But she could not. She did not want Danny to return.

It was not something she could ever tell anyone so she had pushed it deep inside herself and then gone to church with her mother, for the appearance of the thing, and sat in silence.

When they were killed in Bourlon Wood, she knew she had as good as killed them. It was her fault – Danny's death and Alec's. And though she did not regret Danny's death, she was appalled that Alec had been killed too. She had not thought that would happen when she withheld her prayers. But it had. And it had hit her parents hard, hurt the people she loved the best. And it was all her fault. So she had pushed her hurt and outrage even deeper inside.

As she stroked Chrissie's hair and marvelled at the powerfulness of Chrissie's feelings, she realised her own had frozen back then. She had needed her ice shield to deal with her emotional turmoil. Her family and friends had assumed it was the weight of unspeakable grief, never guessing the relief she hid along with the burden of guilt in her heart.

And here she was, as bad as any murderer, being asked to pray for this girl whose only sin appeared to be love.

'Do whatever praying you can,' Janet had instructed.

Lydia found that she wanted to pray for this girl whose cheerful courage had rescued her, and saved Johann's reputation. But how? A memory of sitting on her mother's knee as a child, hands folded, eyes closed, talking simply to God... Maybe since it was for Chrissie, God might listen. Tentatively she reached out towards the God she thought she had known when she was a child.

'Please,' she began. 'For Chrissie.'

It was all she could manage, but maybe it would be enough.

There was a clattering of feet on the stairs. Was that Janet return-ing already? But it was not Janet who arrived in the loft room but the man who had been preaching in the Market Place, Jock Troup. He was not in his smart clothes now but in the working clothes of a cooper in the gutting yard. And with him was a tall lean older man who hesitated in the doorway at the top of the stairs.

'Mrs Foubister said there was a lassie needed help,' Jock announced in his loud voice. 'We came at once.'

Alerted by the sound, Chrissie raised her face from the bed and at sight of Jock Troup, once more burst into noisy tears.

'Nah, nah,' he said in a gentle voice. 'This will never do.'

He nodded politely to Lydia and indicated that he would take over. Lydia glared at him. If it had not been for this man's rabble-rousing in the Market Place and in the church last night, Chrissie would not be in the state she was now. She and Robbie would be continuing as before and everything would be all right.

Lydia's glare said it all. The tall man at the door caught her eye and gave her a reassuring smile but she was not to be placated. Resentfully, she rose from the bed but stayed close.

Jock Troup sat down on the kist beside the bed and said quietly to Chrissie, 'Well now, you'd better tell me all about it.'

'I'm in bad trouble,' Chrissie whispered hoarsely. 'And I'll go to Hell!' The tears exploded again but they did not seem to dismay Jock Troup. With patience and gentleness, he drew the whole story from her.

'And you're hurting now, aren't you?' he asked her.

Chrissie nodded. 'I don't want to go to Hell,' she whispered. 'And I can't do what Johann did...'

The two men exchanged glances.

'The girl who fell in the river?' Jock asked.

Chrissie stared at him. 'Yes!' she said quickly. 'Yes, that's what I meant.'

His gaze was steady, unchallenging, but Chrissie crumbled.

'I lied,' she wailed. 'To the police and the coroner. More sin! Oh, what am I to do?'

'Wait a minute, Chrissie.' Lydia stepped forward, drawing all eyes to her. 'What you did was wrong.' She could have been speaking to any of her ten-year-olds in the classroom at home. She continued, 'But it was my idea, so most of the blame is mine. You don't have to add that burden to what you're carrying.'

'Lyddie, no!' Chrissie protested. 'I went along with it of my own free will. I went to the police and told them...'

'And I went with you,' Lydia reminded her.

Chrissie began to protest again but Lydia held her gaze till Chrissie finally nodded her agreement.

'All right,' she said grudgingly. 'It was your idea.'

Lydia smiled. She stood tall and unflinching under the gaze of the two men.

'Johann was a good girl who had been led astray and we didn't want any more hurt to come to her,' she explained calmly. 'So I thought if we said it was an accident, her parents would have to arrange for her body to be taken home to Lewis... and deal with everything. Much better than a verdict of suicide and a pauper's grave in Yarmouth, disowned by her people and far from her own country.'

Feeling the men's eyes on her, she stumbled on the last few words, but she bit her lip and stood her ground, looking Jock Troup in the eye. Dark, gentle eyes full of compassion and understanding met hers. Surprised, Lydia turned and looked at the other man to see his reaction. She got an impression of strength – and could that be admiration?

Confused and feeling the beginning of a blush start in her cheeks, she stepped back against the wall and focused on Chrissie.

'We're not here to judge you,' Jock Troup said slowly. 'That's for the good Lord to do.' He paused. 'Have her parents done the decent thing?' he asked.

Chrissie nodded. 'Yes. Her body went home on the train on Friday.'

'Well, I see no reason to rake over those coals, do you, Frank?' he asked the man at the door.

'No. It's done now – and what you did, you did out of love,' the man called Frank said in an English accent. 'The Lord understands love.'

'But that's why I'm in trouble!' Chrissie burst out. 'I love Robbie. But now he's a Christian, he won't want to have anything to do with a... a fallen woman like me! I might as well jump in the harbour like Johann!'

'You don't have to do that, lassie,' Jock Troup said. 'What you're feeling is right and proper, though it hurts. It means you've been convicted of sin.'

Chrissie snorted, halfway between a sob and a laugh. 'You can say that again!' she said.

'But you don't need to stay in that place,' Jock Troup explained. 'The Lord Jesus Christ died to take away your sins. He paid the price for them to set you free. If you ask Him, He'll take your sins away and give you a fresh start. He'll cleanse you from your sins and set you off on a whole new way of life – abundant life, eternal life.'

'Would He?' Chrissie asked, the beginnings of hope dawning in her eyes. 'Someone like me? And could I really start fresh? Even with the baby...?'

'You can,' Jock Troup said with a big smile. 'Believe on the Lord Jesus Christ and you will be saved! When you belong to Him, you can trust Him to take care of everything.'

'Oh, I want that!' Chrissie declared in heartfelt tones. 'More than anything!'

'More than Robbie?' Jock Troup asked her.

Chrissie gazed at him and chewed her lip as she considered his question. Finally she nodded. 'I need to get my life put right – for me and the baby – and this is the only way I can see will do it. I can't bear to go on living feeling like this!' She swallowed hard. 'Will you ask your Jesus for me? I don't know what to say... but what you're saying... that's what I want. Clean and saved. A new start. And if Jesus will do that for me, then I'll sign up for Him! And what Robbie decides about me and his bairn... well that's up to him. And I'll trust to your Jesus to sort that out too!'

The two men smiled and Jock Troup prayed the simple words that gave Chrissie into the care of the Lord Jesus.

'It's done now,' he told her. 'You belong to the Lord and He will see to everything for you, and that includes Robbie and the bairn. You'll trust Him with this?'

Chrissie nodded shakily, but in her eyes was that strange light of hope, and the tears had stopped.

Jock Troup looked across at the quiet man at the door and as if at a signal, he prayed then, a simple powerful prayer for Chrissie and Robbie, the baby they had made, for Johann and then surprisingly for Lydia, calling her Lyddie as Chrissie had, encircling them all in God's forgiving love. She looked up uncertainly to find his eyes warm and gentle upon her. A sudden shyness overtook her and she looked away hastily.

Jock Troup rose to his feet.

'I'll need to be getting back to work,' he said matter-of-factly.

'Give us a minute,' Chrissie said decisively. 'We're coming too.' She looked across to Lydia for confirmation. Lydia nodded.

'And you?' Jock Troup asked Lydia. 'Are you all right?'

Lydia looked up and saw the other man was watching her, as if waiting for her answer too. She knew it was not her physical well-being they wanted to hear about, but her spiritual standing. What was the answer? Lydia felt a momentary panic. Her guilt hung heavy on her but it was not something she wanted to talk about, especially not before the rather nice man called Frank. She pulled herself together.

'Thank you,' she finally got out, taking refuge in formality. 'Yes, I'm fine.'

CHAPTER 15

Chrissie's eagerness to return to work surprised Lydia but even more her willingness to announce to the other girls what had happened.

'I saw the error of my ways and the Lord saved me,' she said, smiling as she went to her place amongst the barrels and got on with her work.

'Well done!' came a few voices and 'The Lord be praised!' One of the women started to sing a hymn of praise and the others joined in joyfully.

Janet merely smiled and murmured 'Well done' as she welcomed Lydia back to her place at the farlin. 'We've another lightish catch so you'll easily catch up,' she said. 'You're all right?'

'Fine,' Lydia said and bent to her work, but her mind was racing. This was another unexpected side of these women. They seemed comfortable with matters of faith and religion in a way Lydia had never experienced before.

She looked across to where Chrissie was working, adding some of the day's gutted herring to one of the previous day's packed barrels. She was laughing and joking with the cooper who stood supervising. She seemed to have completely recovered, except for that light in her eyes. There was something different about her. A lightness. A new joy.

~

That night the three of them went to church. There seemed to be meetings every evening in the town's churches and a warm welcome for the fisher lassies and the men whose boats were still kept in harbour by the unseasonal weather.

First, there was hymn singing, the voices a warm mix of Scottish and English accents. Then the minister and the tall older man that had accompanied Jock Troup came in and stood on the platform at the front of the church. Lydia noticed with surprise that he was wearing a clerical collar.

The minister introduced him as the Reverend Frank Everett, a visiting Baptist minister. Lydia allowed herself a moment to admire his fine, upright stance and the smart clothes he was wearing. He was a fine-looking man. Then she noticed that he was carefully scanning the large congregation tightly packed into all the pews and aisles. When his eyes alighted on her, the scanning stopped and he smiled across the crowded church, a smile that felt as though it were just for her. Lydia felt her cheeks warm but she could not resist the warmth in his eyes and she smiled shyly in return.

Janet, who was watching and missed nothing, nudged Lydia. 'Have you got a beau then?' she teased. 'You didn't tell us! You'd do fine with that one!'

'Don't be silly!' Lydia told her fiercely, turning away to hide the tell-tale flame in her cheeks. She had no interest in beaux, she told herself. She was merely being polite. But she had to admit it was a nice surprise that he remembered her, even seemed to have been looking for her.

But before the service proper could begin, Chrissie was elbowing her way to the front. She reached the communion rail and turned to face the congregation.

'Most of you know me,' she said. 'Chrissie Anderson from Wick. And you know what kind of a person I was. Well, I came to the Lord this morning and I want to tell you it's the best thing I've ever done, and if you haven't found the Lord and turned to Him, you should do it too!'

Her words were greeted with a chorus of 'Hallelujah!' and 'Praise the Lord!' and the loudest voice came from a wiry young man who was pushing his way through the crowd to reach her.

'Robbie!' breathed Lydia, her eyes fixed on her brother as he hurried towards Chrissie, joy in his face. But as he reached for her, Chrissie took a step away.

'No,' she said firmly. 'I need to talk to you, but not here.'

Taking his hand she pulled him towards the doors, pausing a moment to look at the two men on the platform. Frank Everett murmured something to the minister at his side and then he spoke to Chrissie and Robbie. As they left, the crowd in the church laughed and cheered, and had to be called to order by the minister. But Frank had his head bowed in prayer and Janet whispered urgently to Lydia, 'Pray like you've never prayed before! She'll be telling him about the baby.'

Pray. It was the second time in one day that Lydia had been told to pray. She had wanted to pray for Chrissie the first time but had felt so inadequate, reaching out for a childish picture of God with a tiny threadbare faith. But now she desperately wanted to pray with a strong, powerful prayer to a strong powerful God. She wanted God to hear her on Chrissie's behalf, and Robbie's. She wanted Him to help Chrissie and Robbie. To make everything all right.

But who was she to think she could make God listen? She had wanted her husband dead and that surely was as bad as killing him herself.

Unaware that tears were rolling down her cheeks, she sat hopelessly beside Janet as the congregation rose and sang, and sat and prayed, and listened to the words of the visiting Baptist minister. His words washed over her, but his voice, a fine clear masculine voice, was strong and sure in such contrast to her own hopelessness.

Young men and women and old men and women went forward and received the Lord Jesus as their Saviour. The very air seemed to crackle with the spiritual electricity that was touching and changing lives.

Then Janet was urging her to stand.

'It's time to go,' she said gently.

Lydia found herself led, almost unawares, out of the pew and down the stairs and into the street.

'May I walk you home?' A male voice.

Lydia came back to herself with a jolt. Standing facing her was Frank Everett.

'I'm sorry,' she said dazedly. 'What did you say?'

Frank and Janet exchanged glances.

'I wondered if I might walk you ladies home?' he said gently. 'It's a fine night...'

'We'd be glad of the company,' Janet said. 'Wouldn't we, Lyddie?'

Lydia tried to pull herself together.

'Yes, of course,' she responded politely and when Frank offered her his arm, she automatically took it, then checked that he had offered his other arm to Janet.

Janet was laughing. 'I hope my husband won't see us and think I've taken up with a fancy man!'

'Dressed like this?' Frank responded cheerfully. 'And not one lady but two?'

'It would be the first time,' Janet agreed.

'What do you think?' he asked Lydia.

'Lyddie?' Janet urged her.

'Oh.' Lydia struggled to remember what they were talking about. 'Well, I think Sandy's sure enough of you not to worry,' she tried.

The walk home was accomplished harmoniously thanks mainly to Janet providing cheerful small talk and Frank responding in kind, both of them clearly pretending there was nothing the matter with Lydia who walked in a kind of daze, aware only of the closeness, the warmth and clean smell of the man walking so closely linked to herself. It had been a long time since a man had been this close and she was surprised at how pleasant it felt. How comfortable. How... safe.

She dragged her thoughts back into order. She was clearly not in her right mind. The emotional upheavals of the past few days had taken their toll and she needed her bed and darkness and a chance to think.

She was glad when they got to the door of their lodgings. She knew she was being discourteous but she could not find the energy to make any effort at conversation. Longing for sleep, she realised it was unlikely to come. Chrissie and Janet would go to sleep secure in their faith, while she struggled in the morass of feelings that had coursed through her at the church. Her head ached and, she realised, so did her heart.

Frank bade Janet goodnight, politely shaking her hand. She smiled at him and swiftly disappeared into the house. Lydia turned to say goodbye and offered her hand. But Frank Everett ignored it.

'You can talk to me, you know,' he said softly. 'About anything.'

Lydia felt herself stare at him. How could she ever tell anyone? Her eyes filled with tears and she shook her head. And suddenly, Frank opened his arms wide and brought them down gently around her, enfolding Lydia in the tenderest, most respectful embrace she had ever experienced, as if she were the most precious, delicate china.

Shocked, she simply stood still within those encircling arms and found she was resting her head upon his chest.

Then he was gone.

CHAPTER 16

Lydia hurried in after Janet and up the stairs to bed. Despite Janet's kindly forbearance, letting her wash and undress in silence, sleep was not to come. Her mind was a whirling confusion of emotions and impressions, with only the feeling of that surprising embrace as a quiet oasis to retreat to.

So much had happened, so much seemed to have changed – for Chrissie, Robbie... And as Lydia relived the experience of Frank Everett's gentle embrace, she was astounded to discover a warming in her heart, a thawing of the permafrost. It seemed maybe she was changing too.

When Chrissie bounced in an hour later bubbling over with her news, there was nothing to be done but for Lydia and Janet to sit up in bed and listen.

'I told him!' Chrissie announced dramatically.

'Hush!' Janet cautioned. 'Don't wake the others. Now tell us, but quietly!' she prompted.

'Robbie says we'll get married,' Chrissie told them joyfully. 'The banns will be read as soon as we get back to Wick at the end of the fishing! So the bairn will be all right... Everything will be all right! That Jock Troup told the truth. His Jesus looked after everything.'

'Praise the Lord,' came Janet's fervent whisper.

Chrissie stopped suddenly and turned to Lydia with appeal in her eyes.

'Oh Lyddie, do you mind? About me and Robbie? I know I'm not as good as your folks...'

'Not as good as...!' Lydia protested.

She thought back to how Chrissie had stood up for her on the train down to Yarmouth and helped her manage on the journey, then had come to her rescue when that horrid man had attacked her and stolen her bag. How Chrissie had brought her to these lodgings and found work for her so she could earn her ticket home... She reached out her arms to hug Chrissie.

'Chrissie love, you're certainly as good as anybody I've ever met! And anyway, I always wanted a sister and you're the best I could ever have!'

She felt Janet's arm steal around her and give her an approving squeeze.

'But what about your mother? I'm afraid she won't be so pleased,' Chrissie confessed.

Lydia considered the truth of what Chrissie had said. Her mother had tried valiantly to hold her head up after marrying a fisherman, marrying beneath her according to Granny Leslie's repeated criticisms. Robbie, her ewe lamb, marrying a pregnant fisher lassie might cause her mother a pang or two but it would incense Granny Leslie. Lydia pushed that thought away. It was hardly Granny Leslie's business (though none of them were probably brave enough to tell her to her face).

Lydia reminded herself that Chrissie was a good-hearted girl who loved Robbie. That, and a grandchild, would surely win her mother's heart.

'My mother may be a bit surprised,' Lydia said with a smile, 'but I'm sure she'll come round.'

'Your Da was lovely...'

'My father?' Lydia asked in surprise. Was there no end to the shocks today was bringing?

'Aye. After Robbie got us all sorted out, he took me to meet his Da,' Chrissie said.

'But where? On the boat?' Lydia was completely puzzled. 'But surely Robbie wouldn't set foot there and in any case, my Dad wouldn't let him!'

'He was at the service too last night,' Chrissie said.

'My Dad at the service?' Lydia echoed in astonishment. She could not remember the last time her father had set foot in a church. He even used to mock her mother for her constant faith.

Chrissie laughed softly. 'Aye, it isn't just Robbie who has come to the Lord. Your Da did too! You should see the pair of them...'

Lydia shook her head in the darkness. It was all too much to take in.

'After you left, it all spilled out on to the pavement outside. You should have seen it! We were surrounded by people on their knees, weeping, praying – and Jock Troup and the minister were going round praying with them. And your Da was one of them. He came to the Lord last night, and when he saw the pair of us' – Chrissie's voice hushed in awe – 'he just reached out to Robbie and Robbie went to him. You should have seen them! Hugging and weeping and...' She stopped for a moment then went on, 'So the good news is that they've made up,' Chrissie said. 'Because of the Lord.'

Lydia was stunned. Could it be possible? If it was true, it was another amazing miracle.

'Your Da has accepted Robbie back on the boat,' Chrissie continued. 'Robbie was only helping out his cousin on the trawler while the other lad was ill. Your Da's even said he'll listen to Robbie's wild ideas!' She snorted in amusement. 'I think Robbie will need to eat some humble pie first, and maybe your Da too!'

'I can't take it in,' Lydia said, in stunned amazement.

Chrissie suddenly leaned over and kissed her on the cheek. 'Well, maybe, big sister-to-be, that's 'cos you're old and...!'

Before she knew it, Lydia had grabbed a pillow and swung it at Chrissie who responded with the other pillow and in a few minutes the pair of them were laughing and giggling together.

'Shh, you two! You'll wake everybody up!' Janet admonished them.

'True enough,' Chrissie said cheerfully. 'Well, my dears, time for sleep.'

And now Lydia slept, warm and comfortable in this bed with her friends – her friend and her sister-to-be, not to mention a niece or nephew-to-be. And Dad and Robbie reconciled. So many amazing, wonderful things had happened. All through one man's preaching the good news of salvation in Jesus Christ.

Lydia was so happy for them, but she felt that somehow she had missed out. The core of permafrost round her guilt remained, blocking her way to God. Though nestled deep in her heart was the tender memory of one gentle embrace.

CHAPTER 17

'*My dearest Jean*,' the letter began.

Jean's hands shook. What could this mean? She stared into the flickering flames of the coal fire, thinking hard. It was a long time since she had known an endearment from her husband. Their love had shrivelled in the face of her mother's bitter disapproval, David's single-minded determination to prove himself as good as her people, and, she had to admit, her own dislike and withdrawal from the man he had become as a result.

Maybe she had judged him as harshly as her mother had. She held his letter in her hands but could not look at it. Had she, she thought for the hundredth time, driven him away from her with her judgment and her criticism? Had it been wrong to side with Robbie against him? Maybe there had been another way, but she had felt torn between the pair of them and Robbie had desperately needed his mother's support.

But what of her husband, that familiar little voice inside reminded her. Did he not deserve her support too? Instead, too often, she had found herself parroting the cruel words her mother said.

'They were right. I never should have married you!'

In her memory she heard her voice flinging the words at him after yet another of the acrimonious arguments they seemed to have every time they were together. And each one more bitter than the last.

Everything seemed to have gone wrong after Alec was killed in the Great War. First David had sunk into a deep depression. All his dreams had smashed. There was no son to share the boat with him and inherit it after him, Robbie written off at the age of seven because he was miserably seasick on his first ever voyage. And when Robbie came home from the war, alive but suffering with the gas in his lungs, David had turned against him worse than ever before.

And that was when he had turned to the drink. Jean had watched him vainly try to drown his misery and despair. The only one who seemed to reach him was young Ewen. Gradually though, David had seemed to put the past behind him and move on. But as a harder man. An unforgiving, angry man who had no time for kind words or gentleness with his family – except for Ewen who remained the apple of his eye.

And Jean had felt jealous. Yet again someone else had taken first place in his heart – that place which should have been hers and hers alone. First there had been Alec. David had idolised him. That was the only word for it. Which had made the pain so much greater when he died in the war. Yet even in death, he was an idol to his father, a hero who had given his life for his country while his worthless brother had come limping back, no use to anyone.

It had not been fair and Jean had tried to fight for Robbie. But it was no good. David had hardened his heart and closed his mind. Only Ewen was acceptable to him. So Jean had watched anxiously each time Ewen took some childhood illness. She could not bear to have David's last hope torn from him. But she could not wrap Ewen in cotton wool.

Somewhere along the way, her faith had become a despairing thing. Something she clung to almost hopelessly. Because there seemed to be no grounds for hope: her marriage a sham, her eldest son killed in the war, her widowed daughter a pale shadow of herself, her younger son outcast by his father, and her grandson seemingly carrying all the hope of the family on his far-too-slender young shoulders. Not to mention her own mother adding her two-pennyworth to the general store of misery: 'You should never have married him. If you'd done as we said...' On and on and on...

And now a letter which was frightening in its gentleness.

'*My dearest Jean...*'

What would make him write like this? What could have happened? Had he met a kinder woman in Yarmouth and was writing to break the news that he would not be coming home?

It was what she feared. She should not be surprised. She had not loved him and stood by him as she should have. She had turned away in her own hurt and pain. He needed love, someone who would care for him...

Jean glanced up at the clock on the mantelpiece. Ewen would be home from school soon. Better get it over with. She turned back to the letter in her hand.

~

'Granny! Granny! What's the matter?' Ewen was shaking her arm and staring into her face, frightened by the tears flowing down her cheeks.

Jean pulled herself together. She should not alarm the child.

'I'm sorry, love.' She gave him what she hoped was a reassuring smile as she struggled to regain control. 'I got a letter.'

'What's happened?' Ewen demanded. 'Is someone dead?'

Jean laughed at the bluntness of youth.

'No, not exactly,' she began.

'Then how exackly?' Ewen persisted, his chubby brow furrowed in perplexity.

'It's good news, not bad news,' Jean said with a wide smile that revealed her joy. She waved the letter. 'Very good news, from your Grandpa. Everything's fine.'

And better than fine, she thought, as she made Ewen his tea. Much better than fine.

'*I have some good news for you,*' David had written. '*On Saturday night, I attended a meeting in the Market Square in Yarmouth and was deeply moved by the preaching of Jock Troup, one of the Wick coopers. I decided I needed to hear more so I went to the church on Sunday...*'

Here Jean had paused in wonder. Her husband had not set foot in a church since Alec's funeral, swearing that he had no more time for the God who had let his son die. So it was very interesting that he had been drawn back to church by Jock Troup's preaching. The Lord's hand, she thought. She should never have doubted...

'*There I came back to the Lord.*'

The simplest of words and the deepest of meanings. More than she could ever have dreamed of. More than she had ever dared to pray for. Eyes swimming with the tears of joy that threatened to overflow, she read on:

'*My dearest Jean, I asked His forgiveness for all that I have done wrong and now I ask yours. I have not been a good husband to you these past years but if you will still have me, I pray the Lord will make the last years we have together better than all those that have gone before.*'

'I haven't been a good wife to you either,' Jean had whispered. 'Dear Lord Jesus, forgive me and give us this second chance!' And that was when the long pent-up tears began to flow.

It was a little later when Ewen had returned. Now with him safely tucked up in bed, a story told and him kissed goodnight, Jean went back down to the warm kitchen, made herself a cup of tea and settled by the fire to reread the amazing letter from her husband.

The wonder of it settled warmly in her heart. The Lord Jesus had done this thing. This wonderful thing. What more was there for her Davey to say? She turned to the next page.

'Robbie was at the service too.'

She found she was holding her breath. There had been such ill feeling between the two men for so many years – since the wee lad was only seven – and it had grown through the years like a rank weed from disappointment to enmity.

'My love, he came to the Lord too and we are reconciled. I have written this letter as fast as I could to get the good news to you. We will work the boat together for this season and then see how we should go forward when we come home.'

Jean was so shocked at the good news that she did not notice the endearment till she went back over the paragraph. David repeated it in his last few lines:

'I long to see you and tell you all this face to face, my bonnie Jean. The autumn fishing is not good this year so we may be home sooner than expected. I pray the Lord will bless our family.

I am, as I always have been, my love,

Yours, but now truly in Christ...'

Jean's tears flowed freely. Tears of joy and hope, and praise to a loving, surprising, wonderful Lord. She remembered that special verse she had found so long ago that had strengthened her when she stood out against her parents and married the man she loved:

'I know the thoughts that I think toward you, saith the Lord; thoughts of peace, and not of evil, to give you an expected end.' (Jeremiah 29:11)

She had clung to that promise through the years, though her hope had all but died. Now it flared into new life and, for the first time in many years, she felt like a young bride longing to see her man safely home after the autumn fishing.

CHAPTER 18

HERRING FISHING
Shoals struck at last

From the northern end of the Wharf down to the Harbour's mouth and also on the Gorleston side of the river, boats were on Wednesday disgorging the silvery fish. Every inch of space for berthing and landing was occupied, and one could scarcely move for the continuous procession of laden motor lorries. Up to 5 o'clock some 400 boats had arrived, total delivery estimated at 20,000 crans.

... As soon as the boats had unloaded they put to sea again.

Yarmouth Mercury, 22 October 1921

Herring Fishing – East Anglian Ports

The Scottish fleet was well among the herring shoals last night and got some very heavy shots.

Upwards of 300 drifters landed over 50 crans each. Owing to the heavy fishing all market space has been used and many shots have been discharged on the opposite side of the harbour.

John O'Groat Journal, 21 October 1921

All Lydia knew was that she had never worked so hard in all her life, or for so long.

The day had begun early as usual. The routine was now familiar: wake-up call at 5 o'clock, cup of tea and get dressed, wrap the clooties round her fingers to protect them after checking the state of any cuts. Then down the stairs and into boots and oilies and on to the waiting lorry ready to start work at 6.

Now she happily joined in the cheerful chatter and the singing as the motor lorry rumbled with its cargo of fisher lassies down to the curing yards. She drew the line at the flirtatious banter the other women seemed to direct at any hapless male they encountered en route to the yard. Interestingly she noticed that Chrissie also abstained, and that Janet had never joined in.

She wondered what else she had never noticed about these women, seeing instead only the stereotype inculcated in her by her grandmother. Well, she was learning fast. Maybe even growing up at last too and making up her own mind about things. Though she was finding it hard to make up her mind about Frank Everett's embrace...

Swiftly, she banished it once again from her thoughts and, arriving at the yard, climbed down from the lorry and went to help Janet and Chrissie top up yesterday's barrels. And then the first lorry laden with silvery fish rolled into the yard. From then on, the work seemed never-ending as lorry after lorry arrived, fully laden.

'Good catch today!' one of the women called out.

'You should see the harbour!' a lorry driver told her. 'Boats on both sides and lining up waiting to get in. I've never seen the like!'

'It's work for us and that's good!' the woman responded cheerfully and the girls agreed as they set to, their hands moving deftly amongst the fish to gut and toss and pack the catch.

'Lyddie!' Janet interrupted the trance she had got into. 'We need to eat. Come on. We'll take a wee break.' She called across the yard. 'Chrissie! Are ye coming with us?'

The three linked arms and Lydia found herself escorted to a tea kiosk nearby. It was a welcome break but brief. Soon they were back at work as the herrings filled the farlin again, a seemingly never-ending harvest.

Nobody complained. Instead the girls sang. Gaelic work songs and familiar hymns. Lyddie loved the harmonies these girls seemed to sing so naturally. The singing made the hours pass more easily, though she longed to own the same fervour that Chrissie and Janet put into their hymn-singing. At church in Wick, such emotion would surely be frowned on by her Leslie grandmother.

Lyddie tossed her head. Granny Leslie was not here so Lydia could sing as loudly as she liked, so she joined in with gusto. It felt good.

Hour after hour, the girls worked. From time to time a crew would stop for a break and have something to eat. But even though the sun began to set, there was no lessening in the mountain of herrings waiting to be gutted.

Lights were lit across the yard so the girls could see to work. Cups of tea and sandwiches were brought to keep their strength up. And on they worked. Still laughing and chatting and singing.

CHAPTER 19

The weather changed suddenly. On Saturday afternoon when the girls were looking forward to their stroll along the river and into the town to meet up with Sandy and Robbie, Yarmouth was struck by a storm of wind and rain that turned to blinding hailstones.

'You're never going out in this!' Mrs Duff, their landlady, protested as they came downstairs in their coats and hats.

The girls exchanged glances. The arrangements to meet their menfolk had been made and they did not want to miss the opportunity of seeing them.

'We'll just go up the road to the café and have a cup of tea there,' Janet suggested.

'What with?' Chrissie asked bluntly. 'The catches may have been better this week but they still haven't made up for the week before. We'll be in debt before the end of the season if we're not careful with our money and I'm going to be needing mine.'

'I do want to see Robbie, though,' Lydia said. 'I need to sort out what I'm going to do.'

'That's your brother?' Mrs Duff asked.

'Yes,' Lydia replied. 'And Chrissie's fiancé. And we're meeting Sandy too. He's Janet's husband.'

'Well, in that case I see no harm in them coming here for a cup of tea. I'm going across the way to my sister's so you can use the parlour,' Mrs Duff offered.

'That's very kind of you,' Lydia said.

'We'll need to get a message to them...' Chrissie began.

'My sister's wee boy will be happy to run to the boats with a message,' Mrs Duff suggested.

So that is what they did and, before long, both Sandy and Robbie had arrived, clean-shaven and smart in their heavy fishermen's sweaters and dark trousers.

Lydia shed tears as she hugged her brother.

'Oh, it's so good to see you!' she cried.

Robbie laughed. There was a new lightness about him, she noticed, a happiness – and that light in his eyes.

'I'm fine, big sister!' he said, gently easing himself from her grip and reaching for Chrissie with an affectionate smile. He held her proudly at his side as he asked Lydia, 'You know our news?'

'Oh yes!' Lydia beamed at them. 'Good news, all of it!'

Robbie sat down in one of Mrs Duff's comfortable chairs with Chrissie perched beside him, Robbie's arm around her waist.

'Chrissie told me you were here,' Robbie said to Lydia. 'But I don't understand why. Shouldn't you be at school?'

'Yes. I'm sorry. It was Mum's idea. She was worried about you,' Lydia explained.

Robbie laughed ruefully. 'That's not news!'

'Yes, well, when she heard you and Dad had fallen out,' Lydia continued, 'she was worried and then she got this mad idea that if I came down here with enough money for your ticket, you would come back with me.'

138

Robbie shook his head in disbelief.

'She really worries about you,' Lydia said.

'Aye, I know. But I was fine. Didn't Chrissie tell you? I went to Granny Nichols and when Cousin George needed an extra hand on his trawler, it seemed heaven-sent.'

'Yes, I know now,' Lydia said. 'But Mum didn't.'

'You should have written and told her,' Chrissie scolded him affectionately.

'I'm not much of a hand at writing,' Robbie said sheepishly. 'And we don't talk much about Granny Nichols and the Lowestoft cousins.'

'That's true,' Lydia said.

'Well, maybe it's time you did,' Chrissie said with characteristic bluntness.

Robbie laughed and ruffled her hair. He looked across at Lydia.

'Granny Nichols would love to meet you. It would be a great surprise for her. What do you think? Would you give it a try?' he asked her. 'I could take you there...'

Lydia hesitated. 'I don't know. Let me think about it.'

'We could go across to Lowestoft on the bus,' Chrissie suggested.

Robbie smiled. 'That would be good. I want you to meet them. They've been good to me.'

'I'm glad about that, Robbie,' Lydia said. 'I think I'd like to meet them but...'

'But everything's fine now,' Robbie said. 'There's nothing for Mum to worry about. Dad and I have made up our differences and I'm back on the *Bonnie Jean* and we're doing fine.' His eyes had a faraway look as he mused, 'It's amazing. Since he came to the Lord, he's changed. He *talks* to me now.' Robbie added with a wondering laugh, 'And he listens when I answer!'

Chrissie poked him in the ribs. 'You've changed a bit yourself,' she told him.

He looked at her fondly. 'Aye, I have. Anyway, enough of that.' He turned back to Lydia. 'If you knew I was all right, what are you doing still here? Shouldn't you be back home?'

Colour flooded Lydia's cheeks. She felt so foolish for having walked into the horrid man's trap and then losing her bag with her ticket and the money. She looked appealingly at Janet and Chrissie for help.

'Lydia had a bit of an accident,' Janet began tactfully. Like Chrissie she was seated on the arm of an armchair, leaning comfortably against her husband.

'Her bag was stolen,' Chrissie stated simply.

'And it had my ticket and all the money Mum gave me for your ticket in it,' Lydia concluded.

Robbie whistled through his teeth. 'So you're stuck here?'

She nodded.

'That's not so good.'

'It is though,' Chrissie assured him. 'I told you we lost Johann, the third girl on the crew?'

Robbie nodded.

'Well, Lyddie was an answer to prayer. She's working with us so she can earn her keep and buy her ticket back home.'

'She's working with you?' Robbie asked. 'In the yard? At the gutting? What will Granny Leslie say to that? You'll never live it down.'

He reached out and took Lydia's hands in his. He turned them over and examined them, seeing the salt sores and the cuts from the sharp knife.

'Well, I can see it's true. I only hope you're earning your keep. It's skilled work and you haven't the experience.'

'She's doing fine.' Janet came quickly to Lydia's defence. 'She's a quick learner and she's getting up to speed.'

Chrissie looked quickly at Lydia and said to Robbie, 'But if you have enough money for her ticket home...'

'I should go home,' Lydia said apologetically. 'I only had the one week off. It was the tattie picking and most of my class would be away for that so I wrote to the Education Board asking for a week's leave of absence. When I knew I'd be here a bit longer, I wrote again. But I really should be going home if you or Dad could find the money for my ticket?' She looked at Chrissie and Janet, wanting them to understand. 'I don't want to leave you. You've been so good to me. And I've had such a good time! But I should really go. There's my wee boy and my job, and Mum will soon start worrying. So if Dad or Robbie can see their way to buy my ticket home...'

'I can't,' Robbie said, shaking his head regretfully. 'I'm sorry. I don't get my cut till the end of the season. And Dad's short as well. The cost of coal is terrible and the price he's getting for the fish is low. It's a poor season all round. We'll be lucky if we get a cut at all!'

Sandy, who had been sitting quietly with Janet, put in, 'I've never seen a Yarmouth fishing as bad as this. The catches are making less than half of what they did last year.'

'But what am I going to do?' Lydia interrupted. 'How am I going to get home? It sounds as if I might not be able to earn enough for my ticket myself!'

'Well, if you stay till the end of the season, you can use Johann's ticket as far as Inverness,' Janet suggested.

'And we can smuggle you the rest of the way!' Chrissie declared with characteristic bravado.

They all laughed.

'But when will that be?' Lydia demanded, serious again. 'Dad came home last year in time for Christmas. If I stay that long, I'm sure to lose my job!'

Robbie and Sandy exchanged glances.

141

'I think the fishing will finish sooner than usual,' Sandy said. 'If the catches and the prices don't improve, it won't be worthwhile anybody staying.'

'So when do you think?' Lydia asked hopefully.

'Middle to end of November,' Robbie suggested.

Sandy nodded.

'But that's weeks away!' Lydia wailed.

'I can't see that there's anything else to do,' Robbie said. 'Unless Mum could send you your fare?'

Lydia shook her head. 'She gave me all she had. And anyway, I wouldn't like to ask her for more.'

'We're happy for you to stay,' Janet reassured her.

'There's a bed here, and food, and work,' Chrissie said.

'But I've got work back in Wick,' Lydia said sadly. 'Or I used to. I don't think they'll keep it open for me till the end of November though.'

A knock at the door interrupted them and Janet went out to see who it was. There was a murmur of voices, then she came back with Frank Everett. Lydia found she could not look at him, the memory of his embrace and the feelings it had aroused in her sending sudden colour into her cheeks. But when he turned away to take off his heavy raincoat, she glanced his way. How smart he looked in neatly pressed flannels, a tweed jacket, and his clerical collar. And how she longed to feel those warm arms round her again. She stamped on the thought and looked away, afraid that her face would give her away.

Frank removed his hat and greeted the company.

'I was passing, so I thought I'd just look in and see how you were doing,' he said, but his eyes were on Lydia. She determinedly avoided his gaze, hoping he would not notice the hot stain in her cheeks.

'That's very nice of you,' Janet said. 'Would you like a cup of tea?' and while she left to put the kettle on again, Chrissie began the introductions.

'This is Janet's man, Sandy. Sandy Foubister. He's from Orkney. This is the Reverend Mr Everett...'

'Frank,' he demurred with a warm smile.

'He and Jock Troup led me to the Lord,' Chrissie announced proudly.

'And how are you doing, Chrissie?' Frank asked her.

He was rewarded by a beaming smile.

'Fine. Just fine. Robbie and I are going to be married when we get back to Wick. Robbie is Lyddie's brother.'

Frank looked across at Lydia again and nodded politely but there was that warmth in his eyes. She knew she was blushing again but could not seem to stop it. It was most annoying. She could have no interest in the man, she told herself fiercely. She would be going home soon.

And she was sure he had no interest in her. He was merely being polite, she scolded herself. That's what ministers did.

But what if he had come to see her? What if he was interested in her? She glanced his way again. He seemed a very nice man. She felt a sigh rise within her. He was someone she would like to get to know better. But it couldn't be.

'Congratulations,' Frank was saying, offering his hand to Robbie. But Robbie seemed not to hear.

'Robbie!' Chrissie nudged him.

Robbie took the outstretched hand with an apologetic grin, but he was clearly puzzling over something, his mind elsewhere. Then his eyes lit with recognition.

'Padre,' he said, shaking the outstretched hand.

Frank looked at him more closely.

'That was a while ago,' he said, acknowledging the wartime military usage. 'Have we met before?' he asked. 'Mr...?' he prompted.

'Ross, Sergeant Robbie Ross,' Chrissie put in with pride.

'Sergeant Ross.' Frank looked full square at Robbie, considering. But Robbie had withdrawn his hand.

'No,' he said bluntly. 'I made a mistake. We've never met before the kirk the other night. You just reminded me of... someone.'

Frank looked at him thoughtfully, then nodded, eyes fixed on Robbie.

'I must have been mistaken too,' he said slowly.

'That's right,' Robbie told him. 'Well, you've probably got plenty to do...'

Lydia's head came up at Robbie's rudeness and she stared at him in surprise. What on earth was the matter with him? Just because Frank Everett had reminded him of someone in the war was no cause for deliberate bad manners. Lydia saw that Frank was looking at Robbie with what she decided was a kind of pity, then he said, 'Yes, you're right. I should go.'

He turned to her and this time, his smile was just for her. 'I'll maybe see you at the church again?'

Lydia, taking pity on the poor man, began to say, 'Yes, maybe,' but Robbie cut across her. 'I don't think so.'

Frank looked sharply at him for a moment but Robbie turned his back on him. Frank reached for his hat and coat.

'I'll be going then. Goodbye, ladies,' he said, nodding to Lydia and Chrissie, then politely to Sandy and Robbie and left the room.

In the lobby outside, Lydia could hear Janet protesting that he was going without his cup of tea. Frank's voice politely making excuses came back clearly, then they heard the sound of the door opening and closing.

Lydia turned on Robbie.

'What was all that about?' she demanded. 'What has the poor man ever done to you?'

'Nothing,' Robbie stated truculently. 'And he can keep his eyes off you too!'

'Don't be so silly,' Lydia protested. 'He was just being polite. And in any case, I'm a grown woman, a widow, and what I do is my business! But if it stops you worrying let me tell you that I have absolutely no interest in the man...'

The lie came surprisingly easily, though Lydia felt her cheeks flame as she said it and her traitorous memory presented her with the picture of being held so tenderly in Frank Everett's arms.

'He does in you though,' Chrissie put in cheekily. 'Anybody can see that!'

'Well, it had better stop right there!' Robbie stormed.

'Nothing has started so there's nothing to stop!' Lydia reacted angrily. Why did Frank Everett have to visit while Robbie was here, she railed silently. Why did he have to spoil...? And at the word, she caught herself. What had she been about to say?

Gingerly, she forced herself to look at it honestly. 'Spoil the lovely feelings he had awakened in her.' That was what she was thinking. Robbie was right. It had to stop, right there. She could not afford to even think about him.

'So you can just stop being so daft about it,' she finished.

'Daft about what?' Janet asked as she returned with the refilled teapot.

'Nothing,' Lydia said wearily.

Slamming the lid shut on Pandora's box was hard work but it had to be done. She could not, dared not get involved with another man. Men, she thought with a sigh. They were nothing but trouble. First her father and Robbie fell out, resulting in her being down here in

145

Yarmouth in the first place – and maybe losing her job. Then Frank Everett with his warm eyes and gentle embrace that had started the slow thaw in her heart. And now Robbie reacting in this strange way to a man he claimed never to have met before.

She glanced quickly at her brother and saw that he was chewing his lip, the way he always did when he was worried, and he seemed far away in his thoughts. There was more to this than met the eye.

The cheerful tea party struggled on with Janet and Sandy and Chrissie trying to pull Robbie out of his megrim. Finally, he stood up and stared out of the window.

'The weather's not so bad now,' he declared. 'You game for a wander?' he asked Chrissie.

She joined him by the window and gave him an encouraging squeeze.

'Yes,' she said. 'I'll go and get my coat and hat.'

Robbie turned back to Lydia. 'We'll go to see Granny Nichols tomorrow. Can you be ready by 10 o'clock?'

Clever Robbie, Lydia thought. It would stop her getting to church and seeing Frank Everett again. The sudden feeling of loss told her that maybe that was no bad thing.

She nodded acquiescence and Robbie turned back to the window and his thoughts.

CHAPTER 20

He had been discharged part-recovered from a gas attack and was on his way back to his unit. He squeezed back against the wall of the farmhouse to let the detail squad and their broken gibbering prisoner push past him. Robbie realised with a pang of regret that it barely touched him any more. He had seen so many...

Then the man raised his stricken face for a moment and Robbie's heart leapt into his mouth in shock. He watched the soldiers drag his brother Alec through the front door and into a room, then turn the key in the lock.

Robbie forced his frozen limbs into motion. He caught up with the officer in charge, saluting smartly.

'What is it, Sergeant?' the officer, a man much his own age, said wearily.

'Sir,' Robbie began. 'That man...' He gestured towards the cell.

'What about him, Sergeant? I'm putting him on a charge, he'll be court-martialled...'

'Sir,' Robbie persisted. 'That's my brother.'

'I beg your pardon?' The young officer was startled.

'I just caught a glimpse of his face. I think it's my brother. Please, will you let me talk to him... just for a minute?'

The officer looked up and down the battered corridor of the farmhouse they had requisitioned as their temporary base. Apart from the two soldiers on guard duty outside the makeshift cell, there was no one else in sight.

'I can't see it will do any harm,' the officer decided. 'He refused an order but if you can talk him into going back... Well, I won't write the charge just yet.' He looked at Robbie with weary sympathy. 'That's the best I can do.'

'Thank you, sir,' Robbie said.

The officer gestured to the guards to let Robbie into the room and left them. In the dim light, Robbie could make out a huddled figure on the plank bed.

'Alec? Is it you?'

The figure moved. A head came out of the blanket, a dirty face, unshaven, hair as wild as the red-rimmed eyes. It was the face of a man suffering the torments of Hell.

'Robbie?' Alec's voice was hoarse, shaking, scarcely recognisable. 'What are you doing here? Come to gloat, have you?'

'No!' Robbie protested, taking a step forward. But Alec pushed himself shakily up on the bed.

'Stay back. I don't want you here. Go away!' His hands shook as he waved them at Robbie.

'Alec,' Robbie pleaded. 'You're not well. I need to get you out of here.'

Alec shook his head. 'No. Let them court-martial me and shoot me. I'll be happy to die. Danny's dead. There's nothing to live for now...' His voice broke.

'What about Dad?' Robbie asked quietly. 'It will hurt him more than anything else you could do.'

'Let it,' Alec said, pulling the blanket around him and huddling down, still shaking, into it. 'I don't care any more.'

Robbie pulled up a camp stool and sat down.

'Alec, you're not well,' he said. 'Please let me help.'

'You? Why? After all I've done to you!' Alec laughed bitterly.

Robbie swallowed hard.

'I know,' he said. 'It's always been you, getting me into trouble with Dad. I always knew I wasn't seasick that first voyage. It was you, wasn't it?'

'Aye, and I did it cleverly,' Alec boasted, a sardonic grin on his shadowed face. 'I was the cook so it was easy to put bad meat on your plate. And then I looked after you, my poor little brother, to save Dad the work or the worry! He thought I was wonderful.'

'But why?' Robbie asked. 'I always wondered why.'

Alec shrugged. 'There was only room for one of us to inherit the boat. Dad loved me and the boat should have been mine alone. I had to make sure you didn't have a chance.'

Robbie nodded sadly. 'Aye, and it worked. I never did have a chance with Dad.'

Alec sighed. 'And it was a total waste,' he said. 'All the times I got you the blame for things you never did. Now you'll get the boat...'

'No,' Robbie stopped him. 'No. I'll never go back on the boat, not after what he's said to me over the years. You won.'

There was a hard silence as they sat with their thoughts. Then, 'I'm sorry,' Alec said slowly. 'It was stupid. And all wrong. I can see that now. When you see the things I've seen over here, it changes you.'

Robbie nodded. He knew the things he had seen had changed him. He contrasted Alec and Danny's bravura as they marched away to war with the broken figure before him.

'So what happened?'

'To our big adventure?' Alec asked bitterly.

Robbie nodded.

'Well, it was good at first, just as we hoped. We came out to France and enjoyed ourselves in the villages with the drink and the local girls...'

'Girls!' Robbie protested. 'What about Lydia! Danny was married to Lydia! He shouldn't have been...'

'You are green, young one,' Alec taunted him. 'You know Lydia was always hanging around, his for the asking – so when we were home on leave, well, Danny was bored. The town was empty, like a ghost town, only the ancient and the very young – and Lydia. So, well, Danny was staying with us, and being Danny, he was making the most of his opportunities – but he got caught and Dad forced him to marry Lydia. It didn't mean a thing to him.'

Robbie sat in stunned silence.

'Then we came back out here. We got involved in the push to Cambrai,' Alec continued. 'It all went well at the start. We thought we were winning. But then it went wrong and the Germans rein-forced and fought back. We were trapped in Bourlon Wood... Danny was killed, right beside me.' Alec's voice cracked. 'Danny. Dead. I still can't believe it but I was there, I saw it with my own eyes! We came out here because he wanted to be a hero! And I came... I came because I always did what he wanted. Because he was... Because he was Danny.'

Alec's voice broke and he began to weep. Looking up to see Robbie waiting patiently, he pulled himself together and went on.

'They said I refused an order.' His eyes were wild and fierce. 'I tell you, I don't remember any order! I was there, with Danny as he died, and I wasn't going to let go. I don't care if I did refuse an order. Don't you see? With Danny dead, what was I doing here? I've seen enough of this war, all the killing and maiming, the mud and the gas and the rats, and I'm not going back out there! I don't care what they do to me. I won't go!'

Robbie listened in horrified silence. If Alec had refused an order and still would not return to the line, then the outcome would be as the officer had said: court-martial, a warrant for his execution signed by General Haig, and then death by firing squad at dawn.

Alec had slumped against the wall, staring blindly into space, his eyes hollowed and tormented.

'They tried to drag me away from Danny,' he said in a hoarse voice. 'They tried to make me keep going forward. I can remember fighting them off.' He gave a bitter laugh. 'Finally they pulled Danny away from me – it took a good few of them, I can tell you! Then they brought me down here.'

'I saw you,' Robbie said. 'I was outside. I followed you.'

But Alec was continuing as if he had not spoken.

'They'll have buried him there,' he said. 'Somewhere in the mud of this hell-hole. Well, they can bury me too! "In death they were not parted..." David and Jonathan they called us at home. Then let us die together and he won't be so lonely in this foreign land so far from home. I'll be there for him, always, like I should be, like I promised.'

A noise at the door startled them. The officer who had admitted Robbie entered, bringing with him a tall lean man in the uniform of a military chaplain.

'I've brought the Padre,' the officer said.

'I was passing,' the man in the padre's uniform said.

'Is there no chance? What about an appeal?' Robbie asked the officer desperately. 'He's not well... He didn't know what he was doing!'

'I'm sorry,' the officer said. 'He refused an order. You know the penalty for that. And anyway, we heard what he said... There are no soundproof walls round here!'

'Padre?' Robbie appealed to the chaplain.

'I can't change the rules, I'm sorry,' the man said. 'But maybe I can help a little, make it easier.'

'Easier!' Robbie exploded. 'How do you make being shot by your own comrades any easier?'

The man pulled up the other camp stool next to Alec's bed and sat down.

'We can talk and I can pray,' he said quietly, as he reached for his Bible.

By the time the officer came to tell Robbie his time was up and that he should go back to his unit, he had to admit that Alec was calmer and had found a strange kind of peace. He had confessed all his misdoings and asked Robbie's forgiveness as well as God's. The padre had pronounced absolution and a blessing, and Alec had straightened his shaking shoulders.

'I'll be fine now,' he said and accepted Robbie's clumsy embrace with a sweetness and humility that brought tears to Robbie's eyes. The padre had clasped his hand and said, 'I'll try to come back.'

'Thank you, padre.'

They both knew a padre was detailed to sit with a condemned man the night before his execution.

As the padre left the makeshift cell with Robbie, they heard the dull rattle of a fusillade of shots outside. And as they ducked out of the door of the farmhouse and into the yard outside to go their separate ways, they heard the whistle of a shell as it approached. They dived for cover behind an old farm wagon. Then they heard the dull thump as the shell exploded behind them.

Robbie turned, horror in his eyes.

'Alec!'

He rushed toward the ruined farmhouse. The walls had caved in and smoke was beginning to rise from the wreckage. It was obvious from the devastation that no-one inside the building could have survived, but he started tearing with desperate hands at the debris nearest to where Alec's cell had been.

The padre joined him and in silence they cleared the rubble till they found Alec's body.

Robbie dropped to his knees by his brother, his head bowed as the tears flowed. The padre put a hand on his shoulder.

'It's maybe for the best,' he said gently.

Robbie looked up wildly.

'How can you say that?' he demanded angrily. 'He's dead!'

'There will be no court-martial now,' the padre said. 'No firing squad. No record of a charge, even. The officer didn't have time...'

And Robbie realised that was true. The shame had been removed. His mother and father would never need to know what might have been. And for their sake, he would guard Alec's secret with his life.

CHAPTER 21

The broadly beaming, sprightly old lady who came to the door and flung her arms round Lydia could not have been more different from Granny Leslie if she had been trying. Dressed in bright colours with a cheerful floral apron around her ample middle, she was like a little robin with beady eyes that twinkled with delight as she welcomed them.

'Oh Robbie!' she cried as she ushered them into her little house. 'This is a lovely surprise!'

Robbie grinned and brought the girls forward.

'Granny, this is my sister Lydia,' he began.

'Lydia!' she exclaimed. 'My very own granddaughter! Can it really be? Now then, let me look at you!' She drew Lydia into the house.

In the tiny sitting-room, crammed with furniture, antimacassars on the chair backs, knick-knacks and big leathery leaved plants on every available surface, the boldly patterned walls crowded with pictures, it was a true Victorian room. But there was room for Granny Nichols to set Lydia in front of her. She put her head on one side and looked closely at her.

'Oh yes!' she declared. 'You look like your granny.'

Lydia looked at her pint-sized, amply built grandmother with disbelief.

'No, no, my dear,' Granny Nichols laughed. 'Your other granny. Mary-Anne. When she was young, she was just like you – a very pretty girl, tall and slender, and that lovely soft hair, the same as yours. It surprised everybody when Murdo Ross chose me. Ah well.' She sighed softly at her memories, then her bright beady eyes spotted Chrissie.

'And who's this?' she smiled on her.

'This is Chrissie.' Robbie brought her forward proudly. 'We're to be wed when we go home.'

Granny Nichols' sharp eyes sized Chrissie up. 'Is that so? And when's the bairn due?' she asked bluntly but not unkindly.

Robbie and Chrissie looked at one another in embarrassment.

'Now, now, my dears,' Granny Nichols said cheerfully. 'You're not the first. It was falling pregnant with Robbie's Dad that was the reason I got Murdo and Mary-Anne didn't! Though it took them all a few months to work it out!'

With a loud chuckle, she turned and left the room, calling behind her, 'Sit yourselves down! Make yourselves at home! I'll make some tea for us all.'

'Well!' Chrissie and Lydia echoed together, and then burst out laughing.

Granny Nichols returned in a short while with a laden tea tray. Robbie jumped up to help her carry it to the table in the window where she presided over the tea things. When everyone had a cup of tea and something to eat, she said, 'It's lovely to meet you at last, Lydia. Now who's going to tell Granny what's going on? What are you all doing here?' Her bright eyes twinkled shrewdly.

The three younger folk shuffled like schoolchildren caught out but first Lydia, then Robbie, with interruptions from Chrissie, told the tale of their adventures in Yarmouth. Granny Nichols exclaimed and laughed and clapped her hands with delight as the story unfolded.

'Well, I never!' she said. 'Isn't that a thing? Well, I'm glad it's worked out so well. The good Lord works in mysterious ways His wonders to perform. And we've got some real wonders here!'

Robbie laughed and Chrissie beamed.

'Not so sure, missy?' Granny Nichols said to Lydia who was sitting quietly, her face shadowed.

'Well...' Lydia began, wondering how to disentangle all that had happened to her in the past days. She had to admit that the sudden appearance of Frank Everett in her life – and that sweet embrace – had to be classed as a wonder. But the rest? Surely it was her own fault she had lost her bag and been reduced to working at the gutting with Janet and Chrissie, maybe at the cost of her teaching position back home?

Granny Nichols topped up their teacups and passed round the plate of food again, then she sat herself down and fixed Lydia with a sharp gaze.

'Don't you be ashamed of working at the gutting – even if it does spoil your pretty hands,' she began firmly.

'I'm not!' Lydia protested, but Granny Nichols carried on as if she had not heard her.

'If it was good enough for Mary-Anne Reid, it's good enough for her granddaughter...'

At Lydia's surprised reaction, she held up her hand for silence. 'Yes, I know you're a trained teacher. I've managed to keep myself in touch with what's been going on with you and your lives.

157

Lydia, my dear, you'll go back to your nice job, so this is not forever...'

'No, that's not what I was thinking about,' Lydia spluttered and tried to gather her thoughts. She started again. 'You said Mary-Anne Reid? My other granny went to the gutting? I never knew. She was always so... so down on the fisher lassies, I never guessed she'd ever been one. She never let on.'

Robbie nodded his head in agreement.

'Ah well,' Granny Nichols said. 'If she hasn't told you the story maybe it's time I did.' She settled herself comfortably. 'You see, we both went to the gutting. And that's how we both met Murdo Ross. He was Mary-Anne's boyfriend first, but that summer she was needed at home. And that's when he and I got friendly.'

Her eyes twinkled and Chrissie giggled.

'Aye, just so.' Granny Nichols smiled. 'So when I found myself in the same condition as you' – she pointed a gnarled scarred finger at Chrissie's stomach – 'Murdo did the decent thing by me. He was a good man. Though I doubt Mary-Anne thought that when she found out.'

Robbie and Lydia stared at her. They had never heard this story before. They knew only of their other granny's hatred of the fisher lassies and of their father. Suddenly now it all made sense. Granny Nichols had stolen Mary-Anne's sweetheart – and the fruit of that union had been David Ross. No wonder Mary-Anne had disapproved of her daughter marrying him.

'That's right,' Granny Nichols cackled as she saw understanding dawn on Lydia and Robbie's faces. 'And she's never forgiven me to this day. It's just a pity though that she's had such a down on David. She made things very difficult for him and your mother.'

'But Dad...' Lydia began. 'I can understand about Granny Leslie now, but... I'm sorry, I don't know how to put this... As far as I know,

Dad doesn't visit you when he comes to Yarmouth, and you don't write? There seems to have been a falling-out...'

Granny Nichols shook her head.

'No, no, my dear. There never was any falling-out.'

Seeing Lydia's puzzled expression, she went on, 'Let me explain. When Murdo was lost at sea, I was left with the three bairns. David was two, Ina was nearly one and a half, and Lena was only a few months old. My mother helped me as much as she could but I had to go to the gutting to make some money for our keep. It was all I knew to do. So I came down here and that's where I met Tommy Nichols. He was another fisherman. When we married, he was happy to take the girls but by then David was five, going on six and had started school. He was settled where he was at home with his granny and I wasn't sure about foisting another man's son on my new husband. I always planned to bring him south but by then I had another family.' She paused thoughtfully, then she brightened and smiled at them. 'I have another son and a daughter, but only a handful of grand-children so you two make a nice addition!'

Chrissie put in, 'Lyddie's got a son so you've got a great-grandson too!'

'That's true,' Granny Nichols said with a delighted smile.

'He's called Ewen,' Lydia said. 'He's five now. His father was killed in the War,' she added briefly.

'Oh my dear, I am sorry,' Granny Nichols said. 'That was terrible.'

But Lydia shook away the sympathy.

'I'm fine. We're doing fine just as we are,' she said stoutly, though her treacherous heart reminded her of the long lonely days and nights that awaited her back home in Wick, and the gentleness of a man she had only just met.

She looked away quickly so Granny Nichol's perceptive eyes could not see her thoughts.

CHAPTER 22

Herring Fishing: Failure at Yarmouth

There has been little improvement in the closing days of October. Some Scottish boats have left, finding it impossible to cover their expenses, and more are likely to follow shortly.

John O'Groat Journal, Friday 4 November 1921

Jean laid the newspaper down and drank her tea. She did not want Davey to have a bad season at the Yarmouth fishing but she wanted him home as soon as could be. She felt like a young bride, she so longed to see him and hear from his own lips what had happened to him. She wanted to see for herself, to hear for herself...

But along with the longing and the excitement was a kind of apprehension. How would it have changed him?

She knew there was no going back in life. You could not turn the clock back. He was no longer the young carefree lad she had fallen in love with. In the years since they married, he had seen much of the world, known great sorrow and loss. And though they had maintained the outward appearance of a marriage, their relationship had withered into chilly formality by the unspoken anger and bitterness between them.

But she had never stopped loving him – although she had maybe given up all hope of him ever returning that love. When he had turned his back on Robbie, she had been cut to the quick. It was as if he had said she had let him down, by not giving him another Alec. After that he had seemed to shift all his love and attention on to Alec who revelled in it, played up to it. Jean stopped herself. That was unkind. Unfair. Though at the time it had rankled when David poured everything into Alec.

When news came of Alec's death in the war at Bourlon Wood, it seemed to cut him down like a great tree in a forest. Felled. That was when he had taken to the drink. And he had seemed to drift further away from her.

But then Lydia had given birth to Ewen and somehow this child seemed able to reach him. Ewen with his bright cheerfulness and his enthusiasm for anything to do with boats and fishing. Like Robbie had been at that age. A pang struck her. She only hoped Ewen would not be seasick on his first trip out!

'Oh please, God!' she prayed earnestly. 'Don't let Ewen inherit the seasickness.'

She wondered should she maybe prevent them finding out? Put a stop to the plans for Ewen to go out in the boat when his grandpa came home? They would both hate her for it. But maybe it would be for the best?

A knock at the door. Hastily Jean set her cup down in its saucer, rose and patted her hair into tidiness before going to the door. She bent and picked up the letters on the mat then opened the door.

'Mother. Won't you come in?' Jean said politely. As always, Mary-Anne Leslie was pushing her way into the hallway. Jean smiled, her politeness her only defence.

'You look terrible,' her mother declared.

Jean snatched a look at herself in the mirror on the wall. She did not think she looked any different from usual.

'Thank you,' she said drily. 'Let me take your coat. Would you like a cup of tea?'

Coming back with the tray, she found her mother poring over the newspaper.

'Another bad season,' Mary-Anne declared in triumphant tones. 'He'll be coming back with his tail between his legs.'

Jean handed her mother her tea.

'I don't think so,' she said mildly.

Her mother looked up with surprise. She pointed to the newspaper article. 'But it says here...'

'But that's not everything,' Jean told her. 'Money and success aren't what really matter in life. And in any case, it's not all the news. David and Robbie will be coming back from Yarmouth with something better than money can buy.'

'What on earth are you talking about?' Mary-Anne demanded, setting the newspaper aside.

'David and Robbie both came to the Lord in Yarmouth, and they are reconciled to Him and to each other. And,' Jean ploughed on determinedly in the face of her mother's silence, 'that means more to me than big catches and monetary success.' She sat back and waited.

Lips pursed, her mother ground out, 'Well, if you want to believe that nonsense...' She lifted her tea cup to her lips and took a long draught of it.

'I do,' Jean replied simply. 'And it's not nonsense.'

'Well, we shall see what wool he's trying to pull over your eyes this time,' Mary-Anne snapped and finished her tea.

After she had gone, Jean cleared away the tea things, then came back to the front room. Her eye caught the letters she had brought in and set on the sideboard while her mother visited. The handwriting on the envelopes told her one was from Lydia and one from Robbie.

She sighed with pleasure. Their letters would surely make up for her mother's acerbic comments! She took them back through to the warm kitchen and settled herself in the battered armchair by the range for a comfortable read.

'*Dear Mum,*' Lydia's letter began,

'*I'm afraid I won't be home for a wee while yet. I'm sorry but the day I arrived my bag was stolen, with my ticket and the money you gave me in it.*'

Jean sat up straight. It was – how long? – four weeks since Lydia had arrived in Yarmouth. What had she been doing since then? Where had she been staying? Where had she got the money for her board and lodgings from?

Hastily, she scanned the letter:

'*I made some friends on the train down to Yarmouth and they have helped me. Robbie's letter will explain everything. Anyway, I've got clean respectable digs and honest work but I need to stay till the other girls come home. I'm not sure when – maybe another week or two. I'll write to the Education Board again and make my apologies. I don't know that they'll keep my job for me. We must hope!*'

And pray, Jean thought.

Lydia's letter did not say much more, and ended with love to her and to Ewen. Jean turned eagerly to Robbie's letter.

'*Dear Ma,*

I've got some great news for you. You'll know that Dad and I both came to the Lord and I'm back on the boat with him and we're getting on just fine. You needn't have worried about me. When Dad threw me off the boat, I went to Granny Nichols in Lowestoft. Then a man went sick on Cousin George's trawler so there was work for me there. The good Lord has been looking after me all the time.

Anyway, the big news is that I'm getting married. You'll love her – she's a Wick girl, Chrissie Anderson. We'll get the banns read before Christmas and be married as soon as we can. She's been a good friend to Lydia, looking after her and letting her share her digs. They're doing fine and we'll all be home when the fishing ends – which is likely to be quite soon. It's been a poor season.

With love from your affectionate son,
Robbie'

Jean set the letters aside. There was a lot to take in. Robbie getting married? It seemed a bit sudden. She wondered if maybe there was a reason for the hurry. The usual reason, she smiled wryly. And who was this girl? Who were her people? But if she had been looking after Lydia, that said a lot for her.

Lydia had reassured her that the digs were clean and respectable. Well, she would not be able to afford the hotel that had been booked for her if she had had her money stolen. But work? What work could she get?

And then the penny dropped. Chrissie was the key. Because what was Chrissie doing in Yarmouth, and how would Robbie know her? She had to be one of the Wick fisher lassies down in Yarmouth to work at the herring gutting. Surely Lydia was not working with the fisher lassies at the gutting? She was not sure her daughter had ever laid hands on a fish that had not already been cleaned and cooked for her in her life!

Jean began to laugh softly. Lydia had assured her that she had made friends and Robbie had assured her that Lydia was doing fine. He had also told her the good Lord had been looking after him. She had to trust that He was looking after Lydia too.

This had turned out to be much more of an adventure than she would ever have guessed, but she was sure it would not do Lydia any harm. '*All things work together for good to them that love God*' from

Romans chapter 8 ran through Jean's mind. She loved God and once, Lydia had too. The war and Danny's death had seemed to change all that. But one thing was certain sure: the Lord loved Lydia and Jean had entrusted her to His care, so everything would work out for good.

Though losing her job at the school could be a problem for her.

Jean stood up. Perhaps she should put on her best coat and hat and maybe pay the Board offices a visit, see what she could do?

CHAPTER 23

Lydia gingerly peeled the cloth strips off her fingers. The salt sores and cuts were red but clean.

'They look worse than they are,' Janet reassured her. 'They're healing fine.'

'They'll scar, though, won't they?' Lydia asked, thinking she would certainly have something to show for her adventure in Yarmouth. 'Like yours.' She pointed to Janet's scarred fingers.

'They're honourable scars,' Janet told her gently. 'Better to have hands that have done honest work than soft idle hands.'

They shared the kettle of hot water, glad of the warmth in the steamy scullery. The day had been cold and wet, with flurries of snow as they worked through the long hours to get the catch gutted and packed in brine. Even Lydia could see that the herring were larger and of better quality than at the beginning of the season.

'Your Dad's pleased,' Chrissie told her. 'Robbie says they're getting better prices.'

'Aye, but are they getting their nets in whole?' Janet asked. 'Sandy says there's a lot of damage and that's costly. His skipper is saying it's not worth staying.'

'I think Lyddie's Da wants to stay a while yet,' Chrissie said.

But Sandy's boat was one of the first to leave. The weather had taken a turn for the worse with lightning and snow added to the gales, so much so that the rough weather put a complete stop to any fishing.

There were a few tears at the parting but Janet steadfastly refused to leave her friends.

'I'll be home soon enough,' she said. 'Our young ones will visit for Christmas and we'll have a grand time. I need to earn a few more pennies so I can spoil them with presents!'

But the following week, the weather turned so stormy with lightning and more snow that the fishing and the supply of herring for gutting came to an abrupt stop, allowing Janet and Chrissie to take Lydia for a wander round the Yarmouth shops, seeing what presents they might like to buy for their families.

'I usually buy mine in Edinburgh on the way home,' Chrissie said. 'You can just get off the train, get digs in Edinburgh for a wee while and have a holiday...'

'A well-earned rest!' Janet put in. 'I used to do that when I was younger.' She smiled warmly. 'But now I like to get home.'

'The shops are lovely in Edinburgh,' Chrissie said.

'I love Princes Street,' Lydia said with a reminiscent smile. 'When I was at college in Edinburgh...' She ploughed to a stop as a man in a long overcoat stopped and raised his hat.

'Good afternoon, ladies,' Frank Everett said. 'Taking advantage of time off work?'

'We're just having a look at the shops,' Chrissie said. 'Oh look, Janet, there's that wool I wanted. If you'll excuse us...' She grabbed Janet's arm and hurried her away, leaving Lydia standing on her own.

Frank laughed. 'Not very subtle,' he said. 'But effective.'

Lydia blushed but had to laugh in agreement. Subtlety was not one of Chrissie's strengths.

'It's cold out here,' he continued. 'May I offer you a cup of tea? And I'd like to hear more about Edinburgh. I was thinking of perhaps paying a visit there myself next year.'

Smoothly, he took her arm and guided her away from the shops and towards a pleasant tearoom. Just the touch of his hand sent a tingle up Lydia's arm and she found herself unthinkingly accompanying him. It felt so natural to walk with her arm in his. She was surprised when they stopped.

'Will here do?' he asked her.

Lydia looked about her. It was a homely respectable-looking place, but not too splendid for the fisher-girl clothes she was wearing.

'Yes. Thank you,' she said, touched by his thoughtfulness.

Inside he held out a chair for her, and when the waitress came, ordered tea and, after consulting her, buttered toasted teacakes.

'Now,' he said, 'you were saying something about Edinburgh?'

'Yes,' she admitted.

'You said you were at college there?' he prompted gently.

'Yes.'

'What were you studying?'

She looked down at the table, unsure whether he would believe her. As far as he was aware, she was simply another of the Scots fisher lassies. And that was who she felt she was now. Mrs Alexander, the respected and respectable primary school teacher in her drab widow's clothes and her soft hair pulled hard back in a tight bun, seemed someone from far away in the past. And if the Education Board responded harshly to her unauthorised continued leave of absence, was someone she might never be again. It was not a happy thought.

She was grateful that the tea arrived. She poured for both of them and handed Frank his cup. Then the teacakes were brought – split, freshly toasted and generously buttered. She gave a little gasp of delighted surprise when she tasted the first mouthful. It was unexpectedly spicy – cinnamon, she thought – and not too sweet.

'You like it?' Frank asked.

'It's lovely,' Lydia assured him. 'I've never tasted them before. I suppose it must be an English thing.'

'We do have some nice food in England,' Frank teased her gently.

'Yes, I'm sure,' Lydia smiled. 'But I've never been to England before.'

'This is your first trip with the girls?' he asked.

She hesitated. To simply answer yes and let him go on thinking she was one of the Wick fisher lassies would be dishonest, and yet, if she lost her teaching position...

She saw his puzzled face and capitulated. There was something about this man that made her want to tell the truth, to be truly herself.

'It's a little complicated. Yes, it's my first trip to Yarmouth,' she confided in him. 'But I'd never met any of the girls before a few weeks ago!'

With an enormous sense of relief, Lydia explained, telling Frank the whole story – about how Robbie and her father had fallen out, her mother's idea of sending her to Yarmouth with money for his ticket home, her leave of absence from her teaching post, the stolen bag with her ticket and the money, Johann's death, and how Chrissie and Janet had come to her rescue.

'Ah, I see. Quite an adventure!' was all he said. But he smiled and drained his tea cup, holding it out to her to be refilled. 'I did my studying at the Pastor's College in London,' he told her. 'Before the war.'

'Were you in the war yourself?' Lydia asked.

'I went as a chaplain,' he said.

'You must have seen much...'

'Too much,' he said. 'And felt I could do too little. At first we were told all we could do was encourage the men, give them cigarettes... And sometimes just be there for a dying man to talk to – but that was perhaps the most worthwhile thing we did.' He seemed to be waiting for her to speak.

'My brother...' Lydia paused. Frank nodded and Lydia continued, 'My older brother and my husband were both killed in the war. At Bourlon Wood.'

At that Frank's head came up sharply and his gaze was piercing.

'Bourlon Wood? Cambrai, 1917?'

Lydia nodded.

'I was there,' he told her. His eyes narrowed, brow furrowed, clearly thinking back. 'Ross,' he said, as if to himself. 'That's right. I thought he looked familiar.' He looked up into her watching eyes. 'I knew I'd met your brother Robbie before. He was there too. That's where I met him.'

'Robbie? At Bourlon Wood?'

'Yes. I'm certain,' Frank said.

Lydia shook her head. 'No, I'm sure that can't be so. Mum and Dad were devastated by Alec's death. If Robbie had been there at the same time, he would surely have said so. There would have been something to help them, to ease their grief. Just knowing he was there when Alec was killed would have helped them.' She shook her head again, decisively. 'I'm sorry. You must be mistaken.'

Frank's gaze held compassion.

'It was a terrible time,' he said. 'We lost over 40,000 men. And the Hun lost at least as many.' He looked down at his tea cup and shook his head. 'It was the terrible waste of lives that got to me.'

Without thinking, Lydia reached out and touched his hand.

'It was,' she said. 'A terrible waste.'

Softly, his hand lifted and covered hers. He left it there for a moment, unthreatening, warm, comforting, then he eased his hand away to take up his tea cup again. Strangely Lydia felt bereft. She wanted to feel his hand on hers again. She pushed the feeling away, annoyed at her weakness. What was it about this man? He was melting her defences. Thawing her heart. It felt terrifyingly wonderful.

But he was speaking again. She forced herself to concentrate.

'You said your older brother and your husband...?'

'They joined up right at the start of the war. We weren't married then.' She blushed as she remembered the shaming circumstances. 'They came home on leave...We were only married a few days before they went back to the fighting.'

Frank nodded and Lydia continued, suddenly wanting to explain. 'Danny was my brother's best friend. I'd tagged along behind them for years. Right little nuisance I must have been! They thought the war would be a big adventure. Over by Christmas, they said.'

'That's what we all thought,' Frank murmured but his eyes were unfocused, his thoughts back in 1917, remembering a man's voice from inside a makeshift cell: 'Lydia was always hanging around, his for the asking... Danny... bored... making the most of his opportunities. It didn't mean a thing to him.' Anger flared briefly in Frank's eyes. Lydia – Lyddie. Of course. He tuned back in to what she was saying.

'But then the war went on and on and so many men were killed, and Alec and Danny among them.'

'I'm sorry,' Frank said, but Lydia had seen something new in his eyes, a sudden flare. She was uncertain what it meant but if it revealed any kind of interest in her, she knew she had to dash it, and quickly. She was not ready – she thought she probably would never be ready – for another relationship with a man, even a man as sweet and gentle as Frank Everett. Once she had thought Danny was sweet and gentle... She had to get away.

'Yes,' Lydia said briefly. 'Me too.' She rose unsteadily to her feet and held out her hand. 'Thank you for the tea. It was very kind of you. But I must go. And... I don't think we should meet again. Goodbye, Mr Everett.' She used the title carefully, deliberately, to underline the finality of her words.

Frank leapt to his feet, his eyes searching Lydia's stricken face.

'Lyddie, I'm sorry. I didn't mean to upset you. What a fool I am, bringing it all back...'

She stood ramrod straight, in her fisher-lassie clothes yet like a duchess in her dignity, her small hand outstretched, waiting. Finally Frank took it, shook it gently, then, unable to stop himself, leaned across and gently brushed her white cheek with his lips. Her hand lifted to her cheek as if in a daze, then she pivoted on her heel and was gone.

Outside she walked heedlessly through the streets, her thoughts a whirling turmoil. What did she think she was doing? Taking tea alone with a man? She was a married woman.

No. She was not.

Danny was dead. She was a widow. But that was not the point. She did not want to become involved with anyone ever again. She dared not risk a second betrayal. Yet for a moment there she had begun to relax the iron grip she kept on her heart. For a moment back there, she had enjoyed Frank Everett's company, and the touch of his hand on hers. She remembered the brief hug the night he had walked them home from church. Her hand lifted, as if by its own volition, and touched her cheek where he had kissed it so gently.

It felt so good, and safe. She was sure he was a good man. A stray memory from Bible verses learnt at Sunday School long ago came to her: an oak of righteousness. Yes, that's what Frank Everett was. For a moment her thoughts lingered on his tall lean elegant figure. Both physically and morally, she was sure he was an oak of righteousness. Yet it still would not do.

It drew a terrible aching yearning from her. Firmly she reminded herself she had Ewen to think of. And she had vowed never to remarry. To put herself again at the mercy of another man, any man, was unthinkable.

More than that, she told herself, she was no wife for Frank Everett. He was a Baptist minister. He needed a Christian wife and though maybe she had once believed in God, what she had experienced of marriage had taken her love and her faith away too. She was not the wife for him. She could not do that to him.

CHAPTER 24

'You're behaving like a silly girl!' Jean chided herself, but she could not repress her smile.

Waiting and watching for the postman had become a habit, as she found herself longing for David's letters just as she had when they were first married and he was away at sea. She laughed ruefully at herself and tried to apply her mind to her sewing. Mrs Hendry's coat needed the hem taken up and the lining neatly shortened to match. And Jean had to admit with a smile that sitting stitching in the good light from the window also gave her the best place to spot the postman coming.

As she stitched, she prayed for her husband and her children. Soon they would be home and how she longed to see them again!

At last the rattle at the door told her the post had arrived. She forced herself to set her sewing down neatly and tidy away her pins and cotton in the basket. Then she walked with scarcely suppressed haste into the hallway to pick up the letters that had arrived. Scanning them quickly, she put David's on the top and brought them all back into the kitchen where she settled herself in the chair by the range and opened it.

'My dearest Jean,

I wish you were here to share all that is happening. I have so much to tell you. Robbie and I are getting along fine. He's a good worker and the men like him. He fits in well. He's learnt new ideas on the Aberdeen trawlers and is keen on the new seine nets for herring. The other skippers don't like them but I'm beginning to see his point.

We'll likely be home early. The fishing has been so bad. We'll have the winter then to think what we do next. With a baby on the way, we'll need to be sure Robbie is able to provide for his family.'

Jean stopped reading in surprise. Then she went back and read the last sentence. 'A baby on the way'? So that was it! Robbie had not mentioned this in his letter. But he had been happy about getting married, she was sure of that. Well, David had been happy about marrying her when she had broken the news to him that she was pregnant.

'I always planned that we would marry,' he had reassured her. 'We'll just get on with it now a bit faster!'

Jean sighed. Such happy memories. Oh, maybe God had answered her prayers and the sad years were behind them? Maybe the years to come would be the best yet! That special verse from Jeremiah came back to her: 'I know the thoughts that I think toward you, saith the Lord; thoughts of peace, and not of evil, to give you an expected end.' Was that promise coming true?

She picked up David's letter again.

'You know Robbie met up with one of his Lowestoft cousins during the War? He's kept in touch with him and when we fell out, he went to them. George is working a trawler belonging to one of the fleets and was a crewman short so Robbie was useful to him. My mother gave the lad board and lodgings.'

Interesting, Jean thought. David hardly ever mentioned his mother and when he did it was with bitterness. The letter continued:

'Robbie showed me that I needed to go and see her. "Honour your mother and your father" he told me and he was right. Well, Robbie said it was time bygones was bygones, so I went. Oh my love, I wish you'd been with me to give me the courage I needed! I think it was one of the hardest things I've ever done. You know how I felt about her taking Ina and Lena to Lowestoft and leaving me behind.'

Jean swallowed hard, half sob, half chuckle, that her brave strong husband would ever admit to needing her there to strengthen him!

'The youngsters were all there and getting on like a house on fire but my mother had a welcome for me. My darling girl, I have been so stupid, my own worst enemy, with my stubbornness and my hardness of heart. And if I have hurt you with it through the years, as I surely have, I beg you to forgive me.'

Jean reached blindly for her handkerchief to mop up the tears that had begun to flow. Yes, it had hurt her to see him change into a hard, stubborn man who turned his face resolutely from his mother and, she had to admit, from her. But it seemed he had changed. Words from the Bible came to mind: 'A new heart also will I give you, and a new spirit will I put within you: and I will take away the stony heart out of your flesh, and I will give you an heart of flesh. And I will put my spirit within you, and cause you to walk in my statutes, and ye shall keep my judgments, and do them.' (Ezekiel 36:26–27) God had indeed worked wonders.

Jean dealt summarily with her tears even though they were tears of joy. She wanted to see what other news this wonderful letter contained.

'My mother would like to meet you and Ewen so we'll have to see what we can arrange.

Lydia seems to be doing fine. She's found good friends in Robbie's girl, Chrissie, and Janet Foubister, the other lass on the crew, an older sensible Christian woman from Orkney. Lydia's coming out of herself *and that white look has gone – though maybe it's being in the rain and the wind at the gutting that's doing it!*

I don't know how we'll keep it from your mother though!'

He finished the letter with endearments that were balm to her soul, but his comment about her mother saddened her. It seemed her family had found new life but her mother was still shackled to her bitterness.

CHAPTER 25

The days toward the end of the season progressed jerkily. Some days there were large catches and the girls had to work hard and late into the evening. Other days the weather was too bad for the fleet to put to sea and there was no work at all in the curing yards.

Some of the curers laid off their staff but Lydia's uncle held firm to his contracts. Other work around the yard, including cleaning offices, was found for the workers. But finally the Scottish skippers called a halt and declared it was time to give up and go home.

Chrissie came back to their lodgings after seeing Robbie on a day when the fleet was stuck in port. She stomped up the stairs and flung into the attic room, furiously banging the door. Janet, making good use of the free time to start packing her kist and instructing Lydia on how to pack Johann's, looked up from her work.

'What's the matter with you?' she asked, taking in Chrissie's high colour and angry eyes.

Chrissie threw herself on the bed.

'It's just not fair!' she exploded. 'These bosses think they can treat us any way they like!'

Janet and Lydia exchanged glances.

'I don't think my Uncle Bill's like that,' Lydia ventured.

Chrissie dismissed him with a shake of her head.

'I wasn't talking about him. It's some of the others,' she declared. 'I met up with those girls from Uist who had digs with us here last year.'

'I remember them,' Janet said. 'They were a nice bunch, and hard workers too. How are they all?'

'They got laid off a few weeks back when the fishing was so bad. The firm told them that if they didn't want to go straight home, they could try and get work some place else – and some of them did – and that the firm would still pay their fare home.' Chrissie paused and announced angrily, 'But now they won't. So the girls are all stuck in Yarmouth. They haven't enough money to get home.'

'But I had a return ticket,' Lydia protested. 'Not just one way.'

'That's what your uncle does,' Janet explained to her, 'but not all the firms do that.' She smiled. 'Another reason we prefer to work for him.' She looked across at Chrissie with an affectionate smile. 'Well, Miss Firecracker, and what are you planning to do about it?'

Chrissie tossed her head at the teasing. 'We have to do something! We can't just go off back home and leave them stranded.'

'I'm not sure we'll have enough money to help them out,' Janet said, thinking carefully about it. 'It has been a poor year. Even if we organised a whip-around of all the fisher lassies in Yarmouth, I doubt we'd get enough for all their tickets.'

'The firm should pay what they agreed,' Chrissie stated firmly. 'A contract's a contract.'

She turned to Lydia and began to explain.

'When they sign you up, they pay you your arles and that holds you. You can't change your mind and switch to another firm. Then they pay for your train ticket, and your standing wages every week.

That pays for your lodgings and food. We don't usually have much left over. The contract the Uist girls are on is that they should get their ticket money with their barrel money at the end of the season – so much per barrel divided up among the crew – but because they were laid off, they'll be getting very little.'

Lydia thought about it. 'It sounds very organised. Is that how it's always been done?'

Janet and Chrissie nodded.

'As far as I know,' Janet said.

'So it's a proper contract, sealed with this money, the arles?' Lydia queried.

'That's right,' Chrissie said. 'That's why it's so wrong...'

Lydia held up her hand to silence her.

'Wait a minute, let me think,' she said. 'If it's a legal contract, the firm can't back out of it. Of course, if there's no work for the girls, they can be laid off, but if the contract included the agreement to pay their fare back home, then the firm has to honour that.'

'And who's going to tell them?' Chrissie said with a bitter laugh. 'The girls went down to the yard to see the management and they got in the mounted police from London. The management said they were frightened there would be a riot!'

'What happened?' Lydia asked, appalled.

'The girls just laughed at them and the police went away again!'

'Oh, good for them!' Lydia exclaimed. 'Well, I think the girls should go to the police themselves! They've been cheated out of what is rightfully theirs. It's a kind of stealing.'

'That's right,' Chrissie said thoughtfully. 'Stealing off the poor fisher lassies and leaving them stranded. It's not good enough. Right, I'll pop down to their digs and see if I can jolly them up to do something about it.' She stood up, then hesitated. 'Lyddie, will you come with me? You can explain it better than me.'

Which is how Lydia found herself one morning standing in the forbidding courtroom in Yarmouth's grand Town Hall making the Uist lassies' case before the magistrates.

The decision handed down was firmly in their favour, and the Uist lassies declared Lydia the heroine of the day.

'Being a teacher comes in handy!' Chrissie said cheekily and Lydia had to agree that the magistrates had appeared as willing as her class of ten-year-olds to hear her out.

'I'd never have done it without you at my side,' she told Chrissie. 'I'd have been far too scared!'

'You, scared?' Chrissie teased her. 'Never! Anyway, I was standing between you and the door. You couldn't get away!' She linked arms with Lydia and after making their farewells, they set off back to the lodgings to report their success to Janet.

As they turned the corner towards the South Quay, Chrissie squeezed Lydia's arm.

'Look who's there!'

Lydia looked in the direction Chrissie indicated. Her heart lurched. The unmistakable tall elegant figure of Frank Everett was walking towards them. Lydia felt her cheeks flame and her breath quickened.

But then she realised he was not alone. Hanging on to his arm and laughing up at him was a woman. Older than herself. Smartly dressed in a long three-quarters length jacket and straight skirt a little below the knee, shoes with kitten heels and with her hair bobbed, she was the picture of modern fashion. A sophisticated older woman. More Frank's type than a Wick fisher lassie, Lydia thought with a sharp pang.

She watched them for a moment and, as if feeling her gaze on him, Frank looked across the street and saw her. Lydia knew her face told the story of her hurt and despair. She could feel the prison door slam shut. She would be going back to Wick soon, to her teaching job if she was lucky, and the rest of her life alone. He was free to make his life the way he wanted it, with whoever he wanted. And it looked, Lydia had to admit sadly, that he had a choice of whoever would share it.

The fragile, fleeting memory of his arms so gently around her, the sudden resurgence of hope that had flickered unexpectedly to life – it had all been a mistake. A misunderstanding of a clergyman's professional kindness to someone he had encountered in the way of his work.

Stricken, Lydia tugged Chrissie's arm.

'Let's go the other way,' she hissed and dragged Chrissie away from the street, away from Frank's eyes, away from what she had to admit to herself she had been thinking. All that she had been dreaming. All that she had been allowing herself to dream.

Mentally she shook herself. Fool! To let her emotions be awakened like this. She should have known better. The pain she had known last time should have taught her a lesson to last her a lifetime. To have allowed someone to touch her heart so that seeing him with someone else felt like betrayal was stupid beyond reason.

Determinedly she chattered brightly to Chrissie, hoping she had noticed nothing. But inside she felt the permafrost start to creep round her heart again.

CHAPTER 26

And at last it was time for the nomadic community of fishermen and shore workers to set off for home. Lydia had concentrated fiercely on her work over the past few days, saying little, her face tight and drawn. Inside she felt she was dying but still the images tortured her – the warm arms around her, the gentle kiss on her cheek, the kindly eyes, and then the memory of him with the other woman that had dowsed the little flame of newly kindled hope, replacing it with the old familiar pain of disillusion and betrayal.

Yarmouth sent its visitors away with special farewell services on the last Sunday evening in the town. Janet went to her own service in the morning, but in the evening she declared she would accompany Lydia and Chrissie to the big Methodist church in the High Street.

Lydia's murmured 'I wasn't planning on going' was met with robust protests from Chrissie and Janet who had discussed their plan and were sure that if they could only get Lydia to where Frank was, everything would be sorted out. They had watched Lydia withdraw into herself, the white stricken look once again taking up residence where more recently there had been vitality and joy.

'Robbie will be there. You'll want to see him before he goes,' Chrissie tried persuading her.

'Your Da will be there too,' Janet put in. 'It will look very odd if you're not there. What will they think?'

'Oh, all right,' Lydia said and did not see the pleased smiles exchanged by the other two. She was too busy thinking how she could avoid Frank Everett, and at the same time how much she wanted to see him – one last time. Just to sit and look at him.

She thrust the images from her. Why was it all so complicated? Yes, she had liked him. More than liked him, her uncomfortable conscience pricked her. But he was not interested in her. He was obviously involved with another woman, a woman who was much more his type. So she needed to just accept that and go home. Put it all behind her – the memory of him... And again the feeling of being in his warm arms returned and the yearning to feel that comfort again started tears in her eyes.

Oh why couldn't she just make up her mind and stick to it? But she found herself choosing to wear her own clothes for the evening, not Johann's.

By the time they had walked to church, Lydia was a bag of nerves. She was glad to see Robbie and her father were waiting at the church for them but Robbie was thunderous when he saw Lydia.

'What are you doing here?' he growled. 'I thought I told you to stay away.'

Janet tucked Lydia's arm in hers. 'Sandy's gone home so I wanted company,' she told Robbie. 'I asked your sister to come with me.' And she sailed past him, smiling cheerily at Lydia's father. 'Are you going to sit with us?'

David Ross was looking bemused by the exchange.

'Robbie can take Chrissie in,' Janet continued.

David smiled. 'That's right. It'll be nice for them.'

He escorted Janet and Lydia into the church and found a pew upstairs with just enough room left for the three of them. The place was packed. Local people and fisher folk filled the building and when the singing began, the volume threatened to raise the roof.

After a few hymns, the local minister appeared from the vestry. With him was Frank Everett. Lydia tensed and shifted sideways so she could hide behind a pillar. While the minister welcomed the congregation and announced another hymn, Frank stood to one side, scanning the gathered throng as he always seemed to do.

Lydia ducked her head, fiddling with her shoes. Janet gave her a sudden sharp nudge and Lydia's head came up sharply to see what was the matter just as Frank's eyes reached her. He smiled and she could see his shoulders relax under his smart dark jacket.

He had a very nice smile, she had to admit to herself. In fact, he was a very nice-looking man. And probably a very nice man too, she thought wistfully. But not for her. He had made his choice and she had to leave him, and all thoughts of him, behind. But it was hard. As the next hymn was announced, Lydia found she needed all her self-control to stand up, pay attention, and sing.

She was glad to sit down and gather her thoughts when the hymn ended. A few latecomers were still filtering into the church and Lydia's sharp eyes suddenly homed in on a smartly dressed woman moving towards a seat at the front of the church.

As she took her place, she beamed at Frank and received an answering warm smile. Lydia's shoulders sagged. It was the woman she had seen him with. If she were here, and publicly recognised by him, then their relationship must be on a sound footing. The last tiny shreds of fragile hope shattered, the broken pieces like sharp glass within her.

Lydia swallowed hard. Somehow she had to get through the service without disgracing herself and then go home to Wick and put it all behind her.

And so the rousing farewell service continued, with Lydia struggling to focus on it and not on the man to one side of the lectern, or the woman who appeared to be gazing at him so fondly from the front pew.

Finally the closing hymn was announced. As they sang 'God be with you till we meet again' there were tears in many eyes. Lydia knew her tears were only waiting for her to be alone before they would spill over and engulf her in the pain she felt. But as she began to sing the words, she realised that the hymn was a prayer that she wanted to pray – even now – for Frank Everett.

> *God be with you till we meet again –*
> *By His counsels guide, uphold you,*
> *With His sheep securely fold you;*
> *God be with you till we meet again.*
>
> *God be with you till we meet again –*
> *'neath His wings securely hide you,*
> *Daily manna still provide you;*
> *God be with you till we meet again.*
>
> *God be with you till we meet again –*
> *When life's perils thick confound you,*
> *Put His loving arms around you;*
> *God be with you till we meet again.*
>
> *God be with you till we meet again –*
> *Keep love's banner floating o'er you,*

Smite death's threatening wave before you;
God be with you till we meet again.

The sentiments of the hymn echoed her finest hopes for this man who had touched her heart and thawed the permafrost that she had encouraged to freeze around her. Fiercely she prayed that the permafrost would not return. Though she had to return to the cold lonely life she had made for herself in Wick, she wanted to continue being able to feel, and laugh, and love...

The word hit her hard. Love? Surely not? Surely she could not have fallen in love with Frank Everett in these short weeks? It was nothing like she had ever felt before. Not at all what she had felt for Danny. Was this, she questioned herself wonderingly, what love – grown-up love – felt like?

Eyes shining with held-back tears, Lydia sang on. Each chorus seemed to mock her. *'Till we meet again.'* She shook her head sadly. Once she left Yarmouth, she knew she would never meet Frank Everett again.

At last it was time to leave the church after the service. As Lydia, Janet and David Ross joined Robbie and Chrissie outside, David asked, 'So who was yon man in the dog collar who had his eye on our Lydia?'

'Nobody!' Lydia and Robbie echoed in unison.

'I see,' their father said, plainly unconvinced. 'You could do worse...'

'No!' Again the protest was in unison.

'Lyddie!'

Lydia turned to see Frank hurrying towards them.

'We're going,' Robbie said determinedly. 'Now!' He grabbed Lydia's arm. But Janet was holding Lydia's other arm and refused to give way as Robbie tugged at her.

'Oh stop it!' Chrissie scolded them crossly, hands on hips. 'Don't be so silly! Robbie, let her go! You too, Janet!'

'You must have nothing to do with that man,' Robbie whispered fiercely to Lydia. He dropped her arm and took Chrissie's instead. 'We're going, but you watch yourself. I know things about him. He's no good for you!' He marched Chrissie away, closely followed by his father and Janet.

'I know,' Lydia whispered softly and started slowly, unwillingly, to follow them. But Frank had caught up with her. To her surprise, he simply reached for her and drew her closely into his arms.

'I couldn't let you go,' he said softly. 'Not without saying goodbye.'

'Don't!' she said. 'Please don't!' and pulling herself out of the comfort of his embrace, she turned and ran after her family and friends.

Running heedlessly, tears pouring down her face, Lydia did not see Frank standing gazing after her with sadness in his eyes.

Nor did she see the elegant woman appear from the church on the arm of her husband.

'Frank!' the woman called.

Frank turned and slowly walked to join them.

CHAPTER 27

Robbie and David Ross walked the three girls back to their digs. Janet and Lydia went in hurriedly to get out of the cold and left Robbie and Chrissie to their goodbyes.

Up in their room, there were a few last things to tuck into the kists which would be collected by the lorry in the morning. Janet and Chrissie had arranged for Johann's kist to be returned to her parents and Lydia had packed it carefully.

'I don't think you'll be needing the oilies or that knife any more,' Janet said. 'You won't be wanting to make a career of the gutting!'

'But you've done a good job and we couldn't have managed without you.' Chrissie's voice was muffled as she helped Lydia close the lid of the kist. She straightened up and put a hand to her aching back. The increasing pregnancy was beginning to tell on her. 'Without you,' Chrissie continued, 'we'd never have been able to pay our way here. There's not a lot of money left, but at least we can pay Mrs Duff.'

'Which is more than some of the crews will,' Janet said. 'I heard some lassies were leaving a lot of debt behind.'

'It was a rotten season but at least your uncle treated us fairly,' Chrissie said.

'And you'll get home safe and sound,' Janet reminded her. With Johann's ticket to Inverness, Lydia had earned enough money to pay for her onward fare to Wick.

The girls continued to chat cheerfully, well aware of Lydia's stricken silence and white face. Now they let the silence run. Finally Lydia spoke. Her voice was thin and despairing.

'It will be good to be home again,' she said.

Chrissie and Janet exchanged glances, then bent to their packing again.

'Though I've no idea what sort of welcome there will be at the school – or whether I've still got a job.' The sigh was heartfelt. 'I need that job, to keep me and Ewen.'

'He'll be glad to see you again,' Janet said. 'He'll have missed you.'

Not as much as she was going to miss Frank Everett, Lydia thought, the pain sharp in her heart.

The kists were duly collected the next day. The train home left on Tuesday. Despite the best efforts of Chrissie and Janet, Lydia refused to budge from their lodgings. They tried all sorts of incentives including the need to buy presents for Ewen and her mother as the chief blandishment. But she sent them on their way with a little of her money, telling them to choose.

'I'm tired' was her excuse. 'And it's a long journey home tomorrow.'

At last they gave up and headed for the shops. And while they were out, Lydia sat on the bed as if frozen, the memories rolling round and round in her head, tormenting her till she wept, carefully mopping up the evidence before her friends returned.

On the journey it was Chrissie who was the more agitated. She plucked at her clothes, now visibly tightening round her tummy.

'You look fine,' Janet reassured her.

'Yes but...' Chrissie's worried eyes darted to Lydia. 'It's your mother I'm worried about,' she told her.

'Mum?' Lydia queried in surprise that anyone could be apprehensive about encountering her loving gentle mother.

'She'll be there at the station to meet you?' Chrissie queried.

'Yes, I should hope so,' Lydia replied, 'and Ewen too. Or I'll want to know about it.'

'Yes, but don't you see?' Chrissie said. 'If she's there to meet you, *I'll* be there getting off the train at the same time.'

'Well, of course,' Lydia said perplexed.

'And... Oh!' Chrissie threw up her hands in frustration at her friends' uncomprehending expressions.

Lydia and Janet exchanged glances. Janet looked pointedly at Chrissie's gently increasing waistline.

'You're worried what she'll think? And what she might say?' Janet probed.

Chrissie nodded. 'I don't want to start wrong,' she said. 'It's important. For Robbie's sake. He loves his mother. She stood up for him all the time. I want to get it right.' She looked down at her swollen body. 'But I can't.'

Lydia reached over and patted her hand.

'Don't you worry,' she told her. 'Mum will be fine. I'm sure of it.'

But Chrissie continued to look worried.

Finally Janet said, 'I don't usually preach at you but this time I think you need it. First of all, where's your faith? We need to take this to the Lord and let Him look after it. And you need to stop worrying about it.'

Surprised at Janet's robust tones, Chrissie nodded.

'Right,' Janet said and bowed her head. 'Lord, Your daughter Chrissie is worried about her reception from Lyddie's Mum. Please look after it for her and make it all work out well, in Jesus' name, Amen.'

Her head came up and she looked over challengingly at Chrissie.

'That's done. Now leave it alone. Trust. And remember who you are. You're God's daughter and you're saved. *"There is therefore now no condemnation to them which are in Christ Jesus".* She quoted the words from Romans chapter 8 verse 1. 'That's you, Chrissie, and don't you forget it. The Lord will see you through.'

Lydia envied Janet's confidence. It seemed to make a real difference to Chrissie too who sat up straighter, the colour back in her cheeks and her usual bouncy manner returning. Would their Lord see her through, Lydia wondered, if she asked? They were saved though. Their sins forgiven. Hers were not. And she could not see how hers ever could be – a woman who had as good as killed her own husband. All she could do was keep going, serving her life sentence of punishment.

When the train reached Perth and the carriages for Aberdeen were uncoupled the farewells from Janet were fond and loud and emotional. Lydia found she was weeping as she and Janet hugged.

'Oh my dear,' Janet told her, stroking her hair as if she were a child. 'I'll be praying for you. It will all work out.' She kissed Lydia's cheek, then grabbing her bag she had to run before the Aberdeen train left. Chrissie and Lydia laughed. It was so typical of Janet!

As she and Chrissie sat down and mopped their tears, ready for the next stage of their journey, Lydia discovered she was feeling genuine sorrow at parting from Janet and there were wet tears still on her face. As she sat, thinking how much she would miss Janet, someone she had only known for a few short weeks, it hit her just how much she had changed since she started on this journey.

And wonderingly, she recognised what her feelings meant. The sorrow and the tears meant that the permafrost round her heart which she had feared would return had not. Despite everything, her feelings had not shut down again. Pandora's box once opened was not going to close. And though she knew it meant she would be able to feel pain, there was a tiny thrill – because it also meant she could feel joy and delight.

And maybe love?

She slammed the lid shut on that one. There was no hope of love for her. Not now. Not ever.

CHAPTER 28

The journey north was as long and as wearisome as Lydia's initial journey down to Yarmouth. But the girl on the train going home, although she was wearing her own clothes again, was very different from the rather stand-offish, emotionally barricaded young woman who had set out from Wick – was it really only six weeks ago?

This time Lydia knew the ropes and joined in the conversations and laughter and singing with enthusiasm. There was also delight in knowing that now the other girls accepted her as one of their own – something she felt was a signal compliment and one that she treasured.

But as the long miles slowly passed by the carriage window, Lydia's thoughts returned to Frank and she probed her feelings like a tongue searching out the sore place in an aching tooth. How could she have been such a fool? How could she have been so mistaken? Surely at her age, she should have been able to tell that his interest in her was merely polite and cursory.

But her treacherous heart reminded her of how warm and tender his embrace had been. It was not the behaviour of a respectable, correct minister towards someone who was the equivalent of a parishioner! And she would have sworn he was not toying with her. Tenderness cannot be faked. Lydia knew that only too well.

But the evidence of her own eyes – seeing him with that woman not just once but twice! – *that* could not be denied. Bitterly she swallowed down the humiliation of her betrayal – all the worse that it was she herself, her own reawakening hope, her own foolish dreams, that had betrayed her.

Tears pricked behind her eyes and she closed them firmly, pretending to sleep, so the others would not see her unhappiness. But it was a tidal wave that threatened to sweep over her and drown her. She had to get home in one piece, she told herself fiercely. Home where she would be safe. Home where she could hide herself away again in the drab clothes of the ultra-respectable war widow. Where she could concentrate on bringing up her son – the only good thing that had ever come out of an encounter with a man. And on her work – if she still had a job.

She shrugged mentally. If the Education Board had not seen fit to keep her job open for her, then she would simply have to find herself another one. That brought a wry smile twitching at her lips. After a season at the gutting, any pride she might have had about stooping to a more menial job was completely gone. She would be glad to tackle any job she could get!

That cheered her. But as the train approached Wick, her stomach began to tie itself in knots. She knew she had changed, but what would her perceptive mother see? And what would she say? There was much about her adventure in Yarmouth that Lydia would be happy to share with her mother, but her foolish broken heart had to be her own secret. Until she got over it. (*If* she got over it, her treacherous heart whispered unkindly.)

So she was glad to see that it was Ewen who came racing up the station platform towards her when the train finally stopped.

'Mum!' he shouted, launching himself towards her as she and Chrissie descended from their compartment.

Lydia scooped him up in her arms. 'My, you've grown! Look at the size of you!' She turned to Chrissie. 'This is my wee boy. Ewen, say hello to your Auntie Chrissie. She and Uncle Robbie are going to be married.'

Ewen's eyes grew huge. Chrissie rewarded her with a big grin.

'Hello, Ewen,' Chrissie said. 'Nice to meet you.'

'H'lo,' Ewen mumbled before burying his head in Lydia's neck.

Lydia looked over the tumbled curls at the approaching figure of her mother and her heart missed a beat.

'Mum,' she said hesitantly but she had no need to worry. Her mother engulfed her in a warm embrace.

'Oh my darling girl, it is so good to see you, and you are looking so well!' She stepped back to inspect her. 'You've got colour in your cheeks and you look...'

'Different?' Lydia asked diffidently. 'Well, maybe I am.' She saw her mother's enquiring gaze and drew Chrissie forward.

'Mum, this is Chrissie Anderson. She's Robbie's fiancée and I don't know what I would have done without her...'

'Chrissie?' Jean interrupted her. 'Robbie wrote and told me.'

There was silence as the two women looked at each other, assessingly. For once Chrissie had no quip or sharp answer. She bit her lip, awaiting the verdict, and her hand came up instinctively to her stomach. She flushed as she saw that Jean had noticed.

'I'm very happy to meet you, Chrissie,' Jean said softly. 'Will you come round and see me once you've got settled at home? We've got a lot to talk about, with plans for the wedding and everything. And I'm looking forward to getting to know my new daughter.' She smiled.

Chrissie smiled back shyly and nodded agreement.

'Good,' Jean said. 'Now we'll need to get moving. You'll be tired after that long journey.'

Lydia set Ewen down.

'You're getting too heavy for me, young man!' she teased him, then she turned to Chrissie and gave her a warm hug. 'I told you it would be all right!' she whispered.

Then they walked, the three women and the little boy, out of the station and into the night. At the top of the Black Stairs, they parted ways – Chrissie going up into Pulteneytown to her aunt's house that had been home to her since her parents died, Jean and Lydia and Ewen going down the Black Stairs to Rose Street and their home.

The house was warm and welcoming and Lydia was glad to get out of her coat and hat and sit in her own chair by the fire. She held her hands out to the welcome blaze as her mother fussed around her. Finally with a cup of tea poured, she sat opposite Lydia, her gaze strong and loving.

'Chrissie's a really good lass,' Lydia began, hoping to deflect the conversation from herself a little longer.

'She certainly seems like a nice girl,' Jean agreed.

'And she's very capable,' Lydia said. 'She and Robbie will make a good pair. I think they'll be fine.'

'I'm glad of that,' was all her mother said. 'But now I want to hear all about what you've been doing.' Her eyes twinkled. 'And I mean all! Your letters were a wee bit skimpy on detail!'

CHAPTER 29

On the Tuesday that the girls left for Wick on the train, a veritable armada of hundreds of boats left Yarmouth, heading north through the storms and squalls. Up the east coast they steamed in convoy, sections of the fleet peeling off as they approached their home ports – Grimsby, Hull, Whitby, North Shields, Eyemouth, Musselburgh and Fisherow, then Anstruther, Whinnyfold and up to Peterhead.

There they discovered that word had spread of the wonderful spiritual revival in East Anglia. The telegraph had been busy – and the local newspapers had taken up the story. In towns where fervent prayer had gone before for the conversion of the hard godless men who had come back from the trenches of the First World War, the returning fishermen were awaited with great joy.

As the boats neared the harbour, some crews sang Gospel songs to praise God and announce the change in their lives. As the words wafted across the water, they were taken up by the crowds that lined the quayside and by the time the boats were tied up, everyone was singing. The fishermen received a welcome home like never before and amidst the embraces and welcomes, there were tears of joy and reconciliation.

At Peterhead, the remaining boats set their course northwards. Robbie and his Dad were in the section of the fleet heading up to Wick but the cooper turned evangelist Jock Troup was not on his way to Wick. He had parcelled up his coopering tools and sent them home to his mother in Wick.

'I don't think I'll be needing them again,' he declared.

Frank Everett had spent the weeks in Yarmouth attached to one of the Baptist churches there but working closely with Jock. He had been inspired by the young evangelist and they had become firm friends. Now that the season was over, he expected Jock to return to Wick and he had thought to go with him. He wanted to see Lydia again, to have a chance of persuading her that they had a future together, and thought that travelling with Jock might open doors for him. But his hopes were dashed.

'Nah,' Jock had said. 'I'm for Fraserburgh.'

'Fraserburgh?' Frank queried in surprise.

'Aye,' Jock said. 'I had a dream...'

Inspired by Jock's fervour for reaching lost souls, Frank decided to throw in his lot with Jock's team of evangelists. Fraserburgh-born Willie Bruce was glad to be going home, while Davey Cordiner was keen for the next stage of their missionary journey. But in the depths of Frank Everett's heart was hope that God would lead them, before too long, to Wick and to Lydia. But first, Fraserburgh.

So they set off by train from Yarmouth for the North. At Aberdeen they needed to change trains for Fraserburgh. They were sitting chatting in the carriage of the little local train when it stopped at a country station and two fishwives climbed tiredly in. The baskets strapped across their backs had started the day filled with fresh haddock which they had sold round the farmhouses but now were thankfully empty.

Once they had got themselves settled in their seats, the women looked around with interest at the young men.

'And where are you going?' one asked.

'We're going to Fraserburgh,' Jock replied with his customary politeness.

'Aye, and what would that be for?'

'I am going to preach the Gospel there. The Lord spoke to me in a dream,' Jock explained.

'Did He now?' the woman said. 'And what did He say?'

'I saw a man praying. He was praying for me to come to Fraserburgh and preach the Gospel there. So that's where we're going.'

'Well, well,' the woman said. 'And where are you going to stay in Fraserburgh?'

'I've no idea,' Jock replied cheerfully.

'Then you'll come and stay with me, son,' the woman said.

So, on arrival in Fraserburgh, they followed the woman to her home and were soon settled in and given a good meal.

'It's a fine night,' Jock said when he had eaten. 'I think I'll take a little walk.'

'I'll come with you,' Frank said and the pair set out for the centre of the town. When they got to the square in Broad Street, they saw that a crowd had gathered there. Jock needed neither invitation nor encouragement. He went straight to the steps of the drinking fountain and began to preach. As always, the crowd drew near and began to grow. But it was a cold night and rain began to fall.

Jock, realising that the people were getting cold and wet, asked, 'Is there anywhere available for a meeting that we can go and get out of the weather?'

'What about the Baptist Church?' came a voice from the crowd.

'Fine,' Jock replied. 'But I only arrived in Fraserburgh today. I don't know where it is!'

'Nae problem!' came the answer from the crowd. 'We'll take you there!'

And as one, the crowd turned and streamed away in the direction of the Baptist Church. Jock began to sing in his loud cheerful voice and soon the crowd had taken up the familiar hymn.

The procession, singing joyfully, spilled through the street to the front of the church. There, just as the crowd arrived, a group of men was getting ready to leave. The Pastor and the elders had been holding a specially convened meeting at which they had decided to send for Jock Troup to come and hold Gospel meetings in Fraserburgh. As directed, the Secretary had drafted the letter to Jock and had it in his pocket ready for posting.

As they stood on the steps of the church, they heard the crowd come singing up the street, and at its head Jock Troup.

Jock looked up at the group on the steps and saw to his amazement the man he had seen in his dream – the man he had seen praying for him to come to Fraserburgh. Joy and wonder filled his heart and he began praising God for leading him step by step to the right place.

Frank by his side was amazed. And as the days in Fraserburgh turned to weeks, he saw more wonders as men and women turned to the Lord and blessings flowed. Working side by side with Jock and his friends, he led many to the Lord and saw their work blessed.

But, although he found real joy and satisfaction in the work, he was aware of an achingly empty place and knew that he wanted Lydia by his side, needed her by his side. Soon, he would have to return to his church in England and settle down to the ministry he had trained for – and he wanted Lydia there, as his wife and helpmeet. If she would have him.

But there was a puzzle there. He was sure he remembered her brother Robbie from those terrible weeks at Cambrai. And he was pretty sure that Robbie remembered him. So why was he denying it? And why was Robbie so set against him seeing Lydia?

Try as he might Frank could not remember the circumstances in which he had met Robbie. That was the problem with the war. So much had happened, so much horror, so many tortured faces – memory graciously smoothed it over to take the edge off the after-effects.

But he was sure there was something. He knew he had briefly remembered something he and Robbie had both been involved in. And it was something that Robbie clearly wanted forgotten.

Frank did not want to cause any problems for Lydia with her brother but he could not let him use the past to keep Lydia away from him. He would have to try to remember – and then tread carefully. So it was with a glad heart that he heard Jock plan to return to Wick in the New Year. Meanwhile, there was plenty of work to do.

CHAPTER 30

'I'm home!'

Lydia drew off her soft cloche hat, unwrapped her warm scarf from round her neck and went to hang them up on one of the hooks in the lobby. But there was no room for her things. All the hooks were occupied with men's coats and caps and scarves. Lydia's face lit with delight.

She dropped her things on the side table and hurriedly pushed open the door to the sitting room. The welcome sight of her family reunited and sitting in cheerful harmony met her delighted eyes.

'Dad! Robbie! You're home!' Lydia cried joyfully. The boat must have arrived in Wick that afternoon after the long sea journey from Yarmouth.

The little room seemed dwarfed by the comfortable presence of the two men sitting companionably by the fire. Her mother, glowing with happiness, presided over the tea tray on the table in the window. Lydia hurried over and gave her father a hug and a kiss of welcome.

He reached for her hand and held her there for a moment, looking searchingly into her face.

'How are you doing?' he asked quietly. 'Is everything all right?'

'Mum went to the Education Board and explained everything,' Lydia told him. 'They hadn't been able to find anyone else to take my job so I've got it back. For the time being anyway.'

She did not mention the gruelling interview she had undergone before they had been willing to reinstate her, nor the probationary nature of her re-employment. Hopefully, she could regain her good reputation. Her absence without leave had damaged her with the other teachers and the Board of Education, though her adventure – and the scars on her fingers – had won her new respect from the children in her class.

She had expected to slip smoothly back into the daily routine, more appreciative than ever before of what Chrissie and Janet would no doubt consider an easy job. But it was more difficult than she had expected to settle back into Wick and her family and her work. She found she missed the easy camaraderie of the other lassies... and so much else. Maybe it would just take time, she told herself determinedly.

She swallowed hard. Time. That was something she was going to have plenty of in the long lonely years she saw yawning empty and cold ahead of her.

But her father seemed satisfied by her answer. 'That's good,' he said. 'So no ill effects from your sojourn down in Yarmouth?'

'Apart from my hands.' Lydia laughed ruefully and held them out to be examined. The salt sores and cuts were healing but the scars would be permanent.

'Evidence of honest toil,' he told her, and let her slip from his grasp to greet Robbie.

'You sit here,' Robbie told her, getting up from his chair. 'I'm off to see Chrissie.'

'Aye,' her father said approvingly. 'You make sure she's all right.'

'Give her our love,' her mother said.

As the door closed behind Robbie, Lydia saw the fond smile pass between her mother and father.

'They're just like we were,' her father said affectionately, reaching out and patting her mother's hand.

Jean blushed. Lydia stared. Her mother blushing? But before she could think about it, Ewen exploded into the room.

'Granddad!' he yelled, hurling himself at his grandfather. 'You're home!'

Laughing, David Ross managed to disentangle himself from Ewen's stranglehold and held the boy out at arm's length.

'Let's have a look at you,' he said. 'My, you've grown while we were away.'

'I have too,' Ewen said importantly. 'I'm nearly as tall as Alistair Stevens in my class and his Dad's going to take him out on his boat overnight soon, so I'll be big enough to come with you soon, Granddad, won't I?' He tugged at his grandfather's hands. 'Won't I? Say you'll take me!'

At his words anxiety flooded Jean's heart. What if Ewen was seasick and gave his grandfather a disgust of him like Robbie had? Such a huge disappointment could push David back to where he was before he went to Yarmouth. Jean shivered. She could not bear it, not now that she had fresh hope for the future, fresh hope for their marriage and their family.

She would have to put a stop to Ewen going out on the boat, but how?

'Don't pester your grandfather,' she chided Ewen with uncharacteristic sharpness. 'He's only just home.'

'He's no bother,' David assured her, surprise in his eyes at her scolding. 'Yes, Ewen, soon you'll come out on the boat wi' me. When the weather's a bit better than this.'

Jean had to be glad of the respite, but just as she promised herself it gave her time to put an immovable spoke in that wheel, Ewen spoke up again.

'Promise!' he demanded fiercely.

David Ross laughed and held up his hand. 'I promise!'

Jean sighed. Whatever she did would upset one or the other of them, but surely it was for their good? Help me, Lord Jesus, she prayed silently. You love them and I love them. Help us with this.

And just as Ewen had to be content with his grandfather's promise, though he returned to the subject several times over the coming days, Jean too had to give her anxiety to the Lord and wait on Him.

CHAPTER 31

Lydia, without the benefit of a live faith, found her wounded heart hard to bear. Her mind kept replaying each meeting with Frank Everett till her skin tingled with the memory of his touch and she ached with longing. Then the shattering memories of the 'Other Woman' as she had dubbed her flooded her mind and bitter tears threatened to overtake her.

She determined to banish the memories and the painful thoughts, but nothing she tried seemed to work. She tried scolding herself soundly. She threw herself into her work at school, into thinking up outings and joint activities with Ewen, and into helping with the wedding preparations for Chrissie and Robbie. But still her heart ached with what now felt like a slap in the face.

Humiliation took hold as she decided he had seen her as just one of the Wick fisher lassies – girls with a reputation, because of their independent and nomadic lifestyle, as more open to men's advances. And those tender memories of Frank's embraces turned to ashes. Though from time to time she found herself fanning the embers alight again and puzzling over why he had seemed attentive, even attracted to her, why he had embraced her, kissed her so tenderly if he was already involved with someone else.

He was not that kind of man, Lydia was almost sure of it. But she did not know for certain. She barely knew him. She only had her instincts, her feelings to rely on – and they were notoriously unreliable, as she told herself severely. She had not known Danny, the real Danny, and had paid a heavy price.

Misery loves miserable company so Lydia took herself off to the one person who would not offer her saccharine platitudes – her grandmother, Mary-Anne Leslie. In her hurting, humiliated frame of mind, she felt it peculiarly appropriate to be welcomed with the customary sniff of disapproval.

'And what are you doing here?'

'I'm visiting my granny,' Lydia replied with answering sharpness.

A wintry smile appeared for a moment.

'Well since you're here, you might as well come in,' Granny Leslie said ungraciously.

'Thank you,' Lydia said, feeling she had won a small victory as she followed her grandmother into the gloomy hallway and through to the chilly front parlour.

'I'll just put a light to this fire,' Granny Leslie said, bending to the task. 'I don't use this room very much nowadays. I don't get many visitors,' she added pointedly.

Not surprising, Lydia thought. Granny Leslie's welcome would drive away the more faint-hearted would-be visitor. For a moment, Lydia wondered what she would be like at Granny Leslie's age. Bitter and alone, like her, in a cold empty house?

Touching the match to the kindling set in the hearth, Granny Leslie struggled to rise.

'Here, let me help you,' Lydia said, but her grandmother brushed her away.

'I can manage,' she said with acerbic dignity and pulled herself up with evident discomfort. 'I'm fine. Just not getting any younger. Now, would you like a cup of tea?'

'Yes please,' Lydia said.

'You just sit there while I see to it. I'll be back in a moment.'

Granny Leslie took herself off to the kitchen – which was probably cosy and warm, Lydia mused, and where she had been sitting comfortably when Lydia arrived. But the kitchen was considered unsuitable for visitors. Appearances had to be maintained, even with her own granddaughter!

Lydia remained obediently in the chilly best room, remembering childhood afternoons sitting obediently still and quiet in her grandmother's house.

'Children should be seen and not heard' was the order of the day and she had been an obedient little girl. Maybe because of that or, Lydia thought, simply because she was the one girl in the family, she seemed to have won her grandmother's grudging approval – or tolerance anyway.

And when it became clear that she was doing well at school, Granny Leslie had provided the financial support so she could stay on past school-leaving age and continue her education. She had also provided a quiet room here in the big old house where she could come after school and at weekends to study. There had been little treats too, little kindnesses given almost surreptitiously as though she disapproved of her own softness towards the young girl.

It did not stop her constant criticism of Lydia's family and her father in particular, 'that man' as she called him. It seemed Granny Leslie had disapproved of David Ross from the start, but of course parental consent is not required for marriage in Scotland and as she never ceased from reminding folk, hers was never asked for. It certainly would never have been given.

It almost seemed that David Ross's success as a fisherman and his rise to being the prosperous skipper of his own boat had only added insult to her injury. She had not a good word for him. Only Lydia appeared to avoid her bitter censure.

Granny Leslie had made it possible for Lydia to pass her exams and win her place at Moray House, the teacher training college in Edinburgh. All had been well between them until Lydia's sudden announcement that she was going to marry Danny Alexander. Then the shutters slammed down and Lydia was thrust out into the cold with the rest of her family.

And when that quiet unassuming man, Grandpa Leslie died, Granny Leslie seemed to shut the door on the whole world. Even when Danny was killed, even when Ewen was born, her grandmother's heart remained closed against her.

She made it plain that in her opinion her only daughter Jean had let her down, and Jean's daughter had then done the same, so now she washed her hands of the lot of them. Except, of course, to come to visit them once a week when David Ross was at sea and give her daughter and granddaughter the benefit of her acid tongue. She made it abundantly plain that she only visited them out of duty.

'A mother's duty,' she declared.

The visit seemed to give her no pleasure and always reduced Jean to a quivering wreck beforehand and floods of tears afterwards. Lydia used to wonder why Granny Leslie persisted in the mutual torment.

She returned now carrying a large tray in a highly polished golden wood with a silver balustrade round it and curly silver handles. On the tray were her silver teapot, matching hot water jug, sugar bowl and milk jug, two fine china cups and saucers, and two delicate tea plates with tiny lace-edged napkins. She set the tray down carefully on the table and returned wordlessly to the kitchen.

When she came back, she was carrying a silver cake stand laden with scones, cake, and shortbread arrayed on lacy doileys. It was going to be a proper afternoon tea.

Memories of Lydia's childhood flooded back. You always got a good tea at Granny Leslie's. And before Lydia knew she had done it, the words had popped out.

'You always did a lovely tea, Granny Leslie.'

The white head jerked upright and two sharp black eyes bored into Lydia's face.

'What did you say, girl?' she snapped.

Lydia faltered, then remembering Janet's teasing comment that Wick girls were fierce, pulled her courage around her. After all, what had she to lose now?

'I said you always made a lovely tea, Granny. I was remembering when I was a little girl...'

'Humph,' the old lady said and went back to pouring tea, but Lydia could see she was pleased.

She accepted her filled cup with thanks.

'Well, help yourself.' Granny Leslie waved at the laden cake-stand.

Lydia smiled. 'Mmm. I'll have a scone. You used to do them for me when I came in from school.' The scone was sweet and soft and delicious. Lydia mopped the crumbs from her mouth with the lace-edged napkin. 'Just as I remembered.'

'Something else?'

'Oh yes please!' She reached for a slice of cake, set it on her plate and without thinking, licked the sweet stickiness off her fingers.

'Lydia Alexander!' her grandmother snapped. 'Have you forgotten your manners?'

Lydia looked down at her now clean fingertips, then back up to the outraged face of her grandmother. Suddenly she had a clear memory of the farlins full of shining herring waiting to be gutted, her own increasing skill with the cuttag, of hosing down the oilies in the yard after work and the smell – that herring smell that they could never get rid of. She saw the clooties tied round her fingers and remembered the pain of the brine in the cuts new every morning.

But Granny Leslie's attention had been drawn to Lydia's fingers and now her thin arthritis-gnarled hands darted out and took hold of Lydia's hands.

'What's this?' she demanded harshly, turning Lydia's hands over to display the cuts. Almost gently, she traced one of the worst scars with a finger. 'What have you been doing? Where did you get these cuts?'

'I went to Yarmouth,' Lydia began, struggling to find the words to tell her grandmother what had happened.

'You went to Yarmouth?' Granny Leslie interrupted. 'For the autumn fishing?'

Lydia nodded unhappily.

'But why would you do that? It's nothing to do with you!' Granny Leslie exclaimed. 'I thought I'd made sure you got a better chance, a good job. You were doing so well! What did you think you were doing?'

'I didn't go because I wanted to go,' Lydia protested. 'It's all a bit complicated. Look, sit down and I'll tell you everything.' She squeezed her grandmother's fingers and looked up at her with earnest appeal.

Granny Leslie dropped Lydia's hands and went back to her seat. She harrumphed and then picked up her cup of tea again.

'Well, then, you'd better tell me,' she said and took a long strengthening draught of tea.

So Lydia began, her tale interspersed by her grandmother's acerbic commentary. Robbie and David's falling-out was greeted by 'No surprise. That man.' Jean's idea of sending Lydia to Yarmouth with money to bring Robbie back drew 'No sense, that girl. Never has.' Though she then looked closely at Lydia and added, 'You're to tell me everything, mind.' And Lydia wondered what her grandmother had seen in her face.

The stolen handbag, rescue and help from Chrissie and Janet and Johann brought a grudging murmur of approval. And when Lydia found herself telling with a little pride how she had learnt to gut herring and got up to speed, her grandmother commented, 'Aye. It's a real skill. I was good and quick at it myself.' Then as if she had been caught out, she snapped, 'Get on with your story, girl. There's more, isn't there?'

Lydia ground to a halt. She had explained why she had to stay in Yarmouth till the end of the season but now she was on dangerous ground.

'There was a religious revival, wasn't there? Your mother said something, some nonsense about it,' Granny Leslie prompted her.

Lydia sighed with relief. This was much safer ground. 'Yes,' she said and told how Robbie and her father had come to the Lord and been reconciled and were back working on the boat together. She mentioned that Chrissie, Robbie's fiancée who had been so good to her, had come to the Lord too.

Granny Leslie's eyes narrowed. 'But not you?'

Lydia swallowed hard. 'No.'

'Mmm,' her grandmother murmured, her sharp black eyes scrutinising Lydia's face. Lydia took refuge in asking for another cup of tea but when it was poured, Granny Leslie sat back and announced, 'But that's not all, is it? Something else happened and you've come back different. And one thing's for sure, you're not happy.'

Lydia laughed at that, a bitter little sound. 'Does that matter? *You're* not happy.'

Her grandmother looked taken aback.

'I'm a widow. Widows aren't happy,' she riposted.

'You weren't happy before,' Lydia responded. 'I don't remember you ever being happy. You were always...' She ground to a halt, embarrassed at the word on the tip of her tongue, the word that so accurately summed up the woman before her.

'Well?' her grandmother challenged her. 'What? I was always what? Spit it out.'

Lydia swallowed hard again. Could she say it? She realised it was what she feared she would become. That was the real reason why she had come to see her grandmother – to see what her life in the future would look like, alone and bitter. The word hung in the air between them till finally Lydia said it, naming not only her grandmother but who she herself was becoming and would be in years to come.

'Bitter.'

Granny Leslie nodded but there was a kind of pride in her face, an eldritch light in her eyes.

'Aye,' she said. 'Bitter. And I've every right to feel bitter...'

Greatly daring, Lydia put in, 'Because Lizzie Nichols stole Murdo Ross from you.'

Granny Leslie's head came up sharply and her eyes stabbed Lydia like the cuttag slicing into a herring.

'And what do you know about that, missy?'

Lydia hesitated only a moment before she told the simple truth. 'We went to visit her and she told us the whole story.'

'Did she now?' Granny Leslie sat back in her chair, her lips pursed in disapproval. She steepled her fingers as she considered Lydia's words. 'That must have been interesting, her side of it,' she said finally, her voice dry and sardonic.

'Well, maybe it's time you told your side of it,' Lydia said.

The wrinkled eyelids flicked up and the sharp black eyes glared at Lydia.

'Do you?' It was a bitter question. 'Do you indeed?'

And Lydia suddenly found herself smiling, her pain and humiliation and bitterness flowing freely through her in a welcome echo of her grandmother's, as she challenged, 'You tell me your story and I'll tell you mine.'

Granny Leslie considered Lydia for a moment, a grudging respect softening her face, and then an unaccustomed and still-bitter smile on her lips as she said, 'All right. I'll make us another pot of tea and then we'll tell each other our stories.'

CHAPTER 32

'In those days a lot of us went to the gutting,' Granny Leslie began. 'It was the heyday of the herring fishing and all hands were needed to get the fish prepared and into the brine so none went to waste.' She sipped her tea and her eyes took on a distance as she looked back. 'Off we'd go, our kists packed and sent on ahead, first to Shetland in May, then back to Wick in August, and then off to Yarmouth for the autumn. We thought it was a grand adventure.'

'I was only 17 that summer in Shetland. We were young and wild and free and when the work was finished on a Saturday, we dressed up and went dancing. And that's where I met Murdo Ross. Oh, I knew him from home but we'd never met properly.' She paused, pondering. 'Maybe I never knew him properly.' She gave a bitter laugh. 'Anyway, I thought myself in love! And more than that, I thought he was in love with me. Oh, he had fine words for a fisherman and sweet ways with him! By the time we'd been to Yarmouth in the autumn for the fishing there, I was as sure we'd marry as if I had the ring on my finger!' She laughed again, full of bitterness.

Lydia waited, almost holding her breath for fear her grandmother would stop.

'But then my mother took ill and I had to stay at home and help nurse her,' she continued. 'All the other girls went off to Shetland as usual. Murdo Ross kissed me goodbye and swore we'd be married when he returned. So I stayed and did my duty.'

She took another sip of her tea, looking over the rim of the cup back sixty years.

'And while I stayed at home and did my duty, Lizzie Nichols set her cap at the lad that was promised to me.' Granny Leslie darted a swift glance at Lydia. 'And more than that. By the autumn fishing in Yarmouth, she knew she was pregnant and he was trapped into marrying her.'

Silence fell as the two women sat and considered her words. Then Granny Leslie picked up the story again.

'The first I knew about it I was sitting in church the first Sunday after they all got home, the shore crews and the Wick boats with all the fishermen. I was wondering why he had not yet come to call.' She gave that bitter little laugh again. 'So there I was in our church in my best hat and coat, all prettied up to meet with him afterwards on a fine December day, and I heard the banns read. Heard that Murdo Ross would be marrying Lizzie Nichols and not me.' She looked across at Lydia then, the outrage as hot and fresh in her eyes as it must have been on that long-ago Sunday morning. 'And I have never stepped foot in a church since that day, and I never will. The only way they'll get me there is in a box for my funeral!'

Lydia marvelled at her grandmother's ramrod-straight posture, head held high in defiant pride.

'And then?' she whispered.

'Then?' Granny Leslie spat the question at her. 'My life was ruined! Finished! All because of that woman.'

'But you married Grandpa Leslie?' Lydia probed.

Granny Leslie tossed her head. 'Yes, and a much better catch than a no-good fisherman!'

Lydia waited and finally Granny Leslie told the rest of the story. She began slowly.

'William Leslie had been after me for years. He was a friend of my father's. My parents liked him but I thought he was too old for me. I preferred Murdo Ross. But when I knew Lizzie Nichols would be marrying him, that I had no chance, I got to thinking. William Leslie owned one of the biggest curing yards in Wick and it was a prosperous business. I knew he'd have me, so I thought...' And here her words speeded up as the long-pent emotion spilled out in searing truth. 'I thought if Lizzie Nichols can take my man, then why shouldn't I get myself a ring on my finger too, and a fine big house, and a man to spend his money on me, and show her that I'm as good as she is at getting myself a man. And I did it!' Triumph gleamed in the old eyes. 'I married one of the richest men in town and we had a grand wedding and came to live in this fine big house. I did much better for myself than she did. I showed them!'

Lydia stared at her grandmother. 'But did you not... care for him?' she asked carefully.

Granny Leslie took a final sip of her tea, then placed the cup and saucer neatly back on the tray. She fixed her eyes on her granddaughter.

'I let myself *care*, as you put it, *once* – and that was enough for me,' she said harshly. 'Marriage is a contract. I fulfilled my side of it and he fulfilled his. He got what he wanted, and I got what I wanted.'

Lydia thought back to her memories of gentle, loving Grandpa Leslie. She was sure he had loved Granny Leslie but yes, she could now recognise the sadness in the man – the sadness of a love that was not, could never be returned. Because Granny Leslie had turned her back on love. Shut it off like a tap. A decision she had kept for the rest of her life.

Granny Leslie interrupted Lydia's thoughts, pursing her lips disapprovingly as she announced, 'Emotion is a waste of time. You have to be sensible in this life.' She glared at Lydia. 'And that's where you young girls go wrong! Look at your mother, getting involved with another one of the Ross clan! He turned her head with his sweet words and charming ways – just like his father – and as no-good! And what about you! Getting married to that Danny Alexander just because he was going back so bravely to the war! All very romantic!'

The bitter sneer stung Lydia but it was the truth of her grandmother's words that really hurt. She knew now that she had been led by innocent romantic dreams and childish hero-worship that had had no foundation. Her marriage had been a terrible mistake.

'Emotion,' Granny Leslie continued. 'That's all it is. Emotion is like the sea. The tide comes in and the tide goes out again. If you've any sense, you'll wait it out and let the tide go out again without getting yourself in too deep and getting hurt.'

The sharp black eyes examined Lydia's face. 'But you've done it again, haven't you? You've let your emotions take over and now you're hurting.'

Lydia felt the blood race into her face. She looked up to find her grandmother nodding.

'Yes. I knew I was right,' she said. 'Well, I think it's time you told your story.'

CHAPTER 33

It was hard to know where to begin. With Danny? Or that hug out of the blue in Yarmouth?

'Well?' Granny Leslie prompted.

'Well,' Lydia sighed in resignation and began her story. 'You're right about Danny. It was a big mistake. I was a silly child...'

Her grandmother laughed briefly.

'Yes, I know. Compared to you, I'm still a child,' Lydia agreed. 'But I was even younger and even more ignorant.' She took a deep breath. 'Yes, I thought it all very romantic, marrying my childhood sweetheart before he went back to the war. The only problem was that he wasn't my childhood sweetheart – just a friend of my big brother's. I'd tagged along after them for years. I adored Alec and I suppose some of that spread over to Danny. But I didn't know Danny really. We never spent any time together – just the two of us – for me to have a chance of getting to know him. And he only married me because my father caught him in my room...'

She paused, gathering her thoughts and her courage. Finally she looked up, straight into her grandmother's eyes.

'He was a brute. I was glad that he didn't come back.'

There. It was said. Out in the open at last. Lydia waited but her grandmother made no comment. She simply reached out and patted Lydia's hand.

'I love Ewen,' Lydia continued determinedly. 'He's the only good thing that came of that marriage, so I can't regret it entirely. But I decided then that I would not ever get involved again with a man. I wouldn't risk being treated like that again.'

Granny Leslie nodded her understanding.

'So I was doing fine, with my job, and staying at Mum's, and bringing up Ewen on my own.' She looked up with a kind of defiance in her eyes. 'I didn't need anyone. I was doing fine,' she repeated.

'That's my girl,' Granny Leslie said approvingly, but Lydia was remembering the train journey where she had needed help from the more experienced fisher lassies. Her innocent blunder that had led to the theft of her bag – and how she had needed Chrissie and Janet to come to her rescue and get her suitcase back. Without them she would not have had a bed for the night. And later how they had enabled her to find honest work that paid for her keep and finally for her return ticket home.

Lydia looked down at her hands, seeing the scars from the cuttag and the brine on her fingers, and she knew what she had said was a lie. She had not been doing fine. She had locked herself away out of fear of being hurt again, and she had hurt herself even more in the process.

In Wick, she had needed her mother's care and love. In Yarmouth she had needed Chrissie and Janet. And for the first time in her life, Lydia realised that needing other people was not weakness, not a bad thing to be ashamed of, but something to be glad of. And suddenly, strangely, she was glad.

But first she had to explain how she had changed so that she would even think that. She continued.

'I set off for Yarmouth thinking I was doing fine and could manage my own life. That I'd get down there, find Robbie and be back home to my comfortable life – just the way I wanted it – in no time at all. But I was wrong.' Lydia leaned forward. Earnestly she said, 'I soon realised I was a babe in arms compared with those fisher lassies – lassies I had been taught, lassies *you* had taught me, to look down on! And now they were the people I needed to help me! On the train, when I ran out of food, they shared theirs with me. They made tea and brought me a cup. When my bag was stolen in Yarmouth, they came to my rescue. And I learnt. I learnt I was wrong – about them, about looking down on people, and about me.

'I've told you about Robbie and Chrissie coming to the Lord. Jock Troup was the man at the head of it but there were others involved.' Her voice quietened as she thought back to the first time she saw Frank Everett, standing at the head of the stairs in their lodgings. Tall, lean, nicely dressed, and with those compassionate eyes.

'There was one man in particular.' Lydia slowed to a stop, her heart quickening with the memories. 'I thought he cared for me. I...' Honesty demanded she face this squarely, if only for her own sake. 'I found my defences vanish. I responded to him... and I began to care in return.' The bleakness returned to her eyes.

'And?' Her grandmother's prompt was gentle, so gentle that tears gathered in Lydia's eyes.

'I got it wrong,' she said simply. 'I was – as far as he was concerned – just one of the Wick fisher-lassies.' (She determinedly banished the memory of their conversation where she had talked of her training in Edinburgh to be a teacher and her job in Wick.) 'He is a minister, a Baptist minister. And he was already involved with someone else. I saw them together. Twice, three times. There was no mistaking it. She's someone more his... class. More suitable.'

Hurt and despair closed down her throat and she was silent.

227

'Oh my poor bairn,' said her grandmother. 'Led on, then betrayed. Like I was.'

'That's how it feels,' Lydia said. 'But maybe I misunderstood. Misinterpreted his interest.' Though how could she misinterpret those hugs, those kisses? Desperately she banished the thought, the memories. 'I got it all wrong,' she declared with a bravado she did not feel. 'So if I'm hurting now, it's all my own stupid fault.'

Grandmother and granddaughter sat in silence, their stories told, their hearts opened to one another.

'It's not your fault,' Granny Leslie said finally. 'Not all of it. You were far from home, in a strange place, and you were tempted to let down your guard.'

Lydia nodded her agreement.

'Don't you blame yourself,' her grandmother admonished her. 'Learn from it!'

'Learn what?' Lydia asked.

'That "*All flesh is grass*".'

The Bible quote was so unexpected Lydia jerked her head up in surprise.

'Oh aye, I can quote the Bible with the best of the churchgoers!' Granny Leslie said. 'And it's true. Men are weak. We're the strong ones. We have to be.'

Thinking of her mother and of herself these past four years, Lydia nodded agreement. They had both had to be strong.

'Men will always let you down,' Granny Leslie told her. 'Fine words will lead you on, but in the end it's always the same. You can't trust them. The only way is to keep yourself to yourself, and then you won't get hurt. If you keep your feelings to yourself nobody can touch them. Nobody can harm you.'

It made sense. If she had not idolised her big brother and his handsome friend and let them see it, there would have been no disastrous marriage – no soul-tearing disillusion and humiliation. And if she had not let the permafrost round her heart melt a little when Frank Everett had first smiled at her, she would not be in the miserable hurting place she was now. Yes, it made sense.

It was the only sense there was for a woman alone in the world. Keep the barriers up. Don't get hurt.

'You're right,' Lydia told her grandmother. 'It's the only way. I won't make that mistake again.' She reached down for the tray. 'Now let me help you take this through to the kitchen.' Without waiting for a reply she picked it up and carried it down the corridor.

CHAPTER 34

'You did what?' her mother exclaimed in amazement when Lydia returned home and said she had had tea with Granny Leslie.

'My mother is a bit of a tartar,' she explained to Chrissie who was comfortably installed next to the fire. Jean and Chrissie had quickly come to warm friendship, bonding over their shared love for Robbie. Chrissie had taken to popping in regularly for tea, comfortably fitting into her role as a second daughter to Jean, and just as welcome.

'She was fine with me when I was little,' Lydia said. 'I've never been really afraid of her.'

'Then you're the only one,' her mother laughed. '*I'm* afraid of her!'

Chrissie's eyes grew round. 'You never are? Of your own mother?'

'I am too!' Jean said. 'She was always hard on us children. Nothing we did pleased her. But when I started walking out with David Ross, you would have thought I was doing something really shocking!'

'But it was, for her,' Lydia put in. 'You and Dad – you were like her and Dad's Dad, Murdo Ross. It must have brought it all back.'

'I know that now,' Jean said gently. 'But at the time, I knew nothing. Lizzie Nichols wasn't living in Wick. What scandal there had been was long gone and long forgotten. And of course nobody spoke about it in our house or to any of us. I just thought my mother had always been like that.'

She rose and began to tidy away her sewing.

'Sad, really,' she said.

'Can I go out to play?' Ewen had come downstairs, changed out of his school clothes and ready to meet up with his friends.

'Yes, of course,' Lydia said. 'But be back in time for your tea.'

'Yes, Mum,' Ewen said obediently, but as he reached for the door handle, he turned back. 'Grandma?'

'Yes, my love?'

'Alistair Stevens in my class is going out on his dad's boat this weekend if the weather's good. He was telling everybody today. And he kept asking when I'd be allowed to go out on Granddad's boat and when I said I didn't know, he said that was because I'm too little to go and wouldn't be allowed for years and years and years and everybody laughed!' The little boy was indignant.

'Oh, that was unkind,' Jean told him, her mind racing. If it was anything to do with her, Ewen would not go out on his grandfather's boat for years and years and years. At least not until they were sure he did not get seasick like Robbie had.

Ewen staggered back as the door was pulled from his grasp and Robbie came in.

'What's this?' he said. 'Somebody being unkind to my favourite nephew? You tell me about it and I'll go and sort it out!'

He winked cheekily at Chrissie who laughed, but Ewen poured out his story again.

'Well, let's see,' Robbie said and stood Ewen up against the wall, pretending to measure his height. 'I don't think you're particularly little for your age, are you? What about this boy, Alistair Stevens – is he a lot bigger than you?'

'No!' Ewen declared. 'He's a wee bit shorter than me!'

'Ah,' said Robbie wisely. 'That's what it's about. He's feeling small so he's talking big to make up for it. Don't you pay him any attention. You'll soon get your chance to go out on the *Bonnie Jean*. Now, off you go and play!'

But Ewen stood his ground a moment longer.

'Promise, Uncle Robbie? Can I tell him it's definite, for sure?'

Robbie tousled his hair affectionately. 'Yes, you can. Certain sure. Now, off you go before it's teatime and time to come back home!'

Ewen laughed and scampered off happily.

Chrissie rose from her seat and went to greet Robbie. 'You did that well, love.' He would make a good father. But Jean's eyes were troubled.

'What's the matter, Mum?' Robbie asked her. 'You're not worried about Ewen coming out on the boat with us? We'll look after him and make sure he's all right. Lydia's not worried. You can trust us.'

'It's not that,' Jean said. 'I do trust you to look after him... But what if...' She paused, the troubled look intensifying as she stumbled on. 'What if he gets seasick like you did? His grandfather would never cope! It would destroy him!'

Robbie and Chrissie exchanged glances.

'I can see that,' Robbie said slowly. 'Well, maybe I can help. Let me think about it. I'll have a wee word with Ewen.'

And Jean had to be content with that. She nodded at Lydia to follow her into the kitchen to give Chrissie and Robbie some privacy. But as she joined her mother, Lydia could hear their laughter even with the door closed. Their delight in one another suddenly felt bitter in her heart, and a surge of unhappy feelings rose up in her throat.

The words forced themselves into her brain. It just was not fair! There was Chrissie – unmarried and pregnant but it was all going to be happy-ever-after for her and Robbie. While Lydia who had carefully trodden the path of scrupulously right behaviour – apart from that one evening when Danny had slipped uninvited into her room and her parents had interrupted Danny's determined seduction – she was left with the dregs of a disastrous marriage and a cold lonely future to look forward to. It was not fair.

The unhappy thoughts roiled round her head as she helped her mother with the preparation for their supper. They grew stronger when her father returned and greeted everyone affectionately, holding Jean a little longer in his embrace.

'How's my girl?' he asked fondly.

That was how he used to greet me, Lydia thought, but now her parents were reconciled, it was clear who was first in his heart. And only right and proper, she scolded herself, but as she sat at table with her family, Chrissie and Robbie chattering happily about their wedding, her mother and father exchanging fond happy glances, she felt awkward. Uncomfortable.

For the first time in her life, she felt she did not belong here in this game of happy families. The widow and her young son were unmistakable reminders of mortality and the misery of life. And the bitter hurt of betrayal and rejection that was taking root in her heart was setting her even further apart from these people.

Just when she felt she could bear it no longer, her mother spoke.

'I've been thinking.' She smiled and looked at her husband for support. 'And we've talked about this, Dad and I. Chrissie, Robbie, you'll be very welcome to stay here with us, after the wedding. We'll be a wee bit squashed but I'm sure we'll manage.'

Chrissie beamed. 'That's very good of you, Mrs Ross.'

'A wee bit squashed,' Lydia thought resentfully. That was a huge understatement. There was just enough room for her and Ewen. And Chrissie would soon be presenting them with another member of the Ross family! A wee bit squashed indeed! The house would be bulging at the seams! She stared at her parents in dismay but they were smiling happily. It seemed a fine idea to them. They clearly had not thought about the effect it would have on her and Ewen.

Talk had moved on to the wedding which was drawing close. Lydia watched as her mother and Chrissie chatted cheerfully about the arrangements. It was obvious the two women were getting on well. And Chrissie was glowing – radiant with the joy of her forthcoming marriage and a healthy pregnancy.

And suddenly it was too much for Lydia. The contrast between her miserable life and Chrissie and Robbie's joyful future here in what had been her home, her refuge, overwhelmed her.

Scarcely trusting her own voice, she told Ewen sharply, 'Time for bed.'

Startled by her tone, he rose at once and followed her out of the room after a swift round of goodnight hugs and kisses. Hurrying him upstairs, she did not see the concerned glance that passed between her parents.

All she cared about was getting away. Being on her own in her misery.

CHAPTER 35

'So what's the matter with you now, missy?'

Lydia looked up from her cup of tea. It had become a regular feature of her week, afternoon tea with Granny Leslie after school finished on a Friday. The old house in Wellington Street was a welcome refuge from the crowded, busy, noisy house she used to call home but that now felt uncomfortable and unwelcoming.

Everything seemed to be focused on Chrissie and the upcoming wedding, followed closely by Chrissie and the arrival of the baby. Jealous, that's what she was, Lydia admitted to herself with a sigh. But it really did not feel she had a home any more. Or a mother, so caught up was Jean in all the preparations for the wedding and the arrival of the baby.

And they were all so happy! That made it much worse when Lydia was struggling with her broken heart. There, she had admitted it to herself. That was what she was suffering from and it would not do. She had to get over it and get on with her life. But that brought her back round to her home, filled to bursting with happy people planning happy futures.

She just did not fit in. Worse, she did not feel there was room for her there any more.

'I can't live there!' It burst from her in anguish. 'They're all so happy, and busy, and there will be the wedding and I'll have to smile and be happy for them, and then there will be the baby, and I'll have to be the delighted auntie. And then they're going to come and live with us! And there's no room. And... I can't bear it,' she finished on a despairing cry.

'Mm-hm,' Granny Leslie said. That all-purpose two-tone Caithness response that at least let you know you were listened to.

Lydia drank her tea and fought back her tears. Why was she so weepy these days? It had never been her way but now tears seemed to come at the slightest opportunity. She looked up to find Granny Leslie's eyes on her.

She seemed to have made up her mind. 'You'll just have to come here,' Granny Leslie said. 'There's plenty of room – too much for me on my own.'

Lydia stared at her grandmother. To get away from that noisy household whose very happiness seemed to mock her loneliness and misery would be wonderful. And this house had always been a refuge for her. There was plenty of room – for them both. Hardly thinking, Lydia replied, 'Yes! Oh, yes please.'

Her grandmother nodded her satisfaction then poured her another cup of tea. 'You just tell your mother when you get home and you can be moved in here before the end of the month.'

When they had finished their tea and Lydia had helped carry through and wash up the tea things, she flew home with wings on her feet.

'I'm home!' she called out as she always used to. But the busy chattering and noise in the sitting room drowned out her voice.

Surprised faces turned to her when she burst into the room with her news, only to be forestalled by Ewen.

'Mum! Mum!' he said excitedly. 'Auntie Chrissie says I can help at the wedding! And I'm to have a suit with long trousers!'

Lydia's gaze snapped from Ewen to Chrissie to her mother.

'And when was I to hear about this?' she asked sharply. 'And where's the money to come from? Maybe someone should have spoken to me first!'

And heedless of Ewen's appalled reaction, she marched through the room and upstairs to her bedroom, her steps loud and angry on the stairs.

Jean and Chrissie exchanged glances as they heard Lydia's bedroom door slam and turned at once to comfort and reassure Ewen.

Lydia sat in her room, the anger and resentment hot in her heart.

'*Auntie Chrissie said!*'

So Chrissie was even taking over her son and deciding what he would do. It was definitely time to move out of this house and get back her independence and her control over her life.

She waited till she heard Chrissie leave, then she went downstairs. Her mother was carrying the tea tray through to the kitchen. Lydia followed her and stood by the sink watching the familiar routine of washing-up till her mother, having put the last plate in the drainer, looked up, waiting for her to speak.

'Ewen and I will be moving,' Lydia announced. 'There isn't enough room here for all of us now that *Chrissie*' – the name came out laden with bitterness – 'will be living here with Robbie, and especially after the baby arrives.'

'And where will you be going?' her mother asked quietly.

'Granny Leslie's,' Lydia said. 'She's invited me.'

Jean reached for a tea towel and started drying the cups and saucers. She handed each one to Lydia who automatically put them away in the cupboard where they belonged.

'Mm-hm,' Jean said. 'I see.' She paused. 'There's plenty of room in that big house – plenty enough for the two of you.'

Glad that her mother was taking her news so calmly, Lydia said, 'Yes. And there's the room I used to use for my schoolwork. I can use that for marking and prep...'

'My mother's not so young as she was,' Jean remarked.

'So it will be good for her to have someone living there with her,' Lydia put in.

'Mm-hm,' Jean responded thoughtfully. 'It's a big house to look after. All the cleaning, and your grandmother's fussy. It's been getting too much for her.'

'True,' Lydia said, not sure where her mother was going with this.

'It's good of you to help her like this but you'll have a lot to do. More than the few bits I'm used to doing for you.' This was said quietly, matter-of-fact.

Lydia thought about those "few bits". As well as keeping the house clean, her mother ensured that meals were cooked for all of them, clothes washed and ironed and mended for her and Ewen who was hard on his clothes as five-year-old boys are...

'I'm not completely useless,' Lydia said stiffly. 'The trip to Yarmouth proved that.'

'That's true, my dear,' her mother said peaceably. 'I never thought you were, but you work hard at the school all day and you'll notice the difference. You'll want to help your granny and not be a burden to her.'

'No!' Lydia declared. 'No – and she did invite me.'

'Ah yes,' Jean said. 'She's invited you. But what about Ewen? Will he be welcome in Wellington Street? He's a lively young chap.

Have you thought about that, and about him? You know how she is with the menfolk.'

That gave Lydia pause. Yes, she knew Granny Leslie did not tolerate any of the males in the family. Had she forgotten that Ewen existed when she issued her invitation? How could she, Lydia's mother-heart protested. Ewen was the apple of her eye!

And suddenly, she was struck that perhaps he had not been the centre of her life for a long while. In Yarmouth, exhausted with the work gutting fish and emotionally carried away with dreams of love and a life with Frank Everett, she had all but forgotten her son. And now it appeared that she had been thinking only of herself again. Granny Leslie was unlikely to provide a welcoming home for a lively, noisy, five-year-old boy.

'I'll talk to Ewen,' she began slowly.

CHAPTER 36

'I'm hungry!' The little boy erupted into the kitchen. 'Mum...'

He ground to a halt and switched his gaze to his grandmother, then back to Lydia. 'What is it? I'm not in trouble, am I?'

Jean laughed. 'No, my dearie.' She tousled his already untidy hair. 'You're in no trouble. But we were just speaking about you.'

Ewen took a step back towards the door, as if readying himself for flight. Cautiously he asked, 'What about? About Uncle Robbie's wedding and the trousers?'

'Not about the trousers. You're not to worry about that.'

'I'm sorry I was cross,' Lydia put in, her guilt overwhelming her. 'I was just...' She faltered to a stop. How could she explain to Ewen all that was going on in her mind?

Her mother came to her rescue.

'Your Mum was surprised because she thought you'd be wearing Uncle Alec's kilt.'

'Uncle Alec's kilt?' Ewen echoed, eyes huge.

'That's right,' Jean said. 'My father had a kilt made for Alec when he was a wee boy like you. I'll have to get it out and make sure the moths haven't eaten it. You can't go to the wedding in a kilt with holes in!'

Ewen laughed. Then ever tenacious, he asked, 'So if it wasn't about the trousers, what were you saying about me?'

Lydia's worried eyes flew to her mother's face but Jean simply nodded reassuringly.

'We weren't talking just about you, my dearie,' she said. 'But about where we're all going to live once your Uncle Robbie and Auntie Chrissie get married.'

Ewen's face cleared and he grinned happily. 'That's not a problem. I've worked that out!' he said proudly.

Mother and daughter exchanged glances.

'Oh yes?' Jean asked him.

'Well, Uncle Robbie and I have been sharing the boys' room now he's back for good,' Ewen began.

Jean smiled. The bedroom that Alec and Robbie had shared as children was always known as the boys' room.

'Auntie Chrissie is a *girl*,' Ewen made the point strongly. 'So she'll share with Mum and that will be the girls' room. So there will be plenty of room for us all!' he concluded triumphantly.

'And when the baby comes?' his grandmother prodded gently, hiding her smile.

Ewen's brow furrowed briefly as he thought about it, then he declared cheerfully, 'If it's a boy, he comes in with us in the boys' room, and if it's a girl, it goes in the girls' room!'

That made Jean and Lydia laugh, but then Jean pointed out, 'I'm not sure that will do, Ewen, my love. Robbie and Chrissie will most likely want a room to themselves – like Granddad and me. And you won't want to share with your Mum...'

Again the young brow furrowed.

'But there may be a better solution,' Jean began.

'What?' Ewen asked curiously.

'Granny Leslie has said that you and your Mum can go and live in her house. There's a lot more room there and you won't be disturbed when the baby starts crying.'

'Granny Leslie's?' Ewen repeated with horror in his voice. He reached behind him for the door handle to make a swift get-away. 'Oh no!' he declared shrilly. 'I won't go! I hate Granny Leslie. She's always nasty to me! I won't go and you can't make me! I'm staying here!' And he pulled the door open and fled, his pounding feet resounding through the house.

'Oh dear,' Jean said quietly. 'I think you may have a wee bit of a problem there.'

'We'll not be moving for a little while,' Lydia said slowly. 'There's plenty of time to sort that out.'

And she put the last cup that she had been holding into the cupboard and went quietly back up to her bedroom where she could think.

Jean allowed herself a small smile. She knew her daughter was suffering, though Lydia had not, unusually for her, shared with her mother what was troubling her. Jean had done what she could – placed her in God's hands. But Ewen was involved too and Ewen's happiness mattered too. She took a deep breath. It would all work out right.

'Please, Lord Jesus,' she whispered.

CHAPTER 37

'I thought you'd like this room best,' Granny Leslie said, standing aside so Lydia could walk into the spacious front bedroom where the tall windows let the light flood in. Wooden shutters and thick curtains plus a pretty little fireplace ensured the room would be cosy in cold weather.

'It's lovely, Granny,' Lydia said as she looked around.

She had escaped Rose Street with its uncomfortable mixture of Ewen's sulky intransigence and the happy excitement of the wedding and the anticipation of the new baby and found the peace of the Wellington Street house soothing, and very appealing to her bruised feelings.

Granny Leslie opened the doors of the big wardrobe. 'Plenty of room for your clothes,' she said, closing the doors and running her gnarled hands over the polished wood of a tall matching chest of drawers placed next to it. An elegant dressing table was set into the window embrasure to catch the best light.

It was a lovely room and much bigger than the one Lydia was used to at home. The girls' room as Ewen had called it. The memory made her smile and then as she remembered she needed to broach the subject of Ewen with her grandmother, the smile faded as worry took hold.

'You can use the small bedroom for your work,' Granny Leslie was saying. 'The one you used before. It's got a fire in it so you'll be warm there too. We can put some shelves in for your books.'

She led the way to the familiar room, furnished with table and chair, as Lydia remembered it, but with the addition of a comfortable armchair.

'I thought maybe you could use somewhere to read,' Granny Leslie said. 'That armchair was your grandfather's.'

'Oh that's lovely,' Lydia said. She hesitated. There would never be a right time so maybe now was as good as any.

'What's the matter?' Her grandmother had picked up on her hesitation. 'Too sentimental to use it?'

'No, no,' Lydia protested. 'It's just... This is all lovely but...'

'But what?'

The old lady was now distinctly displeased. She had clearly gone to a lot of trouble to prepare for Lydia's arrival. Lydia thought it maybe also showed how much she wanted Lydia to join her in the big house where her isolation and loneliness must be only too painful.

Lydia hesitated. She really did not want to upset her grandmother but it had to be said. She searched for the right words.

'I really appreciate this, Granny,' she began. 'You've gone to a lot of trouble to make it lovely for me but...'

'But?' her grandmother repeated sharply.

'But what about Ewen?' Lydia said helplessly. 'You've said nothing about Ewen. Where's he to sleep?'

There was a distinct pause, then her grandmother pursed her lips disapprovingly.

'Do you have to bring the boy with you?' she asked brusquely.

'Wouldn't he be better staying at Rose Street?'

'Not bring him with me?' Lydia echoed in amazement.

'Jean's used to boys. I'm not. He'll be fine there.'

Granny Leslie turned away as though the conversation was ended and stumped downstairs. Lydia followed slowly. It was clear that her grandmother had made no preparations for Ewen. That Ewen was not expected to be moving in with her. She really expected Lydia to leave him behind and move in to the Wellington Street house on her own.

She caught up with her grandmother as she headed down the hallway to the front door. Clearly her visit was terminated for the day.

'He's my son,' Lydia said quietly to her grandmother's back. 'I can't just leave him behind.'

Granny Leslie turned round to face her, her eyes hard.

'I don't see why not,' she replied. 'It's not unusual in your situation.'

Lydia stared at her. 'Not unusual?' she repeated.

'Women on their own have to manage. Lizzie Nichols left her son behind. You are a Ross at the end of the day. Nobody would be surprised.' She opened the door. 'It's up to you. There's plenty of room here for you. You could be very comfortable.'

Lydia opened her mouth to reply but her grandmother cut in. 'Know which side your bread's buttered on, my girl. Don't be stupid and let your *feelings* get in the way of your best interests again.'

And before she knew it, Lydia was out on the street staring at a closed door.

CHAPTER 38

'We're going to be moving again!' the stocky young man with the loud voice declared to the packed congregation in Fraserburgh Congregational Church.

Frank Everett, sitting with the other members of Jock Troup's team, exchanged knowing smiles with his friends. The work in Fraserburgh had made a tremendous impact on the town. The meetings had quickly outgrown their initial base in the Baptist Church but an application to use other buildings in the town was refused because Jock was not an ordained minister. This proved to be no hindrance thanks in part to the support of local ministers in the Congregational and Baptist Churches who had thrown their full weight behind the mission.

Meetings were moved to the larger premises of the Congregational Church but now they had outgrown this venue and needed to move again. This time the Parish Church which could seat 1200 folk was welcoming them. The Kirk Session further demonstrated its approval of the work by pledging to pay the heating bills – a significant contribution in a chilly Scottish winter.

As Jock made his announcement, Frank found his thoughts wandering. Convinced that God had called him to accompany Jock to Fraserburgh, he had thought that Jock would soon return to Wick, his home town – Wick where Lydia Alexander lived.

Working with Jock and Willie Bruce and the other folk on the team had been enormously satisfying as the local people flocked to hear Jock preach the message of salvation. There was plenty to do with prayer meetings and gospel meetings every hour of the day, followed by more prayer and counselling as men and women came to the Lord. Some of those were fishermen whose hardened hearts had kept them from receiving the message in Yarmouth, but now back at home, they too came till whole families were attending services. It was said the delivery boys were whistling hymns as they went round the town.

But Frank knew time was moving on and soon he would have to return to England and take up the work that awaited him there. His church had been gracious in allowing him leave of absence but before long, he too would be moving on. 'Moving on' – Jock's words caught his attention.

'*We'll* be moving on too, in the next fortnight,' Jock was saying.

Not simply the shift of venue to the Parish Church then? Frank's heart leapt with hope. In that case, surely they would be going to Wick so Jock could spend Christmas and the New Year with his family? And in Wick, soon, soon, he would see Lydia again. And surely there would be time to spend with her, let her get to know him, so when he asked her...

Jock's words crashed into his hearing.

'But we don't know where we're going yet,' he announced. 'We do know that the Lord is leading us and where He leads, we will go.'

A moment of rebellion struck Frank's heart, like a dart into a bull's-eye. He had hoped – no, he had expected – that their next destination would be Wick. He had planned what he was going to do once he got there... He had been so sure...

But now that certainty was in doubt. Jock had no definite plans. They could end up going to Wick but Jock was waiting on the Lord. And that meant they could be going almost anywhere. Glasgow. The United States of America. Willie Bruce was talking about China.

Frank mocked his stupid thoughts, but it was true. If the Lord was sending them somewhere other than Wick, it put real delay into his plans to see Lydia again and get her to agree to marry him before he returned south. Briefly he considered parting company with Jock and simply going on up to Wick on his own but, remembering Robbie Ross's hostility, he knew that simply turning up on the Ross family's doorstep would not be a good idea. He first needed to remember what it was from their time in the Great War that had so turned Robbie against him.

In any case, he reminded himself, he too should wait on God's leading. He remembered Luke's reports in the Acts of the Apostles of Paul's missionary journeys, of how some workers had split off from Paul and their reputations had not been enhanced. Then he recalled how when Paul and his companions had wanted to go to Bithynia, '*the Spirit suffered them not*'. Instead they went in the other direction and so were in the right place when Paul had a vision of a man begging them to come to him in Macedonia. Rather like the Baptist Church leaders in Fraserburgh whose prayer had been answered.

Frank shook himself mentally. How could he doubt that God had His hand firmly on their lives? Yes, he wanted to be reunited with Lydia. Yes, he wanted to marry her and spend the rest of his life with her. But that life would only be blessed – both their lives would only be blessed – if they were following God's leading.

It appeared that God might not be leading him to Wick right away. But alongside that disappointment was a gentle glow of assurance. He would at some time be travelling to Wick. He would see Lydia again. And that time would be the right time. He was sure of it.

All he had to do was wait, and trust.

CHAPTER 39

She walked. It was what Lydia always did when she needed to clear her head and sort out her thoughts, and today she badly needed that clarity.

Granny Leslie obviously wanted her to move into the big house in Wellington Street. And just as obviously, she did not want Ewen to come too. Lydia knew her mother would welcome the lad. There would be room for him. Once she moved out, he could have her room. Chrissie and Robbie could share the boys' room.

And there would be love for Ewen at Rose Street. He was the apple of his Granddad's eye as well as his grandmother's. And both Robbie and Chrissie loved him. Which could not be said, it had to be admitted, for Granny Leslie.

And what of herself? How much did she love Ewen? She had headed off for Yarmouth with scarcely a thought of him. She had known he would be well looked after by his grandmother, she chided herself. You cannot keep children in cotton wool. But then Frank Everett had appeared in her life and all thought of anything else, anyone else, had vanished. And that, she admitted sadly, had included Ewen.

Lydia paused. She had reached the Fisherman's Rest, the sheltered viewpoint overlooking the harbour. She walked to the path along the cliff edge, rested her arms on the railing and stared out over the bay, barely seeing the beauty of the waves and the rocks and the sky, heedless to the cries of the gulls, drawn inexorably back as metal to a magnet to that sudden, unexpected dawning of hope. One tender embrace...

But it had all come to nothing. And now would never come to anything. She was back in Wick, alone, and he was... wherever he was, getting on with his own life with the lady she had seen accompanying him. And from nowhere a brief prayer for their happiness surfaced in her heart. Because she still cared for him. And if she truly cared, then his happiness was paramount, not her desires and dreams.

She swallowed hard. That was in the past. Like everything else in her life. And she was determined that no man would in the future disturb her hard-won peace. A little sob escaped her – half-laughter, half-pain – as she recognised that the problem now was another male, but this time a young one, Ewen. Her own son.

What was she to do? She felt torn in two. If she turned down her grandmother's offer, the ensuing scene would likely sever the tenuous connection she had managed to weave between them. For her grandmother's sake, she did not want to do that. And, she had to admit, the big house in Wellington Street offered her more space, more comfort, more peace and quiet.

But to go to Wellington Street meant that she would have to leave Ewen behind. Granny Leslie had flung at her that she was a Ross so nobody would expect anything better than a repeat of her other grandmother's behaviour in leaving her son behind. That had stung, but she recognised Granny Nichols' blood did flow in her veins. If she was even considering leaving Ewen with her mother, that proved it if nothing else!

But despite Granny Nichols' assurances that there had never been any falling-out between her and Lydia's father, Lydia knew that being left behind when his mother began her new life in Lowestoft had hurt him deeply and left scars. How could she consider doing that to Ewen?

But it's not the same, came an insistent whisper. It's not as though you'll be far away. You'll just be a few streets away. You can see him every day if you want to.

Lydia was not sure that was strictly true. She could not bring him home to Granny Leslie's for tea. She would have to go to Rose Street to see him – and the whole point of the exercise was to get away from Rose Street and the game of happy families that was being played out there. A game in which she felt she had no part, would never have a part.

Wellington Street offered escape. But not just that – it was a big comfortable house and she could enjoy the spaciousness and the peace and quiet to rebuild her life. But rebuild it, how? The question was harsh, and the answer even harsher. Living with Granny Leslie, it was more than likely that she would find herself rebuilding her life like Granny Leslie's.

She plunged her face into her hands. What was she going to do? She did not want to end up like Granny Leslie, isolated and bitter – but she could not bear to go on as she was at Rose Street, the resentment building every day against the happiness of the people she loved the best. There seemed to be no sensible solution that would not end up hurting somebody!

A hand on her shoulder roused her.

'What's the matter, Lyddie? Is there anything I can do?' Chrissie stood by her side, looking into her face with concern.

'No, no,' Lydia denied shakily. 'I'm just a bit confused.' She pulled herself up straight and tried for some composure. Just at this moment

Chrissie was the last person she wanted to see. 'I was just trying to sort things out in my mind, what's best to do.'

'About moving out of Rose Street and going to your Granny's?' Chrissie asked with characteristic bluntness.

Lydia's eyes flew to Chrissie's face. Surely the guilt gave her away.

Chrissie nodded. 'Yes. Well, it's a hard decision.' She paused, then touched Lydia's arm. 'Is it because of me that you're going? Me and Robbie making the house overcrowded? I know it will be a squeeze...'

Lydia began an emphatic denial but Chrissie's truthfulness stopped her.

'It is, isn't it?' Chrissie said. 'I'm sorry. You shouldn't feel you have to move out. It's your home.'

Tears came to Lydia's eyes then. The Rose Street house had been home since her birth but since she came back from Yarmouth nowhere felt like home any more. She felt very lost and alone.

Seeing the misery in Lydia's face, Chrissie tucked her arm into hers the way they used to in Yarmouth. She wheeled her round.

'Let's walk,' she said. 'And you can tell me all about it!'

And although Lydia shook her head, firmly determined she would not spoil her friendship with Chrissie by letting her know what was troubling her, little by little it all came out. And as she spoke, the hurt in her heart of her dashed hope to one day be part of a new happy family spilled out and coloured her words.

By the time they reached the rock-cut swimming pool known as the Trinkie, they were both happy to rest. Standing side by side, elbows on a dry-stone wall, they gazed out over the wave-tossed bay towards the North Head.

'It's a pity I don't have relatives with room to spare,' Chrissie said. 'That would be the best solution.'

Lydia knew Chrissie had lived with an aunt after her mother died. A real tartar by reputation, which perhaps had assisted in making Chrissie the strong young woman she was now. On hearing the news of Chrissie's impending marriage, she had decided to up sticks and move to live with her sister in the country. The house was already sold and the new owners waiting to move in.

'Oh Chrissie, I'm sorry!' Lydia said. 'I'm being horrible when you've been nothing but good to me! It's not you, really it's not! It's just...'

'I know,' Chrissie said. 'You came back from Yarmouth with your heart bruised and hurting, and you're still hurting. That's what's making everything so difficult for you.'

Lydia stared at her. Had she been so transparent?

'I should think you're sick of the lot of us!' Chrissie added cheerfully. 'There we are, all so happy. And planning the wedding, and looking forward to the baby coming!'

Lydia gulped.

'Yes?' Chrissie probed with an encouraging grin.

'Yes,' Lydia acknowledged. 'Yes, I am.' It was a huge relief to get the words out, to tell the truth about her feelings.

'Well, it's a real problem. So let's take it to the Lord.' And before Lydia could open her mouth, Chrissie was praying out loud, as naturally as she had been speaking to her, as if Jesus had come to join the two women as they stood on the close-cropped grass overlooking the sea.

Chrissie set out the situation clearly and ended, 'So we ask You to sort it out for the best for all of us, and that includes Granny Leslie, please, Lord Jesus.' She cast a swift glance at Lydia and added with a mischievous twitch of her mouth, 'And heal Lyddie's broken heart too. Put that right for her and give her back her hope and her joy in life.' Blithely ignoring Lydia's protest, she sailed on into, 'Thank you, loving Lord. We know we can trust You. Amen.'

She looked at Lydia. 'There. I think that about covers it, don't you?'

Lydia shook her head in amazement. She had no words.

Chrissie linked arms again and said, 'I think we should be getting back. We don't want your mother to worry.'

But Lydia did not budge. She sighed. 'It's all very well praying,' she said. 'But what am I going to *do*?'

'Don't be so silly,' Chrissie told her. 'You don't have to do anything now. We've given it to the Lord and now He'll see to it. Come on. Your tea will be waiting.'

And she tugged Lydia back the way they had come.

He'll see to it? Lydia wondered at Chrissie's new-found confidence in her God. She could see the new strength and poise she seemed to have. Not the brittle self-assurance Lydia had first noticed but a new lovely confidence, not in herself but in this God who Chrissie seemed to believe really cared about them and their little problems.

Granny Leslie would pour scorn both on the girl and her faith. But Lydia knew she felt only envy for Chrissie's assurance that Someone would care enough to sort things out for them. She only wished it was true.

CHAPTER 40

The opportunity to discover Granny Leslie's opinion of Chrissie came sooner than expected. Lydia, Chrissie and Jean were sitting having tea together the next afternoon when they were surprised by a sharp knock on the front door.

Only one person knocked like that but she never visited when David Ross was at home. Lydia and her mother exchanged worried glances.

'What's the matter?' Chrissie asked.

'It's my mother,' Jean said.

'Shall we hide?' Chrissie teased with a grin.

That made Jean laugh. 'No, no, my dear. You just sit tight and we'll see what she wants.' And she went off to open the door with a smile on her face. Which was quickly removed by her mother's acerbic greeting.

'Do you always have to keep me standing in the cold?'

Chrissie looked across at Lydia and raised an eyebrow comically.

'Sshh!' Lydia whispered.

'You really are all scared of the old besom,' Chrissie said in surprise.

'You wait and see,' Lydia said. 'And don't let anything she says upset you. She will try, you know.'

Granny Leslie sailed into the little sitting room like a big black crow in her long black coat and glared at the two girls.

'Humph!' she said disapprovingly. Lydia found herself shrinking back into her seat.

Granny Leslie's beady black eyes fixed on Chrissie.

'Is this the trollop Robbie's having to marry?'

Chrissie's sharp intake of breath was audible.

Jean had followed in her mother's wake and now she moved quickly to stand protectively beside Chrissie, putting a gentle reassuring hand on her shoulder.

'This is Chrissie Anderson,' Jean said quietly. 'And yes, she is Robbie's fiancée.' She squeezed Chrissie's shoulder. 'And we're delighted about it.'

Granny Leslie looked Chrissie up and down.

'And expecting!' she declared with relish. 'Trollops, the lot of you, and the trollops that go to the gutting are the worst!'

She stood glaring down at Chrissie but Chrissie did not blanch under her gaze. Instead she stood up and squared up to her antagonist.

'But that includes yourself, Mrs Leslie, doesn't it?' Chrissie responded steadily. 'You were one of us, and no better than any of us, if what Lizzie Nichols – Lizzie Ross, that was – told us when we had tea with her in Yarmouth.'

Granny Leslie's eyes flashed. Chrissie remained standing, waiting calmly for what she might say. Jean and Lydia remained frozen in their places. The silence hung menacingly between them as they waited for her answer.

But instead a grudging smile nudged Granny Leslie's mouth.

'Well, well,' she said slowly. 'Robbie's getting a girl with a bit of spirit.'

Chrissie smiled sunnily at her. 'I should hope so!' she declared. 'Now I belong to the Lord Jesus, it's *His* Spirit that's in charge.'

The beady eyes narrowed. 'We'll see about that.' And as Chrissie began to speak again, Granny Leslie waved her away. 'You'd better sit down, girl. In your condition.' She turned and glared at Jean. 'And is there a seat for me in this house? And a cup of tea?'

'Yes, mother,' Jean said peaceably. 'There has always been a seat for you in this house, and a cup of tea.' She nodded to Lydia who hurried into the kitchen to bring another cup, saucer and plate. 'And there are fresh-made pancakes and my rhubarb jam.'

Granny Leslie humphed again but settled herself comfortably in the chair nearest the fire. Once she was provided with tea and food, she glared over her cup at Chrissie.

'You're an Anderson?' she asked.

Chrissie nodded.

'From where?' Granny Leslie demanded.

'Vansittart Street,' Chrissie answered. 'Kath Anderson is my father's sister. Donnie Anderson, he was.'

That brought the sharp eyes back to Chrissie's face.

'Auntie Kath brought me up after my mother and father died,' Chrissie added.

'Mm-hm,' murmured Granny Leslie as she chewed her liberally spread pancake, then dabbed her lips with the napkin Lydia had carefully provided. 'So why are you and Robbie not going there when you're married? There's room enough in that house surely?'

'Auntie Kath's sold it,' Chrissie said simply.

'What?' Granny Leslie said in surprise. 'Where's she going to go?'

'To Auntie May in Lyth.'

Granny Leslie absentmindedly accepted another pancake and spread it with jam, clearly thinking hard. After she had polished off the pancake in two bites, dabbed her lips, and finished off with a swallow of tea, she asked sharply, 'Why? Has she washed her hands of you?'

At that, Chrissie laughed, a clear joyous sound that broke the tense atmosphere in the room. 'No, not at all!' she declared. 'My auntie loves me.'

Mary-Anne's bitter unbelieving cackle cut through her words but Chrissie continued calmly, 'She does. She's like you. She doesn't show it but she loves me just the same.'

Lydia and Jean froze in horror at Chrissie's outrageous statement, their eyes glued to Granny Leslie's face, waiting for the inevitable explosion. But Mary-Anne simply rapped out, 'That doesn't answer my question, girl, and well you know it. So tell me *why* she decided to move when she could have shared that house with you and Robbie?'

'She wanted to be with her sister,' Chrissie said calmly.

'Don't talk rubbish!' Granny Leslie told her derisively. 'Kath and May were at each other's throats as girls and they won't have changed now! Tell me the truth: what was the matter?'

'Nothing was the matter,' Chrissie began, but Granny Leslie's eyes suddenly lit with angry fire and she announced, 'Don't lie to me, girl! It was Robbie, wasn't it?'

Chrissie spluttered and started to speak but Granny Leslie was not having any of it.

'Not good enough for her, was that it?' she demanded. 'Black sheep of the family! The Prodigal Son. And you'd gone and got yourself pregnant...' Clearly she felt she had the monopoly on criticising her family and was outraged by the supposed slight to one of them.

'Lydia.' Jean broke into the diatribe. She held out the teapot to Lydia. 'I think we could do with a fresh pot.'

Lydia fled gratefully into the kitchen, busying herself with filling the kettle and putting it on the stove, all the time with one ear to the sitting room, but she could hear nothing. It seemed the three women were simply sitting in silence. However, when she brought back the fresh pot of tea and set it on the tray for her mother to pour, she was aware that the atmosphere had subtly changed.

'Thank you,' Granny Leslie said when Jean poured her a fresh cup. For a moment Jean faltered. Politeness was a rarity from her mother. Gathering herself together, she moved on to refill Chrissie's cup and received a naughty wink which made her smile.

But Granny Leslie had caught it.

'I don't know what you're smiling about!' she declared sourly. 'I'd have thought you had too much to do! How many days to the wedding? And how soon after that is this child due?' It was said with a sneer but Chrissie answered her calmly.

'The wedding is at noon next Sunday at the Pulteneytown Parish Church manse and we're having a little gathering at the Rosebank Hotel afterwards. You're invited to both and we hope you'll come. And the baby is due in May.'

Again, Jean and Lydia waited with bated breath for Granny Leslie's tart response. Lydia noticed her mother had her eyes closed. Either she could not bear to watch or she was praying for help. It seemed a good idea but Chrissie seemed placidly unaware or unconcerned.

'Humph' was all Granny Leslie said.

CHAPTER 41

'You did what?' Robbie exclaimed when he was told. 'Invited that miserable old baggage to our wedding?'

Chrissie, sitting next to him at the dinner table, smiled and patted his hand. 'Don't worry about it. It was the right thing to do.'

'It was,' Jean agreed. 'Of course she had to be invited. She's family.'

'She won't come though?' Robbie queried hopefully.

'No,' his mother said sadly. 'I shouldn't think she will.'

But Granny Leslie surprised them all. First, Lydia received a peremptory instruction to bring Chrissie with her to tea, not on her usual Friday afternoon but earlier in the week. The two girls duly went, Lydia in fear and trembling, still unsure about her decision to move into Granny Leslie's house at the end of the week. Chrissie however maintained the new calm and poise that Lydia so admired and envied.

They were greeted without ceremony at the door and shown into the front parlour. To Lydia's surprise, the room was warm, a good fire blazing in the hearth.

Granny Leslie, noticing Lydia's raised eyebrows, said, 'It's not good for a woman who's expecting to get chilled. Now, I'll just go and get the tea.' She turned and left the room. In another woman, Lydia thought, that might look like embarrassment. Could Granny Leslie possibly be thawing?

She sat down in her usual place but realised that Chrissie was already halfway down the corridor and chatting to Granny Leslie. Chatting! How could she do it, Lydia wondered. But maybe being brought up by another cantankerous woman had had some benefits. Still, Lydia was amazed when the two women returned in apparent good humour with one another, Chrissie carrying the cake stand laden with buttered scones, shortbread and fruit cake in one hand and the tea plates and napkins in the other.

Laughing, she deposited the cake stand on the tea table, drawn up beside Granny Leslie's chair, and turned to Lydia.

'I know I'm eating for two but this is a grand feast!'

'Oh you'll need it once the child arrives. It's hard work, you know,' Granny Leslie said with only a little of her accustomed harshness.

'Did you find it hard work, Mrs Leslie, with your two?' Chrissie asked.

Granny Leslie's hand pouring the tea paused for a moment. Then she finished her task and handed the cups to the girls.

'No,' she told Chrissie. 'I was the eldest in my family so I was used to helping with the younger ones. Families were big in those days and I had ten younger brothers and sisters. My own two...' And here a reminiscent smile touched her face. 'My two were no bother at all. I had lovely things for them. And I had help in the house.' She looked across at Lydia. 'Your grandpa...' Again a pause, then she shook her head and the words came out slowly. 'Your grandpa was good to me.'

Lydia's eyes, filled with surprise at this revelation, met Chrissie's. The two girls drank their tea in silence. Granny Leslie seemed embarrassed and started fussing with offering more tea.

'But that was only right,' Chrissie announced suddenly. 'You were a bit of a prize...'

The old black eyes came up sharply to her face, searching as if to see if she were being mocked.

Chrissie persisted, 'That's what my Gran used to say...'

'Your Gran?'

'My Mum's Mum – Bella Flett,' Chrissie explained. 'She always went to the gutting and she said...'

'Bella Flett,' Granny Leslie murmured. 'I remember her. She was younger than us...'

Chrissie smiled. 'Yes, but she knew who everyone was. She used to tell us great stories, and she always said...' She paused and her voice changed as she mimicked her grandmother, 'That Bill Leslie, he was a canny man, biding his time till Mary-Anne would look at him. And once she said yes, he would have given her the moon if she'd asked for it, he loved her that much.'

Lydia watched in amazement as the colour spread into her grandmother's cheeks. For a moment they seemed to be teetering on the edge of an outraged explosion, then Granny Leslie set down her cup. She pulled her handkerchief out of her pocket and sat twisting it between her hands, deep in thought.

After a moment she nodded and said gruffly, 'That's true. He loved me that much. I could have had the moon if I'd wanted it.'

She turned fierce eyes on the two girls who sat in stunned silence. 'Never forget what you're worth! The only man worth having is one who knows your worth and treats you right. That Danny Alexander – I could have told you if you'd have listened to me, Lydia. He was no good. He didn't value what he was getting...'

Lydia nodded dumbly. It was true. Danny had not valued her, and she would not have listened if anyone had tried to tell her. Sadly she had had to find it out for herself.

'You, Chrissie...'

But Chrissie was undaunted.

'I know that me being pregnant looks bad – but that was before either of us came to the Lord. Before we knew any better. But we've got that sorted out now and we know our true worth – in God's sight. The Lord Jesus gave his life for both of us. That's who we are and that makes all the difference to how we treat each other and what kind of a life we'll have together. Oh, we won't get it right all the time – maybe not even half the time!' She laughed. 'But that's all right. So long as we forgive one another the way God has forgiven us, we'll be all right.'

She reached over to the cake stand for a slice of fruit cake and bit into it happily. Lydia's eyes flew to her grandmother's. Love and forgiveness? Was that the key?

Sadly, she realised she had had neither to offer Danny. Adolescent hero-worship was what she had felt – not grown-up love. Not what she had felt for Frank Everett. Sudden pain rose in her and she fought it down. That had been then, in the past. And if now she knew the difference between grown-up love and the hero-worship she had felt for Danny, that was something to be grateful for, she told herself resolutely.

The hero-worship that was all she had felt for Danny would never have been a proper basis for marriage and a lifetime together. And when she had discovered so shockingly that her hero had clay feet, her hero-worship had turned to disgust and hatred. She had had no forgiveness to give him.

With a sharp pang, Lydia realised that she had held on to that unforgiveness. Hoarding it like a miser. Checking on it at regular intervals to make sure it was still there. Even after news had come that he had been killed in action, she had gone on holding on to that unforgiveness, carrying it with her. Even now. And just as suddenly, she realised she did not want it any more.

In a decisive gesture, she set her plate down on the table.

'No more?' Chrissie asked.

Lydia shook her head decisively. 'No more,' she said in a firm voice, but she did not mean the plentiful food Granny Leslie had provided but the unforgiveness she had held in her heart since her disastrous wedding seven years ago.

'Forgiveness?' Granny Leslie said slowly. 'Just forgive and let them do what they like? Is that how you intend to live your life?' The harshness had come back into her face. She shook her head decisively. 'No. That's not the way. You have to stand up for yourself, make sure you get what you want. And you don't let anyone away with anything! That's how you show that you value yourself!'

Lydia looked from Granny Leslie, her head held high in bitter self-righteousness, to Chrissie who was gently shaking her head, love and kindness so apparent in her face. Two different ways of living. And she realised she had been tempted to join Granny Leslie in her self-imposed self-righteous exile from love and laughter and family and – Lydia found a smile curving her lips as she added – and noise and untidiness and being squashed in together and getting on one another's nerves, and forgiving and going forward together in love.

And she knew in that instant what she really wanted, more than anything in the world. She wanted a noisy happy untidy home – a home of her own, a family of her own, and a loving good man who valued her truly and loved her as her husband. And in her mind's eye the man she saw there was Frank Everett. The one man she could not have.

CHAPTER 42

The girls made their farewells – but only after Chrissie had cheerfully overruled Granny Leslie and carried the tea things through to the kitchen and washed them up.

'Humph! Treating this house as though it were her own!' Granny Leslie had complained, but it seemed a token jibe, said without the usual harshness.

And that had put the idea into Lydia's head. Would it not be better for Chrissie and Robbie to move to Granny Leslie's? The child Chrissie was expecting would surely not be the only one they would have, so they would be needing a family home for their children to grow up in. There was plenty of room and a nice big garden at Wellington Street.

Granny Leslie seemed to like, and even respect, Chrissie. Maybe she reminded her of herself in her young days. Having been brought up by a difficult great-aunt, Chrissie was well-used to older folk and their tempers! And of course Chrissie's stalwart faith that she so relied on – that would help her cope with Granny Leslie. Maybe it could even help Granny Leslie?

The bitterness and resentment, the entrenched unforgiveness that Granny Leslie displayed saddened Lydia. Now she could see the damage that it had done to her grandmother and the lives of her family. So much waste! Maybe Chrissie's Lord could reach Granny Leslie through Chrissie.

She put it to her mother after school the next afternoon. Ewen had gone out to play, David Ross was down at the boat and Robbie was working in the back garden. Chrissie was at her aunt's and Jean and Lydia were on their own in the kitchen.

'So you're not going to go to Wellington Street?' Jean asked.

'I don't want to,' Lydia confessed. 'Not now. And Ewen is happy here.'

'I can see it would be a grand solution for Chrissie and Robbie, but would your grandmother countenance it? She's so against the menfolk in the family – though when Robbie was young, she did have a soft spot for him. I thought it was only because he'd got on the wrong side of his father. You know, "my enemy's enemy is my friend" sort of thing!' She paused thoughtfully. 'It's a good idea, though.'

Lydia hesitated. 'Em, maybe... pray about it?' she suggested hesitantly. It was what Chrissie would do.

Jean's eyes brightened in joy. 'Yes, my dear!' she declared happily. 'That's what we should do,' and she seized Lydia's hands and there and then, brought it to the Lord. 'Your will be done for each one of us, my Lord,' she ended. 'And we will trust You for the outcome, for You know what is best for our truest happiness.'

Briefly opening her eyes, she saw her daughter, eyes tight closed, her face intent, nod her head decisively. Jean smiled and said a silent thank you, before declaring 'Amen.'

'Amen,' Lydia echoed.

And found herself engulfed in her mother's arms in a warm happy hug.

'There,' Jean said, letting her go. 'Now we have things to do for that wedding. But first you're going to have to tell your grandmother your decision. Tell me when you're going over there and I'll pray for you every moment!'

'Thanks, Mum,' Lydia said and discovered that she meant it.

A loud rapping at the front door broke their peace.

'I'll go!' Lydia said cheerfully and went to the door. Her aunts, Lena and Ina, stood on the doorstep, waiting to be invited in. The inveterate gossips were enthusiastic visitors around the town, gathering news and dispensing rumour. Lydia wondered what scandalous titbits they had brought with them today to exchange for juicy morsels about her own family. She invited them in with a carefully hidden sigh.

'I'll go and get Mum,' she said, once she had hung up their coats and got them settled in the sitting room.

'It's the aunts,' she told her mother. 'Lena and Ina. Shall I make the tea and you go through and defend the household, or do you want to see to the tea...'

Jean laughed. 'That's naughty!'

'But true,' Lydia said.

'Yes, well, maybe once upon a time,' Jean agreed. 'But we've nothing to fear now.' And off she went into the sitting room, greeting her sisters-in-law with affection and unconcern.

A few minutes later Lydia brought in the tea, buttered scones and her Mum's home-made rhubarb jam and the aunts settled themselves down for a good gossip.

When the scones had been polished off, the last cup of tea swallowed, the final item of gossip provided and dissected, Ina

275

looked at Lena. 'Maybe time we were making a move,' she said. 'I promised we'd look in on...'

Just at that moment, the front door cracked open and Ewen burst into the sitting room, dishevelled and grubby from playing with his friends.

'I'm hungry!' he announced.

Aunt Lena stood up. 'Well, you will be, won't you, young man?'

Ewen looked up at her. 'Yes, Auntie Lena,' he answered politely.

'Good lad,' Aunt Ina commented. She squinted at him. 'You're turning into a real Ross,' she added. 'How old are you now?'

'Five and a half,' Ewen told her proudly.

'Well now, that's nearly old enough to go out on your first trip on the boat with your Granddad,' she said.

'Yes!' Ewen said with delight. 'And I will soon. He's promised!'

Ina and Lena exchanged glances. The one tut-tutted. The other's mouth turned down.

'Let's hope there's no repeat of that business with Robbie then,' Lena said ominously.

'That would be bad,' Ina said, her malicious little eyes bright with the prospect.

Ewen stared at them uncomprehending. Lena pounced.

'Oh, don't you know?' she asked with feigned concern

'Know what?' Ewen demanded.

'About your Uncle Robbie? Why he and your Granddad fell out?'

Ewen looked at his mother and grandmother but Aunt Ina put in sharply, 'It's better that he knows. Not good having secrets in a family.'

'No indeed,' Aunt Lena said triumphantly. 'Don't you worry, Ewen. We'll tell you.' She looked at her sister and began, 'It was the first time Robbie went out on the boat.'

'He was about your age,' Ina put in.

'Alec had been out, no problem. He and your Granddad got on fine. Alec was a good help to his father, and soon was working on the boat,' Lena said.

'A born fisherman,' Ina declared.

'He was that,' Lena agreed with a heavy sigh. 'God rest his soul.'

The two gossips lowered their eyes for a pious moment, then Lena continued brightly, 'But Robbie was never any good.'

'No, no good at all,' Ina said.

Seeing Jean about to rush to her son's defence, Lena added quickly, 'He got seasick. First time out on the boat.' She shot a swift challenging glance at Jean. 'You can't deny that, can you? You were there when they brought him in, wrapped in blankets.'

'Granny?' Ewen queried. 'Is that right? Uncle Robbie was *seasick* the first time he went out on the boat?' He made it sound like the worst heresy. 'Was he?' he persisted.

Jean had to answer truthfully. 'He was. Yes, Ewen. It's true.'

'And that's why his father had no time for him. A lad that's seasick is no good to a fisherman,' Ina pointed out.

Ewen nodded slowly. 'There's a boy in my class... His Dad took him out, but just the once. Everybody laughs at him now.'

Ina and Lena nodded their satisfaction.

'That's right. Well, we'll hope that doesn't happen to you,' Lena said cheerfully. 'But of course, seeing that it happened to Robbie, it could happen again.' Her eyes sparkled maliciously. 'No doubt we'll be hearing. Now we must be going.'

Not for the first time Jean and Lydia were glad to see the end of their visit and usher them out the front door.

They returned to a very downcast Ewen.

'Granny? Mum?'

'Yes, my love?' Jean said as she stacked the used crockery on the tea tray.

'Do you think I'll be all right? Or do you think I'll be seasick like Uncle Robbie?' Tears filled the wee boy's eyes. 'I don't want to let Granddad down!'

'Oh Ewen,' Lydia cried as she enfolded him in her arms. 'Nothing you could do would let your Granddad down.'

'Let Granddad down?' It was Robbie. Having left his boots at the back door he had entered the room quietly on stockinged feet.

'If I'm seasick like you were,' Ewen faltered through his tears. 'That would let Granddad down.'

Pity filled Robbie's eyes as he looked down at the distressed little boy. Then he turned decisively to his mother and sister.

'I think me and Ewen need to talk about this. Man-talk, just the two of us.'

Jean nodded and led Lydia out to the kitchen, setting down the tea tray with an unaccustomed clatter and running the tap into the sink noisily. Lydia looked at her in surprise.

'So they know we're not listening,' Jean explained with a gentle smile. 'Though I do wonder what Robbie can say to him that will make any difference.'

'Maybe about why he's not seasick any more,' Lydia suggested.

'Maybe,' Jean said. 'I've never understood that. After he was so ill that first time, he swore he'd never step foot on the boat again. Then when he left home, we heard he was doing fine on the Aberdeen trawlers. I thought maybe it was the bigger size of the trawlers that made the difference or maybe he'd just grown out of the seasickness, for he's fine now.' She exchanged a grin with Lydia. 'Let's find out!'

They crept together to the connecting door between kitchen and sitting room. Jean eased the door open a crack and they set their ears to it.

'You don't have to worry,' they could hear Robbie saying.

'But Auntie Lena said you were seasick!' Ewen protested. 'What if *I'm* seasick? We won't know till I'm out there, like you were! And then it will be too late!'

Tears were threatening to overwhelm the wee boy. Then Robbie's voice came, strong and reassuring.

'No, you don't have to fear. At all. You see...' Robbie seemed to take a deep breath before he announced, 'You see I never was seasick.'

CHAPTER 43

'But you were!' Ewen protested. 'Auntie Lena said you were.'

'Yes,' Robbie said in a sad voice. 'Everybody thought I was. But I wasn't.'

In the kitchen Jean and Lydia exchanged puzzled glances. Ewen, in the sitting room, put their question into words.

'What do you mean?'

'If you'll promise never to tell, I'll tell you,' Robbie said.

'I promise!' Ewen stated. 'Cross my heart and hope to die!' He spoke the schoolboy pledge loud and fervently.

'Well, no need for that,' Robbie told him. 'I'll trust you. Now you see what happened was that there was a lot of jealousy between me and my brother Alec. He was everybody's favourite so they thought it was me that was jealous.'

Lydia saw her mother nod her head.

'But that wasn't the whole story,' Robbie continued. 'Anyway, Alec was working as the cook on the boat – that's the first job you get. He didn't want me on the boat so he fed me some bad meat and I got sick. *Sick*, mind you, not seasick!'

Ewen murmured something.

'Oh, Dad and the other men thought I was seasick. That's what Alec told them. Me, I was too ill to say anything! Then my very kind big brother looked after me – nobody got a chance to come near – till we got back to port and Mum carried me off home. By the time I was well enough to realise what had happened, it was too late.'

'Oh Uncle Robbie, that's not fair!' Ewen exclaimed.

Jean fiercely nodding her agreement reached for the door handle but Lydia held her back.

'It wasn't fair,' Robbie agreed. 'But Alec's dead and everything's all right between me and Dad now.'

'Does Granddad know?' Ewen asked.

'No,' Robbie said, his voice sad. 'Alec is still his golden boy. If only he knew... But there, there's no good raking over the past. So not a word of this to anyone, all right? It's between you and me?'

'Yes, Uncle Robbie,' Ewen said in a serious voice.

'Good lad. You needed to know so you won't be afraid to go out on the boat. Even if it gets very wild out there, always remember: nobody in this family gets seasick. The Rosses are born fishermen!'

Ewen laughed delightedly and it was on his laughter that Jean pushed the door gently closed and turned to Lydia.

'Well, well,' she said. 'I wonder what else we don't know?'

CHAPTER 44

The interview with Granny Leslie was as difficult as Lydia had feared. Her grandmother did not quite say 'Never darken my door again!' but Lydia reckoned it came close.

They had sat stiffly in the now comfortably warm parlour, tea and scones untouched, while she falteringly said her piece.

'I couldn't, not without Ewen. It wouldn't be right.'

Granny Leslie had snorted her disgust. 'You're a fool, girl,' she said. 'I'm giving you a second chance at your life, free and unencumbered. You're a fool not to take it.'

The words stung – but the picture that flew unbidden into Lydia's mind took her back to Yarmouth and the warm embrace of a fine man, a man who had touched her heart and let her dream of a very different kind of second chance. Not the solitary unencumbered future Granny Leslie had offered her but a chance of love and family and joy. Like Robbie and Chrissie were setting out to make their own.

And Lydia knew, so deeply it seemed to be in the very marrow of her bones, that Granny Leslie's kind of second chance – seizing what she wanted in life without any care for what hurt she might do to others – just was not her way, could not be her way. And following closely on its heels came the realization that her love for Frank Everett had not died. If anything, it had strengthened and her longing for the chance to share that love with him, to build a life together, a home, a family.

She swallowed hard. That was not going to be, she told herself. She knew that now. But then the words of her mother's prayer came back to her: 'we will trust You for the outcome, for You know what is best for our truest happiness.' Yes, Lydia thought. That's what Chrissie does. That's what Mum does. So that's what I will do too. She gathered her thoughts and prayed.

'You know what I'd really like, Lord Jesus, but it's no good. I have to put him out of my mind. But I would like a second chance at love and marriage with a good honourable man, so that's what I'm asking You for.' The words her mother had prayed ran through her mind once again, but now Lydia made them her own prayer: 'And I will trust You for the outcome, for You know what is best for my truest happiness.'

And in her heart, there came peace so she was able to face her grandmother and smile.

'I am so grateful for your offer. It really helped me to work out what I should do. And the house is lovely. I would have loved to share it with you.' She paused, then seizing her courage, she offered, 'Chrissie would love it too. Maybe...'

'Humph, yes, well, I'm sure she would,' her grandmother said. 'Maybe she's got more sense than you.'

And then she poured out the tea.

CHAPTER 45

Chrissie glowed with happiness. And Lydia, remembering her brief moment of happiness at Danny's side the moment the minister pronounced that they were man and wife, knew that Chrissie's happiness would not be as fleeting as hers had been. Because beside Chrissie, the happiness shining out of him as much as it was from Chrissie, was Robbie, who had eyes only for his bride. Proud fit to burst, Lydia thought with an affectionate smile.

How very different from her own wedding. When the minister had said the words "man and wife" she had turned towards Danny, happiness surging through her that her dreams had come true, her face lifted expecting his kiss – and saw that he was looking beyond her, with a resigned look on his face, and then he had winked ruefully at the person who was the focus of his attention.

Lydia had looked and found an answering wink and a complicit grin on her brother Alec's face. It seemed once again that the two "big boys" were sharing something that left her out. Just like when they were children, and she was running after them, always trying to keep up but never quite succeeding.

Uncertainly she had turned back to Danny to see a matching shamefaced grin, then it was stripped from his face and he took her arm quite roughly.

'Right,' he said. 'That's done. I need a drink.'

But first there were the well-wishers and family to deal with. Danny was brusque, clearly keen to get away. The moment they were released, he was off, striding away in the direction of the hotel where the wedding reception was to be held, with Alec by his side.

When Lydia and her parents with the rest of their guests caught up with them, the two men were downing drink after drink, their laughter getting rougher and louder. She heard her mother say 'Oh dear' and shake her head.

Stung, Lydia had squared her shoulders and forced a smile on her face. Despite the horrid awareness that Danny and Alec had once more abandoned her and shut her out, she circulated round their guests, fielding the critical comments about her bridegroom, and dispensing sweet smiles that hid her hurt and the terrible betrayal she felt.

She looked now at Chrissie and Robbie, transparently happy with one another. Chrissie need have no fear that Robbie would hurt her as she had been. Danny had finally arrived drunk to their room in the hotel, long after their guests had gone and Lydia had given up and gone to bed. Her initiation into the physical side of their marriage had been brutal and shocking.

She had tried to make allowances. It was the drink, she told herself. Danny was not really like that. But when she had finally protested, he had slapped her. Then she saw the contempt in his eyes and knew that she had made a terrible mistake. Running after her brother and his friend, wanting to be part of their games and adventures, she had created an idealised, false picture of a hero that she had worshipped.

Chrissie loved Robbie – but she loved her Lord Jesus first and foremost. And that seemed to make a huge difference. Lydia knew her idol had had feet of clay and in the shattering of her fantasy, he had broken her heart and her confidence in herself.

Maybe correctly, she pondered, as she watched Chrissie and Robbie move among their guests, smiling and accepting congratulations. For she had done it again, hadn't she? She had let her heart be touched and had allowed herself to dream, once again, of love. Only to find she was mistaken.

Her eyes misted for a moment but she would not let her sorrow for her ruined life spoil this happy occasion.

'Mum!'

Lydia turned. Ewen, who had proudly played his part in the ceremony resplendent in Alec's Ross tartan kilt, was strutting proudly over to her. He came to a sudden halt, confusion plain on his face.

'Mum?' It was now a cry for help.

Granny Leslie was standing on the edge of the group, in her usual black coat and hat, and she was beckoning Ewen.

'Oh no,' Lydia gasped and took a quick step towards them. But a hand stopped her.

'Leave them.' It was Chrissie's voice. 'It will be all right. Look.'

And to Lydia's surprise, Granny Leslie was nodding approval.

'That's a fine kilt,' she said.

'It was Uncle Alec's,' Ewen said hesitantly.

'That's right,' Granny Leslie said. 'Grandpa Leslie had it made for him, his first grandson. So it's right that you should have it now. You're my first great-grandson.'

Ewen nodded uncertainly.

'Grandpa Leslie would be pleased to see you looking so fine.'

'There,' Chrissie whispered. 'I told you it would be all right.'

But Lydia had noticed that her mother and father were moving swiftly across the room to see what was happening.

'Mother,' Jean said, ready to leap to Ewen's defence, but Ewen was stumbling out a thank you before escaping. When he had gone, her mother glared at her.

'Well?' Granny Leslie challenged her. 'Didn't you expect to see me? I was invited.'

'Aye, you were,' David Ross said in a steady voice. 'And you are welcome.' He stretched out a hand to her. 'Will you come through to the tea with us?'

For a moment a deadly silence filled the room. Then Granny Leslie straightened up, back ramrod stiff. She took an unsteady step towards them. Then clearly making up her mind, she stepped forward. David Ross offered his arm to her and she took it. He turned to Jean and with a smile, offered the other to her.

'That's fine,' he said. 'The two Leslie lassies. I'm the luckiest man in the room!' And with a laugh, he bore them off into the room where the wedding tea was waiting.

Lydia let her breath out in a long sigh. She had not realised she had been holding it, but now it seemed all was well. Even between Granny Leslie and her father.

'Come on,' Chrissie said and linking arms with Lydia, led her through to the next room.

They found Granny Leslie installed in a comfortable chair with a table laden with delicious food in front of her. She looked up at the girls as they came in.

'Granny,' Lydia greeted her hesitantly.

'Your wee boy's looking fine,' her grandmother said abruptly, indicating Ewen. 'He looks like Robbie did when he was little. Same curly hair. He takes after our side of the family.'

'Well, I hope this one does,' Chrissie said, patting the bump. Lydia gasped. Surely her grandmother would say something acid and hurtful.

Granny Leslie looked at Chrissie. Chrissie looked back, holding her gaze equably. For a moment neither looked away, then Granny Leslie's gaze shifted to the crowd around Robbie.

'Lydia, will you go and get your brother?' It was a command.

Chrissie looked startled but Lydia, from years of practice, went to obey. She easily extricated Robbie from his friends and brought him back to where Chrissie was waiting with Granny Leslie.

'I hear you're planning on staying at Rose Street,' she began without preamble. 'What will you do when the baby comes?'

Chrissie and Robbie exchanged glances.

'Mum says we can stay,' Robbie began.

Granny Leslie humphed. 'That won't do,' she said. She pursed her lips in disapproval, then clearly coming to a decision she said, 'You'd better come to me. I'm rattling round that big house on my own and it will go to Robbie after my day anyway. I offered it to Lydia but she didn't have the sense to take the chance. What do you say?'

Chrissie's eyes widened, then she bent and impulsively hugged the old lady. 'Oh yes please!'

'Get away wi' you, girl,' Granny Leslie said but it was obvious that she was pleased.

There were tears in Chrissie's eyes.

'You go and enjoy your party,' Granny Leslie said. 'Then come over to me in the next few days and we'll sort it out.'

Chrissie hesitated.

'Go!' Granny Leslie commanded, and Chrissie and Robbie went.

Lydia stood as if frozen. Dumbfounded.

'Not a word,' her grandmother warned her, then reaching for her handbag, removed a tiny handkerchief with lace edging and surreptitiously dabbed the corners of her eyes. She carefully put the handkerchief back in her bag and looked up at Lydia.

'That was a surprise, wasn't it?'

She smiled then and Lydia saw suddenly the resemblance to her own mother – that same little mischievous twitch of the mouth. She hoped the family resemblance would not give her own satisfaction away. It had worked out exactly as she had hoped.

'Get me another cup of tea,' Granny Leslie commanded, back to form, and with a grin, Lydia went off to obey.

She found a group of Robbie's friends chatting excitedly beside the buffet.

'Soon!' one of them was insisting.

'He would surely come back home for New Year,' another said.

'Well, what I heard is that they're moving on from Fraserburgh but they don't know where yet.'

'It was a dream that got him to Fraserburgh,' someone said. 'I wonder if that's God's guiding now.' He caught Lydia's interested gaze. 'Jock Troup,' he explained. 'We're expecting him home soon.'

'Aye, and his team,' someone else added. 'Davey Cordiner's gone back to Peterhead but Willie Bruce and that English lad have stayed with him...'

'Everett,' another put in. 'The English Baptist minister. Frank Everett. He's still with Jock.'

'Anyway,' the first man explained, 'Jock is due home before long and his team will come with him so we can expect great things!'

And the crowd, all young fishermen who had been converted as a result of Jock Troup's ministry in Yarmouth, began excitedly talking about the strengthening revival in Wick once Jock got home.

But Lydia's head was whirling. She did not care about Jock Troup coming home. But bringing Frank Everett with him? That was a different matter entirely.

She still longed to see him. But what was the point? He was not free. Lydia twisted the knife in the wound: maybe he would bring his wife with him. She hoped she would be able to simply hide away so she would not see them and be hurt any more.

CHAPTER 46

As the train chugged along the Aberdeenshire coast heading south, Frank sat with his friends, determined to go with them where the Lord led – even though he felt every mile was leading him in quite the wrong direction.

Time, he reminded himself. The Lord was in charge and it was only a matter of time before he got to Wick and would see Lydia again. Jock's parents were expecting him home for the New Year weekend and that was only a week away. But still Frank felt his impatience tug at its leash.

To distract himself, he thought back to the extraordinary scenes of the previous night. The farewell service in the Congregational Church in Fraserburgh had been a rousing end to their ministry there with every pew packed with people squeezed in for a last glimpse of Jock. Two local ministers – Reverend William Gilmour of the Baptist Church and the Congregational minister Reverend Thomas Johnstone – had paid tribute to Jock and the work he had done in the town. But every time mention was made of their imminent departure, there were interruptions and emotional outbursts from the congregation. Men and women wept like children.

But Jock was adamant. A group of representatives had come from Dundee to meet him. They had discussed the possibility of him leading an evangelistic campaign in the city. And a little later, while Jock and his team were praying for guidance, the formal invitation had arrived. So they were headed south to Dundee.

As the final service in Fraserburgh closed, the congregation rose and sang with heartfelt sincerity 'God be with you till we meet again' and Frank had felt such a pang. He remembered it had been the last hymn they had sung in Yarmouth, in the Methodist Church, with Lydia there in the congregation, and he had sung it to her, and for her, with his whole heart.

But why had she run from him? He had puzzled over that, over and over, these past weeks. Had his embrace been unwelcome, frightening? She had seemed truly distressed. He wondered whether her experience of marriage to her brother's friend had been so bad that she was afraid of men, afraid of physical contact.

And just at that moment, his memory opened a crack and he remembered a man making a contemptuous reference to a young woman named Lydia. 'Danny was making the most of his opportunities – but he got caught and Dad forced him to marry Lydia. It didn't mean a thing to him.'

The crack widened and Frank remembered he had been called on by a young officer to go in to see a soldier arrested for refusing an order to return to battle. His friend had died and he had refused to leave him.

A broken man, like so many others awaiting the firing squad, he was under guard in the old farmhouse but, by some strange chance, his brother had been there and the officer had out of compassion allowed them time together.

As the train rattled over the rails in Scotland, Frank was back in Flanders, the memory vivid. Bourlon Wood, 1917. The man under guard was Lydia's older brother Alec. The younger man was Robbie. The charge would undoubtedly have held up at the court-martial and the penalty would have been a shameful death. But a stray shell from the enemy had hit the farmhouse, taking out the room where Alec was held. He remembered his awkward attempt at comforting a distraught Robbie, clawing at the ruins to find his brother's shattered body. Because the officer, dead too in the rubble, had not had time to write the charge, there was no record of Alec's arrest. There would never be a court-martial now, nor its inevitable shameful verdict. Robbie's parents were spared the shame.

And finally Robbie had realised that in this terrible tragedy there was a glimmer of blessing. Frank had thought they had parted amicably, shaken hands and gone their separate ways. So why now was Robbie so against him? Why did he not want Lydia to have anything to do with him? Surely there had been nothing in his behaviour that day that would cause a caring brother any concern? And there had been nothing in Robbie's behaviour either that Frank could remember that would damage him. In fact, the opposite was true. Robbie had been compassionate and forgiving. The brothers had reached a genuine reconciliation and Alec had found a measure of peace.

Frank continued to puzzle over it. What harm could he do to Robbie or Lydia now? Was there something more to remember, something about Robbie? But try as he might, Frank could not bring any more to his recollection and his thoughts slid effortlessly to Lydia.

What her brother Alec had said suggested that her brief marriage had not been grounded in mutual love and respect. It was possible she feared all men were alike. Surely he could find the gentleness to reassure her?

He longed for her with a longing he had never imagined possible and now he turned to the Lord with it. 'For I need to do Your work,' he said in his heart. 'Keep Lyddie safe and if it is Your will, let us be together. Amen.'

CHAPTER 47

When Lydia returned home after the wedding, the house seemed silent and empty without the cheerful presence of Chrissie and Robbie. She smiled to herself at the thought. Just a few weeks ago she was consumed with resentment focused on the presence of those two, and now she missed them!

She went up to her room and removed her wedding finery. As she put her new frock in the wardrobe, she caught sight of herself in the mirror. Her mother was right. She was getting too thin.

'You're wasting away,' Jean had said. 'This will never do. You must keep your strength up, if only for Ewen's sake.'

Lydia was grateful that her mother, tactful as ever, had not probed for the reason. It felt ridiculous at 25 to be suffering from an adolescent crush. Unrequited love! Such nonsense. Yet, as she put her best coat and hat in her wardrobe, catching sight again of herself and the sad pinched face, she had to admit that it was the pain of unrequited love that ate into her. And hearing that Frank would be accompanying Jock Troup on his return to Wick simply made the pain worse. Seeing the man she loved – knowing he could not be hers – would be unbearable.

What was she going to do? She caught the rising panic and firmly squashed it. Surely Wick was a big enough town to hide in, she told herself. Their paths did not need to meet. She would take pains to avoid him. She had not been accompanying Chrissie and Robbie to the revival meetings so nobody would be surprised by her absence.

Yes, she decided firmly, that was what she was going to do. Just get on with her life. Mind her own business. Ignore his presence in town. It had nothing to do with her. (And hide, her treacherous heart mocked her. Hide like a frightened fieldmouse.)

'Are you ready for a cup of tea?' her mother called up the stairs.

Lydia squared her shoulders. It was time to get on with her life.

'Yes, Mum,' she called and went downstairs.

Ewen had returned from the wedding with her parents and was still proudly strutting about in the kilt.

'I think maybe you should change,' Lydia suggested. 'Especially if you want to go out to play?'

Ewen paused and considered, brow furrowed.

'You don't want to spoil Uncle Alec's lovely kilt,' she added.

But Ewen now looked puzzled.

'I don't know,' he said. 'It's a fine kilt and I like it, but I don't like Uncle Alec so I'm not sure I should like his kilt.'

'Whatever do you mean?' his grandfather asked in surprise. 'Alec was a hero. You know that. He was a fine young man, taken in the flower of his youth in the Great War, and he is a sad loss to this family. We all like him. He was a good lad...'

'He wasn't good to Uncle Robbie,' Ewen put in truculently. 'I like Uncle Robbie but Uncle Alec was bad to Uncle Robbie so I don't like Uncle Alec.'

Jean, coming in from the kitchen with a laden tea tray, exchanged a worried glance with Lydia. She put the tray down on the table and as she busied herself setting out cups on saucers, she said to Ewen, 'You never met your Uncle Alec. It's maybe a wee bit unfair not to like someone you've never met.'

But Ewen stuck out his small chin mutinously.

'I've met Uncle Robbie,' he insisted, 'and he's always been good to me. But Uncle Alec was bad to him...'

'Wait a minute,' David Ross interrupted. 'What's this about Alec being bad to him? This is a lot of nonsense. I never saw him being anything but a good brother – and a good son.'

'That's all you know!' Ewen answered back with surprising rebellion.

'Enough, Ewen,' Lydia stepped in. 'Off you go upstairs and take that kilt off. I'll come up in a minute and put it away. You get into your play clothes, then you can come back and have a scone and jam before you go out.'

The mention of food worked its magic and Ewen did as he was bid.

'What on earth was that about?' David Ross asked Jean and Lydia in puzzlement.

Jean nodded to Lydia who correctly read the signal and rose from her chair.

'I'll go and help Ewen,' she said. 'Mum can tell you.' And she left the room gratefully.

Jean carried David's tea over to him and perched on the arm of his chair.

'What it's about is that Ewen was afraid he'd be seasick when he went out on the boat with you and that he'd let you down,' Jean began. 'He was afraid you and he would fall out like you did with Robbie.'

'Oh, the poor wee laddie,' David exclaimed. 'I never realised...'

'Well, you see, your sisters called last week,' Jean explained. 'They made sure Ewen knew that Robbie had been seasick and that it could just as easily happen to him.'

'They're a pair of troublemakers,' David said. 'I'm sorry, my love. You should have told me. I'd have spoken to him.'

'And what could you have said to him?' Jean's eyes flashed with sudden indignation as she recalled what had happened when Robbie returned ill from his first outing on the boat. 'If he was seasick he'd be no good to you and he'd know it. Like Robbie did – like Robbie has all these years!'

David patted her hand, his face sorrowful.

'I know I did wrong by Robbie, my love. But I've changed. The Lord has changed me and I would never do anything to hurt my family now. I've spoken with Robbie and he has forgiven me. We've made a fresh start and the Lord is blessing us.'

Jean leaned in and kissed his cheek.

'I know, my dear. And I am very glad. It was time it got sorted out.'

David nodded in agreement.

Jean collected her thoughts and began, 'But did you ever ask Robbie what happened that one time he went out on the boat with you? What it was that made him ill?'

David stared at her. 'What was there to ask? Alec came to me and said the boy was mortal bad with seasickness but I didn't need to worry myself, he'd take care of him. And he did. When I went past the little boat, Robbie was hunched up in it, wrapped in blankets, green and ill, and vomiting. It was plain as could be. He was seasick. Nobody needed to ask.'

'Exactly,' Jean said. 'You trusted Alec when maybe you shouldn't have been so quick to dismiss Robbie.' She raised a hand at his instant protest. 'Wait. You need to hear this.'

When he settled again, his perplexity clear on his face, Jean explained. 'Lydia and I were in the kitchen and Robbie was in here with Ewen. He'd offered to talk to Ewen, to reassure him. And he did. Nobody could have done it better. Because Robbie told him that he'd never been seasick.' Jean repeated it. 'Never in his life. So Ewen didn't have to fear being seasick either.'

'But I saw him!' David protested. 'He was green and vomiting and shaking and... and Alec wasn't bad to him! He looked after him all the rest of the voyage so none of the rest of us had to.'

'Ah yes,' Jean said. 'It was easy for Alec.'

'What do you mean?'

'Alec was cook, wasn't he?'

David nodded.

'He fed Robbie something bad that made him sick. Then he told you Robbie was seasick and made sure you didn't get a chance to go near him and find out different.'

Jean watched as David absorbed what she had said. He sat, shaking his head.

'I don't believe it. I can't believe Alec would...'

'Did you never wonder how Robbie managed to work on the trawlers, and now on the boat with you, with never a sign of seasickness?'

'I just thought he'd grown out of it,' David said slowly. He set down his cup and saucer and took both Jean's hands in his. 'I know what I did – what I said – to Robbie and about Robbie that time was wrong and it drove a wedge between him and me...'

'And you and me,' Jean put in softly.

David looked into her eyes and saw the sorrow there.

'Aye, my love. That too.' He sighed deeply. 'But this...'

'You idolised Alec,' Jean said gently. 'You did. You made an idol of him and that's what drove a wedge through our family, and between you and me. All the time, it was Alec, Alec, Alec... There was no room in your heart for any of the rest of us.'

David shook his head but his face was troubled.

'I always felt you weren't able to really see Alec for who he was, what he was. He was your golden boy who could do no wrong,' Jean continued. 'I saw his taunts and jibes against Robbie, how he always managed to put him in the wrong when you were there to see.'

'I never saw any of it,' David protested weakly, running a hand over his face as if to wipe away what he was hearing.

'I know. But I did. I saw it,' Jean said. 'It seemed as if Alec wasn't content with being your favourite. He had to make sure nobody else got a particle of your love, especially Robbie.'

'But why didn't you say anything?' David asked her.

'Would you have listened?' Jean replied sadly. 'We were hardly talking to one another after I saw the state Robbie was in after that first trip. I should have realised that was more than simple seasickness! If *I* didn't guess...'

David patted her hand again and sighed.

'It seems neither of us was seeing clearly,' he reassured her. 'I'm sorry. You know that. What do you think I should do now – tell Robbie I know? Try to put it right?'

'Robbie made Ewen promise not to tell,' Jean told him. 'He's not wanting to taint Alec's memory now.'

'Robbie's a good lad,' David said gruffly. 'And I never saw it.'

'Alec made sure you never saw it,' Jean said gently.

'I fear that is true,' David agreed.

'Lydia and I only heard because the kitchen door was a wee bit open.'

David's eyes twinkled. 'Is that so?'

Jean smiled back at him. 'Oh, away with you! Yes, of course. We both wanted to know what Robbie had to say to Ewen.'

'Well, that seems fair enough to me,' David said with a smile, but then his face grew sombre again. 'I'm glad we know now.'

'But we mustn't let on we know,' Jean insisted gently. 'It's got to come from Robbie. When he's ready to tell us.'

'If he's ever ready,' David said sadly. He kissed Jean's cheek then rose to his feet. 'I'm away for a walk round the harbour. You've given me a lot to think about.'

Jean nodded and remained quietly where she was. There had been major changes in their lives this year already. She wondered what else God had in store for them.

CHAPTER 48

After the sharp cleanness of Fraserburgh and the familiarity of the fisherfolk who had attended meetings in Yarmouth, Dundee was an eye-opener. An industrial city, centre of manufacturing and trade with the Empire, it was a thriving metropolis.

The Steeple Church – St Clement's Parish Church – was the main centre of activity for Jock Troup and his team, and it was obvious from the start that their reputation and the news of the evangelical revival elsewhere had gone before them. At the afternoon service on Boxing Day, just two days after they had arrived, the big church was packed long before it was time for meetings to start. Every pew was crammed full and even after extra seats had been brought in and filled, determined people stood in the aisles and sat on ledges, on the steps of the pulpit, in corridors and passageways, refusing to be turned away.

Again, ministers from the town were present to show their support. Herbert Lockyer, superintendent of Dundee Tent Mission, presided at several services, and seated alongside Jock Troup, Willie Bruce and Davey Cordiner in the pulpit were Reverend Crichton from the United Free Church and Reverend Smith from Ward Road Baptist Church.

Frank, also squeezed into the pulpit ready to move into the vestry to counsel enquirers and lead them to Christ, was impressed by how his friends simply followed the pattern they had developed in Fraserburgh.

First Willie Bruce spoke, then Davey Cordiner. Each gave his testimony, telling of their lives prior to the revival and of how Christ had found them and saved them. The congregation listened attentively but when Jock stood up, it was as if the people in the pews braced themselves for his message.

Even after nearly three months of intense preaching, Jock was still a powerful presence. As he gave his testimony and then preached on a chosen text, he strode backwards and forwards on the pulpit platform, holding his Bible tightly and lifting it up high when he wanted to emphasise a point. There was fire and deep concern for the salvation of his audience in his address, but at times his voice could hardly be heard.

A doctor in Fraserburgh had warned Jock that he could not go on at the relentless pace he was driving himself. A breakdown was inevitable, he said, if Jock would not rest. But Jock, consumed with concern for the peril of those perishing for lack of Gospel preaching, would not rest.

As Frank listened to the usually loud and energetic voice of his friend, he could hear the results of the strain. From time to time, Jock's voice showed signs of breaking and as he forced his way on, there was a new hoarseness.

But he did not stop. On he went, expending huge amounts of energy, striding about, his arms waving, and the deeply felt words surging out of him and into the hearts and minds of his listeners.

'Do not delay!' was the burden of his message and when he came to a close, he added to that appeal with a fervent prayer. Then, as usual, he invited any that were as yet undecided to go to the vestry where Frank and Willie Bruce and Davey Cordiner would speak with them and offer spiritual guidance.

As first one, then another rose from the pews, Frank rose too and moved towards the vestry, squeezing past the folk who clung to every space that they might hear Jock.

As he left, he heard Reverend Smith announce that the Steeple Church had been placed at the disposal of the evangelists. To more cheers and applause, he added that Jock and his friends had been persuaded to remain in Dundee till Thursday.

Thursday, Frank thought. And then where? With God leading Jock, they could be going anywhere. But Jock's parents were expecting him home for New Year, and now New Year was only a few days away. Jock's home was Wick. And Wick meant Lyddie.

Was it possible? Would he be with her again in just a few days? He walked into the vestry. Willie and Davey were already hard at work. Frank set his own concerns firmly aside and plunged into the work.

CHAPTER 49

'It's no place for a young married woman,' Granny Leslie announced with a disapproving sniff. 'And certainly not one in Chrissie's condition!'

Seeing Robbie about to leap into the fray in her defence, Chrissie stepped in first. She was getting good at this, she thought. She had had plenty of practice already in the few days that they had been staying with Mary-Anne. The elderly lady was set in her ways – and in her opinions on men, which did not go down well with Robbie though he was trying hard to live peaceably with his grandmother.

Any slight – real or imagined – towards Chrissie, however, was a different matter and he would defend her, all guns blazing. This glorious display of love and protection, though, was not helping the cause of harmony so Chrissie frequently needed lavish supplies of oil to pour on troubled waters, as now.

'The New Year bonfire is not going to be the same as in the past,' Chrissie said. 'Thanks to the revival, it's going to be an open-air meeting, not...'

'An excuse for drunkenness and wild behaviour,' Mary-Anne said.

'That's right!' Chrissie replied cheerfully. 'It will be quite different. For example, the Salvation Army band will be there.'

'Well, that is a first,' Mary-Anne sniffed again.

'And all the wood for the bonfire has been donated, not stolen, so this year there'll be no trouble about that,' Chrissie added.

In previous years one of the characteristics of the huge bonfire was the stolen barrels and dustbins that made up a large proportion of the fuel, much to the annoyance of local residents. Not to mention the resulting arrests.

'It will be quite safe,' Robbie assured her. 'If it wasn't, Mum wouldn't let Lydia and Ewen attend.'

Before Mary-Anne could comment adversely on this titbit of news, Chrissie continued, 'And then tomorrow night, we're all going to the Salvation Army Social in the Barrogill Hall. You could come too.'

'Humph,' Mary-Anne sniffed. 'All this gadding about. When I was expecting my children, I stayed decently at home.'

'It's different now,' Robbie told her. 'Times have changed.'

'Maybe, and maybe not for the better!'

'Trust Granny Leslie to have the last word!' Robbie laughed later when he and Chrissie were alone.

Though there had been a few fireworks and awkwardnesses to sort out when they moved in, Chrissie was confident that it would all work out. She was glad that they would have several months to get used to one another before the baby arrived.

She loved the room Mary-Anne had given them. Light and airy from the tall windows but warmed by a fire in the pretty fireplace, there was generous storage for their clothes in wardrobe and tallboy.

And just next door was the room for the baby. Chrissie and Mary-Anne had spent some time up in the attics, searching out a cot and a little chest of drawers that would furnish the room.

They had had a chance to talk and get to know one another better.

'She's fine,' Chrissie told Robbie. 'You just need to know how to get along with her.'

'Give in to every whim, more like,' Robbie said. But Chrissie shook her head.

'No, that's completely the wrong way,' she said. 'Too many folk have done that and she's got no respect for anyone that does. I don't and that's why we get along fine.'

'I don't think I've got your nerve,' he told Chrissie fondly. 'I'm a wee mouse compared with you!'

Down in the kitchen, Mary-Anne heard their giggles. Automatically her lips pursed in disapproval but then she relaxed and sat down in the battered armchair by the range. She remembered that kind of laughter when she was courting – Murdo Ross, though, not William Leslie.

Murdo had been what her mother called 'lightsome' – a cheerful, light-hearted man who could always make her laugh, and who had won her heart. Won it and trashed it. So she had no smiles left when William Leslie came along. Even in their wedding photograph, she had had no smile.

That Chrissie was a sharp one, she pondered. Chrissie had noticed, she was sure of it, when they were looking at the family pictures the other day but then, wisely, had said nothing. She had a wisdom beyond her years.

When she had commented on it, Chrissie had given her usual self-deprecating laugh and declared that any wisdom she had worth anything came from her Lord Jesus. As if he was someone real. Someone she knew. Someone related to her and involved in her life.

Mary-Anne sighed. It seemed to have done Chrissie a lot of good, this revival in Yarmouth. Maybe Robbie too, though time would tell.

Time. She sighed again. It was all right for these young ones but it was too late for her.

CHAPTER 50

The revival in Dundee was certainly gathering strength but there was also strong opposition. One of the local ministers, Reverend W. Major Scott, preached fiercely against the methods of the revivalists and his sermon was reported in detail in the local newspaper, the *Dundee Courier*.

But Jock, Willie and Davey continued undaunted. The minister and elders of the Steeple Church remained constant in their support and congregations kept growing. Admittedly some of the number was composed of sightseers and the curious, but weekday meetings were still full to overflowing with every seat in the building occupied a good half-hour before the meeting was due to begin. Doorways were thronged and the choir area overflowed so that the organist was surrounded by people cramming into whatever space was available. It made it more difficult for Jock and his team and the local ministers to reach the pulpit as they had to carefully thread their way through the crush.

And Jock, despite the threat to his health and his vocal cords, was still in fine form, swaying his audience with the sincerity of his message of hope. At the end of the meetings, many folk remained for private counselling and spiritual guidance or for a public prayer meeting, and so the days went on with more and more people turning to the Lord.

Frank stood shoulder to shoulder with his friends as they preached and prayed and counselled, rejoicing with them over the harvest of souls. But when he heard that Jock had been persuaded to remain in Dundee over the weekend rather than head for Wick, he had difficulty hiding his disappointment.

His time seemed to be running out. He would need to come to a decision soon about the direction of his life and he knew it was not to be in the company of the Scottish revivalists for much longer. There was a congregation in England waiting for him and he should return to resume his ministry in the New Year.

But he had hoped he might be returning with Lydia at his side. Or at the least with her promised to him. Now that bright and lovely hope was beginning to dim. It was an effort of will to continue with Jock and his team, fully pulling his weight, as wholehearted as he could be. And he knew he was being tested. Did he love his Lord more than even Lydia? Was he willing to obey Him, even if it meant turning his back on the lovely future he had thought might be possible for them?

In the quiet moments when he got time alone, Frank searched his heart and prayed. It was, he realised, a mini-Gethsemane – when he had to reach his own 'not my will, but Yours' if he was to be able to continue as the Lord's man. And as the year came to a close, he was glad of the pressure of work undertaken by Jock and his team to keep his mind busy and his prayers for others.

It was not unusual for Jock to speak at three services on a Sunday evening. In Dundee that included a 6 p.m. service at Hilltown United Free Church. A taxi was waiting outside to take them on to

St Clements for a Gospel meeting at 8 p.m., and then there were arrangements for overflow services. The hunger for the Gospel seemed never-ending.

But at last, Jock let it be known that they would be leaving Dundee on the second of January, travelling to Inverness en route for Wick.

At the loud cries that greeted this announcement, Jock assured the congregation that he would be back in a fortnight to resume the work in Dundee.

'I don't think I'll be coming back with you,' Frank told him when they were alone later. 'I think I must go back to England to my own work.'

'But you'll come to Wick first?' Jock enquired.

'If that's where we're going!' Frank laughed. He was so used by now to Jock's willingness to change his plans as the Lord directed him, but this time he was praying he might reach Wick and Lydia before it was time to turn round and go south again.

CHAPTER 51

'Mum! Mum!' Ewen was clamouring for Lydia's attention.

She unwrapped his scarf from his neck and helped him out of his warm coat. His round face was red with the cold and he was ready for his tea, but there was clearly something troubling him.

'Mum!' he insisted.

'Yes, my love,' Lydia replied, kneeling down to untie his laces and ease his feet in their thick socks out of his boots.

'Mum, Alistair Stevens says his Dad's going to take him to the bonfire!' Ewen declared in an aggrieved voice.

'That's nice,' Lydia said cautiously, wondering where this was going.

'He says I can't go 'cos I haven't got a Dad!' The wee boy's lip trembled. 'And I want to go!'

Lydia rocked back on her heels and looked into her son's troubled face. For the first time it came home to her that the lack of a father could be a problem for him. Till now, she had thought she was sufficient, but he was growing up and needed male company and support. Lydia had hoped her father and brother would provide what was needed but with Robbie married and a child of his own on the way, he would be occupied with his own little family. And her father was not getting any younger...

'Ewen, love, I'm sorry.' She reached out to give him a hug but he bridled and shrugged out of her reach.

'Here, here, what's all this?' David Ross came out into the hallway. He looked at Lydia's stricken face. 'Ewen, have you been upsetting your mother?'

'No, no,' Lydia protested, getting to her feet. She ruffled her son's hair affectionately. 'He's absolutely right, though.'

Ewen slumped in disappointment.

'It's about the bonfire,' Lydia explained as she ushered Ewen into the sitting room, her father following them through. 'Ewen would like to go. One of the boys in his class is going. Probably a lot of the others too. But it's not somewhere I can take him...'

'And I don't have a Dad to take me,' Ewen put in truculently.

'Well, that's true,' David Ross said, adding 'for the moment.' He looked at his daughter and saw the stain of colour rise in her cheeks. He nodded gently. 'Aye, well, we can't get you a Dad in time for the bonfire, I don't think. That's a bit short notice.' He smiled at Lydia, gently teasing. 'But maybe in time...?'

Lydia shook her head and made a hurried escape into the kitchen to help her mother. She heard her father say to Ewen, 'But maybe Uncle Robbie would take you to the bonfire. What do you say to that?'

'He'd do,' Ewen said ungraciously.

'I thought you liked your Uncle Robbie?'

'Oh I do,' said Ewen. 'But a Dad would be better. Then I'd be like the other boys and they wouldn't tease me 'cos I've just got a Mum. Mummy's boy!' he said in disgust, echoing the mockery of his schoolmates.

And Lydia, coming back into the room with the tea tray at that moment, heard the disgust and misery in her son's voice and her heart turned over. Was her adamant refusal to consider remarriage going to come between her and her son?

Her mother, coming into the room behind her carrying the plate of fresh-baked and buttered scones, put a comforting hand on her arm.

'Let the Lord take it,' she said softly. 'He knows what's best.'

Lydia set the tea tray down on the table in the window and stared out at the chilly scene. If the Lord knew best, why had He let her give her heart only for it to be dashed to pieces, again? She settled into her chair, her face troubled. One thing she was sure of, *she* did not know what was for the best. She had tried, always tried to do what was good, what she thought was for the best, but it had not turned out happily for her. First Danny, then Frank. Betrayal, twice.

Or maybe it was her fault? Maybe she had no sense where men were concerned and always picked the wrong ones? She accepted the cup of tea from her mother and sipped gratefully, but her mind was whirling. Could it be her way was no good but there *was* a better way – the way her mother and Chrissie seemed to live their lives, handing everything over to the Lord Jesus and seemingly able to then trust Him with whatever was worrying them?

I don't know, Lord Jesus. Lydia put words to her prayer in the silence of her heart. You know I don't know. I don't know You the way Mum and Chrissie do, but I'd like to and I want to try their way now. My way never worked. So here I am. Be my Lord like You are to them. Help me to trust You. Sort it all out for me, for me and for Ewen. You're in charge, from now on.

She looked up to find her mother's eyes upon her. She gave her a reassuring smile and was glad to see that Jean smiled back.

CHAPTER 52

The mountains were white with snow and Frank craned his neck to take in as much of the majestic scenery as the compartment window would allow. It was stuffy in the train with Jock and Davey Cordiner and Willie Bruce but obviously freezing outside. But this was the true Highlands, Frank thought, and more beautiful and majestic even than he had imagined.

When Jock had announced that they were leaving Dundee, his heart had leapt and he still could barely believe that he was on his way north at last. North to Lydia and a major turning point in his life.

When the train reached Inverness, there was a deputation awaiting them and Jock was prevailed upon to speak to the crowd.

Frank, standing with Willie Bruce on the platform of the railway station, found worry rushing at him. What if Jock was persuaded to stay and conduct a campaign here in Inverness? The harvest was ripe and the labourers few – and here they were with an inspired evangelist who could win such a harvest of souls in this place. But oh, Frank longed to get back on the train and get to Wick and Lydia.

Battle raged within him. He wanted Jock to hurry up. Stop speaking. Get back in the train.

'Seek ye first the kingdom of God.'

Frank paused. Seek first God's Kingdom. Obey God first. That was what he had promised to do when he first came to Christ so many years ago. And here was a test. Would he continue to choose Christ? He reached in his pocket for his New Testament. The verses he wanted came from somewhere in Matthew. Quietly he leafed through the pages till he found them. Chapter 6, verses 33–34.

'But seek ye first the kingdom of God, and his righteousness; and all these things shall be added unto you. Take therefore no thought for the morrow...'

This came in a section where the Lord Jesus was teaching his disciples and a great crowd of seekers. Frank scanned back a few verses and felt peace settle in him as the Word of God spoke to him anew. Here was reassurance that his Heavenly Father loved him and knew what was in his heart. There was no need to worry because God knew what he needed, what he longed for. God wasn't a God who gave stones to people who needed bread, or snakes to folk who were hungry for fish. He loved them far too much and He wanted only what was good for them.

If a life shared with Lydia was one of the good things God had planned for him, then worrying about getting to Wick in a hurry was not going to assist the progress of God's plans. *'Therefore do not worry about tomorrow.'* The words seemed to repeat in Frank's mind. Instead he should 'seek God's kingdom' and trust Him for everything else.

It was with a calm and happy heart that Frank joined in the Redemptorist hymns and talked with the people around him. God was in charge of his life and all would be well.

CHAPTER 53

'It's hard to believe,' Jean agreed. 'But I was there myself and saw it with my own eyes.'

As Jean spoke to her mother, seated a little grumpily but present nonetheless at the table in the Barrogill Hall at the Salvation Army's New Year Social, she pondered over the many changes she had seen with her own eyes in the past year. The changes in David and Robbie, all for the good. The change in Lydia, squaring up to life, but with a new deeper sadness. Not a change for the better there unfortunately and Jean felt helpless to do anything about it. Until Lydia shared what was troubling her... and that did not seem likely. Another sad change in her daughter.

Jean roused her spirits with the thought of Robbie and Chrissie's happiness and the apparent good influence they were having on her mother. When Mary-Anne had appeared in the Hall, Jean and Lydia had made straight for her side, their first thought that there was an emergency and their help was needed. Mary-Anne would never otherwise have appeared in a public place on an occasion like this, but knowing they would be here, it was the only place she would be able to find them that night.

'Is something the matter?' Jean had asked urgently. 'Is Chrissie all right?'

Mary-Anne had waved her hand in dismissal of the notion and stepped forward to allow Chrissie and Robbie to file in behind her. Jean's jaw dropped in surprise.

'That one persuaded me,' Mary-Anne said shortly, nodding at Chrissie, who grinned happily. 'She said it was a respectable occasion, under the auspices of the Salvation Army. Well, I'd heard about the bonfire and what a change that was, so I just thought I'd take a look in to see for myself.'

Her family exchanged amused glances, hastily hidden.

'You'd better go off to your friends,' Mary-Anne commanded Chrissie and Robbie and they grinned and fled. She let Jean and Lydia usher her to a seat at a table, graciously inclining her head in acknowledgement of people she knew. People, Jean noticed, who gaped in surprise for a moment then responded with cautiously welcoming smiles.

Once settled in her place from where she could view the proceedings, Granny Leslie spotted Ewen playing chase with his friends between the tables. For a moment her mouth pursed in disapproval, then she shook her head.

'What is it, mother?' Jean asked.

'Ach, I'm getting old,' she growled. 'And times are changing.' She seemed to gather herself together, sitting bolt upright in her chair. 'Now, tell me about this bonfire.'

So Jean did.

'And you all went to it?' Mary-Anne queried in surprise.

'We were assured it would be safe,' Lydia said. 'And it was.'

'It was more like an open-air meeting than the New Year bonfire Wick used to have,' Jean put in.

'Well, I never,' Mary-Anne said. 'I'd never have believed it.'

As I would never have believed you would attend this gathering, Lydia thought. Then the Salvation Army struck up a lively tune and the crowd thronging the Hall began to sing. Keeping one eye on Ewen, Lydia allowed herself to enjoy the music. The words were of reassurance, of God's love and saving grace, and Lydia felt them wash over her, gently soothing her. She was glad she had come, though at first she was determined to stay at home.

'Please, Lyddie,' Chrissie had said. 'We'll all be there so you won't be on your own. It's the New Year. A new start...' Head cocked like a little robin, her bright eyes fixed on Lydia, Chrissie's loving gaze had weakened Lydia's resolve.

As planned she had kept close to home since she heard the news that Jock Troup would be returning to Wick for the New Year, bringing Frank Everett with him. He was the last person Lydia wanted to meet, she told herself. (The only person she wanted to see, her treacherous heart insisted.) The Salvation Army Social at the Barrogill Hall was the kind of event Jock Troup and his team of evangelists would attend.

'I can't,' she told Chrissie.

'Why not?' came the typically blunt reply.

'Oh Chrissie...' Lydia wailed.

Chrissie's eyes narrowed. 'What is it?'

'I'm just being silly,' Lydia said. 'Never mind me. I just don't want to go.'

'Yes, you do,' Chrissie said. 'So what's stopping you?'

Lydia flapped a hand. 'It's nothing. I told you. I'm just being silly.'

'Silly,' Chrissie repeated thoughtfully. 'You're not the silly type, so what could you be silly about, I wonder?'

Lydia shook her head but a faint blush began in her cheeks.

Chrissie's gaze sharpened. 'Aha!' she declared. 'There's somebody you don't want to see. Am I right?'

Lydia shook her head vehemently.

'Or somebody you do want to see very much...' Chrissie pondered aloud as Lydia continued to shake her head, the colour rising more deeply now.

'Yes,' Chrissie announced. 'That's it. So who is it?' She laughed that clear joyous sound but Lydia's eyes began to fill with tears.

'What am I getting wrong?' Chrissie murmured to herself. She offered Lydia a handkerchief to mop up the tears. 'Well, I don't know, but if you don't want to come you don't have to. We'll take Ewen with us and your Mum and Dad will be there too. It'll be a grand evening. Just a pity that Jock Troup won't be there. That would make it perfect!'

'But I thought he was coming home for New Year,' Lydia queried in surprise. 'I heard some of Robbie's friends at your wedding saying...'

'No,' Chrissie said. 'They had another change of plan and they're staying in Dundee a bit longer. We haven't heard when they're due here.' With sudden comprehension she grinned mischievously and said, 'So you'd be safe enough coming with us tonight.'

Lydia blushed.

'So it's still that man?' Chrissie teased. 'The English minister?'

'Frank,' Lydia whispered. 'Yes.'

'Oh well, never you mind,' Chrissie said comfortingly. 'The good Lord knows what you need. He loves you and He'll sort it all out for you for the best. You just trust in Him.'

'Oh I try, Chrissie!' Lydia said. 'I do try. I've handed it all over to Him...'

'Well, there you are then,' Chrissie declared, satisfied. 'Now leave it with Him. And come to the Salvation Army Social with us tonight. They're not due back yet so you'll be safe enough. You can relax and enjoy yourself.'

And now, several hours later, she was glad that she had listened to Chrissie. Glad that she had trusted in God. That she was safe. She had enjoyed the joyful hymns and joined in with a new sincerity. The words seemed to make more sense to her and Lydia felt that her faith had revived as well as her trust in God. So she did as Chrissie had bid and relaxed and enjoyed herself.

Ewen seemed to be enjoying the Social too. There was quite a number of youngsters present, including his best/worst friend Alistair Stevens. The two had just started a game of chase around the tables, getting in the way of the ladies serving the tea.

'Ewen!' Lydia called, but over the cheerful hubbub of conversation she could not make him hear her. She rose with a smile to her mother and grandmother and went to fetch him.

But Ewen had other ideas. Seeing his mother approaching, he sent her a mischievous grin.

'Can't catch me!' he called and dived for cover under one of the long trestle tables.

Determined to retrieve her son, Lydia strode in his direction only to hear his voice from further away on one side.

'I'm here!'

She turned and spotted his delighted grin bobbing up from under a long white tablecloth before he vanished once again. Someone laughed and Lydia joined in. If Ewen wanted a game...

At last he broke from cover and raced down the open space between the tables down the length of the Hall towards the front door. Lydia, laughing, turned and hared after him, catching him by his collar.

He laughed up at her. 'You're too fast for me, Mum!'

'That's right,' she told him, smiling into his eyes. 'And don't you forget it!'

At that moment, a cheer went up from the crowd. Holding firmly on to Ewen with one hand, Lydia turned to see what had prompted it. There in the now open doorway stood the stocky figure of Jock Troup. And as Lydia registered his unexpected return, she found herself gazing in shock straight into the eyes of Frank Everett.

CHAPTER 54

'Lyddie,' Frank said, reaching out to her, but she was already turning away in haste, taking with her the small boy she was holding, a small boy whose face was alight with curiosity. For a moment, Frank had seen recognition, shock and a fleeting glimpse of something else in Lydia's eyes before the shutters came down and she turned away, her bright colour drained away.

He tracked her progress back to a table where she sat down, face averted. Two older women leaned over her and he could see her protesting. The small boy – her son, probably – took his opportunity and slipped from her grasp, vanishing among the tables.

'Just a few words,' Jock was saying to the Salvation Army officers who had welcomed them. Willie Bruce exchanged a grin with Frank. Although the signs of exhaustion were clear and Jock had promised he would take some time to rest while he was home with his parents, it was clear that any opportunity to speak on the Lord's behalf was not to be missed.

And so Jock gave a short address to the delighted people in the Hall. His words were greeted with fervent Amens.

Frank and Willie remained by his side, Frank's thoughts racing. Lydia had run from him, once again. And yet... yet she had blushed. That tell-tale stain that told him she must feel something for him. So why turn away? He needed to get that sorted out.

When Jock came to the end of his few words and a hymn was sung, they were soon surrounded by well-wishers, including Jock's family and friends.

'Yes, yes, I will, gladly,' Frank heard Jock saying.

Willie shook his head. 'He won't rest till the Lord makes him,' he said as they heard Jock agree to speak at meetings in the coming days.

Frank nodded agreement. Jock was tireless on his Lord's behalf and since his colleagues accompanied him to meetings and assisted with prayer meetings and counselling, it looked like it was going to be a busy time for all of them.

But he needed to find enough time to see Lydia. To speak with her.

'Hello!'

A cheery Wick voice was accompanied by a tug on his elbow. Frank turned to find a friendly smile on the face of a pretty young woman.

'I'm Chrissie. Remember me, from Yarmouth? You and Jock brought me to the Lord,' she reminded him.

'Yes, of course,' Frank said. Those days in Yarmouth were etched deep in his memory. 'You're engaged to...'

'Married,' Chrissie announced proudly. 'We've been married more than a week now and...'

'What are you doing?' an angry voice demanded. 'Come away at once!'

Lydia's brother Robbie seized Chrissie's arm but she stood her ground, tossing her head defiantly.

'I just thought someone should welcome Mr Everett,' she said.

'No need. He's not welcome here.' Robbie turned and glared at Frank. 'And just you stay away from my sister!'

Frank searched Robbie's face. He could see anger and... could that possibly be fear? As he considered, Chrissie put her hand on Frank's sleeve and tugged urgently. She whispered quickly, 'Pay no mind to him. Go and see her. She needs you!' Then she turned back to her husband. 'All right, Robbie,' she said in a loud cheerful voice. 'You win. I'll be the submissive wife!'

And Robbie had to laugh at that as Chrissie led him away, turning back for a moment to wink at Frank.

'What was that about?' Willie Bruce enquired.

'I met someone in Yarmouth,' Frank told him. 'A Wick lass. I thought we were getting on fine, but her brother doesn't like it. I just don't understand...' He sighed. 'I thought once I was here... But you saw. First she turns and runs as if I'm a bogeyman and then he comes and all but threatens me. It's very odd.'

They stepped aside to let people leave the Hall. The Social was over and people were returning to their homes.

In the crush a heavy hand landed on Frank's shoulder. He turned to see Lydia's father.

'Come and see us,' David Ross said briefly. 'You'll be welcome.'

The woman with him, an older version of Lydia, surely her mother, smiled and added, 'Come for tea. Tomorrow if you can. About 4?'

Surprised and warmed by their invitation, Frank smiled. 'Yes, I will, thank you,' but they had gone.

Tomorrow, he thought and arrowed a prayer swiftly to God. 'If it is Your will, my Lord... oh let it be!'

CHAPTER 55

Frank Everett, Lydia thought.

He was here. In Wick. Jock Troup and his team were in town, she thought wildly, remembering the moment of shock when she found herself staring into Frank's face. Had she given herself away, she worried. What had he seen in her face? She had not been safe going to the Social. Chrissie had lied to her.

No, that could not be true. Chrissie would not lie. Not now that her Jesus so clearly ruled her life. It had to be that Chrissie genuinely had not known. But the shock...

Come on, Lydia, she chided herself. Deal with it. He's here. In town. But it will not be for long. The demands for Jock Troup and his team to conduct evangelical campaigns all over the country would surely take them away again soon. In fact, had she not heard that Jock was only here to see his parents before returning to the work in Dundee? So it would not be long – not long for her to hide herself away and avoid any chance of bumping into Frank.

But oh, he had looked so nice. Just as she had remembered. And as she recalled how it had felt to be in his arms, she longed to feel his arms around her again. Safe and warm and cherished.

No. It could not be, she scolded herself. She had seen with her own eyes that he was in a recognised and respectable relationship with another woman. There was no room for her at his side – much though she would have loved there to be.

And as she kissed Ewen goodnight, she thought longingly and sadly that Ewen deserved a father to help him grow up the way he should go. A decent God-fearing man who would be a good example as well as a teacher and a friend. A man like Frank Everett.

She sighed and turned back to her own room, sitting down at the dressing table and slowly brushing her hair in front of the mirror, as her thoughts lingered on the man she had run from once again.

When she had first met him, she had been hard with bitterness and disillusionment. She had closed her heart to all men, never realising that she had locked herself away in a dark prison unable to reach out and love anyone, even her own son. She had thought she was protecting herself from hurt, but in truth she was just too frightened to let herself feel what she really felt – all the anger against Danny who had so abused her innocent trust, anger that had crystallised into...

Even now it was hard to face the fact that she had not wanted Danny to come home safe and sound from the war to resume their mockery of a marriage. The seed of anger in her heart had festered into something much worse, and that – not to duck it any longer – was a desire for him to simply vanish in France. When the news came of his death, she had felt sudden wild joy, release – and then she had felt like a murderer, as if her wish had been the cause of his death.

Lydia remembered suddenly that Jesus had said something about anger and murder. She rose from the stool in front of the dressing table and went to sit on her bed, reaching into her bedside table for the Bible that had lain there unopened for so many years. What had Jesus said? She started with Matthew's gospel. Yes, there it was: chapter 5 verse 21. '*Ye have heard that it was said by them of old time, Thou shalt not kill; and whosoever shall kill shall be in danger of the judgment: but I say unto you, that whosoever is angry with his brother without a cause shall be in danger of the judgment.*'

Yes, she knew only too well that anger was a murderous thing and that she had indeed harboured anger for Danny. But without cause? Surely she had had cause and enough? But as the memories rose, she knew just as surely that it did not matter. Yes, there had been cause. But now she knew two things. Her vague inchoate longing for Danny not to come back had not caused Danny's death. His death had been caused by a stray shell with his name on it, in a war that neither of them had been responsible for. And she was not guilty of anything other than letting her anger against his unloving treatment of her fester, rather than simply dealing with it and moving on.

It was time for that. Time to forgive him and let the unhappy experience of her marriage to him vanish into God's hands – God who as surely forgave her for her festering anger.

'Oh Lord God,' she prayed, 'this is hard but I know I need to do this. Please help me truly forgive Danny and let go of my anger, my resentment, all the bitterness. Wash me clean and free me from the sadness of my past. Forgive me my sins and let me live like Mum and Chrissie, trusting you and walking with you, through Jesus Christ our Saviour.'

And her thoughts turned again to Frank Everett and the dreams she had had – dreams that had been shattered.

'Dear Lord, I know it cannot be. Please help me accept Your will for my life. Help me trust that You love me and that what You have for my life and my future will be good.' She paused, then with a smile let herself pray what was in her heart. 'Bless us all – Mum and Dad, Chrissie and Robbie and Granny Leslie, Ewen and me, and Frank Everett. Bless each one of us, Lord Jesus, and keep us in Your loving care. Amen.'

She set the Bible on the table and at last she was able to go to bed and sleep.

CHAPTER 56

Heavy snowstorms had closed the roads and the schools and Lydia, stuck at home with her thoughts all day, finally wrapped up warmly, and she thought unidentifiably, and took herself out for a brisk walk. Catching herself looking at everyone she met, part fearing, part hoping it might be Frank, she scolded herself for her foolishness and turned her footsteps back towards home.

Glad to be in out of the cold and the wind, she unwound her scarf and draped it over a hook in the hallway, calling out as usual, 'I'm home!'

As she removed her cloche hat and automatically smoothed her hair with one hand, she heard a murmur of voices from the sitting room. They must have visitors. She opened the door with a smile. Which faded when she saw who the visitor was.

'Come in, Lydia,' her father said. 'You look perished. Come in by the fire.'

She saw her parents exchange glances.

'You know the Reverend Everett... Frank,' her father continued.

Frank was watching her. She bobbed a little nod his way and took herself to the fire to warm her hands, steadfastly ignoring him. What on earth was he doing here?

Her mother busied herself pouring tea and popping a buttered scone on a plate.

'Here,' she said, handing them to Lydia. 'You'll be ready for this.'

'Thank you,' Lydia said, giving in to her fate and sitting down in the only vacant chair, which was uncomfortably close to Frank Everett. She accepted the cup of tea and the scone from her mother with slightly shaking hands which she hoped were not noticeable. Determinedly, she gritted her teeth.

'The snow has shut the schools,' Jean explained to Frank. 'But Lydia needed a breath of fresh air. She's not used to sitting idle.'

'How many children do you have in your class?' Frank asked.

Lydia shot him a glare. How dared he pretend any interest? Why didn't he take the hint and just leave?

'Thirty-five,' she told him in a cool, discouraging tone.

'That's a lot for one person to manage,' he commented.

'Not if you're properly trained,' she found herself snapping at him. For some reason this raised a smile.

'No, of course not,' he agreed. 'Moray House, wasn't it?' and she saw he was teasing her. She nodded and bit into her scone. But then she realised he was also telling her that he remembered. Remembered their conversation...

'These are delicious, Mrs Ross,' Frank was saying. 'Home-made is much nicer than shop-bought, even when they're spicy toasted teacakes. Wouldn't you agree?' He directed the question at her.

Lydia looked at him sharply. Yes, of course she remembered the toasted teacakes in the little tearoom in Yarmouth. Why was he reminding her? Telling her that he remembered too?

She responded with another cool little nod and did not see the look that passed between her parents, or her father's satisfied smile.

The front door banged, then the sitting room door flung open and Ewen catapulted into the room, cap askew, face red with cold and exertion, socks halfway down his calves, grubby and cheerful.

'I'm hungry!' he declared, planting himself in the middle of the room.

'Well, there's plenty to eat,' his grandmother told him with a warm smile. 'Go and tidy yourself. We've got a visitor.'

Ewen turned to stare at Frank, curiosity alive in his bright intelligent face.

'H'lo,' he said cheerfully. 'Saw you last night.'

'Hello, Ewen,' Frank said. 'So you did. It's nice to meet you.'

'How d'you know my name?' Ewen asked. 'I don't know yours.'

'I'm Frank.' It was said with a smile. 'And I know your name because your mother told me. When she was down in Yarmouth. That's where we met – me and your mother and your grandfather and your Uncle Robbie and Auntie Chrissie.'

Ewen, satisfied with the explanation, nodded and reached for a scone.

'Hands, Ewen,' his grandmother reminded him. 'Go and wash them now and take that cap off and pull your socks up.'

Ewen grinned and skipped out into the kitchen where they could hear water splashing.

'He's five?' Frank queried.

'And a half,' put in Ewen, returning speedily. He reached for a plate and piled it with buttered scone and cake, then ambled over to the pouffe in the corner, his eye on Frank all the time. After he had settled himself, he paused, the scone halfway to his mouth.

'So why're you here?' he enquired. The question Lydia wanted to ask but could not. She was grateful for her son's unaffected curiosity.

'Ewen,' his grandfather chided gently. 'We invited Mr Everett. Last night, after the Social.'

Lydia's head shot up and she stared accusingly at her parents. They had invited Frank to tea? Last night? Her parents returned bland gazes. Lydia's eyes narrowed. They were up to something. But what? Surely not matchmaking? She would have to put them right...

'I mean here in Wick,' Ewen explained, interrupting her furious thoughts. 'If you met them all in Yarmouth, why're you not still there?'

'I was in Yarmouth to help with the mission there,' Frank explained. 'I'm a Baptist minister and my church sent me to help. Then when Mr Troup went to Fraserburgh, I went along with him. After that we went to Dundee for a while, then Inverness, and now here.'

Ewen nodded, satisfied, and finished off his scone.

'Do you know how long you'll be staying?' David Ross enquired. Another question Lydia had been longing to ask.

'No, I don't know,' Frank replied. 'I think Jock plans to return to Dundee but he could do with a rest. He's exhausted and his voice is getting hoarse. I don't think he's as well as he should be.'

'Oh no!' Jean exclaimed. 'That fine man! Can you not make him take a rest?'

Frank laughed, a fine rich clear sound. 'I don't think anyone but the Lord can make Jock do anything!' He looked round the room, taking in Lydia's averted gaze. He set down his cup and saucer and his now empty plate. 'I'll be going then. It was very kind of you to invite me. We've got meetings most afternoons and evenings so I'll need to be getting back.'

As he stood up, Lydia's mother rose. 'Well, just you feel you can drop in here any time. We have tea around four.' She looked at Ewen with a warm smile. 'And there's always food for hungry mouths! You'll be very welcome to join us.'

Frank smiled. 'Thank you, Mrs Ross. I really appreciate your welcome.' He turned to Lydia's father. 'Thank you, Mr Ross.'

But David Ross waved it away. 'No, no. We're delighted to see you. And just do as Jean says: drop in any time you're passing by.'

Frank looked at Lydia but she kept her attention on her tea cup.

'I'll say goodbye then,' Frank said and allowed Jean to usher him to the door. Lydia could hear a murmur of voices and wondered what her mother was saying, but then resolutely concentrated on her tea.

There was no future for them, she told herself. There could be no future, not when he was already spoken for. She sighed. It was a pity. She really did like him. She bit into her scone fiercely and did not notice her father's smile.

CHAPTER 57

Frank walked slowly down the street to the harbour and stood, gazing out over the stormy bay, seeing only Lydia's bent head, her refusal to look at him. But her mother had counselled patience.

'Give her time,' she had murmured to him at the door. 'Don't give up.'

Lydia's parents had grilled him when he had arrived at their door for tea as invited. They had wanted to know all about him, his family, his education, his work, his prospects. Exactly what they should do regarding a suitor for their beloved daughter. And oh yes, Lydia's father had broached the subject of Frank's intentions.

'She's been hurt before,' David Ross had said gruffly. 'Rushed into a bad marriage before the war. She'll be chary of making another mistake.'

'I would never hurt her,' Frank assured them. 'Love, honour, cherish – that's what I want to do... if she'll let me.'

Lydia's parents had exchanged glances then and her father had said, 'We would be glad to see Lydia happy. But you'll have to win her.' He had smiled then, leaving the challenge but taking the sting out of it.

Frank had smiled in return.

'I'll do my best – and God willing, I'll be allowed to make Lydia happy.'

They had discussed Ewen then.

'The lad needs a father,' David had said bluntly. 'And I'm getting old.'

'Lydia told me about Ewen,' Frank assured them. 'He comes as no surprise – except...'

Lydia's parents exchanged worried looks.

'No, no!' Frank laughed. 'Nothing to worry about. It's just, last night, I was struck by how much he looks like her. He looks a lively lad and a bright one.'

'You'll need to get to know him,' Lydia's mother, Jean, counselled. 'He has a mind of his own and you'll need him on your side. Hopefully he'll take to you.'

Well, their first encounter seemed to have passed satisfactorily. He liked the lad already but how to win his trust?

The wind blew chill and Frank drew his warm coat around him. Time to be getting back to Jock Troup's parents' house before the evening meeting began.

It was funny, he thought. An evangelistic campaign was designed to turn people's hearts to God. It seemed he was also launched on a campaign to turn Lydia's heart – and Ewen's – to him.

'If it is Your will, Lord Jesus,' he whispered as he began the cold walk back.

CHAPTER 58

Mother and daughter stood, as they so often did, in the kitchen. Jean had her hands in the soapy water in the bowl in the sink. Lydia was wielding the dishtowel to dry the clean cups, saucers and plates her mother handed to her.

Jean stole a glance at Lydia. She was clearly itching to say something.

'Come on, then,' Jean invited. 'Out with it.'

Lydia glared at her and Jean hid a smile. She remembered long-ago tussles with a much younger Lydia when she had been in receipt of that glare.

'There's something you want to say,' she prodded. 'So say it, so we can get it out of the way.'

'Out of the way!' Lydia exploded. 'How can it be out of the way till that man goes away again! You've given him an open invitation to the house. He'll be here all the time. He just doesn't take the hint. What am I going to do? I can avoid him anywhere else but now I can't even find peace in my own home!'

'What's the problem?' Jean asked gently. 'Don't you like him? He likes you and he seems a fine young man.'

Lydia threw down the dishtowel in disgust.

'Is that a no?' Jean suggested.

'No!' Lydia protested, then catching herself. 'What did you say?' She caught her breath in a shaky laugh. 'I don't know what I'm saying!'

'I asked whether you like the man?' her mother said.

'Oh, Mum!' Lydia said, her voice rising into a wail. 'There's no point! It doesn't matter whether I like the man! It's completely useless!'

'And why is that?' Jean turned from the sink and gave her daughter her full attention.

'Because he's already got a lady,' Lydia ground out. 'I saw them. In Yarmouth. And more than once. Chrissie did too.' She slumped against the door. 'So you see. There's no point.'

'I see,' Jean said quietly, turning back to the washing-up in the sink. She splashed a cup through the hot water, giving it a deft wipe with the cloth then handed it to Lydia who took it automatically. 'And you're sure of that?'

'I saw them!' Lydia insisted in a voice thick with hurt. 'She was hanging onto his arm and gooing up at him, the first time I saw them!'

Jean hid her smile. Her daughter's pain was clear to see.

'And then she was in the church, right there at the front, and he acknowledged her, so that means they're a recognised couple.' Lydia slid the cup into the cupboard and turned back to her mother. 'She's probably his wife and he just forgot to mention it,' she said in disgust.

'Mmm,' Jean mused. 'Is that the sort of man he is, then? Is that what you think?'

'No!' Lydia protested. 'Yes! Oh, I don't know! Oh Mum, I just don't understand...'

'But you do like him?'

Lydia threw herself down in the battered armchair by the range and thrust her head into her hands.

'Yes! Yes, I do. Too much. I thought maybe he liked me. I thought... Oh Mum, I got my hopes up that maybe... and then I saw them together. And I saw I was in danger of making a worse fool of myself than I ever did over Danny.' She looked up and Jean could see the tears in her eyes.

'Oh my love,' Jean said and quickly wiping her hands on her apron hurried over and enfolded Lydia in a comforting hug.

'Oh Mum, why is it so hard?' Lydia asked. 'Shouldn't love be easy?'

Jean shook her head sadly, thinking back on the ups and downs of her own life.

'I'm not sure that anything worthwhile ever comes easy,' she said. 'That way we appreciate it when we've got it.'

'It doesn't look as if there's anything for me to look forward to appreciating!' Lydia declared wryly.

'Oh my dear,' Jean chided her. 'The Lord tells us that He thinks good thoughts for us, thoughts of peace for us. So we must trust Him.' She released Lydia and took a step back so she could look in her face. 'Will you trust Him with this?'

'I have prayed about it,' Lydia said shyly. 'I have handed it over to the Lord, but it's so hard when I don't understand what's going on.'

'That's life, my dear,' Jean said with a little chuckle. 'But if it's any comfort, your father grilled Mr Everett about his life and he never mentioned a wife.'

'I know what I saw,' Lydia said stubbornly.

'Aye well,' her mother said. 'Maybe if you come home a little later from school tomorrow afternoon, I'll get a chance to quiz him a bit more thoroughly! If there's another lady in his life, I'll find out about her. Will you trust me to do that?'

Jean was pleased to see a glimmer of hope enter Lydia's eyes as she nodded hesitantly.

'Good girl,' Jean said. 'Now we must get this finished before it's time to start cooking again!'

CHAPTER 59

Despite Chrissie's pleadings, Lydia declined her invitation to go with her to the meeting that night at the Zion Hall.

'Maybe Jock Troup will be there,' Chrissie said, adding 'and the other fellows he's brought with him.'

Lydia shook her head, refusing to be drawn by Chrissie's mischievous grin.

'We'll go with you,' David Ross announced. 'Lydia's had a busy day at school.'

So Chrissie, accompanied by her parents-in-law, set off in good time to get a seat in the crowded hall. They were delighted that Jock Troup delivered a short address, despite the hoarseness of his voice.

Frank, sitting with Willie Bruce and the Salvation Army officers, noticed the Ross family's attendance – and Lydia's absence. He noted too Robbie's glowering presence. It seemed he had more than one member of the family to win over – and as little idea how to do it.

Resolutely he gave his worries to the Lord and concentrated on the meeting, his heart thrilling once more to the sincere testimonies of young fisherfolk who had come to the Lord in Yarmouth.

At the end of the meeting, he received a brilliant smile from Chrissie and a warm handshake from Lydia's father. Her mother bestowed a gentle reminder of their invitation to tea. 'If you are free, Mr Everett.'

'Frank,' he insisted.

'Frank,' she returned with a smile so like Lydia's that his heart caught.

'I'd be happy to,' he told her sincerely. Their kindness renewed his strength. If they were on his side, perhaps he had a chance?

But next day there was an afternoon meeting and he was not able to get away. And the following day, concerns for Jock's health had taken centre stage. He was to go into the local hospital for an operation on Monday. Meanwhile, Willie and Frank took the lion's share of speaking at meetings to spare him.

It was not till the following Tuesday that Frank found himself at the Rosses' door. He had not seen a glimpse of Lydia in the meantime, though he had taken a walk round the little grey town at times when he thought she might be out and about. He had taken himself up past the school where she taught, enjoying the sight of the playground full of cheerful noisy youngsters undeterred by the cold weather, but there was no sign of Lydia. He had hoped she might accompany her parents or her brother and sister-in-law to church or to one of the meetings at the Zion Hall, but she did not appear.

So now, unable to resist, his footsteps took him straight to the house in Rose Street at 4 o'clock. He would be there waiting for Lydia when she got home from school.

'Mr Everett!' Lydia's mother exclaimed with every indication of pleasure at his arrival.

'Frank,' he reminded her gently.

'Yes, of course,' she said. 'Frank. Now take your coat off and hang up your things and come in by the fire. We were hoping you might look in.'

David Ross, comfortably ensconced by the fire, gave him a warm smile and indicated the other big armchair. 'There'll be a cup of tea in a wee while and something to eat,' he said. 'Sit yourself down.'

Frank did as he was bid, aware that the two pairs of eyes were looking at him more quizzically than before. The welcome was as warm however, so he took heart.

David Ross cleared his throat and cast a look at his wife. She sat down and waited, plainly letting him take the lead.

'The thing is...' David began and ground to a halt.

Jean threw him a fond, exasperated look.

He started again. 'It's our Lydia. You see...' and again he seemed to run out of words.

Frank looked at him and then at Jean.

'What's the matter? Is she ill?'

'No, no,' Jean said. 'It's just...' Again that quick telegraphic signal between Lydia's parents. Jean took a deep breath and plunged in. 'We know what you told us when you were here last. About yourself and your life. It's just... maybe... there was something missing?'

'Something missing?' Frank repeated, bemused.

'Something you forgot to mention,' Jean prompted. She smiled encouragingly. 'Maybe a lady...' she said delicately.

Frank shook his head, bewilderment clear in his face. 'There's no lady to forget to mention,' he said forcefully. 'There's only one lady in my life – and that's your daughter. Lydia.'

Jean looked at him thoughtfully, then she said quietly, 'Lydia seems to think otherwise.'

'Otherwise?'

351

'She saw you with someone, in Yarmouth. Walking arm in arm. Chatting as if you knew each other very well.'

Frank's face showed only puzzlement. He shook his head again. 'I've no idea who that could be.'

'And at the last service, this lady came in late and waved to you and you waved back.' Jean added the final piece of evidence.

His eyes gazed into the distance for a moment then his face cleared.

'No,' he said decisively. 'That wasn't a lady...' He stopped and laughed. 'Oh dear, she'd skin me if she heard me say that! She's a lady now, I suppose, but she'll always be my little sister! She's married to the Baptist minister in one of the villages near Yarmouth. It was good to catch up with her...' Frank paused. 'But maybe not so good if Lydia thought...'

Jean nodded. 'Yes. Lydia thought...'

'Oh, I understand,' Frank said, and now he did. Lydia had been keeping clear of him because she thought he was already spoken for. She was an honourable woman – even if wholly wrong!

'I hope you didn't mind me asking,' Jean said. 'But I felt we needed to be clear about it.'

'I'm delighted,' said Frank and he was.

'I'll go and make the tea,' and Jean rose and left the room.

CHAPTER 60

When Jean returned to the sitting room, Lydia had arrived and was sitting stiffly on a hard chair as far away from Frank as she could manage in the small room. Jean hid an affectionate smile at her daughter's rather obvious stratagem and went to set down the tea tray on the table in the window.

'How was school today?' she asked Lydia.

'Fine,' Lydia said. 'The Francis twins were up to mischief again. I think we'll have to separate them.'

'They're girls,' Jean put in, with a smile for Frank. 'And sometimes the girls are worse than the boys.' She handed Frank his tea. 'Do you have brothers and sisters, Frank?'

She was rewarded by a beaming smile as he gratefully picked up the opportunity she had given him.

'I've two brothers and one much younger sister,' he replied. 'And yes, my mother always said my sister was more trouble than the rest of us but she's fine now, happily married and settled down.' He looked directly across at Lydia. 'You'll have seen her in Yarmouth,' he stated blandly. 'She was in the front pew at that last service. Came in late, as usual, and then instead of settling herself in inconspicuously, she waved at me!'

David Ross chuckled. 'Aye, we saw her. A bonnie lass.'

'I love her dearly,' Frank went on. 'It was good to see her again, but despite being married to a decent Baptist minister, she's still a minx at heart!'

Frank observed Lydia as the information sank in. It was like watching a sea anemone unfurl. Her eyes opened wide, her lips softened, and the tension seemed to leave her body. As finally she looked at him properly for the first time, he let himself smile gently into her eyes, willing her to see his love and his understanding.

A faint blush began to creep into her cheeks and she dropped her eyes again, focusing all her attention on her tea, but as gradually she was drawn into the conversation, he could see what he now knew had been distrust in him disappear.

He was telling them about Jock Troup's planned operation.

'It seems he had an accident at work a while back and it went bad, turned into an abscess. The surgeon will remove it on Monday and they'll try to keep Jock in for a few days' convalescence and rest.'

'He needs it, that lad,' Jean said wisely. 'Maybe this is the Lord making him rest!'

'Maybe so,' Frank agreed. 'Willie Bruce and I will carry on the work while he's out of action. There are a lot of meetings planned and the converts keep coming.'

The front door opened and banged shut.

'Ewen,' Jean smiled. But then the inner door opened and as well as Ewen bounding in to seize a scone, came Robbie.

'Mum, Dad,' he began genially then he caught sight of Frank. 'What's he doing here?' Robbie demanded, finger pointing at Frank.

'Robbie!' Jean exclaimed.

'We invited Mr Everett to tea,' David Ross said in a firm voice. 'I think this is still my house and I can invite who I wish to it.' His eyes held Robbie's for a moment, challenging him.

'Would you like a cup of tea?' Jean put in. 'And there are fresh-made scones.'

'Yes, please,' Robbie said sulkily and planted himself on a hard chair from where he watched Frank from hostile eyes. Jean and David exchanged puzzled glances.

'I think maybe I'd better be going,' Frank said quietly, rising to go.

'No, no!' David began.

'Good idea,' Robbie put in.

'Granddad,' Ewen interrupted, oblivious to the tense atmosphere around him, his words slightly muffled by a mouth full of scone. 'Alistair Stevens says the weather's getting better so I should be able to go out on the boat with you soon. Is that right? Will we go soon?'

David smiled at the young lad. 'Aye, that's right. It looks like we may get a few days set fine and then you can come with us.'

'It'll be my first time,' Ewen told Frank proudly. 'I'm going to be a fisherman like Granddad and Uncle Robbie.' He smiled round at them all, before pinning Frank with a curious gaze. 'Are you a landlubber?' Ewen stumbled slightly on the word.

Frank started to speak but Ewen was in full flow. 'Alistair Stevens says landlubbers get seasick. I'm not going to get seasick 'cos we're not landlubbers. We Rosses,' he announced proudly, 'never get seasick. If you're a landlubber, do you get seasick?'

'I'm not a fisherman,' Frank said. 'But I don't get seasick.'

'That's good,' Ewen said, then became aware of the horrified faces of his family. 'What's the matter?' he demanded. 'I never said anything bad. I only asked...' He caught sight of Robbie's anguished expression. Seeing his reaction Ewen gulped. 'Oh, I'm sorry, Uncle

Robbie! I wasn't supposed to say anything about being seasick! I forgot!'

And with that, Ewen hastily grabbed another scone and made himself scarce.

Robbie swallowed hard. He stared down at the floor between his feet, not meeting anyone's eyes.

'Don't blame Ewen,' David Ross told him. 'He let a little bit spill out the other day and I got the rest of it out of him.'

Robbie's eyes came up to search his father's face.

'And did you believe him?' Robbie asked, his voice flat with hopelessness.

Jean and David exchanged looks filled with sadness.

'Aye,' David said. 'Aye, we believed him. It made sense. I always wondered how you managed on every boat after that without the seasickness coming back, but... I'm sorry. I should have paid more attention.'

He let the silence stand while Robbie absorbed what he had said.

'We've thought about it and talked about it and prayed about it, your mother and I, and it would seem that maybe we never knew Alec, and certainly I never gave you a chance. I just swallowed whatever Alec told me. Robbie, I'm mortal sorry.'

'Oh, Dad!' Lydia whispered.

Frank Everett coughed quietly to remind the Ross family of his presence. 'I really should go...' he began.

Robbie looked up at him, as if suddenly reminded of his presence. Frank paused as doubt chased torment across Robbie's face.

'What is it, Robbie?' his mother probed.

'Is there something else you need to tell us?' David asked, swallowing hard. 'About Alec?'

'This is hard...' Robbie began.

'*The truth shall make you free*,' his father quoted.

'Yes but...' Robbie began. 'I don't want to take away from Alec's memory...'

'I think we've had enough secrets in this family,' David told him. 'Now we belong to the Lord, let us tell the truth and shame the devil! What do you say, Frank?'

All eyes turned on Frank: Lydia tender and curious, Jean peacefully waiting for him to speak, David braced for the truth, and Robbie – Robbie suddenly flung his head into his hands. When he lifted his head, his eyes were wild and desperate.

'Go on, then!' he cried. 'You tell them! You were there too, weren't you, Padre?'

CHAPTER 61

'Yes, Robbie,' Frank agreed. 'I was there.' He turned to Jean and David. 'I was at Bourlon Wood, Cambrai, that day in November 1917.'

Jean gave a little gasp and her hand came up to her mouth. David reached out for her and held her hand firmly in his.

'And Robbie knows I was there because...' Frank looked over at Robbie and waited for him to speak.

Finally Robbie, his eyes still averted from his family, said in a low voice, 'Because I was there too.'

There was a moment's stunned silence then David Ross ground out, 'You were there, at the same time as Alec? At the same place?'

Robbie nodded.

'But you never said,' Jean cried. 'You could have told us. Surely you could have told us!'

But David, suddenly alert to the tension in the two men, held up a warning hand.

'Wait a minute. Why didn't you tell us?' he asked Robbie. 'Was there something that you didn't want us to know?'

'And if there had been, would you have believed anything I said?' Robbie exclaimed, and all the old bitterness was back in his voice. 'Who was I? The useless one! Not the golden boy, the hero. You'd have thought I was simply trying to blacken his memory now he was dead and couldn't speak for himself!'

'We know different now,' Jean said softly. 'We know Alec wasn't the perfect son he pretended to be.'

'Just tell us,' David said sadly. 'We're ready to hear it now.'

Frank caught Robbie's eye and nodded. Robbie stared at him for a moment as if drawing strength and courage from him, then he began.

'I'd been caught in a gas attack and taken to a field hospital for a few days to recover. I'd been discharged and was working my way back up the line to my regiment when...' He looked at his parents with pity in his eyes. 'When I saw Alec.'

'Yes?'

'Was he alive?'

'He was alive,' Robbie faltered then went on. 'But he was under arrest. He was being led away between two guards.'

'But why? What had he done?' his father demanded in shocked tones.

'When Danny was killed,' Robbie said, 'Alec had refused to leave his body, refused an officer's order to return to the line. He was being taken to the guardroom to await court-martial.'

'But... But we were never told that,' his father protested. 'We were told that he was killed at Bourlon Wood.'

'That's because a shell came over and took out the farmhouse where they were keeping him,' Robbie said simply. 'That's how he died. In the guardroom, not the trenches.'

'So how did you get involved?' David asked Frank. 'I know the Padre is there before the firing squad, but if Alec was killed by a shell...'

360

'I was passing,' Frank said. 'Robbie had seen his brother and asked permission to speak with him. That delayed the officer writing up the charge. That's why it never came out...'

'How was he?' Jean interrupted. 'You saw him last, before he died.'

Robbie and Frank exchanged glances, Robbie's eyes deeply troubled.

'Frank?' Jean pleaded. 'Please tell us.'

Frank sighed. 'The men had been on the front line for too long,' he said. 'They were all exhausted and just wanted it all to finish. Alec was no different from all the rest. His friend's death had been the last straw for him.'

Lydia saw the gratitude in Robbie's glance. He picked up the story.

'But we had time to talk. Time to put things right between us,' Robbie said.

'I can vouch for that,' Frank said.

'Thanks,' Robbie said gruffly.

Frank gave him a swift smile and went on, 'We prayed together and he was at peace. He didn't want to go back to the line. He was prepared for the sentence of the court-martial. The shell simply took him sooner, and maybe more kindly. He wouldn't have known what happened.'

There was silence in the little sitting room as Alec's mother, father and sister took in what they had heard.

'Thank you, both of you,' David Ross said. He looked at his wife, gently mopping tears from her eyes. 'We needed to know.'

'I thought...' Robbie began. 'I thought since Alec and I had sorted it out between us, there was no need for you to know.'

'It's better to know,' David said. 'Now we can get on with our lives based on the truth.'

Robbie nodded. He stood and offered his hand to Frank.

'I recognised you that day you came to the girls' lodgings in Yarmouth. I was afraid you'd let slip something to Lydia...' He looked across at Lydia with a smile. 'And if I was right about your intentions regarding my sister' – he grinned at her as she blushed and ducked her head – 'I couldn't let you turn up here to pay your addresses to my parents in case they asked you about the war and it all came out.'

Frank took the proffered hand in a firm grip.

'I understand,' he said and the two men shook hands in fine accord.

'I don't.'

It was Ewen who had crept back into the room unnoticed. He was standing in the doorway munching another scone.

'What don't you understand, my love?' his grandmother asked.

'About his address,' Ewen said. He waved the scone at Frank. 'What does where he lives matter to you?'

CHAPTER 62

As the adults dissolved into uproarious laughter, Ewen stared at them in perplexity.

'I didn't say anything funny,' he complained.

'No,' Frank agreed solemnly. 'But maybe my address does matter.' He looked round the room. 'My home is in England, in a small town not much bigger than Wick. I'm to be minister of a Baptist church there.'

He looked across at Lydia.

'Does that make a difference?'

Lydia looked into his beloved face, saw the hope and the longing there and knew just what this man was asking her. And she knew her answer. She would go anywhere to be with him. But what about Ewen?

'It makes no difference to me,' Lydia said with a smile and as Frank reached out his hand to her, she put him off gently, turning to her son. 'What do you say, Ewen?'

'Would you like to see my address?' Frank asked him. 'Come to England with us?'

Ewen stuffed the remains of the scone into his mouth and chewed thoughtfully as he looked from one to the other.

'With you? You and Mum?' he queried.

'If she'll have me,' Frank said.

Lydia slipped her hand into his.

'There's your answer,' Robbie said with a grin.

Jean and David clapped their hands in delight.

'Can I wear my kilt at the wedding?' Ewen asked.

Lightning Source UK Ltd.
Milton Keynes UK
UKOW01f0914030217
293511UK00002B/124/P